A DEADLY DISCOVERY

The man who'd pursued her walked down the stairs and stood over her. The second intruder appeared from the door to the living room and looked down at the silent and unmoving figure. He knelt beside her and pressed his fingertips to the side of her neck.

After a moment he looked up angrily. "You weren't supposed to kill her," he snapped.

Alberti looked down at his handiwork and shrugged. "She wasn't supposed to be here. We were told the house would be empty. It was an accident," he added, "but she's dead and there's nothing we can do about it."

Rogan straightened up. "You're right about that. Let's finish what we've got to do and get out of here."

Without a backward glance, the two men returned to the living room. Rogan picked up the hammer and chisel and continued to chip away at the remaining sections of old plaster about the huge stone lintel that spanned the entire width of the fireplace.

The work took very little time, and in some twenty minutes the entire area was exposed. Both men stood in front of the fireplace, staring at the letters carved into one of the stones. . . .

THE
FIRST APOS†LE

James Becker

A SIGNET BOOK

SIGNET
Published by New American Library, a division of
Penguin Group (USA) Inc., 375 Hudson Street,
New York, New York 10014, USA
Penguin Group (Canada), 90 Eglinton Avenue East, Suite 700, Toronto,
Ontario M4P 2Y3, Canada (a division of Pearson Penguin Canada Inc.)
Penguin Books Ltd., 80 Strand, London WC2R 0RL, England
Penguin Ireland, 25 St. Stephen's Green, Dublin 2,
Ireland (a division of Penguin Books Ltd.)
Penguin Group (Australia), 250 Camberwell Road, Camberwell, Victoria 3124,
Australia (a division of Pearson Australia Group Pty. Ltd.)
Penguin Books India Pvt. Ltd., 11 Community Centre, Panchsheel Park,
New Delhi - 110 017, India
Penguin Group (NZ), 67 Apollo Drive, Rosedale, North Shore 0632,
New Zealand (a division of Pearson New Zealand Ltd.)
Penguin Books (South Africa) (Pty.) Ltd., 24 Sturdee Avenue,
Rosebank, Johannesburg 2196, South Africa

Penguin Books Ltd., Registered Offices:
80 Strand, London WC2R 0RL, England

Published by Signet, an imprint of New American Library, a division of Penguin
Group (USA) Inc. Previously published in a Transworld Publishers edition. For
further information contact Transworld Publishers, a division of Random House
Ltd., 61–63 Uxbridge Road, London W5 5SA, England.

First Signet Printing, March 2009
10 9 8 7 6 5 4 3 2 1

Copyright © James Becker, 2008
All rights reserved

 REGISTERED TRADEMARK—MARCA REGISTRADA

Printed in the United States of America

PUBLISHER'S NOTE
This is a work of fiction. Names, characters, places, and incidents either are the
product of the author's imagination or are used fictitiously, and any resemblance
to actual persons, living or dead, business establishments, events, or locales is
entirely coincidental.
   The publisher does not have any control over and does not assume any
responsibility for author or third-party Web sites or their content.

For Sally,
as ever.

ACKNOWLEDGMENTS

I'd like to start by thanking Luigi Bonomi, the best literary agent in London and a man I'm pleased to call a good friend, for suggesting the idea for this book in the first place, and for his perseverance in shepherding it through a series of incarnations until it met his exacting standards.

At Transworld, I'd like to thank Selina Walker and Danielle Weekes, two of the most charming and talented ladies I have ever had the privilege of working with—and formidable editors as well—and Francesca Liversidge for her obvious enthusiasm for the book from the first. Publishing, of course, is a team effort, and I'm grateful to everyone involved at Transworld for their dedication and professionalism.

—James Becker
Principality of Andorra, 2008

PROLOGUE

In the center of the group of silent watching men, the naked Jew was struggling violently, but it was never going to make a difference. One burly Roman soldier knelt on each arm, pinning it to the rough wooden beam—the *patibulum*—and another was holding his legs firmly.

General Vespasian watched, as he watched all the crucifixions. As far as he knew, this Jew hadn't committed any specific offense against the Roman Empire, but he had long ago lost patience with the defenders of Jotapata, and routinely executed any of them his army managed to capture.

The soldier holding the Jew's left arm eased the pressure slightly, just enough to allow another man to bind the victim's wrist with thick cloth. The Romans were experts at this method of execution—they'd had considerable practice—and knew that the fabric would help staunch the flow of blood from the wounds. Crucifixion was intended to be slow, painful and public, and the last thing they wanted was for the condemned man to bleed to death in a matter of hours.

Normally, victims of crucifixion were flogged first, but Vespasian's men had neither the time nor the inclination to bother. In any case, they knew the Jews lasted longer on the cross if they weren't flogged, and that helped reinforce the general's uncompromising message to the besieged town, little more than an arrow-shot distant.

The binding complete, they forced the Jew's arm back onto the *patibulum,* the wood rough and stained with old blood. A centurion approached with a hammer and nails. The nails were about eight inches long, thick, with large flat heads, and specially made for the purpose. Like the crosses, they had been reused many times.

"Hold him still," he barked, and bent to the task.

The Jew went rigid when he felt the point of the nail touch his wrist, then screamed as the centurion smashed the hammer down. The blow was strong and sure, and the nail ripped straight through his arm and embedded itself deep in the wood. Compounding the agony of the injury, the nail severed the median nerve, causing continuous and intense pain along the man's entire limb.

Blood spurted from the wound, splashing onto the ground around the *patibulum.* Some four inches of the nail still protruded above the now blood-sodden cloth wrapped around the Jew's wrist, but two more blows from the hammer drove it home. Once the flat head of the nail was hard up against the cloth and compressing the limb against the wood, the blood flow diminished noticeably.

The Jew screamed his agony as each blow landed, then lost control of his bladder. The trickle of urine onto the dusty ground caused a couple of the watching soldiers to smile, but most ignored it. Like Vespasian, they were tired—the Romans had been fighting the inhabitants of Judea off and on for more than a hundred years—and in the last twelve months they'd all seen too much death and suffering to view another crucifixion as much more than a temporary diversion.

It had been hard fighting, and the battles far from one-sided. Just ten months earlier, the entire Roman garrison in Jerusalem had surrendered to the Jews and had immediately been lynched. From that moment on, full-scale war had been inevitable, and the fighting bitter. Now the Romans were in Judea in full force. Vespasian commanded the fifth legion—*Fretensis*—and the tenth—*Macedonica*—while his son Titus had recently arrived with the fifteenth—*Apollinaris*—and the army also included auxiliary troops and cavalry units.

The soldier released the victim's arm and stood back as the centurion walked around and knelt beside the man's right arm. The Jew was going nowhere now, though his screams were loud and his struggles even more violent. Once the right wrist had been properly bound with fabric, the centurion expertly drove home the second nail and stood back.

The vertical section of the T-shaped Tau cross—the *stipes*—was a permanent fixture in the Roman camp. Each of the legions—the three camps were side by side on a slight rise overlooking the town—had erected fifty of them in clear view of Jotapata. Most were already in use, almost equal numbers of living and dead bodies hanging from them.

Following the centurion's orders, four Roman soldiers picked up the *patibulum* between them and carried the heavy wooden beam, dragging the condemned Jew, his screams louder still, over the rocky ground and across to the upright. Wide steps had already been placed at either side of the *stipes* and, with barely a pause in their stride, the four soldiers climbed up and hoisted the *patibulum* onto the top of the post, slotting it onto the prepared peg.

The moment the Jew's feet left the ground and his nailed arms took the full weight of his body, both of his shoulder joints dislocated. His feet sought for a perch— something, anything—to relieve the incredible agony coursing through his arms. In seconds, his right heel landed on a block of wood attached to the *stipes* about five feet below the top, and he rested both feet on it and pushed upward to relieve the strain on his arms. Which was, of course, exactly why the Romans had placed it there. The moment he straightened his legs, the Jew felt rough hands adjusting the position of his feet, turning them sideways and holding his calves together. Seconds later another nail was driven through both heels with a single blow, pinning his legs to the cross.

Vespasian looked at the dying man, struggling pointlessly like a trapped insect, his cries already weakening. He turned away, shading his eyes against the setting sun. The Jew would be dead in two days, three at the most. The crucifixion over, the soldiers began dispersing, returning to the camp and their duties.

Every Roman military camp was identical in design: a square grid of open "roads," their names the same in every camp, that divided the different sections, the whole surrounded by a ditch and palisade, and with separate tents inside for men and officers. The *Fretensis* legion's camp was in the center of the three and Vespasian's personal tent lay, as the commanding general's always did, at the head of the *Via Principalis*—the main thoroughfare, directly in front of the camp headquarters.

The Tau crosses had been erected in a defiant line that stretched across the fronts of all three camps, a constant reminder to the defenders of Jotapata of the fate that awaited them if they were captured.

Vespasian acknowledged the salutes of the sentries as he walked back through the palisade. He was a soldier's soldier. He led from the front, celebrating his army's triumphs and mourning their retreats alongside his men. He'd started from nothing—his father had been a minor customs official and small-time moneylender—but he'd risen to command legions in Britain and Germany. Ignominiously retired by Nero after he fell asleep during one of the Emperor's interminable musical performances, it was a measure of the seriousness of the situation in Judea that he'd been called back to active service to take personal charge of suppressing the revolt.

He was more worried than he liked to admit about the campaign. His first success—an easy victory at Gadara—might almost have been a fluke because, despite the best efforts of his soldiers, the small band of defenders of Jotapata showed no signs of surrendering, despite being hopelessly outnumbered. And the town was hardly strategically crucial. Once he'd captured it, he knew they'd have to move on to liberate the Mediterranean ports, all potentially much harder targets.

It was going to be a long and bitter struggle, and at fifty Vespasian was already an old man. He would rather have been almost anywhere else in the Empire, but Nero was holding his youngest son, Domitian, as a hostage, and had given him no choice but to command the campaign.

Just before he reached his tent, he saw a centurion approaching. The man's red tunic, greaves or shin protectors, *lorica hamata*—chain-mail armor—and silvered helmet with its transverse crest made him easily identifiable among the regular soldiers, who wore white tunics and *lorica segmenta*—plate armor. He was leading a small group of legionaries and escorting another prisoner, his arms bound behind him.

The centurion stopped a respectful ten feet from Vespasian and saluted. "The Jew from Cilicia, sir, as you ordered."

Vespasian nodded his approval and gestured toward his tent. "Bring him." He stood to one side as the soldiers hustled the man inside and pushed him onto a wooden stool. The flickering light of the oil lamps showed him to be elderly, tall and thin, with a high forehead, receding hairline and a straggly beard.

The tent was large—almost as big as those normally occupied by eight legionaries—with separate sleeping quarters. Vespasian removed the brooch that secured his *lacerna,* the purple cloak that identified him as a general, tossed the garment aside and sat down wearily.

"Why am I here?" the prisoner demanded.

"You're here," Vespasian replied, dismissing the escort with a flick of his wrist, "because I so ordered it. Your instructions from Rome were perfectly clear. Why have you failed to obey them?"

The man shook his head. "I have done precisely what the Emperor demanded."

"You have not," Vespasian snapped, "otherwise I would not be stuck here in this miserable country trying to stamp out yet another rebellion."

"I am not responsible for that. I have carried out my orders to the best of my ability. All this"—the prisoner gestured with his head to include Jotapata—"is not of my doing."

"The Emperor does not agree, and neither do I. He believes you should have done more, far more. He has issued explicit orders to me, orders that include your execution."

For the first time a look of fear passed across the old man's face. "My execution? But I've done everything he asked. Nobody could have done more. I've traveled this world and established communities wherever I could. The fools believed me—they still believe me. Everywhere you look the myth is taking hold."

Vespasian shook his head. "It's not enough. This rebellion is sapping Rome's strength and the Emperor blames you. For that you are to die."

"By crucifixion? Like the fisherman?" the prisoner asked, suddenly conscious of the moans of the dying men nailed to the Tau crosses beyond the encampment.

"No. As a Roman citizen you will at least be spared that. You will be taken back to Rome under escort—by men I can ill afford to lose—and there you will be put to the sword."

"When?"

"You leave at dawn. But before you die, the Emperor has one final order for you."

Vespasian moved to the table and picked up two diptychs—wooden tablets with the inside surfaces covered in wax and joined with wire along one side as a rudimentary hinge. Both had numerous holes—*foramina*—pierced around the outer edges through which triple-thickness *linum* had been passed, thread that was then secured with a seal bearing the likeness of Nero. This prevented the tablets being opened without breaking the seal, and was common practice with legal documents to guard against forgeries. Each had a short note in ink on the front to indicate what the text comprised, and both had been personally entrusted to Vespasian by Nero before the general left Rome. The old man had seen them many times before.

Vespasian pointed to a small scroll on the table and told the prisoner what Nero expected him to write.

"And if I refuse?" the prisoner asked.

"Then I have instructions that you are not to be

sent to Rome," Vespasian said, with a smile that didn't reach his eyes. "I'm sure we can find a vacant *stipes* you can occupy here for a few days."

A.D. 67–69

Rome, Italy

The Neronian Gardens, situated at the foot of what are now known as the Vatican Hills, were one of Nero's favored locations for exacting savage revenge on the group of people he saw as the principal enemies of Rome—the early Christians. He blamed them for starting the Great Fire that almost destroyed the city in A.D. 64, and since then he'd done his best to rid Rome and the Empire of what he called the Jewish "vermin."

His methods were excessive. The *lucky* ones were crucified or torn to pieces by dogs or wild animals in the Circus Maximus. Those he wanted really to suffer were coated in wax, impaled on stakes placed around his palace and later set on fire. This was Nero's idea of a joke. The Christians claimed to be the "light of the world," so he used them to light his way.

But Roman law forbade the crucifixion or torture of Roman citizens, and that rule, at least, the Emperor was forced to obey. And so, on a sunny morning at the end of June, Nero and his entourage watched as a swordsman worked his way steadily down a line of bound and kneeling men and women, beheading each one with a single stroke of his blade. The elderly man was the second to last and, as specifically instructed by Nero, the executioner slashed at his neck three times before his head finally tumbled free.

Nero's fury at the failure of his agent extended even beyond the man's painful death, and his body was unceremoniously tossed into a cart and driven miles out of Rome, to be dumped in a small cave, the entrance then sealed by rocks. The cave was already occupied by the remains of another man, another thorn in the Emperor's side, who had suffered crucifixion of an unusual sort three years earlier, at the very start of the Neronian Persecution.

The two diptychs and the small scroll had been handed to Nero as soon as the centurion and his Jewish prisoner arrived in Rome, but for some months the Emperor couldn't decide what to do with them. Rome was struggling to contain the Jewish revolt and Nero was afraid that if he made their contents public he would make the situation even worse.

But the documents—the scroll essentially a confession by the Jew of something infinitely worse than treason, and the contents of the diptychs providing unarguable supporting evidence—were clearly valuable, even explosive, and he took immense care to keep them safe. He had an exact copy made of the scroll: on the original, he personally inscribed an explanation of its contents and purpose, authenticated by his imperial seal. The two diptychs were secreted with the bodies in the hidden cave, and the original scroll in a secure chest in a locked chamber in one of his palaces, but the copy he kept close to him, secured in an earthenware pot just in case he had to reveal its contents urgently.

Then events overtook him. In A.D. 68, chaos and civil war came to Rome. Nero was declared a traitor by the Senate, fled the city and committed suicide. He was succeeded by Galba, who was swiftly murdered by Otho. Vitellius emerged to challenge him, and defeated the new Emperor in battle: Otho, like Nero before him, fell upon his sword.

But Otho's supporters hadn't given up. They looked around for another candidate and settled on Vespasian. When word of events in Rome eventually reached him, the elderly general left the war in Judea in the more than capable hands of his son Titus and traveled to Italy, defeating Vitellius's army on the way. Vitellius was killed as Vespasian's troops secured the city. On 21 December A.D. 69, Vespasian was formally recognized by the Senate as the new Emperor, and peace was finally restored.

And in the confusion and chaos of the short but bitter Roman civil war, a locked wooden chest and an unremarkable earthenware pot, each containing a small papyrus scroll, simply disappeared.

1

I

For a few moments Jackie Hampton had no idea what had awoken her. The digital display on the radio alarm clock showed 3:18, and the master bedroom was entirely dark. But something had penetrated her slumber—a sound from somewhere in the old house.

Noises weren't unusual—the Villa Rosa had stood on the side of the hill between Ponticelli and the larger town of Scandriglia for well more than six hundred years—the old wood creaked and groaned, and sometimes cracked like a rifle shot, in response to changing temperatures. But this sound must have been something different, something unfamiliar.

Automatically she stretched out her hand to the other side of the bed, but her probing fingers met nothing but the duvet. Mark was still in London and wouldn't be flying back to Italy until Friday evening or Saturday morning. She should have been with him, but a last-minute change in their builders' schedule had forced her to stay behind.

And then she heard it again—a metallic pinging sound. One of the shutters on the ground-floor windows must have become unlatched and was banging in the wind. Jackie knew she wouldn't get back to sleep until it was secured. She snapped on the light and slipped out of bed, slid her feet into her slippers and reached for the gown draped over the chair in front of the dressing table.

She switched on the landing light and walked briskly down the wide oak staircase to the central hall. At the foot of the stairs, she heard a noise again—slightly different from the previous sound, but still unmistakably metal on stone—and it was obviously coming from the huge living room that occupied most of the ground floor on the east side of the house.

Almost without thinking, Jackie pushed open the door. She stepped inside the room, turning on the main lights as she did so. The moment the two chandeliers flared into life, the source of the metallic knocking sound became obvious. She raised her hands to her face with a gasp of fear, then turned to run.

A black-clad figure was standing on a dining chair and chipping away with a hammer and chisel at a section of the plaster over the massive inglenook fireplace, his work illuminated by the beam of a flashlight held by another man. Even as Jackie backed away, both men turned to look at her with startled expressions on their faces. The man with the flashlight muttered a muffled curse and began running toward her.

"Oh God, oh God, oh God." Jackie sprinted across the wide hall, heading for the staircase and the safety of the master bedroom. The wood on the door was more than an inch thick and there was a solid steel bolt on the inside. Beside the bed was an extension phone, and her cell phone was in her handbag on the dressing table. If she could just get inside the room, she knew she'd be safe and could call for help.

But she wasn't dressed for running, and the man behind her was. The slipper fell off her right foot as she reached the third stair, and she could hear the pounding of her pursuer's trainers on the stone-flagged floor of the hall, just yards behind her. Her feet scrabbled for grip on the polished wooden treads, then she stumbled, missed a step and fell to her knees.

In an instant the man was on her, grabbing at her arm and shoulder.

Jackie screamed and twisted sideways, kicking out with her right leg. Her bare foot smashed into the man's groin. He moaned in pain, and in a reflex action swung his flashlight at her. The heavy-duty aluminum tube crashed into the side of Jackie's head as she tried to stand. Dazed, she lurched sideways and grabbed at the banister, but her grasping fingers missed it. She fell heavily, her head smashing into the rail, instantly breaking her neck. Her body tumbled limply down the staircase and came to rest on the hall floor, her limbs spread out, blood pouring from the wound on her temple.

Her pursuer walked down the stairs and stood over her. The second intruder appeared from the door to the living room and looked down at the silent and unmoving figure. He knelt beside her and pressed his fingertips to the side of her neck.

After a moment he looked up angrily. "You weren't supposed to kill her," he snapped.

Alberti looked down at his handiwork and shrugged. "She wasn't supposed to be here. We were told the house would be empty. It was an accident," he added, "but she's dead and there's nothing we can do about it."

Rogan straightened up. "You're right about that. Come on. Let's finish what we've got to do and get out of here."

Without a backward glance, the two men returned to the living room. Rogan picked up the hammer and chisel and continued to chip away at the remaining sections of old plaster above the huge stone lintel that spanned the entire width of the fireplace.

The work took very little time, and in some twenty minutes the entire area was exposed. Both men stood in front of the fireplace, staring at the letters carved into one of the stones.

"Is that it?" Alberti asked.

Rogan nodded uncertainly. "It looks like it, yes. Get the plaster ready."

As Alberti left the room carrying a bucket to collect some water, Rogan removed a high-resolution digital camera from his pocket and took half a dozen shots of the stone. He used the screen to check that they all clearly showed the inscription carved on it. Then, for good measure, he wrote down the words in a small notebook.

Alberti reappeared with the water. From the detritus left by the builders, he picked a wooden mixing board and trowel, then selected a bag of plaster from the pile stacked against one wall. A few minutes later, once he had a firm mix, he carried the board over to the fireplace.

The lintel rested on a steel plate, obviously a fairly recent repair to compensate for an unsightly crack that ran diagonally through the stone about two feet from the left-hand edge. The steel projected about half an inch in front of the lintel, and provided a firm base for the plaster.

Alberti clearly had some experience of the technique, and in about half an hour had produced a smooth and professional finish that neatly matched the new plaster on the right-hand side of the fireplace. The other side still had old plaster on it—the builders hadn't got that far yet—but there was nothing they could do about that.

Fifty minutes after Jackie Hampton died, and almost ninety minutes after the two Italians had forced the rear door of the house, they walked away from the property, heading for the nearby lane where they'd left their car.

II

Chris Bronson swung his silver Mini Cooper into a space on the second floor of the Crescent Road multi-story parking garage, which was directly opposite the police headquarters in Tunbridge Wells. For a few moments he sat in the driver's seat, lost in thought. This morning, he anticipated, was going to be difficult, very difficult.

It wasn't the first time he'd had problems with Harrison, though the way he was feeling it might well be the last. Detective Inspector Thomas Harrison—"Tom" to his few friends, and "the fat bastard" to almost everyone else—was Bronson's immediate superior, and they hadn't got on from day one.

Harrison considered himself to be an old-school policeman, who'd come up through the ranks, as he never tired of telling anyone who asked and most people who didn't, and he resented Bronson for a number of reasons. The D.I. was particularly scathing about "smart-arse coppers": officers who joined the force after university and enjoyed certain privileges as a result. He'd lumped Bronson in with this group, though he didn't have a degree and had joined the army on a short-service commission straight from school. In short, Harrison believed that Bronson—whom he normally referred to as "Death Wish"—was just "playing" at being a policeman: the fact that he was clearly a highly competent officer cut no ice with him.

In the six months that Bronson had been stationed at Tunbridge Wells he'd been reprimanded virtually on a weekly basis by Harrison for something or other but, because he really did want a career in the police force, he'd tried his best to ignore the man's obvious dislike. Now he'd had enough.

He'd been told to report to the station early that morning, and Bronson thought he knew exactly why. Two days earlier, he'd been involved with other officers—uniformed and plainclothes—in the apprehension of a gang of young men suspected of dealing in Class A substances. The gang's normal turf was East London, but they'd recently expanded their operations into Kent. The arrests hadn't gone as smoothly as everyone had hoped and in the resulting scuffles two of the young men had suffered minor injuries. Bronson suspected that Harrison was going to accuse him of using unnecessary force during the arrest, or even assaulting a suspect.

He climbed out of the car, locked it and walked down the stairs—the elevators in the parking garage didn't start running until eight—to the street.

Ten minutes later he knocked on the door of D.I. Harrison's office.

III

Maria Palomo had lived in the Monti Sabini area all her life, and still, at seventy-three years of age, worked a fifty-hour week. She was a cleaner, though it wasn't work she enjoyed, and she wasn't all that good at it. But she *was* honest—her clients could leave a pile of euro notes on a desk and be quite certain that all of them would still be there when Maria had finished—and reliable, in that she'd arrive more or less when she said she would. And if the odd corner remained unswept and the oven didn't get cleaned more than once a year, well, at least the windows sparkled and the carpets were clean.

Maria, in short, was better than nothing, and in her

voluminous handbag she had the keys to some thirty properties in the Ponticelli–Scandriglia area. Some houses she cleaned, others she simply checked for security while their owners were away, and in a few she watered the plants, sorted out the mail and checked that the lights and taps worked and that the drains hadn't overflowed.

Villa Rosa was one of the houses she cleaned, though Maria wasn't sure how long the arrangement was likely to last. She was fond of the young Englishwoman, who used Maria's visits to polish her Italian, but her customer had voiced some dissatisfaction recently. On her last two visits, in particular, she'd pointed out several areas where the cleanliness could have been much improved, to which Maria had responded as she always did, with a smile and a shrug. It wasn't easy, she'd explained, to keep everything clean when the house was full of builders and their tools and equipment. And dust, of course.

That clearly hadn't pleased Signora Hampton, who'd urged her to try a little harder, but Maria was beyond the stage where she took very much notice of what people asked her to do. She'd go to the house every week, do as little as she thought she could get away with and see what happened. If the Englishwoman sacked her, she'd find work somewhere else. It really wasn't much of a problem.

A little after nine that morning, Maria pottered up the drive to Villa Rosa on the elderly Vespa she'd used to get around the area for the last fifteen years. The scooter didn't belong to her, and she'd been lent it so long ago that she barely remembered who did own it. This confusion extended to the Vespa's documentation—it wasn't licensed and hadn't been tested for roadworthiness in a number of years, but that didn't concern Maria, who'd never bothered applying for a driving license. She just took care to avoid the *Polizia Municipale* and the less frequently seen *Carabinieri* when she was riding it.

She stopped the scooter in front of the house and pulled it onto its stand. Her helmet—she complied with the law to that extent—went onto the seat, and she strode across to the front door. Maria knew Jackie was at home, so she left the keys in her bag and rang the bell.

Two minutes later she rang it again, with the same lack of response. That puzzled her, so she walked over to the double garage that stood to one side of the house and peered behind the partially open door. The Hamptons' car—an Alfa Romeo sedan—was there, just as she had expected. The house was too far from Ponticelli for her employer to go there on foot, and in any case she knew Jackie wasn't much of a walker. So where was she?

The garden perhaps, she thought, and walked around the side of the house to the rear lawn, studded with shrubs and half a dozen small flower beds, that rose gently away from the old building. But the back garden was deserted.

Maria shrugged and returned to the main door of the house, fishing in her bag for her bunch of keys. She located the Yale, slid it into the lock and turned it, ringing the bell again as she did so. "Signora Hampton?" she called, as the door swung wide open. "Signora . . ."

The word died in her throat as she saw the sprawled figure lying motionless on the stone floor, a pool of blood surrounding the woman's head like a dark red halo.

Maria Palomo had buried two husbands and five other relatives, but there was a world of difference between the anticipation of seeing a sheet-draped figure in a mortuary chapel and what she was looking at. A scream burst from her throat and she turned and ran out of the house and across the gravel drive.

Then she stopped and turned to face the building. The door was fully open and, despite the brightness of the early-morning sun, she could still see the shape on the floor. For a few seconds she stood unmoving, working out what she should do.

She had to call the police, obviously, but she also knew that once the *polizia* were involved, everyone's life would be placed under the microscope. Maria walked over to the Vespa, pulled on her helmet, started the engine and rode the scooter down the drive. When she reached the road, she turned right. Half a mile away was a house owned by one of her numerous extended family, a place where she could safely leave the Vespa and get a lift back to the Hamptons' house.

Twenty minutes later Maria stepped out of the front passenger seat of her nephew's old Lancia and led the way over to the still-open front door of the property. They walked into the hall and looked at the body. Her nephew bent down and felt one of Jackie's wrists, then crossed himself and took a couple of steps backward. Maria had known what to expect, and barely reacted at all.

"Now I can call the *polizia,"* she announced. She picked up the phone that stood on the hall table and dialed 112, the Italian emergency number.

2

"You've really screwed up this time, Death Wish," Harrison began.

Right, Bronson thought. That's it. He was standing in front of the D.I.'s cluttered desk, a swivel chair beside him that Harrison had pointedly not invited him to sit in. Bronson glanced over his shoulder, a puzzled expression on his face, then looked back.

"Who are you talking to?" he asked quietly.

"You, you little shit," Harrison snapped. This was laughable, as Bronson stood three inches taller than his superior, though he weighed substantially less.

" 'My name's Christopher Bronson, and I'm a detective sergeant. You can call me Chris. You can call me D.S. Bronson, or you can just call me Bronson. But, you fat, ugly bastard, you can't call me 'Death Wish.' "

Harrison's face was a picture. "What did you call me?"

"You heard," Bronson said, and sat down in the swivel chair.

"You'll bloody well stand when you're in my office."

"I'll sit, thanks. What did you want to see me about?"

"Stand up!" Harrison shouted. Outside the glass-walled cubicle, the few officers who had arrived early were starting to take an interest in the interview.

"I've had it with you, Harrison," Bronson said, stretching out his legs comfortably in front of him. "Ever since I joined this station you've complained about pretty much everything I've done, and I've gone along with it because I actually like being in the force, even if it means working with incompetent arseholes like you. But today, I've changed my mind."

Small gobbets of spittle had gathered around Harrison's mouth. "You insubordinate bastard. I'll have your warrant card for this."

"You can certainly try. I suppose you've worked out some scheme to charge me with assaulting a prisoner or using excessive force during an arrest?"

Harrison nodded. "And I've got witnesses," he growled.

Bronson smiled at him. "I'm sure you have. I just hope you're paying them enough. And do you realize that's almost the first sentence you've spoken since I walked in here that didn't have a swearword in it, you foulmouthed, illiterate idiot?"

For a few moments Harrison said nothing, just stared at Bronson, his eyes smoldering with hate.

"It's been lovely, having this little chat," Bronson said, standing up. "I'm going to take a day or two off work now. That'll give you time to decide whether you're going to carry on with this charade or start acting as if you really were a senior police officer."

"You can consider yourself suspended, Bronson."

"That's better—you actually got my name right that time."

"You're bloody well suspended. Give me your warrant card and get the hell out of here." Harrison held out his hand.

Bronson shook his head. "I think I'll hang on to it for the moment, thanks. And while you decide what you're going to do you might like to take a look at this." Bronson fished in his jacket pocket and pulled out a slim black object. "To save you asking, it's a tape recorder. I'll send you a copy of our conversation, such as it was. If you want an inquiry, I'll let the investigating officers listen to it.

"And this," Bronson extracted a buff envelope from another pocket and tossed it on the desk, "is a formal request for a transfer. Do let me know what you decide to do. You've got my numbers, I think."

Bronson clicked off the recorder and walked out of the office.

II

The telephone in the apartment in Rome rang just after eleven thirty that morning, but Gregori Mandino was in the shower, so the answering machine cut in after half a dozen rings.

Fifteen minutes later, shaved and dressed in his usual attire of white shirt, dark tie and light gray suit, Mandino prepared a large *café latte* in the kitchen and carried it into his study. He sat down at his desk, pressed the "play" button on the machine and leaned forward to ensure he heard the message clearly. The caller had used a code incomprehensible to an eavesdropper, but the meaning was clear enough to Mandino. He frowned, dialed a number on his Nokia, held a brief conversation with the man at the other end, then sat back in his leather chair to consider the news he'd been given. It wasn't, by any stretch of the imagination, what he had wanted or expected to hear.

The call was from his deputy in Rome, a man whom he had come to trust. The task he had given Antonio Carlotti had been simple enough. Just get a couple of men inside the house, get the information and get out again. But the woman had been killed—whether it had been a genuinely accidental death he neither knew nor cared—and the information the men had obtained added almost nothing to what he already knew.

For a few minutes Mandino sat at his desk, his irritation growing. He wished he'd never become involved in this mess. But it hadn't been his choice, and the instructions he'd been given years ago had been both clear and specific. He couldn't, he rationalized, have disregarded what they'd found out through the Internet, and the Latin phrase was the most positive clue they'd ever unearthed. He had no choice but to get on with the job.

Just, in fact, as he had no real choice about what to do next. Distasteful though it might be to him, in view of what had happened, at least one man would have to be informed.

Mandino crossed to his wall safe, spun the combination lock and opened the door. Inside were two semi-automatic pistols, both with loaded magazines, and several thick bundles of currency secured with rubber bands, mainly U.S. dollars and middle-denomination euro notes. At the very back of the safe was a slim volume bound in old leather, its edges worn and faded, and with nothing on the front cover or the spine to indicate what it contained. Mandino took it out and carried it across to his desk, released the metal clasp that held the covers closed, and opened it.

He turned the handwritten pages slowly, scanning the faded ink lettering and wondering, as he did every time he looked at the volume, about the instructions it contained. Almost at the end of the book one page contained a list of telephone numbers, clearly a fairly recent addition, as most had been written using a ball-point pen.

Mandino ran a finger down the list until he found the one he was looking for. Then he glanced at the digital clock on his desk and picked up his cell phone again.

III

In his office in the City, Mark Hampton had shut down his computer and was about to go off for lunch—he had a standing arrangement with three of his colleagues to meet at the pub around the corner every Wednesday—when he heard the knock. He shrugged on his jacket, walked across the room and opened the door.

Two men he didn't recognize were standing outside. They didn't, he was certain, work for the firm: Mark prided himself on knowing, if only by sight, all of the employees. There were stringent security precautions in place in the building as all four companies housed there were involved in investment and asset management, and their offices held financially critical data and programs, which meant that the men must have been properly checked in by the security staff.

"Mr. Hampton?" The voice didn't quite match the suit. "I'm Detective Sergeant Timms and my colleague here is Detective Constable Harris. I'm afraid we have some very bad news for you, sir."

Mark's mind whirled, making instant deductions based on nothing at all, and almost immediately dismissing them. Who? Where? What had happened?

"I believe your wife is at your property in Italy, sir?"

Mark nodded, not trusting himself to speak.

"I'm afraid there's been an accident there. I'm very sorry to have to tell you that your wife is dead."

Time seemed to stop. Mark could see the police officer's mouth opening and closing, he even heard the words, but his brain completely failed to register their meaning. He turned away and walked across to his desk, his movements mechanical and automatic. He sat down in his swivel chair and looked out of the window, seeing but not seeing the familiar shapes of the high-rise buildings that surrounded him.

Timms had continued talking to him. "The Italian police have requested that you travel out there as soon as possible, sir. Is there anybody you'd like us to contact? Someone who can go with you? To handle the—"

"How?" Mark interrupted. "How did it happen?"

Timms glanced at Harris and gave a slight shrug. "She was found by your cleaning lady this morning. It looks as if she had a bad fall on the stairs sometime last night. I'm afraid she broke her neck."

Mark didn't respond, just continued to stare out of the window. This couldn't be happening. It must be some kind of mistake. It's somebody else. They've got the name wrong. That must be it.

But Timms was still there, still spouting the kind of platitudes Mark assumed policemen had been trained to say to bereaved relatives. Why didn't he just shut up and go away?

"Do you understand that, sir?"

"What? Sorry. Could you say that again?"

"You have to go to Italy, sir. You have to identify the body and make the funeral arrangements. The Italian police will collect you from the nearest airport—I think that's probably Rome—and drive you to the house. They'll organize an interpreter and whatever other help you need. Is all that clear now?"

"Yes," Mark said. "I'm sorry. It's just—" A racking sob shook his whole body, and he sank his face into his hands. "I'm sorry. It's the shock and . . ."

Timms rested his hand briefly on Mark's shoulder. "It's quite understandable, sir. Now, is there anything you want to ask us? I've a note here of the contact details for the local police force in Scandriglia. Is there anyone you'd like us to inform on your behalf? You need somebody to stand by you at a time like this."

Mark shook his head. "No. No, thank you," he said, his voice cracking under the strain. "I have a friend I can call. Thank you."

Timms shook his hand and handed him a single sheet of paper. "Sorry again, sir. I've also included my contact details. If there's anything else you need that I can help with, please let me know. We'll see ourselves out."

As the voices faded away, Mark finally let himself go, let the tears come. Tears for himself, for Jackie, tears for all the things he should have said to her, for all that they could and should have done together. In an instant, a few words from a well-meaning stranger had changed his life beyond all recognition.

His hands shaking, he flicked through his Filofax and checked a cell phone telephone number. Timms, or whatever his name was, had been right about one thing: he definitely needed a friend, and Mark knew exactly whom he was going to call.

3

I

"Mark? What the hell's wrong? What is it?"

Chris Bronson pulled his Mini to the side of the road and held the cell phone more closely to his ear. His friend sounded totally devastated.

"It's Jackie. She's dead. She—"

As he heard the words, Bronson felt as if somebody had punched him in the stomach. There were few constants in his world, but Jackie Hampton was—or had been—one of them. For several seconds he just sat there, staring through the car's windshield, listening to Mark's tearful explanation but hearing almost none of it. Finally, he tried to pull himself together.

"Oh, Christ, Mark. Where did . . . ? No, never mind. Where are you? Where is she? I'll come straight over."

"Italy. She's in Italy and I have to go there. I have to identify her, all that. Look, Chris, I don't speak the language, and you do, and I don't think I can do this by myself. I know it's a hell of an imposition, but could you take some time off work and come with me?"

For a moment, Bronson hesitated, sudden intense grief meshing with his long-suppressed feelings for Jackie. He genuinely didn't know if he could handle what Mark was asking him to do. But he also knew his friend wouldn't be able to cope without him.

"I'm not sure I've got a job right now, so taking time off isn't a problem. Have you booked flights, or what?"

"No," Mark replied. "I've not done anything. You're the first person I called."

"Right. Leave it all to me," Bronson said, his firm voice giving the lie to his emotions. He glanced at his watch, calculating times and what he would need to accomplish. "I'll pick you up at the apartment in two hours. Is that long enough for you to sort things out at your end?"

"I think so, yes. Thanks, Chris. I really appreciate this."

"Don't mention it. I'll see you in a couple of hours."

Bronson slipped the phone into his pocket, but didn't move for several seconds. Then he flipped on the turn signal and pulled the car back out into the traffic, working out what he had to do, keeping his mind focused on the mundane to avoid dwelling on the awful reality of Jackie's sudden death.

He was only a few hundred yards from his house. Packing would take him no longer than thirty minutes, but he'd need to find his passport, pick out whichever cards had the most credit left on them, and get to the bank and draw some euros. He'd have to let the Crescent Road station know he was taking unpaid compassionate leave and confirm they had his cell phone number—he would still have to follow the rules despite his problems with Harrison.

And then he'd have to fight his way through the London traffic to get to Mark's crash pad in Ilford. Two hours, he guessed, should be about right. He wouldn't bother trying to book tickets, because he wasn't certain when they would reach Stansted, but he guessed EasyJet or Ryanair would have a flight to Rome sometime that afternoon.

II

The direct-line telephone in Joseph Cardinal Vertutti's sumptuous office in the Vatican rang three times before he walked across to the desk and picked it up.

"Joseph Vertutti."

The voice at the other end of the line was unfamiliar, but conveyed an unmistakable air of authority. "I need to see you."

"Who are you?"

"That is not important. The matter concerns the Codex."

For a moment, Vertutti didn't grasp what his unidentified caller was talking about. Then realization dawned, and he involuntarily gripped the edge of his desk for support.

"The what?" he asked.

"We probably don't have a great deal of time, so please don't mess me about. I'm talking about the Vitalian Codex, the book you keep locked away in the Apostolic Penitentiary."

"The Vitalian Codex? Are you sure?" Even as he said the words, Vertutti realized the stupidity of the question: the very existence of the Codex was known to a mere handful of people within the Vatican and, as far as he knew, to no one outside the Holy See. But the fact that the caller was using his external direct line meant he was calling from *outside* the Vatican walls, and the man's next words confirmed Vertutti's suspicions.

"I'm very sure. You'll need to arrange a Vatican Pass for me to—"

"No," Vertutti interrupted. "Not here. I'll meet you outside." He felt uncomfortable about allowing his mystery caller access to the Holy See. He opened a desk drawer and pulled out a map of Rome. Quickly his fingers traced a path south, from the Vatican Station. "In the Piazza di Santa Maria alle Fornaci, a few streets south of the Basilica di San Pietro. There's a café on the east side, opposite the church."

"I know it. What time?"

Vertutti automatically glanced down at his appointments book, though he knew he was not going to meet the man that morning: he wanted time to think about this meeting. "This afternoon at four thirty?" he suggested. "How will I recognize you?"

The voice in his ear chuckled. "Don't worry, Cardinal. I'll find you."

III

Chris Bronson drove his Mini into the long-term parking at Stansted Airport, locked the car and led Mark toward the terminal building. Each man carried a carry-on and Bronson also held a small computer case.

Bronson had reached the Ilford apartment just more than an hour after leaving Tunbridge Wells, and Mark had been standing outside waiting when he pulled up. The journey up to Stansted—a quick blast up the M11—had taken them well less than an hour.

"I really appreciate this, Chris," Mark said for at least the fifth time since he'd climbed into the car.

"It's what friends do," Bronson replied. "Don't worry about it."

"Now don't take this the wrong way, but I know being a copper doesn't pay much, and you're helping me out here, so I'm picking up the tab for everything."

"There's no need," Bronson began a halfhearted objection, though in truth the cost of the trip had been worrying him—his overdraft was getting near its agreed limit and his credit cards couldn't take too much punishment. He also wasn't certain whether Harrison was going to try to suspend him or not, and what effect, if any, that would have on his salary. But Mark's last bonus had been well into six figures: money, for him, wasn't a problem.

"Don't argue," Mark said. "It's my decision."

When they got inside the airport, they realized they'd just missed the midafternoon Air Berlin flight to Fiumicino, but they were in good time for the five thirty Ryanair, which would get them to Rome's Ciampino Airport at just before nine, local time. Hampton paid with a gold credit card and was given a couple of boarding cards in return, and they made their way through the security control.

There were a few empty seats at the café close to the departure gate, so they bought drinks and sat down to wait for the flight to be called.

Mark had said very little on the journey to the airport—he was clearly still in shock, his eyes red-rimmed—but Bronson desperately needed to find out what had happened to Jackie.

"What did the police tell you?" he asked now.

"Not very much," Mark admitted. "The Metropolitan Police received a message from the Italian police. They'd been called out to our house this morning. Apparently our cleaning woman had gone to the house as usual, got no answer and used her key to get inside." He squeezed his eyes shut for a brief moment, then took out a tissue and dabbed at them. "Sorry," he said. "She told the police she'd found Jackie dead on the floor of the hall. According to the Italian police, she'd apparently stumbled on the stairs—they found both of her slippers on the staircase—and hit the side of her head against the banister."

"And that . . ." Bronson prompted.

Mark nodded, the depth of his despair obvious. "And that broke her neck." His voice cracked on the last word, and he took a sip of water.

"Anyway," he went on, "Maria Palomo—she's the cleaner—told the police that I worked in London. They traced me through the British Embassy in Rome, and they contacted the police here."

That was the limit of his knowledge, but the paucity of information didn't stop him speculating. Indeed, for the next hour or so he did little else but hash and rehash possible scenarios. Bronson let him—it was probably good therapy for him to get it out of his system—and, to be selfish, it gave Bronson a chance simply to sit there, contributing little to the conversation, as his mind spanned the years and he remembered Jackie when she'd been plain Jackie Evans.

Bronson and Mark had first met at school, and had formed a friendship that had endured, despite the very different career paths they'd followed. They'd both known Jackie for almost the same length of time, and Bronson had fallen helplessly, hopelessly in love with her. The problem was that Jackie only really ever had eyes for Mark. Bronson had hidden his feelings, and when Jackie married Mark, he had been the best man and Angela Lewis—the girl who would become Mrs. Bronson less than a year later—was one of the bridesmaids.

"Sorry, Chris," Mark muttered, as they finally took their seats in the rear section of the Boeing 737. "I've done nothing but talk about me and Jackie. You must be sick of it."

"If you hadn't, I'd have been really worried. Talking is good for you. It helps you come to terms with what's happened, and I don't mind sitting here and listening."

"I know, and I do appreciate it. But let's change the subject. How's Angela?"

Bronson smiled slightly. "Perhaps not the best choice of topic. We've just finalized the divorce."

"Sorry, I didn't think. Where's she living now?"

"She bought a small apartment in London, and I kept the little house in Tunbridge."

"Are you talking to each other?"

"Yes, now that the lawyers are finally out of the picture. We *are* talking, but we're not on particularly good terms. We just weren't compatible, and I'm glad we found out before any kids arrived to complicate things."

That, Bronson silently acknowledged, was the explanation both he and Angela gave anyone who asked, though he wasn't sure if Angela really believed it. But that wasn't why their marriage failed. With the benefit of hindsight, he knew he should never have married her—or anyone else—because he was still in love with Jackie. Essentially, he'd been on the rebound.

"Is she still at the British Museum?"

Bronson nodded. "Still a ceramics conservator. I suppose that's one of the reasons we split up. She works long hours there, and she had to do field trips every year. Add that to the antisocial hours I work as a cop, and you'll see why we started communicating by notes—we were almost never at home at the same time."

The lie tripped easily off Bronson's tongue. After about eighteen months of marriage he'd begun to find it easier to volunteer for overtime—there was always plenty on offer—instead of going home to an unsatisfactory relationship and the increasingly frequent rows.

"She loves her job, and I thought I loved mine, but that's another story. Neither of us was willing to give up our career, and eventually we just drifted apart. It's probably for the best."

"You've got problems at work?" Mark asked.

"Just the one, really. My alleged superior officer is an illiterate idiot who's hated me since the day I walked into the station. This morning I finally told him to shove it, and I've no idea if I'll still have a job when I get back."

"Why do you do it, Chris? There must be better jobs out there."

"I know," Bronson replied, "but I enjoy being a cop. It's just people like D.I. Harrison who do their best to make my life a misery. I've applied for a transfer, and I'm going to make sure I get one."

4

Joseph Vertutti changed into civilian clothes before leaving the Holy See and, striding down the Via Stazione di Pietro in his lightweight blue jacket and slacks, he looked like any other slightly overweight Italian businessman.

Vertutti was the cardinal head, the Prefect, of the dicastery of the Congregation for the Doctrine of the Faith, the oldest of the nine congregations of the Roman Curia and the direct descendant of the Roman Inquisition. Its present-day remit hadn't changed much since the times when being burned alive was the standard punishment for heretics, only now Vertutti ensured that it was somewhat more sophisticated in its operations.

He continued south, past the church, before crossing to the east side of the street. Then he turned north, back toward the piazza, the bright red and green paintwork of the café building contrasting with the Martini umbrellas that shaded the tables outside from the afternoon sun. Several of these tables were occupied, but there were three or four vacant at the end, and he pulled out a chair and sat down at one of them.

When the waiter finally approached, Vertutti ordered a *café latte,* leaning back to look around him and glancing at his watch. Twenty past four. His timing was almost perfect.

Ten minutes later the unsmiling waiter plopped a tall glass mug of coffee down in front of him, some of the liquid slopping into the saucer. As the waiter moved away, a heavyset man wearing a gray suit and sporting sunglasses pulled back the chair on the other side of the table and sat down.

At the same moment, two young men wearing dark suits and sunglasses each took a seat at the nearest tables, flanking them. They looked well built and very fit, and exuded an almost palpable air of menace. They glanced with disinterest at Vertutti, then began scanning the street and the pedestrians passing in front of the café. Although he'd been watching the road carefully, Vertutti had no idea where the three men had come from.

The moment his companion was seated, the waiter reappeared, took his order and vanished, taking Vertutti's slopped drink with him. In less than two minutes he was back, two fresh *lattes* on a tray, together with a basket of croissants and sweet rolls.

"They know me here," the man said, speaking for the first time.

"Who exactly are you?" Vertutti demanded. "Are you a church official?"

"My name is Gregori Mandino," the man said, "and I'm delighted to say I've got no direct link to the Catholic Church."

"Then how do you know about the Codex?"

"I know because I'm paid to know. More important," Mandino added, glancing around to ensure they weren't overheard, "I've been paid to watch for any sign that the document the Codex refers to might have been found."

"Paid by whom?"

"By you. Or, more accurately, by the Vatican. My organization has its roots in Sicily but now has extensive business interests in Rome and throughout Italy. We've been working closely with the Mother Church for nearly a hundred and fifty years."

"I know nothing of this," Vertutti spluttered. "What organization?"

"If you think about it you'll realize who I represent."

For a long moment Vertutti stared at Mandino, but it was only when he glanced at the adjoining tables, at the two alert young men who hadn't touched their drinks and who were still scanning the crowds, that the penny finally dropped. He shook his head, disbelief etched on his florid features.

"I refuse to believe we have ever been involved with the *Cosa Nostra*."

Mandino nodded patiently. "You have," he said, "since about the middle of the nineteenth century, in fact. If you don't believe me, go back to the Vatican and check, but in the meantime let me tell you a story which has been omitted from official Vatican history. One of the longest-serving popes was Giovanni Maria Mastai-Ferretti, Pope Pius IX, who—"

"I know who he was," Vertutti snapped impatiently.

"I'm glad to hear it. Then you should know that in 1870 he found himself virtually besieged by the newly unified Italian state. Ten years earlier the state had subsumed both Sicily and the Papal States, and Pius encouraged Catholics to refuse cooperation, something we'd been doing for years. Our unofficial relationship began then, and we've worked together ever since."

"That's complete nonsense," Vertutti said, his voice thick with anger. He sat back in the chair and folded his arms, his face flushed. This man—virtually a self-confessed criminal—was suggesting that for the last

century and a half the Vatican, the oldest, holiest and
most important part of the Mother of all Churches,
had been deeply involved with the most notorious
criminal organization on the planet. In any other context it would have been laughable.

And to cap it all, he, one of the most senior
cardinals of the Roman Curia, was now sitting in a
pavement café in the middle of Rome, sharing a drink
with a senior *Mafioso*. And he had no doubts that
Mandino *was* high-ranking: the deference exhibited by
the normally surly waiters, the two bodyguards, and the
man's whole air of authority and command proved
that clearly enough. And this man—this gangster—
knew about a document hidden in the Vatican archives, a document whose very existence Vertutti had
believed was one of the most closely guarded secrets
of the Catholic Church.

But Mandino hadn't finished. "Cards on the table,
Eminence," he said, the last word almost a sneer. "I
was christened a Catholic, like almost every other Italian child, but I've not set foot inside a church for forty
years, because I know that Christianity is nonsense.
Like every other religion, it's based entirely on
fiction."

Cardinal Vertutti blanched. "That's blasphemous
rubbish. The Catholic Church can trace its origins
back for two millennia, based upon the life and deeds
and very words of Jesus Christ our Lord. The Vatican
is the focus of the religion of countless millions of
believers in almost every country in the world. How
dare you say that you're right and everyone else is
wrong?"

"I dare say it because I've done my research, instead of just accepting the smoke and mirrors the
Catholic Church hides behind. Whether or not huge
numbers of people believe something has no bearing
whatsoever on its truth or validity. In the past, millions

believed that the earth was flat, and that the sun and the stars revolved around it. They were just as wrong then as Christians are today."

"Your arrogance astounds me. Christianity is based upon the unimpeachable authority of the words of Jesus Christ himself, the son of God. Are you really denying the truth of the Word of God and the Holy Bible?"

Mandino smiled slightly and nodded. "You've gone right to the crux of the matter, Cardinal. There's no such thing as the Word of God—only the word of man. Every religious tract ever written has been the work of men, usually writing something for their own personal gain or to suit their individual circumstances. Name me one single thing—anything at all—that proves God exists."

Vertutti opened his mouth to reply, but Mandino beat him to it. "I know. You have to have faith. Well, I don't, because I've studied the Christian religion, and I know that it's an opiate designed to keep the people in line and allow the men who run the Church and the Vatican to live in luxury without actually doing a useful job of work.

"You can't prove God exists, but I can almost prove that Jesus *didn't*. The only place where there's any reference to Jesus Christ is in the New Testament, and that—and you know this just as well as I do, whether you admit it or not—is a heavily edited collection of writings, not one of which can be considered to be even vaguely contemporary with the subject matter. To come up with the "agreed" gospels, the Church banned dozens of other writings that flatly contradict the Jesus myth.

"If Jesus was such a charismatic and inspiring leader, and performed the miracles and all the other things the Church claims he did, how come there's not *one single reference* to him in any piece of contemporary Greek, Roman or Jewish literature? If this man was so important, attracted such a devoted following and was such a thorn in the side of the occupying Roman army, why didn't anybody write something about him? The *fact* is that he only exists in the New Testament, the "source" that the Church has fabricated and edited over the centuries, and there's not a single shred of *independent* evidence that he ever even existed."

Like every churchman, Vertutti was used to people doubting the Word of God—in an increasingly Godless world, that was inevitable—but Mandino seemed to harbor an almost pathological hatred of the Church and everything it stood for. And that begged the obvious question.

"If you hate and despise the Church so much, Mandino, why are you involved in this matter at all? Why should you care about the future of the Catholic religion?"

"I've already told you, Cardinal. We agreed to undertake this task many years ago, and my organization takes its responsibilities seriously. No matter what my personal feelings, I'll do my best to finish the job."

"You're lucky to be living in this century if you harbor such heretical views."

"I know. In the Middle Ages, no doubt, you'd have chained me to a post and burned me alive to make me see things your way."

Vertutti took a sip of his drink. Despite his instant and total loathing for this man, he knew he was going to have to work with him to resolve the present crisis. He put the mug back on the table and looked across at Mandino.

"We must agree to differ in our views of the Church and the Vatican," he said. "I'm much more concerned about the matter in hand. You obviously know something about the Codex. Who told you about it?"

Mandino nodded and leaned forward. "My organization has been involved in the quest to find the source document since the beginning of the last century," he began. "The task has always been the sole responsibility of the head—the *capofamiglia*—of the Rome family. When that mantle fell upon my shoulders, I was given a book to read, a book that to me made little sense. So I sought clarification from your dicastery, as the source of the original request, and your predecessor was kind enough to supply me with some additional information, facts that he believed would help me to appreciate the critical nature of the task."

"He should never have done so." Vertutti's voice was low and angry. "Knowledge of this matter is restricted to only a few of the most trusted and reliable senior Vatican officials. What did he tell you?"

"Not a great deal," Mandino replied, his tone now conciliatory. "He simply explained that the Church was seeking a document lost for centuries, an ancient text that must never be allowed to fall into the hands of anyone outside the Vatican."

"That was all?" Vertutti asked.

"More or less, yes."

Vertutti felt a surge of relief. If that genuinely was all the information his predecessor had divulged, then little real damage had been done. The Vitalian Codex was certainly the darkest of all the multitude of secrets hidden in the Apostolic Penitentiary and it seemed that for now this particular secret was safe. But the crux of the matter was whether he trusted Gregori Mandino enough to believe him.

"We've established you know about the Codex. But what I still don't know is why you called me. Do you have some information? Has something happened?"

Mandino appeared to ignore the question. "All in good time, Eminence. You're obviously not aware that a small group of my people has been constantly watching for the publication of any of the significant words and phrases contained within the Codex. This is in accordance with the written instructions given to us by your dicastery more than a hundred years ago.

"We have monitoring systems in all the obvious places, but since the arrival of the Internet, we've also focused on dead language translation sites, both the online programs and those supplying more professional services. With the agreement of your predecessor, we set up a small office here in Rome, ostensibly charged with the identification, recovery and study of ancient texts. Under the guise of scholarly research, we requested all Latin, Hebrew, Greek, Coptic and Aramaic translators we were able to identify to advise us whenever they received passages that contained the target words, and almost all of them agreed.

"We've also approached the online programs, and most of these have been easier—it's amazing what co-operation you get if people think you work for the Pope. We've simply supplied the same word list for each language service, and in every case the Web site owners have agreed to notify us whenever anyone requests a translation that fits the parameters. Most of the sites have automatic systems that send us e-mails containing the word or words, and any other information they have about the person making the request. This sometimes includes their name and e-mail, but we always get their IP address."

"Which is what?" Vertutti asked.

"It's a set of numbers that identify a location on the Internet. We can use it to find the person's address, or at least the address of the computer they used. Obviously if an inquiry comes from an Internet café there's no easy way of identifying the person who made it."

"Is all this relevant?"

"Yes, just bear with me. We've cast our net wide

and we've specified a huge number of words to ensure that nothing gets past us. We also have programs in place that scan the e-mails we receive and identify the most likely matches. They're known as syntax checkers. Until last week, no expression scored more than forty-two percent.

"And then two days ago we received this." He reached into his jacket pocket and extracted a single sheet of paper. He unfolded it and handed it to Vertutti. "The syntax checkers rated it at seventy-three to seventy-six percent, almost double the highest score we'd seen previously."

Vertutti looked down at the page in front of him. On it, typed in capital letters, were three words in Latin:

HIC VANIDICI LATITANT

5

I

"And this came from where, exactly?" Joseph Cardinal Vertutti asked, still staring down at the paper in his hand. Below the Latin was a translation of the words into Italian.

"An online translation program on a server located in America—Arlington, Virginia, to be exact. But the inquiry originated here in Italy, at an address only a few miles outside Rome."

"Why would they choose an American site?"

Gregori Mandino shrugged. "On the Internet, geographical locations are irrelevant. People pick whatever site they find the easiest to use or the fastest or most comprehensive."

"And the translation? Is this what the program provided?"

"No, though it's fairly close. The American site suggested 'In this place or location the liars are concealed,' which is clumsy at best. My language specialist's interpretation is much more elegant: 'Here lie the liars.' "

"The Latin is clear enough," Vertutti murmured.

" '*Hic*' is obviously 'here,' and I would perhaps have expected '*vatis mendacis*'—'false prophets'—rather than '*vanidici*,' but why '*latitant*'? Surely '*occubant*' would have been more literal?"

Mandino smiled slightly and extracted two photographs. "We anticipated that question, Eminence, and you would have been right if this inscription had been found at a grave site. '*Occubant*'—'buried' or 'resting in the grave'—would have been far more likely. But this inscription isn't on a tombstone. It's carved on a small oblong stone that's part of the wall above a fireplace in a six-hundred-year-old converted farmhouse in the Monti Sabini region."

"What?" For the first time, Vertutti was shocked. "Let me see those pictures," he instructed.

Mandino passed them over and Vertutti studied them for a few moments. One was a close-up view of the inscription, and the other several stones over a large fireplace. "Then why," he asked, "are you so certain this has anything at all to do with the Codex?"

"I wasn't at first, and that's why I decided to investigate further. And that, I'm afraid, is when things went wrong."

"You'd better explain."

"The person who made this inquiry left their e-mail address—it's one of the conditions of using this particular site—and that made tracing them a lot easier. We identified the house from which the request for the translation was made. It's located a short distance off the road between Ponticelli and Scandriglia, and was bought last year by an English couple named Hampton."

"And then what did you do?" Vertutti demanded, fearing the worst.

"I instructed my deputy to send two men to the house when we believed the owners would be away in Britain, but what we didn't know was that Signora

Hampton was still on the property. For some reason she hadn't accompanied her husband. The men broke in and began searching for the source of the Latin phrase, and quickly located it carved into the stone above the fireplace. It had been covered in plaster that a team of builders are replacing and only part of the stone had been exposed. That section contained the inscription.

"They'd been ordered to find the Latin phrase and anything else that might be relevant, and their first task was to check the entire stone for any other inscriptions. The men began chipping away the plaster but Signora Hampton heard them, and came down to investigate. When she saw what was happening she ran away. One of the men chased her, and in a scuffle on the stairs she fell against the banister rail and broke her neck. It was a simple accident."

This was even worse than Vertutti had expected. An innocent woman dead. "A simple accident?" he echoed. "Do you really expect me to believe that? I know the way your organization works. Are you sure she wasn't pushed? Or even beaten to death?"

Mandino smiled coldly. "I can only repeat what I've been told. We'll never know what really happened in that house, but the woman would have had to die eventually. I understand that the provisions of the Sanction are unambiguous."

In the middle of the seventh century, Pope Vitalian had written the Codex by hand, not wishing to entrust his recommendations to even the most devoted of scribes. Down the centuries, the contents of the Codex had been known to only a handful of the most senior and trusted men in the Vatican, including the reigning pope. None had recorded any reservations about the steps Vitalian had suggested—known as the Vitalian Sanction—should any of the forbidden relics surface, but that was hardly surprising.

"Don't you dare presume to lecture *me* about the Sanction. How do you even know about it?" Vertutti demanded, his eyes flashing with annoyance.

Mandino shrugged. "Again, from your predecessor. He told me that anyone who finds this document or has knowledge of its contents would be considered so dangerous to the Church that his or her life would be forfeit. For the good of the Church, obviously."

"The cardinal exaggerated." Vertutti leaned forward to emphasize the point. "This document must be recovered, and under no circumstances must it be allowed to enter the public domain. That much *is* true. The provisions of the Sanction are secret, but I can tell you that assassination is *not* one of the options suggested."

"Really, Eminence? The Church has openly sanctioned assassinations in the past. In fact, it's even condoned them inside the Vatican, and you know that as well as I do."

"Rubbish. Name one single incident."

"That's easy. Pope Pius XI was almost certainly assassinated in 1939 to prevent him making a crucial speech condemning Fascism at a time when the papacy had decided to embrace it. It was no surprise when his successor, Pius XII, openly supported the Third Reich."

"That's a frivolous allegation that has never been proven."

Mandino spat back, equally angry, "Of course it hasn't. But that's because the Vatican has refused to allow independent investigations into events that occur inside the Holy See. But just because the Vatican refuses to acknowledge something, that does not mean it hasn't happened or doesn't exist."

"Some people will try anything to besmirch the good name of the Church." Vertutti sat back, convinced he'd scored a point. "And your hypocrisy astounds me. *You* trying to lecture *me* about morality and murder."

"It's not hypocritical at all, Eminence." Again, Mandino sneered the word. "At least the *Cosa Nostra* doesn't hide behind the trappings of religion. Just like us, the hands of the Catholic Church have been stained red with blood throughout the centuries, and still are today."

For a few moments both men remained silent, glaring at each other across the table, then Vertutti dropped his gaze.

"This is getting us nowhere, and obviously we'll have to work together." He took another sip of his coffee to emphasize the change of mood. "Now, was the search by these men successful? What else did they find?"

"Nothing much," Mandino replied calmly, as if they hadn't, a few seconds ago, exchanged harsh words. "The same Latin text that the Hamptons found. My two men cleared all the plaster off the stone and photographed it, and made a written copy as well, but they found no other words on it."

Vertutti shook his head. Not just a death, but a completely pointless one. "So you're saying that the woman died for nothing."

Mandino gave a tight smile. "Not entirely. We did find something that the Hamptons probably dismissed as unimportant. Look closely at this photograph and you'll see it."

Vertutti took the picture from Mandino—it was the close-up of the inscription—and stared at it for a few seconds. "I can't see anything else," he said.

"It isn't another word, just eight letters: one group of two and another of three, close together, and a further group of three letters. They're at the bottom of the inscription, and very much smaller, almost like a signature." Mandino paused, savoring the moment.

"The first two groups of letters spell 'PO' and 'LDA,' and I think we can both work out what they mean. The final three are 'MAM,' and we believe they stand for 'Marcus Asinius Marcellus.' And that, I think, is all the proof we need."

II

They knew the house should be deserted, but even so Rogan and Alberti waited until just after ten thirty in the evening before they approached the building: it was just possible that the police might have left an officer there. Rogan walked around to the back, checking for any telltale lights shining or cars parked outside, but saw nothing. Satisfied, he and Alberti walked to the back door.

Both men were keenly aware that Mandino and his deputy Carlotti were extremely unhappy with them because of the death of the woman and, though the orders Carlotti had given them didn't make a lot of sense, they were determined to carry them out perfectly.

Alberti produced a collapsible jimmy from his pocket, inserted the tip between the door and the jamb and levered gently. With a slight splintering sound, the screws holding the lock in place pulled easily out of the wood, just as they'd done the previous evening, and the door swung open.

Leaving Alberti to replace the lock—they'd leave by the front door, as before—Rogan walked through the house to the staircase, lighting his way with a pencil flashlight, and ascended to the first floor. He wasn't sure exactly where he'd find what he was looking for, so he tried every room, but without success. It had to be downstairs somewhere.

It was. Four doors opened off the hall, and the third one revealed a small study. On the desk the light of the flashlight revealed a flat-panel computer monitor, keyboard and mouse, with the system unit on the floor beside it. There was also a telephone and a combined scanner and printer, plus a scatter of papers, pens, Post-it notes and the usual stuff to be found in any small office.

"Excellent," Rogan murmured. He walked across to the window, glanced through the glass to confirm that the outside shutters were closed, then drew the curtains. Only then did he turn on the main light.

He sat down in the leather swivel chair behind the desk and switched on the computer and screen. While he waited for the machine to load the operating system, he quickly checked the papers on the desk, looking for any notes that might refer to the inscription. He found a single sheet of paper on which the three Latin words had been written, with an English translation underneath. He folded the page and put it in his pocket, then continued his search, but found nothing else.

When the Windows desktop was displayed, Rogan used the mouse to open Internet Explorer. He selected "Internet Options" and cleared the history of recently visited Web sites. He also checked the "Favorites" list, looking for anything resembling the Web sites Carlotti had specified, but found nothing. Then he scanned the sent and received e-mails in Outlook Express, again following Carlotti's precise instructions, but once more his search was fruitless. Rogan checked his written instructions one final time, shrugged and then shut down the computer.

He took a last look around the room, switched off the light and walked out. Alberti was waiting in the hall.

"We'll check the living room again," Rogan said, and led the way. The new plaster over the fireplace was still slightly damp to the touch, but was a good match for that on the adjacent wall.

The two men inspected the room thoroughly, looking for pictures or drawings that might show the now-invisible inscription, but found nothing.

"I think that's it," Rogan said. "We've done everything the *capo* wanted. Let's get out of here."

They were twenty-five minutes and nearly thirty kilometers away from the house when Rogan suddenly realized that he'd forgotten to open the curtains in the study. He eased his foot off the accelerator pedal while he debated whether or not they should go back, but eventually decided it didn't matter. After all, what could anyone possibly deduce from a set of drawn curtains?

6

It was almost midnight when the taxi turned into the gravel drive, the car's headlights washing over the old stone walls of the Villa Rosa and startling a fox that was making its solitary way through the garden. Mark looked wrecked, staring at the house with a kind of horrified fascination as the car pulled to a halt. They lifted their bags out of the trunk and watched as the taxi drove away.

"Wait here, Mark. I'll go in first."

Hampton nodded, but didn't respond. He pulled a bunch of keys from his jacket pocket and passed it over. Bronson left his bag on the drive, walked over to the front door of the property and undid the lock. The door swung open and he stepped inside, turning on the hall lights as he did so.

Inevitably, the first place he looked was the stone floor at the foot of the wide oak staircase. It wasn't anything like as bad as he'd feared: the mark where Jackie's head wound had bled was still just visible as an almost circular discoloration, but somebody—probably the cleaning woman, Maria Palomo—had cleaned off the blood. There was an oblong rug beside the hall table, and Bronson dragged it over the floor until it completely covered the mark on the flagstones.

Waves of sadness rolled over him. He imagined Jackie, her body crumpled on the floor, unable to call out for help and probably knowing that she was dying. What a terrible, lonely, appalling way to die. He felt the tears welling up, and angrily brushed them away. He had to be strong. For himself, for Jackie and especially for Mark.

The stairs and hall had obviously been cleaned, and every attempt made to conceal the fact that a fatal accident had occurred in that part of the house. There was even a vase of fresh flowers on the table. Bronson made a note to give the cleaner some extra money.

He quickly walked around the rest of the property, upstairs and down, checking that the Italian police and forensic people hadn't left any debris or equipment, then went back outside.

"OK, Mark?"

Mark nodded, quite obviously anything but "OK," and followed Bronson to the door of the house.

"Go through to the kitchen," Bronson suggested. "We'll have a drink and then get to bed. I'll sort out the bags."

Mark didn't respond, just stared at the staircase and the hall floor for a few seconds, then walked down the short passage that led to the rear of the property. Bronson stepped back outside, collected their two bags and returned to the house.

He left the bags in the hall and walked through to the kitchen. Mark was sitting in an upright chair, staring at the wall. Bronson opened cupboards, finding tea and coffee, then a tin of drinking chocolate and a half-full jar of Horlicks. That wasn't what he wanted, but in a floor-level cupboard he found a selection of bottles of spirits and pulled out two of them.

"Whiskey or brandy?" Bronson asked. "Or do you want something else?"

Mark looked up at him, almost as if he was surprised to see him there. "What?"

Bronson repeated the question, holding up the bottles for emphasis.

"Oh, brandy, please. I can't bear that other stuff."

Bronson sat opposite his friend and slid a half-full tumbler across the table.

"Drink that, then get up to bed. It's been a long day and you must be exhausted."

Mark took a sip. "You should be exhausted as well."

"I am," Bronson said with a slight smile, "but I'm more concerned about you. Which bedroom do you want to use?"

"Not the master suite, Chris," Mark said, a distinct tremor in his voice. "I can't face that."

Bronson had already checked the master bedroom. Someone had tidied it—probably the cleaner—because the bed was made and Jackie's clothes neatly folded on a chair.

"No problem. I'll take your bag up to one of the guest rooms." Bronson put down his tumbler and left the kitchen, but was back in a few minutes, a small brown tablet bottle in his hand. "Here," he said, "take one of these. They'll help you sleep."

"What are they?"

"Melatonin. I found them in the bathroom. They're good for jet lag because they relax you and help you get to sleep. And they're nonaddictive, not like normal sleeping pills."

Mark nodded, and washed down the tablets with the rest of his brandy.

Bronson rinsed their glasses and put them in the sink. "Go on up. I'm just going to check the house, make sure all the doors and windows are locked, then I'll follow you."

Mark nodded and left the room. In the hall, Bronson bolted the main door, then walked around the ground floor, room by room, checking that all the windows were locked and the outside shutters bolted.

He finished his security check back in the kitchen and, as he made sure the key was turned in the backdoor lock, he glanced down at the floor. There was something on it, some small brown particles. He bent down to look more closely, picked up a couple of the larger fragments and rolled them between his forefinger and thumb. They were obviously small pieces of wood, and Bronson glanced up at the ceiling above him, wondering if the old house had a woodworm or termite problem. But the beams and floorboards were blackened with age and looked absolutely solid. The fragments weren't residue from insects either. Boring insects reduce wood almost to dust, and what he was holding in his hand were more like small wooden splinters.

Bronson unlocked the door to check the outside of it and immediately noticed on the doorframe, and level with the lock itself, a small section of compressed wood about one inch square. He knew immediately what had caused it—he'd been to enough burglaries in his short career as a police officer to recognize the marks made by a jimmy or crowbar. Obviously someone had forced the door, and fairly recently. The fragments of wood had almost certainly been ripped out when the lock was torn off.

He examined the lock carefully. Even with his bare hands, he could move it very slightly—all the original screws were there, but had barely enough purchase to keep the lock in position on the door. Somebody had broken into the house—that much was obvious—then replaced the lock and presumably left the property by the front door, which would self-lock because of the Yale. He guessed that the burglars had done this—if the cleaning woman had found the lock ripped off, she would presumably have left a message or told the police, and if the police had found it, they would hopefully have done more than just shove the screws back in the holes.

What puzzled Bronson was why any burglar would waste his time replacing the lock. In his experience, most people who broke into houses chose the easiest point of entry, picked up every item of value they could carry, and then left by the simplest route. Fast in, fast out. But in the Hamptons' property they must have taken several minutes to refit the lock. The only possible reason he could come up with was that the burglars hadn't wanted anyone to know they'd been inside the house, and that really didn't make any sense. Why should they care? The homeowner would know immediately that he'd been robbed. Unless, of course, the burglars didn't take anything, but if that were the case what was the point of them breaking in?

Bronson shook his head. He was tired after the flight and could no longer think clearly. He'd try to work out what the hell was going on once he'd got some sleep.

He looked around the kitchen and selected one of the upright chairs that flanked the wooden table. He picked it up and wedged its back under the door handle, kicking the legs to jam it firmly into position. He placed another chair behind it, so that even if somebody did force the door, the noise they'd make getting in would awaken him.

Then he went up to bed. The forced door was a puzzle that would have to wait until the morning.

7

I

Bronson woke early. His sleep had been restless and his dreams peopled with unaccountably vivid pictures of Jackie on her wedding day, smiling and radiant, contrasting with his constructed image of her crumpled body lying dead on the cold and unyielding flagstones of the hall floor.

He padded down the staircase at just after seven and went straight into the kitchen. While he waited for the kettle to boil, he removed the chair he'd used to jam the door the previous night and looked again at the damage. In daylight, the marks were even more clearly visible.

He walked around the room, opening cupboards and looking for a screwdriver. Under the sink he found a blue metal box where Mark kept a good selection of tools, a necessity in any old house. But there were no screws, which were what he needed to secure the lock properly.

Bronson made a pot of coffee, and ate a bowl of cereal for breakfast, then took a set of keys and went out to the garage. He found a plastic box half full of woodscrews on a shelf at the back. Ten minutes later, he'd fixed the lock back on the door using thicker screws about half an inch longer than the originals, but because the screws had been torn out of the wood when the door was forced, the holes had been enlarged and the wood weakened. He was certain that, even with the bigger screws in place, quite gentle pressure on the door from the outside would probably rip the lock off again. He could find a couple of bolts to fit on the door but he would have to check that with Mark before he did it. Next, he inspected the entire building for other signs of forced entry, but found nothing else.

The property stood on the side of a hill, honey-colored stone walls and small windows under a red-tiled roof, in the center of a pleasantly overgrown garden of about half an acre, a satisfying mix of lawns, shrubs and trees. Beside the house a lane snaked away up the hill to a handful of other isolated properties. The closest town—Ponticelli—was about five kilometers distant.

Bronson had visited the house twice before, once when the Hamptons had just bought it but hadn't yet moved in, and a second time, a month or so later, before all the renovation works began. He remembered the property well, and had always liked the feel of it. It was a big, rambling, slightly dilapidated farmhouse, which displayed its advanced age with a mix of charm, solidity and eccentricity. The blackened beams and floor timbers contrasted with the thick stone walls: some plastered, but many not. Jackie always used to say, her voice tinged with both pleasure and irritation, that there wasn't a straight wall or a square corner anywhere in the house.

Bronson smiled sadly at his memories. Jackie had loved the old house from the first, adored the relaxed Italian lifestyle, the café society, the food and wine, and the weather. Even when it rained, she'd said, it seemed somehow less wet than British drizzle. Mark had pointed out the logical impossibility of her argument, but that hadn't swayed her.

And now, it finally hit Bronson that he'd never hear her cheerful voice again, never be carried away by her infectious enthusiasm for all things Italian, from the cheap Chianti they bought from a small and dusty shop in the local village to the mind-blowing beauty of the lakes.

He could feel the tears coming, and quickly brought that train of thought to a halt. He forced himself to concentrate on checking the building, looking for any sign that a burglary had occurred.

Of course, with builders' tools and equipment, bags of plaster and pots of paint stacked up in almost every room, the property looked very different from his recollection. Most of the furniture had been shifted into piles and covered in dust sheets to allow the builders space to work, but Bronson was still able to identify most of the more valuable items—the TV, the stereo and computer, and half a dozen decent paintings—and even, in the master bedroom, nearly a thousand euros in notes tucked under a bottle of perfume on Jackie's dressing table.

As he walked around the house, he wondered if Mark would want to keep it, and its tragic mix of memories, or just sell the place and walk away.

A few minutes later, Bronson sat down at the kitchen table and looked at the wall clock. If Mark didn't get up soon, he was going to have to go and wake him: they had things—unpleasant things for both of them—to do today. But even as the thought crossed his mind, he heard his friend's footsteps on the stairs.

Mark looked dreadful. He was unshaven, unwashed and haggard, wearing an old pair of jeans and a T-shirt that had seen better days. Bronson filled a mug with black coffee and put it on the table in front of him.

"Morning," he said, as Mark sat down. "Would you like some breakfast?"

His friend shook his head. "No, thanks. I'll just stick to coffee. I feel about as sharp as a sponge this morning. How long have we got?"

Bronson glanced at his watch. "The mortuary is about a fifteen-minute drive, and we need to be there at nine. You'd better drink that, then we should both go and get ready. Do you want me to ring for a taxi?"

Mark shook his head and took another sip of his coffee. "We'll take the Alfa," he said. "The keys are on the hall table, in the small red bowl."

They left the house thirty minutes later. The temperature was already climbing steeply and there wasn't a single cloud in the sky, a beautiful day. It would have suited their moods better if it had been raining.

II

Joseph Cardinal Vertutti stared at the ancient text in front of him. He was in the archives of the Apostolic Penitentiary, the most secret and secure of the Vatican's numerous repositories. Most of the texts stored there were either Papal documents or material that would never be made public because it was protected by the Seal of the Confessional, the promise of absolute confidentiality for Roman Catholic priests for any information gleaned during the confessional. Because access to the archives was strictly controlled, and the contents of the documents never revealed, it was the ideal place to secrete anything the Vatican considered especially dangerous. Which was precisely why the Vitalian Codex had been stored there.

He was sitting at a table in an internal room, the door of which he'd locked from the inside. He pulled on a pair of thin cotton gloves—the fifteen-hundred-year-old relic was extremely fragile and even the slightest amount of moisture from his fingertips could do irreparable long-term damage to the pages. Hands trembling, he reached out and carefully opened the Codex.

The seventh-century Church of Christ, headed by Pope Vitalian, had existed in chaotic times. The arrival of Muhammad and the subsequent emergence of Islam had been a disaster for Christianity and within a few years Christian bishops had virtually vanished from the Middle East and Africa, and both Jerusalem and Egypt became Muslim. The Christian world had been decimated in just a few decades, despite the strenuous efforts of Vitalian and his predecessors to convert the inhabitants of the British Isles and Western Europe.

Somehow Vitalian had found time to study the contents of the archives. He'd summarized his findings in the Codex that bore his name and which Vertutti was studying yet again.

He had first seen the document just more than a decade earlier, and it had frankly terrified him then. He wasn't even sure why he was looking at it again. There was no information in the Codex he hadn't already studied and memorized.

The conversation he'd had with Mandino had disturbed him more than he was willing to admit, and as soon as he'd returned to his offices in the Vatican, Vertutti had spent more than an hour meditating and praying for guidance. It greatly concerned him that the very future of the Vatican had, almost by chance, been placed in the hands of a man who was not only a career criminal, but—far worse—also a committed atheist, a man who was apparently almost rabid in his hatred of the Catholic Church.

But as far as Vertutti could see, there was no alternative. Mandino held all the cards. Thanks to Vertutti's predecessor in the dicastery, and despite the most explicit prohibitions against the dissemination of such information, the mobster had intimate knowledge of the quest begun by Pope Vitalian almost one and a half millennia earlier. On the plus side, he also had the necessary technical resources to complete the task, and men who were willing to follow whatever orders he gave.

Vertutti's gaze dropped down to the Codex. He'd been turning the pages of the ancient document without really seeing them. Now, as he stared at the Latin sentences, he realized that the open page described the finding of the text that had so terrified Pope Vitalian, and had produced the same effect on his successors through the ages. Vertutti read the words again—words almost as familiar to him as the prayers he offered daily—and shuddered.

Then he carefully closed the Codex. He would replace the document in its climate-controlled safe and then return to his office and his Bible. He needed to pray again, and perhaps the holy book would guide him, reveal to him the best way to try to avert the disaster that was almost certainly just around the corner.

III

To say the identification of Jackie's body had been traumatic was an understatement. The moment the mortuary technician lifted the sheet to reveal his wife's face, Mark virtually collapsed, and Bronson had to grab his arm to steady him. The police officer who'd been waiting for them outside the mortuary opened his notebook and asked formally, and in passable English, if the body was that of Jacqueline Mary Hampton, but all Mark could do was nod, before turning away and stumbling from the viewing room. Bronson sat him down in the waiting room, then returned to talk to the officer.

Bronson was holding it together, just. If Mark hadn't been standing beside him, relying on him for support, he probably wouldn't have been able to handle the moment. He'd been in mortuaries dozens of times as an attending officer, waiting for desperate relatives to confirm their nightmares and identify the corpse on the table, but this was the first time, ever, that he'd been on the other side, as it were.

Jackie looked incredibly peaceful, as though she was merely asleep and might at any moment open her eyes and sit up, and as beautiful as ever. Somebody had taken a lot of trouble over her appearance. Her hair was brushed back and looked freshly washed; her complexion appeared flawless. Bronson forced himself to take a closer look, tried to be professionally detached, and then saw the heavy makeup on her forehead and cheeks, obviously concealing large bruises. And she was pale, much paler than she'd ever been in life.

He shook hands with the police officer, took a long last look at the woman who'd been his first and all-consuming love, and stumbled out of the room.

Once the documentation had been completed, Bronson and Mark headed outside to the parked Alfa Romeo.

"I'm sorry, Chris," Mark said, tears streaming uncontrollably down his face, his eyes red and puffy. "It only really hit me when I saw her body just lying there on that slab."

Bronson just shook his head. He didn't trust himself to speak without breaking down.

Their route out of the town took them past a pharmacy. Bronson pulled the car to a stop at the side of the road, went into the shop and emerged a few minutes later carrying a small paper bag.

"These should help," he said, handing the bag to Mark. "They're mild tranquilizers. They'll help you to relax."

At the house, Bronson poured his friend a glass of water and insisted he take a couple of the tablets.

"I won't be able to sleep, Chris. Everything's just going round and round in my head."

"At least go and lie down upstairs. You need to rest, even if you stay awake all afternoon."

Reluctantly, Mark took the drink and headed for the stairs.

Breakfast seemed an age ago, and Bronson found he was hungry. He looked in the walk-in larder and the big American fridge and found ham, bread and mustard, and made himself a couple of sandwiches and a pot of coffee to wash them down. When he'd finished eating he loaded the plates into the dishwasher and crept upstairs. Outside Mark's bedroom he stopped and listened at the door. He could hear the sound of gentle snoring, so he knew the tranquilizers had done their job. He smiled briefly, then retraced his steps.

Bronson had looked around the house that morning, but he wanted to check the property again. He was still worried about the "burglary," and was sure he must have missed something, some clue that would reveal why the property had been broken into.

He started in a methodical way, in the kitchen where the door had been forced, and then worked his way around the rest of the house. He even checked the garage and the two outbuildings where Mark kept the lawn mower and other gardening tools. Nothing appeared to be missing, and he could find no other sign of damage or forced entry anywhere in the house. It just didn't make sense.

Bronson was standing in the hall, looking up at the staircase where Jackie had fallen, when he heard the crunch of car tires on the gravel drive. He peered out the window and saw that a police car had pulled up outside the house.

"You are Signor Hampton?" the officer asked in halting English, stepping forward and extending his hand.

"No," Bronson replied, in fluent Italian. "My name's Chris Bronson and I'm a close friend of Mark Hampton. You'll appreciate that the death of his wife has come as a severe shock. He's asleep upstairs and I really don't want to disturb him unless I have to."

The officer, seemingly relieved at Bronson's command of the language, reverted to his native tongue. "I've been sent here to give Signor Hampton the results of the autopsy we carried out on his wife."

"That's no problem," Bronson replied. "Come on in. I can explain everything to him when he wakes up."

"Very well." The policeman followed Bronson into the kitchen, sat down at the table and opened the slim briefcase he was carrying. He extracted a buff folder containing several typed sheets of paper, some photographs and diagrams.

"It was a tragic accident," he began, and passed two pictures across to Bronson. "The first photograph shows the staircase of the house, taken from just inside the hall. If you look here"—he took a pen out of his uniform jacket pocket and pointed—"and here, you'll see two slippers on the stairs, one close to the bottom and the other nearer the top. And this one shows the victim's body lying on the floor at the foot of the staircase."

Bronson braced himself to look at the image, but the picture wasn't anything like as bad as he'd feared. Again, the photograph had been taken from just inside the hall, and had probably been intended only to show the position of the corpse in relation to the staircase. Jackie's face was not visible, and Bronson found he was able to study the picture almost emotionlessly.

"Reconstructing the sequence of events," the officer continued, "it seems clear that she ran up the stairs but lost her footing near the top and her slippers fell off as she tumbled down the staircase. We found a small patch of blood on the banister rail with three hairs adhering to it, and the pathologist has matched those to Signora Hampton. The cause of death was a broken neck, caused by a violent sideways impact to the right side of her head with a blunt object. It seems clear that when she lost her footing on the stairs she hit her head on the rail."

Bronson nodded. The conclusion seemed logical enough based on the available forensic evidence, but he still had some unanswered questions.

"Were there any other injuries on the body?" he asked.

The officer nodded. "The pathologist found several bruises on her torso and limbs that were consistent with an uncontrolled fall down the staircase."

He riffled through the papers and selected a page containing outline diagrams of the anterior and posterior views of a human body. The drawings were annotated with a number of lines pointing at areas of the body, and at the end of each was a brief note. Bronson took the sheet and studied it.

"May I have a copy of this?" he asked. "It will help me explain to Mr. Hampton exactly what happened to his wife."

"Of course. This copy of the report is for Signor Hampton."

Ten minutes later Bronson closed the door behind the police officer and walked back into the kitchen.

He spread the pages and photographs out on the table in front of him and read the report in its entirety.

Halfway down the second page he found a single reference that puzzled him. He looked carefully at the injury diagrams to cross-refer what he'd read, but that merely confirmed what the report stated. He walked out into the hall and up to the top of the stairs, and looked very carefully at the banister rail and the stairs themselves. Frowning, he returned to the kitchen to look again at the pathologist's report.

Half an hour later he heard the sound of movement upstairs, and shortly afterward Mark walked into the kitchen: he looked a lot better after a couple of hours' sleep. Bronson poured coffee and made him a ham sandwich.

"You're probably not hungry, Mark, but you have to eat. And then we need to talk," Bronson finished.

"What about?"

"Finish that, and I'll tell you."

He sat quietly as Mark drained his cup and sat back in his chair.

"So talk to me, Chris," Mark demanded.

Bronson paused for a second or two, choosing his words with care. "This won't be easy for you to accept, Mark, but I think we have to face the possibility that Jackie didn't die from a simple fall."

Mark looked stunned. "I thought the police said she'd hit her head on the banister."

"She probably did, but I think there's more to it than that. Take a look at this."

Bronson got up and led Hampton across to the kitchen door. He opened it and pointed to the compressed area of wood on the frame close to the lock.

"That mark was made by a jimmy or something very similar," he said. "When I checked the lock on the inside of the door, I found that all the screws had been pulled out. But the lock had then been refitted on the door and the screws replaced. Someone broke into this house and made every effort to keep that fact a secret."

"You mean a burglar?"

Bronson shook his head. "Not unless it was a very strange kind of burglary. I've investigated dozens back in Britain, and I've never encountered one where the criminals tried to hide the fact that they'd broken in. Most thieves take the easy way in, grab whatever they can, and get out again as quickly as possible. They're interested in speed, not stealth. I've looked around the house and I haven't found any sign of anything missing. It's difficult to tell, because of all the work being done, but your TV sets and computer are still here, and there's even some jewelry and money lying on the dressing table in the master bedroom. No thief would ignore stuff like that."

"So what are you saying—someone broke in but didn't take anything? That doesn't make sense."

"Exactly. And the other thing I've found relates to Jackie. I'm really sorry about this, but we need to consider the possibility that she didn't just fall. She may have been pushed."

Mark studied his friend's face for a moment. "Pushed?" he echoed. "You mean someone . . . ?" Bronson nodded. "But the police said it was an accident."

"I know, Mark, but while you were asleep an officer brought the autopsy report to the house, and after he left I studied it very carefully. There's one thing that doesn't make sense." Bronson selected one of the sheets of paper and showed it to Mark. "Jackie's body had numerous bruises on it, obviously caused by her fall down the staircase, and I've no doubt that what actually killed her was hitting her head on the banister. But this one injury here really worries me.

"On the left side of her head the pathologist found a single compressed fracture of the skull: that's on the opposite side to the more severe injury. In his opinion, that wound had been caused by a roughly spherical object about three to four centimeters in diameter. It would have been a painful injury, but certainly not fatal, and had been inflicted at about the time death occurred."

Mark nodded. "She probably hit her head on the stairs or something when she fell."

"That's obviously what the local police thought, but that injury bothers me. I've looked all the way up the staircase and in the hall, and I can't find anything of the right size and shape to have inflicted the wound, and which she could possibly have hit when she fell."

For a few moments Mark didn't reply. "So what are you suggesting?" he asked eventually.

"You know exactly what I'm suggesting, Mark," Bronson said. "Take the fact that someone has obviously broken into the house, and that Jackie had an injury on her body that I don't think could have been caused by her falling, and there's only one possible conclusion. I think she disturbed the burglars, and was hit on the head by a bludgeon or something like that. And then she fell against the banister rail."

"Murdered? You mean Jackie was murdered?"

Bronson looked at him steadily. "Yes, I think she was."

8

"What do you know about ciphers, Cardinal?" Mandino asked.

The two men were sitting at a busy pavement café in the Piazza del Popolo, just east of the Ponte Regina Margherita, people bustling past on the street. Vertutti would under no circumstances allow the man to enter the Vatican: it was bad enough having to deal with him at all. This time Mandino had three men in attendance. Two were bodyguards, but the third was a thin, bespectacled man with the air of an academic.

"Virtually nothing," Vertutti confessed.

"Neither do I, which is why I've asked my colleague—you can call him Pierro—to join us." Mandino gestured toward the third man sitting at their table. "He's been involved in the project as a consultant for about three years. He's fully aware of what we're looking for, and you can rely on his discretion."

"So this is someone else who knows about the Codex?" Vertutti demanded angrily. "Do you tell everyone you meet, Mandino? Perhaps you should publish information about it in the newspapers?"

Pierro looked uncomfortable at Vertutti's outburst, but Mandino appeared unruffled.

"I've only ever told those people who needed to know," he explained. "For Pierro to analyze the snippets of dead languages we've been translating, he needed to know what we were looking for and why. He can read Greek, Latin, Aramaic and Coptic, and he's also something of an expert on first- and second-century encryption techniques. I was lucky to find him."

The glance Pierro directed at Mandino immediately suggested to Vertutti that the "luck" might have been somewhat one-sided, and he guessed that Mandino had used threats or some kind of pressure to persuade the academic to work with him.

"You're obviously familiar with the Latin phrase we found, Cardinal," Pierro said, and Vertutti nodded.

"Good. We know that all early ciphers were very simple and basic. Until about the fifth century, illiteracy was the norm for the majority of the population, and not just in Europe but throughout the whole of the Mediterranean region. The ability to read and write, in any language, was almost the sole preserve of religious communities and working scribes. And it's worth remembering that many of the monks were essentially copyists, reproducing manuscripts and books for use within their own communities. They didn't need to understand what they were duplicating: the skill they possessed was that of making accurate copies of the source documents. The scribes, or amanuenses, on the other hand, *did* have to understand what they were writing, because they were producing legal documents, taking dictation and so on.

"Because of such widespread illiteracy, there was rarely any need to encrypt information, simply because so few people would have been able to read anything that had been written. But in the first century the Romans did begin to use a simple plain-text code for some important messages, particularly those relating to military matters. The code was, by modern standards, childishly simple: the hidden text was formed from the initial letters of the words in the message. As a further refinement, sometimes the hidden message was written backward. The problem with this type of encryption was that the plain-text message was almost invariably stilted, just to accommodate the secret text, and so it was often obvious that there *was* a concealed message, which rather defeated the object of the exercise.

"Another common cipher was known as Atbash, a simple substitution code originally used in Hebrew. The first letter of the alphabet was replaced by the last, and so on."

"So are you suggesting that *'Hic Vanidici Latitant'* contains a cipher?" Vertutti asked.

Pierro shook his head. "No, I'm not. In fact, I'm quite convinced it doesn't. We can eliminate an Atbash cipher immediately, because anything encoded in Atbash invariably resulted in gibberish, and the Latin phrase is far too short for a plain-text code to work. As a precaution, I've run several analysis programs on the Latin words, but without result. I'm certain that there's no hidden meaning."

"So why am I here?" Vertutti demanded. "If there's nothing more to be learned from this inscription, I'm just wasting my time. And you, Mandino, could have told me all this over the telephone. You do have my number, don't you?"

Mandino gestured to Pierro to continue.

"I didn't say there was nothing else to be learned from this phrase," the scholar persisted. "All I said was that there was no hidden message in the words— that's not the same thing at all."

"So what *did* you find out?" Vertutti snapped.

"Patience, Cardinal," Mandino said. "That stone's been waiting for someone to decipher the inscription for about two thousand years. I'm sure you can wait a few more minutes to hear what Pierro has to tell you."

The lanky academic glanced uncertainly from one man to the other, then addressed Vertutti again. "My analysis of the Latin phrase has only confirmed the literal meaning of the words. *'Hic Vanidici Latitant'* means 'Here lie the liars,' and the most plausible explanation for the inscription is that the stone was originally in one of two places. The first possible location is obvious: it was placed in or close to a tomb or burial chamber that contained at least two bodies. If there was only a single corpse, the Latin should read *'Hic Vanidicus Latitat.'*"

"I *do* read and understand Latin, Signor Pierro," Vertutti murmured. "It is the official language of the Vatican."

Pierro colored slightly. "I'm only trying to show you the logic that I was using, Cardinal. Please hear me out."

Vertutti waved his hand in irritation, but leaned back and waited for Pierro to continue.

"I rejected that explanation for two very simple reasons. First, if that stone had been in or close to a tomb, there's a very strong chance that whoever found it would also have found the bodies. And we can be reasonably certain that didn't happen, because there would certainly have been a record of the discovery. Even in the Middle Ages, the significance of the burial would have been quite obvious."

"And the second reason?"

"The stone itself. It's simply not the right size or shape to be a grave marker."

"So what was the other possible location? Where was that?" Vertutti asked.

Pierro smiled slightly before replying. "I have no

idea. It could be anywhere in Italy, or even in another country."

"What?"

"When I said there were two possible locations for the stone, what I meant was that if the stone wasn't a grave marker—which I think I've demonstrated—there's only one other thing it could possibly be."

"And that is?"

"A map. Or, to be precise, half a map."

II

Mark studied the autopsy diagram with care, and listened as Bronson translated the Italian description of the injury to the side of Jackie's head. Then he nodded agreement.

"You're a police officer, Chris, and you know what you're talking about. What you say makes sense. I can't think of anything that shape on the staircase or down in the hall."

Bronson could tell that Mark's grief was slowly being displaced by anger. Anger at whoever had violated his property and—deliberately or by accident—killed his wife.

"So what should we do now? Tell the Italian police?"

"I don't think that would help much. They've already decided this was just an accident, and absolutely the only evidence we've got is an unusual wound and the fact that the back door of the house was forced. They would point to the fact that nothing was stolen, not even the cash that we found lying about, and you could interpret the injury to Jackie's head in more ways than one. They'd nod politely, offer their condolences, walk away and do nothing."

"So what do we do?"

"I think," Bronson said, "that the first thing we

should do is to try to find out what the burglars—or whatever they were—were looking for. I've been around the house a couple of times, and I've not noticed anything missing, but if we do it together we might spot something."

"Good idea."

But twenty minutes later, having checked every room, they'd found nothing. Everything of value— money, jewelry and expensive electronic equipment— was, as far as Mark could tell, present and correct.

The two men walked down the stairs to the kitchen where Bronson filled the kettle and switched it on. "Forget anything missing, Mark. Did you see anything out of place, anything in one room that should be in another, that kind of thing?"

"Bloody difficult to tell. Half the furniture in the house is covered with dust sheets, and some bits have been moved into different rooms to give the builders space to do their work."

"You didn't see anything that looked as if it had been disturbed or moved that *wasn't* to do with the builders?"

Mark thought for a few seconds. Finally he said, "Only the curtains in the study."

"What do you mean?"

"We haven't owned this place very long, and there are a lot of things that need changing. The study curtains came with the house, and they're hideous, which is probably why the sellers left them. Jackie couldn't stand the sight of them, so we always left them pulled back, so you can't really see the pattern. But when we were in the study I noticed they were drawn across the window."

"And Jackie wouldn't have done that?"

Mark shook his head. "Absolutely not. There are shutters on the outside of that window, and we've al- ways kept them closed—that helps stop reflections appearing on the computer screen—so there would never be any need to draw the curtains."

"Well, somebody must have done," Bronson said. "The police would have had no reason to do so. Maybe the burglars closed the curtains because they were looking for something in the study and wanted to ensure no light shone through the window."

"But we've checked the study," Mark protested, "and there's nothing missing."

"I know, so we need to go back and check it again."

In the study, Bronson switched on the computer, and asked Mark to check every drawer and cupboard in the room, just in case they'd missed something. While he waited for the operating system to load, Bronson rummaged through the papers scattered over the desk, and found invoices, estimates and quotations for the work the Hamptons were doing on the property, plus the usual collection of utility bills. There were also several sheets of A4 paper that he presumed Jackie had used to write herself notes, as he found shopping lists and to-do lists on a few of them. One of these interested him, and he put that piece of paper to one side, together with another, apparently blank, sheet.

When the computer was ready for use, Bronson checked what programs were installed and then scanned through the "My documents" folder, looking for anything unusual, but found nothing. Then he checked the e-mail client, looking in both the "Inbox" and "Sent items," again without result. Finally, he opened the Web browser—like most people, the Hamptons had used Internet Explorer—and looked at the Web sites Jackie had visited recently. Or rather, he tried to. There were no sites listed in the history, so he checked the program settings. That puzzled him, and he leaned back in the black leather office chair with a frown.

"What is it?" Mark asked, closing the door of the cupboard they used to store their stationery.

"I don't know that it's anything, really. Was Jackie an experienced computer user? I mean, would she have fiddled about with program settings, that kind of thing?"

Mark shook his head. "Not a chance. She used the word processor and the spreadsheet, sent and received e-mails and did a bit of surfing on the Internet. Nothing else. Why?"

"I've just checked the settings for Internet Explorer, and pretty much everything uses the default values, including the history, which is set for twenty days."

"So?"

"Despite the default setting, there are no sites at all listed in the program's history, so somebody must have deleted them. Could Jackie have done that?"

"No," Mark said firmly. "She would have had no idea how to do it and, in any case, why would she have wanted to?"

"I've no idea."

Back in the kitchen, Mark made coffee while Bronson sat down at the table, the papers in front of him.

"Right, then," Mark said, carrying two mugs across the room. "What have you found?"

"Apart from the anomaly with the computer, I picked up a shopping list and what looks like a blank piece of paper."

"That doesn't sound promising—or even very interesting."

Bronson shrugged. "It might be nothing, but it's a bit odd. The shopping list, for example. It's got the usual kinds of things you'd expect to find on it, like groceries and stuff, but right at the bottom is 'Latin dictionary.' There's a line through the words, so either Jackie changed her mind or she went out and bought one and then crossed out the entry when she'd done so."

"She bought it," Mark said. "I saw a Latin-Italian dictionary on the bookshelf in the study. I didn't bother mentioning it, because it didn't seem important. But why would she want a Latin dictionary?"

"Maybe because of this," Bronson said, holding up the blank sheet of paper. "There's no writing on either side of this sheet, but when I looked at it I saw faint indentations, as if Jackie had written something on another piece of paper on top of this one. There are four letters altogether, printed in block capitals, and they're reasonably clear. The letters are 'H,' 'I,' 'C' and 'V.' Those letters, in that order, are not a part of any word I can think of in English."

" 'CV' could refer to someone's curriculum vitae," Mark suggested.

"But what about the 'HI'?"

"Apart from the obvious, I've no idea."

"I think the dictionary Jackie bought might be a clue. I studied Latin, believe it or not, and *'Hic'* is a Latin word. It means 'here' or 'in this place,' as far as I remember, and the 'V' could be the first letter of another word. There's what looks like a dot between the 'C' and the 'V' on this page, and I think the Romans sometimes separated words with a symbol like that."

"Are you serious? Jackie had enough trouble with Italian. Why would she be messing about with Latin?"

"I'm guessing here. Apart from this piece of paper, I've seen nothing anywhere in this house that looks like a Latin text, but I suspect Jackie found or was given something that had a Latin phrase written on it. That would certainly explain the dictionary."

Bronson paused for a few seconds, because what he was about to suggest was less a leap of logic than a quantum leap.

"What is it?" Mark asked, seeing the uncertainty on Bronson's face.

"I'm trying to make some sense of this. We've got a newly bought Latin dictionary, and the impression of what could be a Latin word on a sheet of paper, but no sign of the top sheet. That means somebody's definitely been into the study, unless Jackie herself removed the top sheet and then destroyed it. But what worries me most of all is the deletion of the browsing history from Internet Explorer."

"I'm not following you."

"I don't want to make too much of this, but suppose Jackie found something, here in the house or maybe in the grounds, something with a Latin expression written on it. She didn't understand what it meant, so she bought a Latin dictionary. She'd probably have preferred a Latin-English version, but couldn't find one. She tried to translate the text, but found she couldn't make sense of it with the Italian dictionary.

"So Jackie did what most people in that situation would do. She logged on to a search engine, found a Latin translation service and input the phrase. Now," Bronson said, "the next stage is pure conjecture, but it does make sense, to me at least.

"Maybe some organization, somewhere, put a form of Internet-monitoring service in place, watching for any requests to translate certain expressions from ancient languages. Technically, it wouldn't be all that difficult to set up, as long as the translation service Web sites were willing to cooperate. When Jackie input the Latin phrase into the search engine, it raised a flag, and perhaps even identified the address where the computer that generated the query was located—"

"Hang on a minute," Mark interrupted. "Why the hell would anyone today have the slightest interest in somebody trying to translate a two-thousand-year-old—or whatever—bit of Latin?"

"I've not the slightest idea, but nothing else seems to make sense. If I'm right, whoever put the monitoring service in place then came here, to this house, to search for whatever Jackie had found. It was *that* important to them. They obviously recovered the object, sanitized the computer so there would be no record of Jackie's searches, and took away anything they could find that referred to the Latin text."

"And, in the process," Bronson finished sadly, "I think Jackie just got in their way."

III

Pierro reached into his jacket pocket and pulled out a brown envelope. He looked around the café, checking that nobody else was in earshot—a superfluous precaution with Gregori Mandino's two men acting as watchdogs—and placed several photographs on the table in front of Vertutti.

He recognized the images immediately: they were close-up views of the inscribed stone.

"When I'd concluded that there was no secret message hidden in the inscription," Pierro went on, "I started looking at the stone itself, and there are two obvious clues in its shape. First, look at the four edges of the slab."

Vertutti bent forward over the table and stared at two of the pictures, side by side, but saw nothing he hadn't previously noticed. He shook his head.

"The edges," Pierro prompted gently. He took a short ruler out of his pocket, placed it on one of the photographs and aligned it with the top of the stone. He repeated the process with the left and right sides of the image.

"You see now?" he asked. "The top edge and both sides of the slab are absolutely straight. But now do the same to the bottom of the stone."

Vertutti took the ruler and positioned it carefully. And then he saw what the academic was driving at: with the ruler in place, it was obvious that the bottom edge of the stone was very slightly out of true.

"That's the first point," Pierro said. "If the Romans—or whoever prepared this slab—could get three of the edges straight, why couldn't they do the same with the fourth? And the second clue is related to the first. Look closely at the position of the carving. If you study it, you'll see that the words are centered on the stone from left to right, but not from top to bottom."

Vertutti peered at the photograph in front of him and nodded. The gap between the letters and the top of the stone was much larger than that at the bottom. Now that Pierro had pointed it out, the discrepancy was quite obvious. A classic case, he mused, of not being able to see the wood for the trees.

"And that means what?" he asked.

"The most obvious conclusion is that this stone"— Pierro tapped the photograph with his finger for emphasis—"was originally part of a larger slab, and at some point the lower section was removed."

"Can you be certain of that?"

Pierro shook his head. "Not without examining the stone for myself, but these photographs are fairly clear. In one of them are what look to me like marks made by a chisel, which would have been the obvious tool to split the slab in two. I think this stone was made as a kind of pointer, a device that would lead to the 'Tomb of Christianity,' which is how I believe Pope Vitalian described it in the Codex."

Vertutti glanced angrily at Mandino as Pierro confirmed the depth of his knowledge of the secret Codex.

"I believe the lower half of the slab almost certainly had a map or directions of some sort carved on it," Pierro finished.

"So what are you suggesting?" Vertutti demanded. "Where is the missing section? And how do we find it?"

Pierro shrugged. "That's not my problem," he said, "but it seems logical that whoever decided to split the stone would not have discarded the lower half. If this stone had been incorporated in the wall of the house purely as a decoration, why didn't they keep it intact? Why go to the trouble of cutting it in two? The only scenario that makes sense is that this section of the stone was placed in the wall for a purpose, as a definite pointer for somebody who knew what they were looking for. Unless you know the identity of the 'liars,' this stone is merely a curiosity. And that means—"

"That means," Mandino interrupted him, "that the other half of the stone is probably concealed somewhere in the property, so I'm going to have to send my men back to the house to find it."

9

I

Bronson walked across the hall to the front door and pulled it open. Standing on the doorstep was a short, dark-haired man dressed in grubby white overalls. Behind him was an old white van, the diesel engine clattering noisily, with three other men sitting in the cab.

"Can I help you?" Bronson asked in Italian.

"We would like to speak with Signor Hampton. We need to know about the work."

Bronson guessed they were the builders who'd been employed to do the renovations on the property.

"Come in," he offered, and led the four men through to the kitchen.

Mark greeted them in halting Italian.

Bronson immediately took over, explaining that he was a family friend and offering wine—an offer that was gratefully accepted. Once Bronson had opened a couple of bottles and filled glasses, he asked what the men wanted.

"We had a small job to do on Wednesday morning and so we arrived here in the afternoon," the foreman said, "but when we drove up we found that the police were here. They said there'd been an accident, and told us to go away and not come back for at least two days. Later we heard that the *signora* had died. Please accept our sincere condolences for your loss, Signor Hampton."

Bronson translated, and Mark nodded his understanding.

"What we need to know," the foreman continued, turning back to look at Bronson, "is whether or not Signor Hampton wants us to continue with the work. We have other clients waiting for us if he doesn't, so it's not a problem. We just need to know."

Bronson relayed the question to Mark, who immediately nodded his head in agreement. The renovations weren't even half finished, and whether he decided to keep the house or sell it, the work would obviously have to be completed. That response generated broad smiles all around, and Bronson wondered briefly just how many "other clients" the builders had.

Ten minutes later, having each drunk a second glass of red wine, the four builders were ready to leave. They would, the foreman promised, be back at the house first thing on Monday morning, ready to continue their labors.

Bronson led the way back to the hall, but as the procession passed the door to the living room—which was standing wide open—one of the builders glanced inside and came to an abrupt halt. He said something to his companion, which Bronson didn't hear clearly, then stepped inside the room.

"What is it?" Bronson asked.

The foreman turned to face him. His former good humor seemed to have vanished. "I know Signor Hampton has had a dreadful shock, but we do not appreciate him trying to take advantage of us."

Bronson hadn't the slightest idea what the man was

talking about. "What? You need to explain what you mean," he said.

"I mean, Signor Bronson, that he's obviously employed another builder to do some work here since last Tuesday, and that builder has probably been using our tools and materials."

Bronson shook his head. "As far as I know, nobody else has done any work here. Signora Hampton died sometime on Tuesday night or early on Wednesday morning. The police were probably here for most of Wednesday, and we arrived late last night, so when could . . . ?" His voice died away as a possible explanation occurred to him. "What work has been done?" he demanded.

The foreman swung around and pointed at the fireplace. "There," he said. "There's new plaster on the wall, but none of us put it there. We couldn't have, because we were waiting for Signora Hampton"—he made the sign of the cross on his chest—"to decide about the lintel."

Bronson felt the conversation slipping away from him.

"Wait there," he said, and walked quickly back to the kitchen. "Mark, I need your input here."

Back in the living room, Bronson asked the foreman to explain exactly what he meant.

"On Monday afternoon," the Italian said, "we were stripping the old plaster off the wall here above the fireplace. When we exposed the lintel, we called Signora Hampton, because the stone had a big crack in it, just about here." He sketched a diagonal line directly above one side of the fireplace. "It had a steel plate underneath it, so it was safe enough, but it wasn't very attractive. The *signora* had wanted the lintel exposed, as a feature, but when she saw it was broken she couldn't decide what to do. She asked us to wait, and just carry on stripping the old plaster, which we did. But now, as you can see, that whole area has fresh plaster on it. Somebody else has been working in here."

Bronson glanced at Mark. "Do you know anything about that?"

His friend shook his head. "Nothing. As far as I know, Jackie was perfectly happy with these builders. If she wasn't, I can guarantee she'd have told them so. She was always very forthright."

That, Bronson thought, was an understatement. Jackie had never, to use an old expression, been backward in coming forward. It was one of the many things he'd found attractive about her. She always said exactly what she thought, politely but firmly.

Bronson turned back to the foreman. "We're certain no other builders have been in here," he said, "but you obviously know what stage you'd reached in the renovations. Tell me, when you removed the plaster, did you find anything unusual about the wall, apart from the crack in the lintel?"

The foreman shook his head. "Nothing," he said, "apart from the inscribed stone, but that was just a curiosity."

Bronson looked at Mark with a kind of triumph. "I think we've just traced what Jackie found," he said, explaining what the builder had told him. And without waiting for Mark to respond, he switched back to Italian.

"Strip it," he ordered, pointing at the wall. "Strip the new plaster off that wall right now."

The builder looked puzzled, but issued instructions. Two of his men seized club hammers and broad-bladed masonry chisels, dragged a couple of stepladders over to the fireplace and set to work.

Thirty minutes later, the builders left in their old van, again promising to return early on Monday morning. Bronson and Mark walked back into the living room and stared at the Latin inscription on the wall. Bronson took several pictures of it with his digital camera.

"The first four letters are the same as those I found impressed on that piece of paper in the study," Bronson said. "And it *is* a Latin inscription. I don't know what it means, but that dictionary Jackie bought should help me decipher it."

"You think she was searching for a translation of that—of those three words—on the Internet, and that was enough to get her killed? That's just bloody ridiculous."

"I don't know it got her killed, Mark, or not deliberately, anyway. But this is the only scenario that makes sense. The builders exposed the inscription on Monday. Jackie wrote down the words—that's confirmed by the paper in the study—and bought a Latin dictionary, probably on Tuesday, and if she did do a search on the Internet, she most likely did it that day. Whatever happened, somebody broke into the house—my guess is late on Tuesday night—and on Wednesday morning Jackie was found dead in the hall.

"Now, I know it probably seems stupid that anyone would care enough about a three-word Latin inscription carved into a stone, maybe two thousand years ago, to risk a burglary, far less a charge of manslaughter or murder, but the fact remains that somebody did. Those three words are vitally important to someone, somewhere, and I'm going to find out who and why.

"But I'm not," he added, "going to use the Internet to do it."

II

Alberti and Rogan reached the town early that evening, following telephoned instructions—this time from Gregori Mandino—to enter the property for the *third*—and what they both hoped would be the *last*— time. They cruised slowly past the house as soon as they arrived in Monti Sabini and saw lights shining from windows on both floors. That complicated things, because they had hoped to be able to get inside and complete their search for the missing section of the stone without detection. But, ultimately, it wouldn't matter, because this time Mandino's instructions gave them far more latitude than before.

"Looks like the husband's home," Alberti said, as Rogan accelerated away down the road. "So do we wait, or what?"

"We wait for a couple of hours," his partner confirmed. "Maybe he'll be asleep by then."

Just more than two and a half hours later, Rogan drove their car up the lane that ran beside and behind the house, and continued climbing the hill until they were out of sight of the building. Then he turned the car around, pointed it down the slope and extinguished the headlights. He waited a couple of minutes for his eyes to adjust to the gloom, then allowed the vehicle to roll gently down the gradient, using only the parking lights to see his way, until they reached a section of the grass verge that offered a good view of the back and side of their target. There he eased the car to the side of the road and switched off the lights and engine. As a precaution, Rogan turned off the interior light, so that it wouldn't come on when they opened the doors.

A light was still burning in one of the downstairs rooms of the old house, so they settled down to wait.

III

Chris Bronson closed the dictionary with a snap and sat back in the kitchen chair, rubbing his tired eyes.

"I think that's the best translation," he said. " 'Here are lying the liars,' or the short version: 'Here lie the liars.' "

"Wonderful." Mark sounded anything but impressed. "What the hell is that supposed to mean?"

"I've not the slightest idea," Bronson confessed, "but it must be important to somebody. Look, we're not getting anywhere with this, so let's call it a night. You go on up. I'll check the doors and windows."

Mark stood up and stretched. "Good idea," he murmured. "Your subconscious might have a flash of inspiration while you sleep. Good night—I'll see you in the morning."

As Mark left the kitchen, Bronson took one of the upright chairs and wedged it under the handle of the back door, then walked out of the room and switched off the light.

He checked that the front door was locked and bolted, and that all the ground-floor windows were closed and the outside shutters secured, then went up to his bedroom.

In the car parked on the hill road behind the house, Alberti nudged Rogan awake and pointed down the slope.

"The downstairs light just went out," he announced.

As the two men watched, slivers of brightness appeared behind the closed shutters of one of the bedrooms, but after about ten minutes this light, too, was extinguished. A dull glow was still visible behind two other shutters, but the men guessed this was probably just the landing light.

"We'll give it another hour," Rogan said, closing his eyes and relaxing again in the car seat.

In the guest bedroom, Chris Bronson booted up his Sony Vaio laptop. He checked his e-mails, then turned his attention to the Internet. As he'd told Mark, he certainly wasn't prepared to input the Latin phrase into a search engine or online dictionary, but there were other ways of trying to find out its significance.

First he ran a small program that generated a false IP address—the Internet protocol numbers that identified his geographical location. Then he made it look as if he was accessing the Web from a server based in South Korea, which, he thought with a smile, should be far enough away from Italy to throw anyone off the scent. Even so, he still wasn't going to do a direct search. Instead, he began looking at sites that offered translations of Latin phrases in common use at the height of the Roman Empire.

After about forty minutes, Bronson had discovered two things. First, a surprising number of expressions he was already familiar with in both English and Italian had their roots in the dead language. And, second, the words *Hic Vanidici Latitant* were not recorded anywhere as being part of an aphorism or expression in common usage two thousand odd years ago. That wasn't exactly a surprise—if the phrase had been well known, it would presumably have had no special significance for the people who had broken into the house—but at least it eliminated one possibility.

But he really wasn't getting anywhere and eventually decided to give up. He shut down the laptop, then opened the shutters and one of the windows to provide fresh air, switched off the main light and got into bed.

Rogan looked along the back of the house. He nodded to Alberti, who produced a jimmy from one of the pockets of his jacket. He inserted the point of the tool between the door and the frame, changed his grip on it, and levered, pushing toward the door. It gave slightly, but then stuck: something seemed to be jamming it.

Rogan took out his flashlight and shone it through the window, the beam dancing over the interior of the kitchen as he tried to see the cause of the problem. He directed the flashlight downward, and muttered a curse. A chair had been wedged below the door handle. Rogan shook his head at Alberti, who removed the jimmy and stepped back.

The two men walked cautiously along the back wall of the house to the nearest window. Like all of the windows on the ground floor of the property, it was protected by full-height wooden shutters, but Rogan didn't think that would be a problem: it was just going to be a noisier solution. He used his flashlight to check the lock, and nodded in satisfaction. The shutters were held closed by a central catch that not only locked the two halves together, but also secured them to the wall using bolts at the top and bottom. It was a simple design with a single flaw. If the catch was undone, both bolts would immediately be released and the shutters would swing open.

Rogan took the jimmy from Alberti and slid its point between the two shutters. Then he moved it up until it touched the underside of the catch, and rapped the other end sharply. With a scraping sound, the catch lifted and both shutters swung outward. Rogan opened them fully and clipped them back using the hooks fitted to the wall.

In his bedroom almost directly above, Bronson was still wide awake, lying silently in the dark and puzzling over the meaning of the three Latin words.

He heard noises—a metallic click followed by a creaking sound and other clicks—and climbed out of bed to investigate. He walked across to the window and looked down cautiously.

At the back of the house he saw two dark figures, bulky in the shadows cast by the moon, the beam of a small flashlight playing over one of the downstairs windows. The shutters that he'd locked an hour or so earlier were now wide open.

Bronson slowly moved away from the window and walked back across the room to where he'd left his clothes. He pulled on a black polo-neck sweater and dark-colored trousers, and slid his feet into his trainers. Then he eased open the bedroom door and made his way across the landing and down the stairs.

There were no guns in the house, as far as he knew, but there were several stout walking sticks in an umbrella stand beside the front door. He picked out the biggest one and hefted it in his hand. That, he thought, would do nicely. Then he walked over to the living-room door, which was fortunately ajar, and pushed it open just far enough to allow him to slide into the room.

The open shutters were obvious—every other window was black—and Bronson moved across the room to his left, keeping low. Their unwelcome visitors were not visible through the window but that simply meant that they hadn't yet broken one of the panes of glass to get in.

The window was wood-framed with twelve small single-glazed panes of glass, and Rogan had come prepared. He hadn't anticipated that they wouldn't be able to use the back door again, but whenever he was tasked with a burglary he always had a backup plan. And for an old house like this, with very basic security, breaking a window and getting inside that way was the most obvious option.

He took a roll of adhesive tape from his pocket and tore off several strips, handing each to Alberti, who stuck them on the glass in a star pattern, leaving a protruding "handle" in the middle, formed from the central sections of the tape. Then Alberti held the tape in his left hand, reversed the jimmy and rapped the rounded end sharply against the taped window. The glass broke instantly, but stuck to the tape, and he easily pulled out the broken pane. He handed the glass to Rogan, who placed it carefully on the ground, then reached inside and lifted the catch to open the window.

Although he'd been as quiet as he could, there was obviously a possibility that the noise had been heard inside the house. So, before he climbed in, Alberti took the pistol from his shoulder holster, checked the magazine and chambered a round by pulling back the slide. He set the safety catch, then grasped the left side of the window frame, rested his right foot on a protruding stone in the wall and pulled himself up and into the open window to lower himself into the room.

At that moment, Bronson acted. He'd seen and heard the glass break, and guessed what the intruders' next move would be, and he also knew that if the two men managed to get inside the house, he wouldn't stand a chance.

So as Alberti leaned forward, his right arm extended, ready to jump down inside the room, Bronson stepped away from the wall and smashed the walking stick down with all his force, instantly breaking the Italian's right arm a few inches below the shoulder. The intruder screamed with pain and shock, dropped the automatic and in a reflex action threw himself backward, landing heavily on the ground outside.

For the barest of instants Rogan had no clue what had happened. He'd stepped back to give Alberti room to hoist himself up through the window, and just a split second later his companion had tumbled backward, yelling in agony. Then, in the moonlight, he saw Alberti's arm and realized it had been broken. That could mean only one thing. He stepped forward to the window and lifted his own pistol.

An indistinct shape moved inside the darkness of the house. Rogan immediately swung the weapon toward his target, took rapid aim and pulled the trigger. The bullet shattered one of the unbroken panes of glass and slammed into a wall somewhere inside the room.

The report of the pistol was deafening at such close range, the sound of breaking glass following moments later. Bronson's military training took over and he dropped flat on the floor. But if the intruder hoisted himself up and looked down into the room, Bronson knew he'd be clearly visible. He had to get out of sight, and quickly.

The base of the ground-floor window was higher than usual and the second man would have to be standing almost on tiptoe—not the ideal shooting stance by a long way. If he moved quickly, he might be able to make it to safety.

Bronson jumped to his feet and ran across the room, ducking and weaving. Two more gunshots rang out, their reports a thunderous assault on the silence of the night. He heard the bullets smashing into the solid stone walls of the room, but neither hit him.

Before the builders had arrived, the living room had contained a large wood-framed three-piece suite, a couple of coffee tables and about half a dozen smaller chairs, all of which were now stacked in a heap more or less in the middle of the floor.

Bronson had no illusions that a collection of furniture, no matter how solid, would be sufficient to stop a bullet, but if the intruder couldn't see him, he'd have nothing to aim at. So he dived behind the sheet-covered mound and flattened himself against the wooden floorboards.

Then he waited.

Alberti had staggered to his feet, clutching his broken arm and howling with pain. Rogan knew there was now no chance of getting inside the house that night. Even if Hampton, or whoever it was inside the property, hadn't called the *Carabinieri*, somebody in the neighborhood would probably have heard the shots and made a call. And he was going to have to get Alberti to a hospital, if only to shut him up.

"Come on," he snapped, holstering his pistol and bending down to help his companion to his feet. "Let's get back to the car."

Within a couple of minutes the two men had vanished into the night.

Bronson was still crouching behind the stack of furniture when he heard the sound of footsteps above him. Moments later, the hall lights flared on. Bronson knew he had to stop his friend from walking into a gunfight, so he risked a quick glance toward the open window, then jumped up and ran across to the door, wrenched it open and stepped out into the hall.

"What the hell's going on, Chris?" Mark demanded, rubbing his eyes. "Those noises sounded like gunshots."

"Spot on. We've just had visitors."

"What?"

"Just give me a minute. Stay here in the hall—don't go into the living room. Where's the switch for the security lights?"

Mark pointed at a group of switches at the end of the hall, next to the corridor leading to the kitchen. "Bottom right."

Bronson stepped over to the panel and flicked the switch.

"Don't go into the living room, Mark," he warned again, then ran up the stairs. On the first floor, he opened each window in turn and peered outside, checking the area around the house. The security lights the Hamptons had installed were fitted directly below the bedroom windows, mainly to make changing the high-power halogen bulbs as easy as possible. This had the accidental benefit of permitting anyone on the first floor to observe the perimeter of the property without being visible from below.

Bronson checked twice but the men, whoever they were, had gone. The only sound he could hear—apart from the animals of the night—was the noise of a car engine receding rapidly, probably the two burglars making their getaway. He checked all the windows once more, then walked back down the staircase to the hall, where Mark was obediently waiting.

"I think those guys were probably the same ones who broke in here before," Bronson explained. "They decided to come in through the window because I'd jammed the back door with a chair."

"And they shot at you?"

"At least three shots, maybe four. Wait here while I close the shutters in the living room."

Bronson opened the door carefully and peered inside, then strode into the room. He walked across to the open window, looked out to check that there was nobody in sight and reached out to pull the shutters closed. He shut and locked the window itself, then switched on the main lights. As Mark followed him into the room, Bronson noticed something lying on the floor close to the broken window, and in a moment realized it was a semiautomatic pistol.

Bronson picked it up, removed the magazine and ejected the cartridge from the breech. The pistol was a well-used nine-millimeter Browning Hi-Power, one of the commonest and most reliable semiautomatics.

He replaced the ejected cartridge in the magazine, re-loaded the weapon but didn't chamber a round, and tucked it in the waistband of his trousers.

"Is that yours?" Mark asked.

Bronson shook his head. "The only people in Britain who own handguns these days are criminals, thanks to the coterie of idiots and spin doctors who allegedly govern the country. No, this was dropped by the guy who tried to climb in through the window. These people are serious, Mark."

"We'd better call the police."

"I *am* the police, remember? Plus, there's nothing they would be able to do."

"But these men tried to break in and they've shot at you, for God's sake."

"I know," Bronson said patiently, "but the reality is that we have no clue who they are, and the only physical evidence we've got—assuming they weren't stupid enough to drop their wallets or something outside the house—is a forced door, a broken window and a couple of bullet holes."

"But you've got that pistol. Can't the police trace . . . ?" Mark's voice died away as he realized the futility of what he was suggesting.

The kind of people who break into houses never carry weapons that can be traced. They may be criminals, but they're not stupid.

"But we've got to do *something*," Mark protested.

"We will," Bronson assured him. "In fact, we are already." He pointed to the exposed stone above the fireplace. "Once we've found out what that means, we'll probably know why a couple of bad guys were prepared to break in here waving pistols. More important, we might be able to work out who sent them."

"What do you mean?"

"My guess is those two men were just a couple of thugs, employed for the job. Even if we'd caught them, they probably wouldn't know anything, more than the specific orders they'd been given. There's a plan behind whatever's going on here, and that's what we need to understand if we're going to make any sense of this. But that inscription's at the very heart of it."

IV

Just outside Rome, Rogan pulled the car to a halt in the parking area and switched off the engine. Alberti was huddled in the passenger seat next to him, moaning and clutching his shattered arm. Rogan had driven as quickly as he could—stopping only once, to call Mandino and explain what had happened—but it had taken them the better part of an hour to reach their destination. Alberti's pain was obvious, but still Rogan wished he'd shut up.

"Give it a rest, will you? We're here. In a couple of minutes they'll slide a needle into your arm and when you wake up it'll all be over."

He got out of the car, walked around and pulled open the passenger door.

"Don't touch me," Alberti said, his voice hoarse and distorted, as he struggled out of his seat, levering himself up using only his left arm.

"Stand still," Rogan ordered. "I'll take off your holster. You can't go in wearing that."

Rogan eased his companion's jacket off his shoulders, unbuckled the strap and removed the holster.

"Where's your pistol?" he asked.

"What?"

"Your Browning. Where is it? In the car?"

"Hell, no," Alberti gasped. "I was holding it when I went in through the window. It's probably inside the house somewhere."

"Oh, shit," Rogan said. "That's all we need."

"What's the problem? The weapon's clean."

"I know that. I also know it's got a full magazine, which means the son of a bitch who did this to you is now armed, and I've still got to go back there and finish the job."

Rogan turned away and pointed toward the low-lying building, ablaze with lights, on the opposite side of the parking lot.

"There you go," he said. "The emergency admissions section is on the right-hand side. Tell them you had a bad fall or something."

"OK." Alberti stumbled away from the car, still gripping his right arm.

"Sorry about this," Rogan murmured quietly. He drew his own pistol and with a single fluid movement released the safety catch, pointed the weapon at the back of Alberti's head and pulled the trigger.

The other man fell lifeless to the ground as the sound of the shot echoed off the surrounding buildings. Rogan stepped forward, turned over the body, avoiding looking at the shattered red mess that was all that was left of his companion's head, and removed his wallet. Then he got back in his car and drove away.

A couple of miles down the road, Rogan stopped the car in a turnout and rang Mandino.

"It's done," Rogan said, as soon as Mandino answered.

"Good. That's the first thing you've got right today. Now, get back to the house and finish the job. I need you to find that missing stone."

10

"I think we need help."

Bronson and Mark were sitting over breakfast in the kitchen the following morning.

"You mean the police?" Mark asked.

Bronson shook his head. "I mean specialist help. This house has been standing for about six hundred years, but I think that stone's a hell of a lot older, maybe a couple of thousand years, otherwise why use Latin for the inscription? If it was contemporary with the house, I'd have expected it to be written in Italian. We need someone who can tell us what the Latin means, and why it's so important."

"So who do you—oh, you think Angela could help us?"

Bronson nodded, somewhat reluctantly. His former wife was the only person he knew who had any connection with the world of antiquities, but he wasn't sure how she would react if he approached her. Their separation had been less than amicable, but he hoped she'd regard this problem as an intellectual challenge and respond professionally.

"She might, I hope," Bronson said. "I know Latin inscriptions on lumps of stone are well outside her field of expertise, but she'll certainly know someone at the British Museum who could help. She knows some Latin herself, because she specializes in first- to third-century European pottery, but I think we need to talk to an expert."

"So what? You'll call her?"

"No. She probably wouldn't answer if she saw my cell phone number on her phone. I'll send her a couple of photographs in an e-mail. I hope she'll be curious enough to open that."

Bronson went up to his bedroom and returned with his laptop. He double-clicked the first image and angled the screen so that Mark could see it as well.

"We need to pick out two or three maximum," he said, "and make sure they show the inscription clearly. How about this?"

"It's a little blurred," Mark said. "Try the next one."

Within five minutes they'd selected two pictures, one taken from a few feet away and indicating the stone's position in relation to the wall itself, and the second a close-up that showed the inscription in some detail.

"They should be fine," Mark said, as Bronson composed a short e-mail to his ex-wife, explaining where the stone was and how they'd found it.

"It'll take her a while to reply," Bronson guessed.

But he was wrong. Just more than an hour later, his Sony emitted a musical double-tone indicating that an e-mail had been received. It wasn't from Angela, but from a man named Jeremy Goldman, and was a couple of pages in length.

"Listen to this," Bronson said. "As soon as she saw the pictures, Angela sent them off to a colleague—an ancient-language specialist named Jeremy Goldman.

He's supplied a translation of the Latin, but it's exactly the same as we'd already worked out: 'Here lie the liars.' "

"So that was pretty much a waste of time," Mark commented.

"No, it's not. He's also given us some information about where the stone may have come from. First, he looked at the inscription itself. He doesn't know what the 'liars' were, but he's suggested the word might have referred to books or texts, something like that, some documents that whoever carved the inscription believed were false.

"He doesn't think the text refers to a grave, because it's the wrong verb. He thinks it just means something that's been hidden or secreted somewhere. The letters, he says, were fairly crudely carved and their form suggests that the inscription is very old, maybe dating from as early as the first century A.D.

"He's also looked at the shape of the stone, and again it doesn't fit with a grave marker. He thinks it might have been part of a wall, and he suggests that in its original location there would have been one or more inscribed stones below it, and those would probably have displayed a map showing the location of whatever the inscription referred to.

"He finishes up by saying that as a curiosity the stone is interesting, but it has no intrinsic value. He guesses that when this house was being erected, the builders found the stone and decided to incorporate it in the wall as a kind of feature. And then, over the years, tastes changed and the wall was plastered over."

"Well, I suppose that's helpful," Mark acknowledged, "but it doesn't get us very much further, and we still don't know why these 'burglars' have been breaking in."

"Oh, I think we do," Bronson said. "Whatever

those three words refer to, someone, somewhere, is very concerned that they should remain hidden, otherwise why would they replaster the wall? And that person obviously knows exactly what these 'liars' are, and is desperate to find their hiding place. They're after the missing bit of the inscription, the map or whatever that shows where the relics were hidden."

"So what should we do now?" Mark asked.

"That, I think, is fairly obvious. We find the missing stone before the burglars come back."

II

Joseph Cardinal Vertutti's caffeine intake was rising rapidly. Yet again he'd been summoned by Mandino, and yet again they'd met in a busy pavement café, this time on Piazza Cavour, not far from the Vatican. As usual, Mandino was accompanied by two young bodyguards, and this time, Vertutti hoped, he'd have some good news.

"Have your men found the rest of the stone?" he asked, more in hope than expectation.

Mandino shook his head. "No. There was a problem," he said, but didn't seem inclined to elaborate.

"So what now?"

"This matter is occupying more and more of my time, Cardinal, as well as incurring significant expenses. I'm aware that we're contracted to resolve this problem on behalf of your employer, but I need to make you aware that I'm expecting these expenses to be met by you."

"What? You're expecting the *Vatican*"—Vertutti lowered his voice as he said the word—"to pay *you*?"

Mandino nodded. "Exactly. I anticipate our total expenses will be in the region of one hundred thousand euros. Perhaps you could make arrangements to have that sum ready to transfer to us once we've sorted out this matter. I'll advise you of the account details in due course."

"I will do no such thing," Vertutti spluttered. "I have no access to funds of that size and, even if I had, I wouldn't contemplate transferring a single euro to you."

Mandino looked at him without expression. "I was rather expecting that reaction from you, Cardinal. Put simply, you're in no position to argue. If you don't agree to meet these modest expenses, I may decide that the interests of my organization would be better served by *not* destroying the relic or handing it over to you. Perhaps making our findings public would be the optimum solution. Pierro is very interested in what we've found so far, and he believes his academic career would be greatly enhanced if he could discover this object and submit it to scientific scrutiny. But, of course, ultimately it's your choice."

"I think that's called blackmail, Mandino."

"You can call it anything you like, Eminence, but don't forget who you're dealing with. My organization is incurring necessary expenses in carrying out this operation on your behalf. It seems only reasonable that you should meet them. If you decide not to, then as far as I'm concerned our contractual obligation to you is at an end, and we would then be free to do whatever we thought most appropriate with anything we manage to recover. And don't forget that I'm no friend of the Church. Whatever happens to this relic wouldn't bother me."

Vertutti glowered at him, but both men knew he had no choice, no choice at all.

"Very well," Vertutti grated. "I'll see if I can arrange something."

"Excellent." Mandino beamed. "I knew you'd see

things my way eventually. I'll let you know as soon as
we've resolved the situation in Ponticelli."

III

"Jeremy Goldman's pretty sharp," Bronson said. He
was rereading the e-mail and had only just realized
the significance of another of Goldman's suggestions.

"In what way?" Mark asked.

"He spotted something else about the inscribed
stone. He says that the Latin text is centered on the
stone left and right, but not vertically. The words are
closer to the base of the stone than they are to the
top. And that could mean that the stone isn't complete, that someone's cut away the lower section of it.
Let's go and take a look."

The two men walked through into the living room
and stood in front of the fireplace to stare up at the
stone. It was immediately obvious that Goldman was
right.

"Look at this," Bronson said. "If you know what
to look for, you can clearly see the marks where someone's chiseled off the lower part. This section of
stone—the bit that has the inscription carved on it—
was once part of a much larger slab, probably twice
this size. So all we need do now is find the lower half,
the bit that presumably contains the map or directions
or whatever."

"That could be tricky. This house is built of stone,
and so's the garage. That used to be a stable block
and before that a small barn. The house is surrounded
by about half an acre of garden, and most of that has
rocks buried in it, some of them obviously worked
stones with shaped sides and edges. Even if the stone
is somewhere here, it could take a hell of a long time
to find it."

"My guess, Mark, is that if it's here it'll be cemented into a wall somewhere in the house, just like this one. The stone was split into two carefully—the cut edge is almost straight—and I don't believe whoever took the time to do that would simply dump the other section."

"So we start checking inside the house. The problem is—which wall do we start with?"

Bronson grinned at his friend. If nothing else, the search was taking both their minds off Jackie's death. "We check them all, and we might as well begin right here with this one."

Just more than half an hour later, the two men were again standing in the living room, looking at the stone above the fireplace. All but three of the walls in the house had already been stripped of any covering before the Hamptons purchased the property, and they'd just inspected every exposed stone in the house and found precisely nothing. That left only two rooms where they were going to have to get their hands dirty: the dining room, with two plaster-covered walls that the builders hadn't started work on yet, and the living room itself, where about half of the fireplace wall still had the original plaster on it.

"Is this really necessary?" Mark asked, as Bronson donned a pair of overalls left by the builders and picked up a hammer and chisel.

"I think so, yes. The only way to resolve this is to find the missing half of that stone."

"And what do we do then?"

"Until we locate the stone and decipher what's on it, I've no idea," Bronson said.

Then he turned around and studied the wall beside the fireplace. The old plaster began just to the left of the cracked lintel and extended all the way to the back wall, which had already been stripped.

He took a firm grip of the chisel, positioned the tip

about three inches from the edge of the plaster, and rapped it sharply with the hammer. The chisel drove about half an inch into it, and a section of plaster fell to the floor, revealing part of the stone underneath. It looked as if stripping the wall wouldn't take him too long.

Rogan was stiff, tired, uncomfortable, bored and pissed off. He'd slept as best he could in the car for what was left of the night after he'd got back to Monti Sabini, then driven into the town for an early-morning coffee and a couple of pastries. He'd returned to the house straight afterward and had spent the rest of the morning watching the property through a set of powerful binoculars.

He'd seen two men inside—not one, as he'd been expecting—and had watched as one of them had pulled on a pair of overalls and started chipping away at the wall of the living room. It looked as if Hampton and the other man were going to do the job for him.

The old house was surrounded by lawns dotted with shrubs and trees, and the Italian found it easy enough to reach the property without being seen. He flattened himself against the wall and eased up into a standing position. From there he could see into the living room at an oblique angle and watch what was happening.

Removing all the plaster didn't take long. Every time Bronson used the chisel, he knocked off a chunk two or three inches square and, just more than ninety minutes after he'd started work, the entire section of the wall was bare. Then he and Mark checked every single stone he'd revealed. Several of them bore chisel marks, but none had anything on them that could possibly be either a map or any form of writing.

"So what now?" Mark asked, staring at the debris piled up along the base of the wall.

"I still think it's here somewhere," Bronson replied. "I don't believe that inscribed stone was incorporated in the wall purely as a decoration. That Latin phrase means something today, and must have meant something when this house was built. In fact . . ." He broke off and looked again at the stone above the fireplace. Maybe the clue had been there all the time, literally staring him in the face.

"What is it?"

"Is this a riddle inside a riddle? According to Jeremy Goldman, that inscription probably dates from the first century, but the house is about six hundred years old."

"So?"

"So the carving was already about fifteen hundred years old when the house was built. If the stone *was* just intended to be a decoration, where would the builders have put it? Over the fireplace, probably," Bronson said, answering his own question, "but not exactly where it is now. They'd have positioned it centrally, directly over the lintel. But it isn't—it's well off to one side. That had to have been done deliberately, as a sign to show that the stone wasn't just a decorative feature but had a special meaning.

"Suppose whoever built this house found the stone and tried to follow the directions to these 'liars'— whatever they are—but couldn't follow the map or work out the clues. They might have decided to split the stone and hide the map section somewhere for safekeeping, but leave a clue to its location for future generations. So one part of the stone indicates the location of the other section, which is a map to some sort of long-buried relics.

"If I'm right, maybe the *'Hic'*—the Latin word meaning 'here'—is the most important part of the inscription. Could it be telling us exactly where the missing section of the stone has been hidden?"

"You mean 'here' as in 'X marks the spot,' that kind of thing?"

"Exactly."

"But where is it, then?" Mark asked. "That's a solid wall almost a meter thick. The other stones below that one are not only unmarked, but they're also a different kind of rock, so what could the *'Hic'* refer to?"

"Not something *in* the wall, necessarily, but perhaps below it. Maybe the hiding place is under the floor."

But that looked unlikely. The fireplace in the old farmhouse was a collection of solid lumps of granite, and the floor in front of it was made of thick oak floorboards. If there was a hiding place either under the fireplace or below the floorboards, it would require major work—not to mention lifting gear—to find it.

"I don't expect what we're looking for will be under something as simple and obvious as a trapdoor in the floor," Bronson said, "but equally I doubt if we'd need to demolish half the house to get at it."

He looked at the wall again. "That's about a meter thick, you said?"

Mark nodded.

"Well, maybe there's something on the other side of the wall. Have you got a tape measure, something like that?"

Mark went out to the workshop at the back of the garage and returned a couple of minutes later with a carpenter's steel tape. Bronson took it and, using the floor and the edge of the doorway leading into the dining room as datum points, measured the exact position of the center of the stone. Mark jotted down the coordinates on a sheet of paper, then they stepped through into the dining room itself.

This was much smaller than the living room, and the wall it shared with the living room was fully plastered. The furniture hadn't been moved, though it was covered in the ubiquitous dust sheets. The Hamptons had planned to knock a large doorway through the southern wall of the dining room and build a conservatory, but they were still waiting for planning permission.

Using the coordinates and the tape measure, Bronson made a cross in the corresponding area on the dining-room wall. To confirm that they had the right place, they checked the measurements in the living room again, then repeated the process in the dining room.

Then Bronson picked up the hammer and chisel, climbed back up the stepladder and struck a single blow just below the cross he'd drawn. The plaster cracked, and after two more blows a large chunk fell off the wall. He wiped his hand across the exposed stone, trying to clear away some of the dust and debris.

"There's something here," he said, his voice rising with excitement. "Not a map, but what looks like another inscription."

Half a dozen more blows from the hammer and chisel shifted the rest of the old plaster and revealed the whole face of the stone.

"Here," Mark said, and passed up a new three-inch paintbrush.

"Thanks," Bronson muttered, and ran the brush briskly back and forth over the stone. A few sharp raps from the handle of the hammer cleared away the remaining pieces of plaster. They could both now see exactly what had been carved into the stone.

It was an inscription that hinted at the blood-soaked history of another country—an inscription that was worth killing for.

Rogan watched with interest as the man in the overalls stripped all the old plaster off the wall in the living room, and smiled at their total failure to find what they were looking for. At the very least, they were saving him a job.

At first, he hadn't understood why they had taken such trouble to measure the exact position of the inscribed stone in the wall, though he realized they'd worked something out when the two men had walked through into the small dining room. The moment they vanished from sight, Rogan dropped down into a crouch and scuttled along the wall until he was beyond the end of the first of the two dining-room windows. Then he eased up slowly until he could just see inside the room, though he guessed he could have cavorted naked outside the window and the chances were neither of the men would have seen him. Their attention was entirely directed at the dining-room wall.

As Rogan watched, his view slightly distorted through the thick old glass of the dining-room windows, he saw the man uncover something. It looked as if the missing section of the stone that Mandino had sent him to find *had* been in the house after all.

The stone didn't appear to have a map carved on it—from Rogan's viewpoint, and through the admittedly distorting glass of the window, it looked to him more like a couple of verses of poetry. But whatever the content of the carving on the stone, the simple fact that there *was* another inscription was enough for him to report back to Mandino. He wasn't prepared to try to get inside the house himself, because he was outnumbered, plus one of them was probably armed with Alberti's pistol. Mandino had promised to send another man from the Rome family to join him, but he hadn't appeared so far.

The important thing, Rogan decided, was to let Mandino know what he'd seen, and then await instructions. He dropped down into a crouch, crept back along the wall of the house until he was well clear of the dining room and living room windows, then ran swiftly across the lawn to the break in the fence where he'd entered the property, and walked back to his car and the cell phone he'd locked in the glove box.

"What the hell is it, Chris?" Mark asked, as Bronson climbed down the stepladder and looked up at the inscribed stone.

Bronson shook his head. "I don't know. If Jeremy Goldman's deduction was right, and if our interpretation of the first stone was correct, this should be a map. I don't know what it is, but a map it ain't."

"Hang on a minute," Mark said. "Let me just check something."

He walked into the living room and looked at the inscribed stone, then returned a few moments later. "I thought so. This stone's a slightly different color. Are you sure the two are related?"

"I don't know. All I am certain of is that this stone has been cemented into the wall directly behind the other one, to the inch, as far as I can see, and I don't think that's a coincidence."

"It looks almost like a poem," Mark observed.

Bronson nodded. "That's my guess," he said, looking up at ten lines of ornate cursive script arranged in two verses, underneath an incomprehensible title that consisted of three groups of capital letters, presumably all some kind of abbreviations. "Though why a stone with a poem carved into it should have been stuck in the wall at this exact spot beats me."

"But the language isn't Latin, is it?"

"No, definitely not. I think some of the words might have French roots. These three here—*ben, dessús* and *perfècte,* for example—aren't that dissimilar to some modern French words. Some of the others, though, like *calix,* seem to be written in a completely different language."

Bronson climbed back up the ladder and had a

closer look at the inscription. There were several differences between the two, not just the languages used.
Mark was right—the stones were different colors, but
the form and shape of the letters in the verses was
also unfamiliar, completely different from those in the
other inscription, and in places the stone had been
worn away, as if by the touch of many hands over
countless years.

IV

The ringing of the phone cut across the silence of
the office.

"There's been a development, Cardinal." Vertutti
recognized Mandino's light and slightly mocking
tone immediately.

"What's happened?"

"One of my men has been carrying out surveillance
of the house in Monti Sabini and a few minutes ago
he watched the discovery of another inscribed stone
in the property, on the back of the wall directly behind
the first one. It wasn't a map, but looked more like
several lines of writing, perhaps even poetry."

"A poem? That makes no sense."

"I didn't say it *was* a poem, Cardinal, only that my
man thought it *looked* like poetry. But whatever it is,
it must be the missing section of the stone."

"So what are you going to do now?"

"This matter is now too sensitive to be left only to
my *picciotti,* my soldiers. I will be traveling to Ponticelli early tomorrow morning with Pierro. Once we've
got inside the house, I'll have both inscriptions photographed and copied, then destroy them. Once we have
this additional information, I'm sure Pierro will be
able to work out exactly where we should be looking.

"While I'm away, you should be able to contact me
on my cell phone, but I'll also send you the telephone

number of my deputy, Antonio Carlotti, in case of an emergency."

"What kind of an emergency?"

"Any kind, Cardinal. You'll receive a text listing the numbers in a couple of minutes. And please keep your own cell phone switched on at all times. Now," Mandino continued, "you should also be aware that if the two men in the house have worked out—"

"Two men? What two men?"

"One is, we believe, the husband of the dead woman, but we don't know who the second man is. As I was saying, if these men have found what we're seeking, I will have no option but to apply the Sanction."

11

"I think these verses are written in Occitan, Mark," Bronson said, looking up from the screen of his laptop. He'd logged onto the Internet to try to research the second inscription but without inputting entire phrases. He'd discovered that some of the words could have come from several languages—*roire,* for example, was also found in Romanian—but the only language that contained all the words he'd chosen was Occitan, a Romance language originally spoken in the Languedoc region of southern France. By trawling through online dictionaries and lexicons and cross-referencing, he had managed to translate some of the words, though many of those in the verses simply weren't listed in the few Occitan dictionaries he'd found.

"What's it mean?" Mark asked.

Bronson grunted. "I've no idea. I've only been able to translate the odd word here and there. For example, this word *'roire'* in the sixth line means 'oak,' and there's a reference to 'elm' in the same line."

"You don't think it's just some medieval poem about husbandry or forest maintenance?"

Bronson laughed. "I hope not, and I don't think so. There's also one oddity. In the last line but one there's the word *'calix,'* and I can't find that in any of the Occitan dictionaries I've looked at. That might be because it seems to be a Latin word, rather than Occitan. If so, it translates as 'chalice,' but I've no idea why a Latin word should appear in a verse written in Occitan. I'll have to send a copy of this to Jeremy Goldman in London. Then we might find out what the hell this is all about."

He'd already taken several photographs of the inscription, which he'd transferred to the hard drive of his laptop, and had also typed the text into a Word file.

"What we need to do now," he said, "is decide what we should do with this stone."

"You think these 'burglars' will be back?"

Bronson nodded. "I'm sure of it. I hurt one of them badly last night, and probably the only reason they haven't been back already is because they know we've got a pistol in the house. I suspect that they *will* be back, and sooner rather than later. And that stone"—he pointed—"is almost certainly what they've been looking for."

"So what do you suggest? You think we should cover it up again?"

"I don't think that would work. The fresh plaster would be obvious the moment they walked into this room. I think we need to do something more positive than simply hiding the stone. I suggest we leave the plaster just as it is, but take a hammer and chisel to that inscription and obliterate it. That way, there'll be no clues left for anyone to follow."

"You really think that's necessary?"

"I honestly don't know. But without that inscription, the trail stops right here."

"Suppose they decide to come after us? Don't forget, we've seen both these carved stones."

"We'll have left Italy by then. Jackie's funeral is tomorrow. We should leave soon after that's over, and be back in Britain tomorrow evening. I hope that whoever's behind this won't bother following us there."

"OK," Mark said. "If that's what it'll take to end this, let's do it."

Twenty minutes later Bronson had chipped away the entire surface of the block, obliterating all traces of the inscription.

II

Gregori Mandino arrived in Ponticelli at nine thirty that morning and met Rogan by arrangement in a café on the outskirts of the town. Mandino was, as usual, accompanied by two bodyguards, one of whom had driven the big Lancia sedan from the center of Rome, as well as the academic Pierro.

"Tell us again exactly what you saw," Mandino instructed, and he and Pierro listened carefully as Rogan explained what he'd witnessed through the dining-room window of the Villa Rosa.

"It definitely wasn't a map?" Mandino asked, when they'd heard the explanation.

Rogan shook his head. "No. It looked like about ten lines of verse, plus a title."

"Why verse? Why are you so sure it wasn't just ordinary text?" Pierro asked.

Rogan turned to the academic. "The lines were different lengths, but they all seemed to be lined up down the center of the stone, just like a poem you see in a book."

"And you said the color of the stone looked different. How different?"

Rogan shrugged. "Not very. I just thought it was a lighter shade of brown than the one in the living room."

"It could still be what we're looking for," Pierro said. "I'd assumed that the lower half of the stone would contain a map, but a verse or a few lines of text could give directions that will lead us to the hiding place of the relic."

"Well, we'll soon find out. Anything else?"

Rogan paused for a few seconds before replying, Mandino noticed.

"There is one other thing, *capo*. I believe that the men in the house are armed. When Alberti tried to break in and was attacked by one of them, he dropped his pistol. I think it's in the house and that the men have found it."

"We're well rid of Alberti," Mandino snarled. "Now we'll have to wait until they've gone out. I'm not risking a gunfight in that house. Anything else?"

"No, nothing," Rogan replied, sweating slightly, and not because of the early-morning sun.

"Right. What time's the funeral?"

"Eleven fifteen, here in Ponticelli."

Mandino glanced at his watch. "Good. We'll drive out to the house and, as soon as these two men have left, we'll get inside. That should give us at least a couple of hours to check what this verse says and arrange a reception committee for them."

"I really don't want—" Pierro began.

"Don't worry, *Professore,* you won't need to be anywhere near the house when they get back. You just decipher this verse or whatever we find in the place, and then I'll get one of my men to drive you away. We'll handle the rest of it."

III

Like every day since they'd arrived in Italy, the morning of Jackie's funeral presaged a beautiful day, with a solid blue sky and not the slightest hint of a cloud.

Mark and Bronson were up fairly early, and ready to leave the house by a quarter to eleven, in good time to attend the service at eleven fifteen in Ponticelli.

Bronson locked his laptop and camera in the trunk of the Hamptons' Alfa Romeo when he went out to the garage at a few minutes to eleven. As an afterthought, he went back into the house, collected the Browning pistol from his bedroom and slipped it into the waistband of his trousers.

Two minutes later, Mark sat down in the passenger seat and strapped himself in as Bronson slipped the Alfa into first gear and drove away.

Mandino's driver had parked the Lancia about a quarter of a mile down the road, between the Hamptons' house and Ponticelli, in the parking lot of a small out-of-town supermarket, and Rogan's car was right next to it. The site offered an excellent view of the road, and the gateway of the house.

A few minutes before eleven, a sedan car emerged from the gateway and headed toward them.

"There they are," Mandino said.

He watched as the Alfa Romeo drove past them, two indistinct figures in the front.

"Right, that was both of them, so the house should be deserted. Let's go."

The driver pulled out of the parking space and turned up the road toward the house. Behind them, one of Mandino's bodyguards turned the opposite way out of the supermarket in Rogan's Fiat and fell into place about two hundred yards behind the Alfa, following the vehicle toward Ponticelli.

The Lancia sedan swept in between the gateposts. The driver turned the car so that it faced back up the drive and stopped it. Rogan climbed out and walked around to the back of the house. He slipped a knife from his pocket and released the catch on one set of shutters outside the living room. As he had hoped, the pane of glass Alberti had broken during their last, abortive, attempt to break in still hadn't been repaired, and he needed only to slip his hand through the window and release the lock.

With a swift heave, he pulled himself up and through the window, landing heavily on the wooden floor of the living room. Immediately, he pulled his pistol out of his shoulder holster and glanced around the room, but there was no sound anywhere in the old house.

Rogan walked through the room into the hall and pulled open the front door. Mandino led Pierro and his remaining bodyguard inside, waited for one of them to shut the door and then gestured for Rogan to lead the way. The three men followed him through the living room and into the dining room, and then stopped dead in front of the featureless surface of the honey-brown stone.

"Where the hell is it? Where's the inscription?" Mandino's voice was harsh and angry.

Rogan looked like he'd seen a ghost. "It was here," he shouted, staring at the wall. "It was right here on this stone."

"Look at the floor," Pierro said, pointing at the base of the wall. He knelt down and picked up a handful of stone chips. "Somebody's chiseled off the inscribed layer of that stone. Some of these flakes still have letters—or at least parts of letters—on them."

"Can you do anything with them?" Mandino demanded.

"It'll be like a three-dimensional jigsaw," Pierro said, "but I should be able to reconstruct some of it. I'll need the stone to be pulled out of the wall. Without that, there's no way I can work out which piece goes where. There's also a possibility that we could try surface analysis, or even chemical treatment or an X-ray technique, to try to recover the inscription."

"Really?"

"It's worth a try. It's not my field, but it's surprising what can be achieved with modern recovery methods."

That was good enough for Mandino. He pointed at his bodyguard. "Go and find something soft to put the stone chips in—towels, bed linen, something like that—and collect every single shard you can find." He turned to Rogan. "When he's done that, get the stepladder and start chipping out the cement from around that stone. But don't," he warned, "do any more damage to the stone itself. We'll help you lift it down when you've loosened it."

Mandino watched for a few moments as his men started work, then walked toward the door, motioning to Pierro to follow him. "We'll check the rest of the house, just in case they were helpful enough to write down what they found."

"If they did that to the stone," the professor replied, "I doubt very much if you'll find anything."

"I know, but we'll look anyway."

In the study, Mandino immediately spotted the computer and a digital camera. "We'll take these," he said.

"We could look at the computer here," Pierro suggested.

"We could," Mandino agreed, "but I know specialists who can recover data even from formatted hard disks, and I'd rather they checked it. And if these men photographed the stone before they obliterated the inscription, the images might still be in the camera."

Mandino yanked the power cable and connecting leads out of the back of the desktop computer's system unit and picked it up. "Bring the camera," he ordered, and led the way to the hall, where he carefully placed the unit beside the front door.

They walked back into the dining room, where Rogan and the bodyguard were just lifting the stone clear of the wall. When they'd lowered it to the floor, Mandino examined the surface again, but all he could see were chisel marks. Despite Pierro's optimism, he didn't think there was even the remotest chance of recovering the inscription from the pathetic collection of chips and the surface of the stone itself.

The best option they had was to talk to the men themselves.

Funerals in Italy are normally grand family affairs, with posters pasted around the town announcing the death, an open casket and lines of weeping and wailing mourners. The Hamptons knew few people in the town—they'd only been there, off and on, for a matter of months, and had spent most of that time working on the house rather than getting to know their neighbors.

Bronson had arranged for a simple service in the anticipation that there'd be only three people there—himself, Mark and the priest. In fact, there were about two dozen mourners, all members of Maria Palomo's extended family. But it was, by Italian standards, a very restrained, and comparatively brief, ceremony. Within thirty minutes the two men were back in the Alfa, and heading out of the town.

Neither of them had noticed the single man in a nondescript dark-colored Fiat who had followed them into Ponticelli. When they'd parked near the church, he'd driven past but within moments of Bronson pulling away from the curb, the car was behind them again.

Inside the vehicle, the driver pulled a cell phone from his pocket and pressed a speed-dial number. "They're on the way," he said.

*   *   *

Mark had barely said a word since they'd left Ponti-celli, and Bronson hadn't felt like talking, the two men united in their grief for the death of a woman they'd both loved, albeit from different perspectives. Mark was trying to come to terms with the final, irrevocable chapter of his short marriage, while Bronson's aching loss was tempered by guilt, by the knowledge that for the last five years or so he'd been living a lie, in love with his best friend's wife.

The funeral had been Mark's last farewell to Jackie and, now it was over, he was going to have to make decisions about his life. Bronson guessed that the house—the property the Hamptons had intended to retire to—would go on the market. The memories of their time together in the old place would probably be too painful for Mark to relive for very long.

As he neared the house, Bronson noticed a Fiat sedan coming up fast behind them.

"Bloody Italian drivers," he muttered, as the car showed no signs of overtaking, just maintained posi-tion about ten yards behind the Alfa.

He braked gently as he approached the gateway, turned on his blinker and turned in. But the other car did the same, stopping actually in the gateway and completely blocking it. In that instant, as Bronson glanced toward the old house, he realized they were trapped, and just how high the stakes really were.

Outside the house, a Lancia sedan was parked, and beside the front door—which looked as if it was slightly ajar—was an oblong gray box and a cubical sandy-colored object. Behind the car, two men were standing, staring at the approaching Alfa, one with the unmistakable shape of a pistol in his right hand.

"Who the hell . . . ?" Mark shouted.

"Hang on," Bronson yelled. He swung the wheel to the left and accelerated hard, powering the car off the gravel drive and across the lawn, aiming straight for the hedge that formed a boundary between the garden and the road.

"Where was it?" Bronson shouted.

Strapped into the passenger seat, Mark immediately guessed what Bronson was asking. When they'd bought the house, the driveway was U-shaped, with two gates, but they'd extended the hedge and lawn across the second entrance. And that was now their only way out. He pointed through the windshield. "A little farther to the right," he said, braced himself in the seat and closed his eyes.

Bronson twitched the wheel slightly as the Alfa rocketed forward. He heard the cracks of two shots behind them, but he didn't think either hit the vehicle. Then the nose of the car tore into the hedge, the bushes planted barely a year earlier. Beyond the windshield, their view turned into an impenetrable maelstrom of green and brown as the Alfa smashed the plants under its chassis, branches whipping past the side windows. The front wheels lifted off the ground for a moment when the car hit the low bank that formed the base of the hedge, then crashed down again.

And then they were through. Bronson lifted his foot off the accelerator pedal and hit the brakes for an instant as the car lurched across the grass verge, checking the road in both directions. It was just as well he did.

A truck was lumbering up the hill directly toward them, just a few yards away, a black cloud of diesel belching from its exhaust. The driver's face wore an almost comical look of shock, having just seen the bright red car materialize from a hedge right in front of him.

Bronson slammed the accelerator pedal down again, and the Alfa shot straight across the road, missing the back of the truck by perhaps three feet. He hit the brakes, swung the wheel hard left and, the moment the car was aiming down the hill, accelerated again. The Alfa fishtailed as he fed in the power, but in moments it was screaming down the road at well more than sixty miles an hour.

"What the hell's going on?" Mark demanded, turning around in his seat to look back toward his house. "Who were those people?"

"I don't know *who* they were," Bronson said, "but I know *what* they were. That cubical object was the stone from your dining-room wall, and the gray box was the system unit from your computer. They were the people who broke in to read the first inscription, and who've been trying to get back inside ever since to find the second one."

Bronson glanced in his mirror as he accelerated hard down the hill. About two hundred yards behind them he saw two cars emerge from the gateway one after the other and start chasing them. The first was the Fiat that had blocked the drive behind them, and the second was the Lancia.

"I don't—" Mark began.

Bronson interrupted. "We're not clear yet. Both cars are chasing us."

His eyes were scanning the instruments, checking for any abnormal readings that might have been caused by the harsh treatment he'd given the car, but everything seemed OK. And he hadn't detected any problems with the handling, though there appeared to be various bits of greenery attached to the front of the car.

"What do they want?"

"The inscription, obviously. They know we erased it, so now we're their only lead, simply because we saw it. Whatever it means, it must be a hell of a lot more important than I thought."

Bronson was pushing the Alfa as hard as he dared,

but the roads were fairly narrow, twisting and not that well surfaced and, though he couldn't see the other cars behind him, he knew they had to be close. He was a very competent police-trained driver, but he wasn't familiar with the car or the area, and he was driving on the "wrong" side of the road, so the odds were stacked against him.

"You'll have to help me, Mark. We've got to get the hell away from here, as quickly as possible." He pointed ahead to a road sign indicating a crossroads. "Which way?"

Mark stared through the windshield, but for a moment he didn't respond.

"I need to know," Bronson said urgently. "Which way?"

Mark seemed to rouse himself. "Left," he said. "Go left. That's the quickest route to the autostrada."

But as Bronson paused in the center of the road, waiting for a group of three cars coming in the opposite direction to pass, the Fiat appeared in his rearview mirror about a hundred yards behind.

"Shit," Bronson muttered, and accelerated as quickly as he could the instant the road was clear.

"A quick check, Mark," he said. "My laptop and camera are in the car, and my passport's in my pocket. Is there anything you have to collect from the house?"

Mark felt in his jacket pocket and pulled out his wallet and passport. "Only my clothes and stuff," he said. "I hadn't finished packing."

"You have now," Bronson said grimly, alternating his gaze between the road in front and his mirrors.

"We need to take the next road on the right," Mark instructed. "Then the autostrada's only a couple of miles away."

"Got it."

But though Bronson slowed as the Alfa neared the junction, he didn't take the turn.

"Chris, I said turn right."

"I know, but we need to lose this guy first. Hang on."

The Fiat had closed to less than fifty yards behind the Alfa when Bronson acted. He slammed on the brakes, waited until the car's speed had dropped to about twenty miles an hour, then released the brakes, spun the wheel to the left and simultaneously pulled on the handbrake. The car lurched sideways, tires screaming in protest as it slid across to the other side of the road. The moment it was facing the opposite way, Bronson dropped the handbrake and pressed on the accelerator. The Alfa shot past the Fiat, whose driver was still braking hard, and moments later they passed the Lancia as well, which had just caught up.

"What the hell was that?" Mark asked.

"Technically it's called a J-turn, because that's the shape of the skid mark the tires leave on the road. It's amazing what you can learn in the police force. The important thing is that it should have given us a couple of minutes' breathing space."

Bronson was checking his mirrors constantly and when they reached the turning for the autostrada there was still no sign of either the Fiat or the Lancia behind them. For a second or two he debated ignoring the junction and taking a side road up into the hills, where they might be able to find somewhere to hide for a few minutes. But he decided that speed was more important, and hauled the Alfa across the road, barely slowing, and within three minutes they were taking a ticket at the barrier.

"Where are we going?" Mark asked.

"We're heading for the Italian border. I'm going to put as much distance as possible between us and them, and the sooner we're in another country the better, as far as I'm concerned."

Mark shook his head. "I still don't really understand

what's going on. Stealing the computer makes sense, I suppose—it's possible we could have stored the pictures of the verses on that—but the stone? You completely destroyed the inscription, so why would they bother taking it?"

"They probably think they can recover it by using some kind of high-tech process. You can use X-rays to read the number of a car engine after it's been ground off the block, so maybe there's a similar technique that can be applied to stone. I really don't know. But to go to the trouble of hacking that stone block out of the wall—not to mention shooting at us—that means they're *really* serious about finding that inscription."

12

I

Gregori Mandino was furious. He'd ordered the stone and computer unit to be taken out to the Lancia, and he'd planned to have Pierro drive the vehicle away from the house, leaving the three of them in the property to await the return of Hampton and his companion. But the call from his bodyguard, telling him the two Englishmen were already heading back to the house, had changed all that.

The maneuver by his bodyguard had worked perfectly, completely blocking the entrance to the driveway, but the way the car had escaped had been totally unexpected. That, and the way the Alfa had evaded them minutes later, had convinced Mandino that the driver was either desperate or an expert.

They'd turned to give chase as quickly as possible, but by the time they'd reached the first junction, the Alfa Romeo was nowhere in sight, and there were three possible routes the driver could have taken. Mandino had guessed Hampton and the other man would head for the autostrada, and he'd ordered the Lancia driver to take that route, but they'd seen no sign of their quarry before they reached the tollbooths and, without knowing which way the Alfa had gone, any further attempt at pursuit was pointless.

Mandino hated making mistakes. He'd *assumed* that the two Englishmen wouldn't be returning to the house for at least two hours, and *assumption,* as an American colleague had been fond of saying, was the mother of all screwups. But it was too late now.

"Search the house," he ordered. "Look for any documents that identify the second man, and anything that might help us find the two of them."

As his men dispersed to do his bidding, Pierro walked over to Mandino. "What would you like me to do?"

"Take another look around the place, just in case my men miss anything."

"Where do you think the Englishmen have gone?"

"If they've got any sense," Mandino replied, "they'll be heading for England. They'll have picked up the autostrada and headed north, out of Italy."

"Can't you stop them? Get the *Carabinieri* to intercept them?"

Mandino shook his head. "I have some influence with them, but this whole matter is supposed to be handled as discreetly as possible. We'll have to find these two using our own resources."

II

Mandino was right—Bronson *had* taken the autostrada and turned north, heading for the Italian border.

"Do you think they'll be following us?" Mark asked, as the Alfa rounded a gentle curve at an indicated speed of one hundred and forty kilometers per hour.

"Not unless they've got a helicopter or something,"

Bronson said, keeping his eyes on the road. "We lost the Fiat and Lancia well before we picked up the autostrada."

"Which route are we taking, so I can program the navigation system?"

"Just in case those guys are planning on a roadblock or something, we'll take the short route out of Italy. The closest frontier is with Switzerland, but as the gnomes aren't yet a part of the E.U. we'll probably be asked for paperwork. So we'll turn north just outside Modena and head up through Verona and Trento to Austria, then on through Innsbruck into Germany and Belgium.

"This is going to be a bloody quick trip. I plan to stop for petrol, food, coffee and the loo, and nothing else. When we're too tired to drive on, we'll find a hotel somewhere. But that won't be until at the very least we've crossed two borders and are well inside Germany."

III

They'd met absolutely no problems on their very rapid drive across Europe. Bronson had been as good as his word, and he'd driven as fast as the traffic would allow, staying on the toll roads as much as possible, up through Italy, and crossed western Austria before entering Germany just north of Innsbruck.

They'd driven on to Munich, then turned west to Stuttgart and on to Frankfurt, but by then Bronson was really feeling the strain. He'd pulled off the autobahn at Montabaur and headed north. At Langenhahn they'd found a small hotel and fallen into bed.

The next morning, Bronson pushed the Alfa hard on the back roads until he picked up the autobahn just southeast of Cologne. After that it was toll roads all the way to the south of Aachen, where they en-

tered Belgium, and on to the French border near Lille.
And then it was only a short hop to the Channel Tunnel terminal just outside Calais, where Mark handed over a small fortune for the privilege of sitting in his own car for the brief journey under *La Manche.*

"I'll tell you this, Chris," he said, as Bronson drove the Alfa onto the train. "The next time I cross to France I'm taking a ferry."

An hour later, Bronson dropped Mark off at his apartment in Ilford, and then picked up the southbound M25 and opened the front door of his house only seventy minutes after leaving his friend.

He left his computer bag in the living room and spent a few minutes transferring the photographs of both inscriptions onto a high-capacity USB memory stick, because he didn't want to drag his laptop all the way up to London with him.

He hadn't eaten since his breakfast in Germany, what seemed like a week ago, so on his way to the railway station he grabbed a packet of sandwiches and a can of soft drink from a convenience store.

Thirty minutes later he was sitting in a train heading for Charing Cross Station and the British Museum.

IV

Gregori Mandino had returned to Rome as soon as it was clear that his quarry wouldn't be going back to the house. He had managed to track down Mark Hampton's home address in Ilford and his place of work in the City of London. The second man was proving more elusive: an Englishman who spoke fluent Italian, and who had introduced himself to the staff of the funeral home as "Chris Bronson."

But there were ways of tracing people, and Mandino knew the two Englishmen had flown to Rome from

Britain, and the *Cosa Nostra* had extensive connections at all levels of Italian bureaucracy. So he dialed a number and issued certain orders.

Just more than three hours later Antonio Carlotti called with the result.

"Mandino."

"We have a match, *capo*," Carlotti said. "Our contact in passport control in Rome has identified the man as Christopher James Bronson, and I have an address for him in Tunbridge Wells."

Mandino grabbed a pencil and paper as Carlotti dictated Bronson's address and telephone number to him.

"Where is this Tunbridge Wells?" Mandino asked.

"Kent, about fifty kilometers south of London. And there's something else. The reason the inquiry took so long was because my man had to explain the reasons for his request to the British authorities. Usually, a passport check is just a formality, but in this case they refused to release the information until he had told them why he was making the inquiry."

"What did he tell them?"

"He said that Bronson might have been a witness to a road accident in Rome, and that seemed to satisfy them."

"But why," Mandino asked the obvious question, "were they reluctant to divulge this?"

"Because this man Bronson is a serving police officer," Carlotti explained. "In fact, he's a detective sergeant based at the station in Tunbridge Wells. And, just like in the *Carabinieri,* the British police protect their own."

For a few moments Mandino didn't respond. This was an unexpected development, and he wasn't sure if it was good or bad news.

"Family?" he asked, finally.

"His parents are both dead, he has no children, and

he's recently divorced. His ex-wife's name is Angela Lewis. She's employed by the British Museum in London."

"As what? A secretary or something?"

"No. She's a ceramics conservator."

And that, Mandino knew, definitely *was* bad news. He had no idea what a ceramics conservator actually did, but the mere fact that the Lewis woman worked in one of the most celebrated museums in the world meant that she would have immediate access to experts from a number of disciplines.

Time, Mandino now knew, was fast running out. He needed to get to London as quickly as he could if he was to have any chance of retrieving the situation. But before he ended the call, he obtained Angela Lewis's London address and phone number. He also instructed that changes be made in the Internet monitoring system and added some very specific new criteria to the searches the syntax checkers were to analyze.

The monitoring system he'd put in place was both comprehensive and expensive, but as the Vatican was picking up the tab, the cost didn't bother him. It was based on a product called NIS, or NarusInsight Intercept Suite, which Mandino's people had modified so it could be installed on remote servers without the host's knowledge and operated like a computer virus or, more accurately, a Trojan Horse. Once in place, the NIS software could be programmed to monitor whole networks to detect specific Internet search strings or even individual e-mail messages.

Whenever Bronson accessed the Internet, and whatever he searched for, Mandino was sure he'd find out about it.

13

I

Bronson pulled out his Nokia and dialed Angela's work number. The journey into town from Tunbridge Wells had been quick and painless, and he'd even got a couple of seats to himself on the train so he'd been able to get comfortable.

"Angela?"

"Yes." Her voice was curt and distant.

"It's Chris."

"I know. What do you want?"

"I'm near the museum and I've brought the pictures of the inscriptions for you to look at."

"I'm not interested in them—I thought you realized that."

Bronson's steps faltered slightly. He hadn't expected Angela to welcome him with open arms, obviously—the last time they'd met had been in a solicitor's office and their parting had been frosty, to say the least—but he had hoped she would at least see him.

"But I thought . . . well, what about Jeremy Goldman? Is he available?"

"He might be. You'd better ask for him when you get here."

Five minutes later, Bronson plugged his memory stick into a USB slot in the front of a desktop computer in Jeremy Goldman's spacious but cluttered office in the museum. The ancient-language specialist was tall and rail-thin, his pale freckled complexion partially hidden behind large round glasses that weren't, in Bronson's opinion, a particularly good choice for the shape of his face. He was casually dressed in jeans and shirt, and looked more like a rebellious undergraduate than one of the leading British experts in the study of dead languages.

"I've got pictures of both the inscribed stones on this," Bronson told him. "Which would you like to see first?"

"You sent us a couple showing the Latin phrase, but I'd like to look at those again, and any others you took."

Bronson nodded and clicked the mouse button. The first image leapt onto the twenty-one-inch flat-panel monitor in front of them.

"I was right," Goldman muttered, when a third picture was displayed. His fingers traced the words of the inscription. "There *are* some additional letters below the main carving."

He turned to look at Bronson. "The close-up picture you sent was sharp enough," he said, "but the flash reflected off the stone and I couldn't make out whether the marks I could see were made by a chisel or were actually part of the inscription."

Bronson looked at the screen, and saw what Goldman was pointing at. Below the three Latin words were two groups of much smaller letters that he'd not noticed previously.

"I see them. What do they mean?" he asked.

"Well, I believe the inscription itself to be first or

second century A.D. and I'm basing that conclusion on the shape of the letters. Like all written alphabets, Latin letters changed in appearance over the years, and this looks to me like fairly classic first-century text.

"Now, the two sets of smaller letters might help us refine that date. The 'PO' of 'PO LDA' could be the Latin abbreviation *per ordo,* meaning 'by the order of.' That was a kind of shorthand used by the Romans to indicate which official had instituted a particular project, though it's unusual to find it as part of an inscription on a stone slab. It was more common to see it at the end of a piece of parchment—typically there would be a series of instructions followed by a date and then 'PO' and the name or initials of the senator or whoever had ordered the work to be carried out. So if you can find out who 'LDA' was, we might have a stab at dating this more accurately."

"Any ideas?" Bronson asked.

Goldman grinned at him. "None at all, I'm afraid, and finding out won't be easy. Apart from the obvious difficulty of identifying somebody who lived two millennia ago from his initials and nothing else, the Romans had a habit of changing their names. Let me give you an example. Everyone's heard of Julius Caesar, but very few people know that his full name was Imperator Gaius Julius Caesar Divus, or that he was normally just known as Gaius Julius Caesar. So his initials could be 'JC,' 'GJC' or even 'IGJCD.' "

"I see what you mean. So 'LDA' could be almost anyone?"

"Well, no, not anyone. Whoever had this stone carved was a person of some importance, so we're looking for a senator or a consul, someone like that, which will obviously narrow the field. Whoever the initials refer to will almost certainly be in the historical record, somewhere."

Bronson looked again at the screen. "And these other letters here—'MAM.' What do you think they could stand for? Another abbreviation?"

Goldman shook his head. "If it is, it's not one I'm familiar with. No, I think these letters are probably just the initials of the man who carved the stone—the mason himself. And I don't think you've got the slightest chance of identifying him!"

"Well, that seems to have exhausted the potential of the first inscription," Bronson said. "You thought that this stone might have been cut in half, so we checked throughout the house for the other piece. We didn't find it but, on the other side of the same wall, in the dining room and directly behind the first stone, we found this."

With something of a flourish, Bronson double-clicked one of the images on the memory stick and leaned back as a picture of the second inscription filled the screen.

"Ah," Goldman said, "this is *much* more interesting, and much later. The Latin text on the first inscription was carved in capital letters, typical of first- and second-century Roman monumental inscriptions. But this is a cursive script, much more elegant and attractive."

"We thought it might be Occitan," Bronson suggested.

Goldman nodded. "You're absolutely right—it *is* Occitan, and I'm fairly sure it's medieval. Do you know anything about the language?"

"Not a thing. I put a few words into Internet search engines and those that generated any results were identified as Occitan. All except that word"—he pointed at the screen—"which seems to be Latin."

"Ah, *calix*. A chalice. I'll have to think about that. But the use of medieval Occitan is interesting. It places this carving in the thirteenth or fourteenth century, but Occitan wasn't a tongue in common usage in the Rome area of Italy, where I gather you found this. That suggests the person who carved this had probably traveled to the region from southwest France, from the Languedoc area. Languedoc literally means the 'language of Oc,' or Occitan."

"But what does the inscription mean?"

"Well, it's not a standard Occitan text, as far as I can tell. I mean, it's not a prayer or a piece of poetry that I've ever seen before. I'm also puzzled by that word *calix*. Why put a Latin word in a piece of Occitan poetry?"

"You think it's a poem?" Bronson asked.

"That *is* what the layout suggests." Goldman paused, took off his glasses and cleaned the lenses thoughtfully.

"I can translate this into modern English, if you like, but I won't be able to vouch for the absolute accuracy of the translation. Why don't you go and have a cup of coffee or take a look around the museum? Come back in about half an hour and by then I should have a finished version ready for you."

As Bronson walked out of Goldman's office, he glanced around expectantly. He *had* hoped to see Angela while he was in the museum, and her refusal to meet him had been a disappointment.

He wandered out into Great Russell Street and went down one of the side roads. He took a seat in a café and ordered a cappuccino. The first sip he took made him realize just how bad most English coffee was in comparison to the real Italian stuff. That started him thinking about Italy again and, inevitably, about Jackie.

As he sat there, drinking the bitter liquid, his thoughts spun back over the years, and he remembered how excited she and Mark had been when they completed the purchase of the old house. He'd gone out to Italy with the Hamptons because they didn't speak the language well enough to handle the transaction, and had stayed with them in a local hotel for a couple of days.

A vivid picture swam into his mind: Jackie, dancing on the lawn in a bright red and white sundress while Mark stood beside the front door, a broad grin on his face, on the day when they'd finally got the keys.

"Stay here with us, Chris," she'd said, laughing in the spring sunshine. "There's plenty of room. Stay as long as you like."

But he hadn't. He'd pleaded pressure of work and flown back to London the following afternoon. Those two days he'd spent with them in Italy had rekindled feelings for Jackie that he'd really thought he'd got over, feelings that he knew were a betrayal of both Mark and Angela.

Bronson shook himself out of his reverie, and drained the last of his coffee, grimacing as he tasted the gritty grounds. Then he sat back and, in a sudden moment of gloomy introspection, seriously wondered if his life could do anything except improve.

Jackie was now—to his eternal regret—dead and gone. Mark was an emotional wreck, though Bronson knew he was strong and he'd pull himself out of it, and Angela was barely speaking to him. He wasn't sure he still had a job and, for some reason he still couldn't fathom, he'd got embroiled with a gang of armed Italian thugs over a couple of dusty old inscriptions. As midlife crises went, Bronson reflected, it pretty much ticked all the boxes on the debit side. And he wasn't even middle-aged. Or not quite, anyway.

Three-quarters of an hour later he walked back into Goldman's office.

If Bronson had been hoping for a clue that would

lead them to the missing section of the first inscribed stone, or even a written description of its contents, he was disappointed. The verses that Goldman handed him appeared to be little more than rambling nonsense:

GB•PS•DDDBE

From the safe mountain truth did descend
Abandoned by all save the good
The cleansing flames quell only flesh
And pure spirits soar above the pyre
For truth like stone forever will endure

Here oak and elm descry the mark
As is above so is below
The word becomes the perfect
Within the chalice all is naught
And terrible to behold

"You're sure this is accurate, Jeremy?" he asked.

"That's a fairly literal translation of the Occitan verses, yes," Goldman replied. "The problem is that there seems to be a lot of symbolism in the original that I'm not entirely sure we can fully appreciate today. In fact, some of it would be completely meaningless to us, even if we knew exactly what the author of this text was driving at. For example, there are some Cathar references, like the statement 'As is above so is below,' which, without a thorough grounding in that religion, would be impossible to understand completely."

"But the Cathars were prevalent in France, not Italy, weren't they?"

Goldman nodded. "Yes, but it's known that after the Albigensian Crusade some of the few survivors fled to northern Italy, so maybe this verse was written by one of them. That would also explain the use of

Occitan. But as to what it actually means, I'm afraid I haven't got a clue. And I think you'd be hard-pressed to find a Cathar you could ask. The crusaders did a very efficient job of exterminating them."

"What about the title—this 'GB PS DDDBE'? Is that some kind of code?"

"I doubt it," Goldman replied. "I suspect they refer to some expression that would have been familiar to people who saw the stone back in the fourteenth century."

Bronson looked blank.

"There are a lot of initials in common use today that would have been completely meaningless a hundred years ago, and might be just as incomprehensible to future generations. Things like . . . oh, 'PC' for 'personal computer' or even 'politically correct'; 'TMI' for 'too much information'; that kind of thing. OK, a lot of these kind of initials refer to slang terms, but nobody today would have any trouble telling you that 'RIP' stands for 'rest in peace,' and that's the kind of thing you'll frequently find carved on a piece of stone. Maybe the initials we have here had a similar significance in the fourteenth century, and were so familiar to people that no explanation was ever needed."

Bronson looked again at the paper in his hand. He'd hoped that the translation would provide an answer, but all it had done was present him with a whole new list of questions.

II

Early that evening, and a mere five hours after they'd landed at Heathrow, Rogan braked the rental car to a halt about a hundred yards from Mark Hampton's Ilford apartment.

"You're sure he's here?" Mandino asked.

Rogan nodded. "I know somebody is. I've made

three telephone calls to that apartment and they've all been answered. I did one as a wrong number, and the other two as telesales calls. In all three cases, a man answered, and I'm reasonably certain it was Mark Hampton."

"Good enough," Mandino said. He picked up a small plastic carrier bag from the footwell of the Ford sedan, opened the passenger door and headed along the street, Rogan at his side.

Time was of the essence. With every hour that passed, Mandino knew that more people would be likely to see copies of the inscriptions as Hampton and Bronson tried to work out what they meant.

He and Rogan walked the short distance to the building. At the entrance door, Mandino glanced in both directions before pulling on a pair of thin rubber gloves, and then pressed the button on the entry-phone. After a few seconds there was a crackle and a man's voice issued from the tiny speaker grill.

"Yes?"

"Mr. Mark Hampton?"

"Yes. Who is it?"

"This is Detective Inspector Roberts, sir, of the Metropolitan Police. I've got a few questions to ask you about your wife's unfortunate death in Italy. May I come in?"

"Can you prove your identity?"

Mandino paused for a few seconds. In the circumstances, Hampton's response was not unreasonable, or unexpected.

"You don't have a videophone, sir, so I can't show you my warrant card. But I can read you the number, and you can check it with either the Ilford police station or New Scotland Yard. The number is seven four six, two eight four."

Mandino had not the slightest idea what number or numbers might be found on a Metropolitan Police warrant card, but he was prepared to bet that Hampton wouldn't either. It all depended on whether the Englishman would bother to check.

"What questions?"

"Just some simple procedural matters, sir. It will only take a few minutes."

"Very well."

There was a buzz and the electric lock on the front door of the building clicked open. With a final glance up and down the street, Mandino and Rogan stepped inside, walked straight to the elevator and pressed the button for Mark's floor.

When the doors opened, they checked the apartment numbers, then strode down the corridor. At the correct door they stopped and Mandino knocked, then stepped to one side.

The moment the door came off the latch, Rogan kicked against it, hard. The door flew backward, knocking Mark off his feet and sending him sprawling onto the floor of the narrow hallway. Rogan stepped forward quickly, knelt down and hit him on the side of his head with a bludgeon. The blow was just hard enough to knock Mark unconscious, and was sufficient to disable him for the few minutes they needed.

"There," Mandino said, walking into the living room and pointing at a carver dining chair. "Tie him in that."

Rogan pulled the chair into the center of the room. Together, the two men dragged Mark over to the carver and sat him in it. He slumped forward, but Mandino pulled his shoulders back and held him in place while Rogan did his work. He took a length of clothesline from the bag Mandino had been carrying, looped it twice around Mark's chest and tied it behind the back of the chair, holding him upright. Then he took some cable ties, wrapped one around each wrist and used a pair of pliers to pull them tight. He re-

peated the process around Mark's forearms and el-
bows, and then secured his ankles in the same fashion
to the chair legs. In less than three minutes, he was
completely immobilized.

"Check the place," Mandino ordered. "See if he
brought a copy of the inscription back with him."

While Rogan began looking around the apartment,
Mandino walked through into the kitchen and made
himself a mug of instant coffee. It was nothing like
the Italian *latte* he was used to, but it was better than
nothing, and the last drink he'd had was a can of
orange juice on the flight from Rome.

"Nothing," Rogan reported, as Mandino walked
back into the room.

"Right. Wake him up."

Rogan stepped across to Mark, lifted his head and
then roughly forced his eyes open. Their captive
stirred, then regained consciousness.

When Mark came to, he found himself staring at a
well-dressed and heavily built man sitting in an easy
chair opposite him, sipping a hot drink from one of
his own mugs.

"Who the hell are you?" Mark demanded, his voice
harsh and slurred. "And what are you doing in my
apartment?"

Mandino smiled slightly. "I'll ask the questions,
thank you. We know about the two inscribed stones
you found in your house in Italy, and we know you
or your friend Christopher Bronson decided to obliterate the carving in the dining room. Now you're going
to tell me what you found."

"Are you the bastards who killed Jackie?"

The smile vanished from Mandino's face. "I said I'll
ask the questions. My associate will now emphasize
the point."

Rogan stepped forward, the pliers in his hand,

reached down and placed the jaws around the end of the little finger on Mark's left hand and slowly levered backward. With a snap that was audible to both Italians, one of the bones broke, the sound followed immediately by a howl of pain from Hampton.

"I hope the soundproofing here is good," Mandino remarked. "I wouldn't want to disturb your neighbors. Now," he continued, raising his voice above Mark's groans, "just answer my questions, quickly and truthfully, and then we can get you proper medical attention. If you don't tell us what we want to know, you've seven more fingers that my associate can work on."

Rogan waved the pliers in front of Mark's face.

Through a red haze and tears of pain, Mark stared in disbelief at the Italian.

"OK," Mandino said briskly, "let's begin. What did you find on the second inscribed stone? And don't even think about lying to me. My colleague here was watching through the window of the house when Bronson uncovered it."

"A poem," Mark gasped. "It looked like a poem. Two verses."

"In Latin?"

"No. We thought it was a language called Occitan."

"Did you translate it?"

Mark shook his head. "No. Chris tried, but he could only find a few of the words on the Internet, so we've no idea what the verses were about."

"What *did* you manage to translate?"

"Only a couple of words about trees—oak and elm, I think—and there was a Latin word as well. Something about a cup or chalice. That's all we could do."

"Are you quite sure?" Mandino asked, leaning forward.

"Yes, I—" Mark screamed as Rogan tapped the

pliers sharply on his fractured finger, already badly swollen and bleeding.

Mandino waited for a few seconds before continuing. "I'm inclined to believe you," he said, in a conversational tone. "So where is the inscription? I presume you copied it or something before your friend destroyed it."

"Yes, yes," Mark sobbed. "Chris photographed it."

"And what's he doing with it?"

"His ex-wife put him in contact with a man named Jeremy Goldman at the British Museum. He'll be taking the pictures to show him, to try to get it translated."

"When?" Mandino asked softly.

"I don't know. We only got back from Italy today. He's been driving for two solid days, so he'll probably go there tomorrow. But I don't know," he added hastily, as Rogan lifted the pliers threateningly.

Mandino raised a calming hand. "And do you have a copy of those photographs?"

"No. There didn't seem any point. Chris is the one who's interested in this—I'm not. All I wanted was my wife back."

"Are there any other copies, apart from those Bronson has?"

"No—I've just told you that."

It was time to finish it. Mandino nodded to Rogan, who walked behind their captive, picked up a roll of adhesive tape and tore off a strip about six inches long, which he stuck roughly over Mark's mouth as a rudimentary gag. Then he cut about a two-foot length of clothesline and knotted the ends together to form a loop.

Mark's terrified stare never left the Italian as he made his preparations.

Rogan dropped the loop of cord over Mark's head and walked into the kitchen, returning a few seconds later with that most mundane of kitchen utensils, a rolling pin. He stood directly behind Mark, awaiting instructions.

"Neither you nor your policeman friend have any idea what you've stumbled into," Mandino said. "My instructions are explicit. Anyone with any knowledge of these two inscriptions—even the limited knowledge you appear to have—is considered too dangerous to remain alive."

He nodded to Rogan, who slipped the rolling pin into the loop of cord and began twisting it to form a simple but effective garrotte. Mark immediately began to struggle in a desperate effort to free himself.

When the cord tightened around the Englishman's neck, Rogan paused for a moment, awaiting final confirmation.

Mandino nodded again, and watched Mark as the noose began to bite, seeing the flush rise in the man's face as his struggles intensified.

Rogan grunted with the effort as he held the rolling pin tight, waiting for the end.

Mark jerked violently once, then a second time, then slumped forward as far as the rope would allow. Rogan maintained the pressure for another minute, then released the cord and checked for a pulse in Mark's neck. He found nothing.

Mandino finished his coffee, then stood up and carried the mug through into the kitchen where he washed it thoroughly. He wasn't too bothered about the possibility of his DNA being found in the apartment, as there was nothing whatsoever to link him or Rogan to the killing, but old habits died hard.

Back in the living room, Rogan had already released Mark from the chair and dragged his body to one side of the room. Then they trashed the place, trying to make it look as if a violent struggle had taken place. Finally, Mandino produced a leather-bound Filofax, opened it, tore several pages and smeared the organizer with blood from Mark's broken finger, then dropped it beside the body. The name in the front of the document was "Chris Bronson," and it was one of the items Mandino's men had found when they searched the house in Italy.

They made a final inspection of the apartment, then Rogan opened the door and checked up and down the corridor. He nodded to Mandino and they left the apartment, pulled the door closed behind them and walked to the elevator.

Outside, they strode unhurriedly down the street to their rental car. Rogan started the engine and pulled away from the curb. As they neared the end of the road, Mandino pointed to a public phone booth.

"That will do. Stop beside it."

He got out, stepped across to the phone, checked he still had his gloves on, then lifted the receiver and dialed "999." The call was answered in seconds.

"Emergency. Which service do you require?"

"Police," Mandino replied, speaking quickly and with what he hoped was the sound of panic in his voice.

"There's been a terrible fight," he said when the officer came on the line. He gave the address of Mark's apartment, then ended the call just as the officer began asking for his personal details.

"Drive back up the road. There's a side street not far from the apartment building. Take that turning."

Rogan parked the car where Mandino directed, facing the main road. Mark's building was just visible from their position.

"Now what?" Rogan asked.

"Now we wait," Mandino told him.

Twenty minutes later they heard the unmistakable sound of a siren, and a police car drove swiftly past the end of the road and squealed to a stop outside the apartment block. Two officers ran toward the building.

"Can we go now?" Rogan asked.

"Not yet," Mandino said.

After about another fifteen minutes, three more police cars, sirens screaming, tore down the street. Mandino nodded in satisfaction. *He* hadn't been able to find Bronson so far, but he had no doubt that the British police force would be able to track him down quickly. They would almost certainly have enough evidence to arrest him on suspicion of the killing of Mark Hampton.

Faced with the possibility of a murder charge, deciphering an ancient Occitan inscription would be the last thing on Bronson's mind. Mandino's organization had good contacts within the Metropolitan Police, and he was certain he would be able to find out where Bronson was being held and, more important, when and where he would be released.

"Now we can go," he said.

III

Bronson unlocked the front door of his house and stepped inside. He'd caught one of the fast trains out of Charing Cross, and had got back home quite a bit sooner than he'd expected. He walked through into the kitchen and switched on the kettle, then sat down at the table to study the translation of the inscription again. It still wasn't making any sense.

He looked at his watch and decided to give Mark a call. He wanted to show him the translation, and suggest that they meet up for a meal. He knew his friend was in a fragile emotional state. He'd feel happier if Mark wasn't left alone on his first evening back in Britain immediately after his wife's funeral.

Bronson picked up the landline phone and dialed

Mark's cell phone, which was switched off, so he called the apartment. The phone was picked up after half a dozen rings.

"Yes?"

"Mark?"

"Who's calling, please?"

Immediately, Bronson guessed something was wrong.

"Who is this?" the voice asked again.

"I'm a friend of Mark Hampton, and I'd like to speak to him."

"I'm afraid that won't be possible, sir. There's been an accident."

The "sir" immediately suggested he was talking to a police officer.

"My name's Chris Bronson, and I'm a D.S. in the Kent force. Just tell me what the hell's happened, will you?"

"Did you say 'Bronson,' sir?"

"Yes."

"Just a moment."

There was a pause, then another man picked up the phone.

"I'm sorry to have to tell you that Mr. Hampton is dead, Detective Sergeant."

"Dead? He can't be. I only saw him a few hours ago."

"I can't discuss the circumstances over the telephone, but we are treating the death as suspicious. You said you were a friend of the deceased. Would you be prepared to come over to Ilford to assist us? There are several matters that we think you could help us to understand."

Bronson was in shock, but he was still thinking clearly. It was far from normal procedure to ask an officer from another force to just pop over to the scene of a suspicious death.

"Why?" he asked.

"We're trying to establish the last movements of the deceased, and we hope you can assist us. We know you're acquainted with Mr. Hampton, because we found your Filofax here in his apartment, and the last few entries suggest you've just returned from Italy with him. I know it's not the usual routine, but you really could be of great assistance to us."

"Yes, of course I'll come over. I've got a couple of things that I've got to do here, but I should be there within about ninety minutes, say two hours maximum."

"Thank you, D.S. Bronson. That's very much appreciated."

The moment Bronson put down the phone, he dialed another number. It rang for a very long time before it was answered.

"What do you want, Chris? I thought I told you not to ring me."

"Angela, don't hang up. Please just listen. Please don't ask questions, just listen. Mark's dead, and he's probably been murdered."

"Mark? Oh my God. How did—"

"Angela. Please listen and just do as I say. I know you're angry and you don't want to have anything to do with me. But your life is in danger and you have to get out of your apartment right now. I'll explain why when I see you. Pack the minimum possible— enough for three or four days—but bring your passport and driver's license with you. Wait for me in that café where we used to meet in Shepherd's Bush. Don't say the name—it's possible this line has been bugged."

"Yes, but—"

"Please, I'll explain when I see you. Please just trust me and do what I ask. OK? Oh, and keep your cell phone switched on."

"I . . . I still can't believe it. Poor Mark. But who do you think killed him?"

"I've got a good idea, but the police have a completely different suspect in mind."

"Who?"

"Me."

14

Though he was used to the traffic in Rome, Mandino was still surprised at the sheer number of cars on London's streets. And at the treacle-slow pace at which the traffic moved, from red light to road works to another red light.

The distance between the apartment in Ilford and Angela Lewis's apartment in Ealing was only about fifteen miles, about a quarter-hour drive on an open road. But it had taken them more than an hour so far. Rogan was inching his way down the Clerkenwell Road, silently cursing the traffic, and the navigation system for bringing them this way.

"We're coming up to Gray's Inn Road," Mandino said, consulting a large-format London A–Z he'd bought at a newsagent's fifteen minutes earlier, when they had been stationary for even longer than usual. "When we reach the junction, ignore what that piece of electronic junk tells you and turn right, if you're allowed to."

"Right?"

"Yes. That'll take us up to King's Cross, and if we turn left there we'll be able to get on the Euston Road, and that will take us straight to the motorway. That's a longer way around, but it has just got to be faster than staying in this." Mandino gestured at the nearly motionless traffic all around them.

A mere ten minutes later, Rogan was pushing the Ford sedan up to fifty on the A40.

"If there are no more holdups," Mandino said, calculating distances on the map, "we should reach the Lewis woman's building in under twenty minutes."

In her north Ealing apartment, Angela replaced the telephone and stood in the living room for a few seconds, irresolute. Chris's phone call had scared her, and for a moment she wondered if she should ignore what he'd asked her to do, bolt the doors and simply stay inside the apartment.

Chris was right—she *was* still angry with him, because in her opinion the breakup of their marriage had been his fault, due entirely to the fact that he'd always been in love with his best friend's wife. He'd never talked about his feelings for Jackie—but then again, Chris had never been very good at talking about *any* of his feelings. But you only had to watch his reaction when Jackie appeared—his whole face would light up. The sad reality was that in her and Chris's marriage there had *always* been three people.

And Mark was dead! This shocking news, coming so soon after Jackie's fatal accident in Italy, was almost unbelievable. In just a few days, two people she'd known for years were dead.

Angela felt the tears coming, then shook her head angrily. She wasn't going to turn into a weeping wreck, and she knew what she had to do. Chris had many faults that she could—and indeed had—expound in great detail during their brief marriage, but he'd never been given to flights of fancy. If he said her life was in danger, she was perfectly prepared to believe him.

She walked briskly into the bedroom, pulled put her favorite bag from under the bed—it was a Gucci knockoff she'd picked up in a Paris street market years earlier—and quickly stuffed clothes and makeup inside. She took a smaller bag and grabbed a selection of her favorite shoes, checked her cell phone was in her handbag, unplugged the charger from its usual socket by the bed and tucked that in the overnight bag as well, then chose a coat from her wardrobe.

Angela made a final check that she'd got everything, then picked up her bags, locked her door and took the two flights of stairs down to street level.

She'd only walked about a hundred yards down Castlebar Road when she spotted a vacant black cab in the northbound traffic. She waved her hand and whistled. The cabbie made a sharp U-turn and stopped the vehicle neatly beside her.

"Where to, love?" he asked.

"Shepherd's Bush. Just around the corner from the Bush Theatre, please."

As the cab gathered speed down Castlebar Road toward the Uxbridge Road, a Ford sedan made the turn into Argyle Road from Western Avenue, and stopped outside Angela Lewis's apartment building.

II

Bronson put down the phone, ran upstairs, pulled an overnight bag from his wardrobe, grabbed clean clothes from his wardrobe and chest of drawers and stuffed them into it. He made sure he left one particular item on the bedside table, then went back downstairs.

His computer bag was in the living room, and he

picked that up, checked that the memory stick was still in his jacket pocket, seized Jeremy Goldman's translation of the inscription from the kitchen table and shoved that into his pocket as well. Finally, he opened a locked drawer in his desk in the living room and removed all the cash, plus the Browning pistol he'd acquired in Italy. He slipped the weapon into his computer bag, just in case.

And all the time he was doing this he was checking outside the windows of his house, watching for either Mark's killers or the police to turn up. The Met now knew he was a serving officer with the Kent force, and it would take only a few phone calls to find his address. Whether or not his agreement to drive over to the apartment in Ilford had actually served to allay their suspicions he had no idea, but he wasn't prepared to take any chances.

Less than four minutes after he'd called Angela, he pulled his front door closed behind him and ran across the pavement to his Mini. He put his bags in the trunk and drove away, heading north toward London.

About two hundred yards from his house, he heard sirens approaching from ahead of him, and took the next available left turn. He drove down the road, made another left at the end, and then left again, so that his car was pointing back toward the main road. As he watched, two police cars sped through the junction in front of him. He guessed that he'd got out of the house by the skin of his teeth.

An hour later, Bronson parked the car in a street just off Shepherd's Bush Road and walked the short distance to the café. Angela was sitting alone at a table in the back, well away from the windows.

As Bronson threaded his way through the tables toward his ex-wife, he felt a rush of relief that she was safe, mingled with apprehension as to how she might be feeling. And, as always when he looked at her, he was struck anew by her appearance. Angela wasn't a beauty in the classical sense, but her blond hair, hazel eyes and lips with more than a hint of Michelle Pfeiffer about them gave her a look that was undeniably striking.

As she pushed her hair back from her face and stood up to greet him, she drew appreciative glances from the handful of men in the café.

"What the hell is going on?" Angela demanded. "Is Mark really dead?"

"Yes." Bronson felt a stab of grief, and swallowed it down quickly. He had to stay in control—for both their sakes.

He ordered coffee, and another pot of tea for Angela. He knew he should eat something, but the thought of food made him nauseous.

"I rang Mark's apartment," he said, "and a man answered the phone. He didn't identify himself, but he sounded like a police officer."

"What does a policeman sound like?" Angela asked. "Still, I suppose you would know."

Bronson shrugged. "It's the way we're told to use 'sir' and 'madam' when we're talking to members of the public. Almost nobody else does that these days, not even waiters. Anyway, when I gave him my name, he told me that Mark was dead, and they were treating the death as suspicious. Then another man—definitely a copper, and probably a D.I.—asked if I could drive over to Ilford and help explain some things."

He put his head in his hands. "I can't believe he's dead—I was with him earlier today. I should never have left him alone."

Angela cautiously reached for his hand across the table. "So why didn't you just drive over to Ilford, as the policeman asked?"

"Because everything changed when they found out my name. The second man—the D.I.—told me they knew I was a friend of Mark, because they'd found my Filofax in the apartment, and that there were notes about the trip to Italy in it."

"But why did you leave your organizer with Mark?"

"I didn't, that's the point. The last time I saw my Filofax was in the guest bedroom of Mark's house in Italy. The only way it could have been found in his apartment was if the killers had dropped it there in a deliberate attempt to frame me for his murder."

He went on to explain about the "burglaries" at Mark's house following the uncovering of the first inscription, and the possibility that Jackie had been killed during the initial break-in.

"Oh, God. Poor Jackie. And now Mark—this is a nightmare. But why are you and I in danger?"

"Because we've seen the inscriptions on the stones, even if neither of us has a clue why they're important. The fact that Mark was killed in his apartment—or at least, that's where the body was found—means the killers found out where he lived. And if they found *his* address, they could just as easily find mine and, more important, yours. *That's* why I wanted you to get out of your apartment. They're going to come after us, Angela. They've killed our friends and we're next."

"But you still haven't explained why." Angela banged the table in frustration, spilling some of her tea. "*Why* are these inscriptions so important? Why are these people killing anyone who's seen them?"

Bronson sighed. "I don't know."

Angela frowned, and Bronson could tell that she was thinking it through. She had a fierce intellect—it was one of the things that had attracted him to her in the first place. "Let's just look at the facts here, Chris. I talked to Jeremy about these stones and he told me that one inscription dates from the first century and contains exactly three words written in Latin. The second is fifteen hundred years later, written in Occitan, and appears to be a kind of poem. What possible link can there be between them, apart from the fact that they were discovered in the same house?"

"I don't know," Bronson repeated. "But the two people who owned the house where the stones were hidden are now dead, and the Italian gang that I believe is responsible has made a pretty professional attempt to frame me for Mark's death. We have to stop them. They can't get away with this."

Angela shivered slightly, and took a mouthful of her tea. "So, what's your plan now? You have got a plan, haven't you?"

"Well, we've got to do two things. We have to get ourselves out of London without leaving a paper trail, and then we have to sit down and decode those two inscriptions."

"Got anywhere in mind?"

"Yes. We need somewhere not too far from London, but with easy access to a reference library and where a couple of researchers like us won't stand out. Somewhere like Cambridge, maybe?"

"Bicycle city? Yes, OK. That sounds as good as anywhere. When do we leave?"

"As soon as you've finished your tea."

A couple of minutes later they stood up to leave. Bronson glanced at Angela's luggage.

"Two bags?" he asked.

"Shoes," Angela replied shortly.

Bronson paid the bill and they walked out of the café. He turned right, not left toward where he'd parked the Mini Cooper, but to an ATM machine outside a bank off the Uxbridge Road.

"I thought guys on the run didn't use plastic?" Angela said, as Bronson took out his wallet.

"You've been watching too many American films.

But you're right. That's why I'm using this machine, not one up in Cambridge."

Bronson withdrew two hundred pounds. He wasn't bothered that the transaction would pinpoint his location, because they wouldn't be staying in the area for more than a few minutes.

He stuffed the cash in his pocket and led the way to his Mini. He repeated the process, each time drawing a few hundred pounds, at four further ATMs about a mile apart, but always staying in the Shepherd's Bush–White City area. He reached his credit limit at the last one.

"Right," he said, as he got back into the driving seat of the Cooper after the final withdrawal. "Hopefully that will convince the Met that I've gone to ground somewhere in this area. From now on, we're only going to use cash."

15

I

Angela stepped out of the cramped shower cubicle, wrapped a towel around her and walked across to the sink. As she dried her hair, she stared at herself critically in the small mirror and again wondered just what the hell she was doing.

In the last twenty-four hours her world had been turned completely upside-down. Before, her life had been ordered and predictable. Now, one of her best friends had been killed and her ex-husband was apparently the prime suspect, and she was on the run with him, trying to avoid both the police and a gang of Italian killers.

But, strangely, she was beginning to enjoy herself. Despite the failure of their marriage, she still liked Chris, and enjoyed being in his company. And, though she would never admit it to anyone else, she found his dark good looks just as attractive now as when she'd first met him. It still gave her a thrill inside when he walked into a room, instantly commanding attention.

Perhaps, she reflected as she dressed, that was part

of the problem. Chris *was* attractive, and perhaps that had clouded her judgment when he'd proposed. Maybe if she'd looked at him more carefully she'd have realized that his real affection was directed elsewhere, at the unattainable Jackie. It would have saved her a lot of heartache if she'd deduced that at the time.

She jumped slightly at the knock on the door.

"Good morning," Chris said. "Have you had breakfast yet? Because we need to get to work."

"I'll grab something later," Angela replied. "I'll go and make the calls, and take a look around. You stay here until I get back."

Outside the hotel, she walked briskly down the street until she found a working public telephone, fed a phone card into the slot and dialed the number of her immediate superior at the British Museum.

"It's Angela," she croaked. "I'm afraid I'm going down with something, Roger. Flu or something. I'm going to have to take a couple of days off."

"God, you sound like death. Don't you dare come anywhere near here until you're better. Seriously, is there anything you need—food, medicine, anything like that?"

"No, thanks. I'm just going to stay in bed until it's gone."

Angela and Bronson had discussed their plan on the train to Cambridge the previous evening. She was using a public phone because that left no trace—Bronson knew that switching on their cell phones would locate them to the nearest few yards immediately, so both of their Nokias were in his overnight bag, their batteries removed as a precaution.

Angela made one more call, then she walked back along East Road, stopping at the bakery along the way.

"Here," she said, as she walked into Bronson's hotel

room and passed him a small paper bag. "I bought a couple of pastries to keep us going until lunch."

"Thanks. You made the calls?" Bronson asked.

Angela nodded. "Roger will be fine. He's paranoid about any kind of cold or flu."

"And Jeremy?"

"Well, I called him and passed on the message. I explained about Mark and that we think his death had something to do with the inscriptions. I warned him he might be a target too but he laughed it off. He still thinks that the verses are meaningless to anyone in this century."

Bronson frowned. "I wish I could believe he's right," he said. "Well, you did your best."

"Right," Angela said, brushing crumbs off her lap. "Let's get started. Have you had any thoughts?"

"Not really. The problem with the Occitan verses is that they seem tantalizingly clear in what they say, but I've got no idea about their actual meaning. So I did just wonder if our best option was to start with the Latin inscription—or rather with the initials below it—and see if we can identify the man who ordered the stone to be carved."

"That makes sense," Angela said. "There are a couple of cybercafés not far from here, full of unshaven, scruffy students probably accessing high-quality porn sites." She paused and looked critically at him. "You'll fit right in."

Bronson had opted for a rudimentary disguise. He'd stopped shaving, though it would take a couple of days before his beard became really noticeable, and had discarded his usual collar and tie for a sloppy T-shirt, jeans and trainers.

Ten minutes later they entered the first of the Internet cafés Angela had identified. Three machines were available, so they ordered two coffees and started trawling the Web.

"Are you happy with Jeremy's suggestion about the 'PO' standing for *per ordo*?" Angela asked.

"Yes. I think we should just take that as established and try and find out who 'LDA' was. The other thing he suggested was that the carving was probably first century A.D. And, Angela, we have to be quick. After what happened to Jackie, I'm only staying on this machine for an hour. Whether or not we've found anything by then, we get up and leave. OK?"

Angela nodded her agreement. "Let's start the simple way," she said, typed "LDA" into Google, pressed the return key and leaned forward expectantly.

The result didn't surprise them: almost one and a half million hits, but as far as they could see from a quick scan, none of any use unless you *were* searching for the London Development Agency or the Learning Disabilities Association.

"That would have been too easy," Bronson muttered. "Let's refine the search. Try and find a list of Roman senators and see if any of them fit the bill."

That was easier said than done, and by the end of the hour Bronson had allotted, they'd found details about the lives of numerous individual senators but no list they could peruse.

"OK," Bronson said, with a quick glance at his watch. "One last try. Put 'Roman senate LDA' and see what comes up."

Angela input the phrase and they waited for the search engine to deliver its results.

"Nothing," Angela said, scrolling down the page.

"Wait," Bronson said. "What's that?" He pointed at an entry entitled "Pax Romana" that included a reference to "LDA and Aurora." "Try that," he said.

Angela clicked on it. On the left-hand side was a long list of Roman names, below the title "Regular members."

"What the hell is this?" Bronson wondered aloud.

"Oh, I know," Angela said, scrolling up and down. "I've heard of this. It's a kind of online novel about ancient Rome. You can read it, or write material for it, if you want. You can even learn quite a bit."

Bronson ran his eyes down the list of names, then stopped. "I'll be damned. Look—is that serendipity or what?" And he pointed at the name "Lucius Domitius Ahenobarbus" about three-quarters of the way down. "The contributors must be using the names of real historical Romans."

Angela copied the name and input it into Google.

"He certainly was real," she said, looking at the screen, "and he was a consul in sixteen B.C. Maybe Jeremy was wrong about the age of the inscription. It could have been fifty or so years older."

Bronson leaned over and clicked the mouse. "It might be even simpler than that," he said. "It seems this was a fairly common family name. On this list there are nine people all called Domitius Ahenobarbus, five of them with the first name Gnaeus, and the other four Lucius. Three of the four named Lucius Domitius Ahenobarbus were consuls: the one you found in sixteen B.C., plus two others, in ninety-four B.C. and fifty-four B.C."

"What about the fourth Lucius?"

Bronson clicked another link. "Here he is—but he looks a bit different. 'Like the others, this man was born Lucius Domitius Ahenobarbus, but his full name was Nero Claudius Caesar Augustus Germanicus, also known as Nero Claudius Drusus Germanicus. Just to complicate things, when he ascended the imperial throne in fifty-four A.D., he took the name Nero Claudius Caesar Drusus.' "

He scrolled down, then chuckled. "But he's better known to us as the emperor who fiddled while Rome burned."

"Nero? You think that inscription might refer to Nero?"

Bronson shook his head. "I doubt it, though that does fit better with Jeremy's estimated date. He suggested that the initials probably referred to a consul or senator. Just say for a moment that the inscription *was* prepared on Nero's orders—wouldn't it be more likely to read 'PO NCCD,' to reflect his imperial name?"

"Perhaps the inscription was carved before he became emperor?" Angela suggested. "Or maybe it was intended to be personal, to emphasize that whoever had carved the stone knew a lot about Nero, and maybe was even related to him."

"We're out of here," Bronson said, looking at his watch and standing up to leave. "So you reckon Nero's worth another look?"

"Absolutely," Angela agreed. "Let's find another cybercafé."

II

They walked the quarter mile or so to the second cybercafé Angela had located earlier. This one was almost empty, presumably due to the time of day, and they sat down at the PC at the end of the line, closest to the back wall of the café.

"So where do we go from here?" Angela asked.

"Bloody good question. I'm still not convinced we're even on the right track, but we've got to start somewhere. Look, forget 'LDA' for the moment. Jeremy suggested that the other letters on the stone—'MAM'—were probably those of the mason who carved it. But what if there's another explanation?"

"I'm listening."

"This is a bit tenuous, so bear with me. Assume

that the 'PO LDA' does mean 'by the order of Lucius
Domitius Ahenobarbus,' and that we *are* talking about
Nero himself. Jeremy guessed that meant the *stone*
was inscribed on Nero's instructions. But let's suppose
it wasn't. Maybe Nero ordered something completely
different to be done—some other action—and another
person, someone with the initials 'MAM,' decided that
this event should be recorded."

"I'm sorry, you've lost me."

"Take a present-day example. You'll quite often see
monuments and inscribed stones in Britain commemo-
rating some event: the names of local residents who
died in a war, or details of a building that once stood
on the spot, that kind of thing. Sometimes there's a
note at the end explaining that the stone, or whatever,
was paid for by the Rotary Club or some other group.
The point is that the people who paid for the stone
had nothing to do with the event the inscription described. They just arranged for the memorial to be
erected. Maybe this is something similar."

"You mean that Nero did something that could be
described by the expression 'here lie the liars,' but
someone else—'MAM'—ordered the stone to be prepared as a record of what Nero had done?"

"Exactly. And that suggests that whatever Nero did
might have been illegal or private, nothing to do with
his position as emperor. So what we have to do is find
out if he was connected to anyone with the initials
'MAM.' If he was, we might have something. If he
wasn't, it's back to the drawing board."

That search took very little time. Within a few minutes they had a possible match.

"This guy might fit the bill," Angela said. "His
name was Marcus Asinius Marcellus, and he was a
senator during the reigns of both Claudius and Nero.
What's most interesting is that he should have been
executed in A.D. sixty because of his involvement in a

plot to forge a will. All his accomplices were put to the sword, but Nero spared his life. I wonder why?"

"That's worth chasing."

Angela scrolled down the page. "Ah, here we are. Marcellus was distantly related to the Emperor. That's probably why Nero gave him a break."

"Yes, that could be the link."

"I'm not following you."

Bronson paused for a moment to order his thoughts. "Suppose the Emperor saved Marcellus because he was a relative, certainly, but also for some other reason. Nero wasn't known for his compassion. He was one of the most ruthless and bloodthirsty of all the Roman emperors—if my memory serves me correctly, he even had his own mother executed—so I don't think killing a fifth cousin or whatever Marcellus was would have made him lose any sleep.

"But suppose Nero wanted the services of someone who owed him a debt of allegiance, someone whom he could trust completely. In that case, this inscription makes more sense. Nero had ordered something done, something private or illegal or both, and Marcellus had been told to carry it out, maybe against his will. And it's *that* action which the inscription on the stone has recorded."

"You're quite right—it *is* tenuous. But what orders did Nero give?"

"I haven't got the faintest idea." Bronson stood up and stretched. It had been a long morning. "And there's something else. How would you describe the inscription we found on that stone—the three Latin words?"

"Cryptic, probably."

"Exactly. Assuming we're right about this, why did Marcellus feel the need to have a cryptic inscription prepared? Why didn't he carve something that explained the situation? Or was that exactly what he did on the missing lower section of the stone? Maybe that Latin phrase we found was just the title of the inscription?"

He paused and looked at Angela. "We need to do a *lot* more research."

Two hours later, Angela was in Bronson's room surrounded by books on the Roman Empire. They now knew a great deal more about Nero, but information on Marcellus was tantalizingly sparse. He seemed an extremely shadowy figure, and they found almost nothing about him that they hadn't already known. And they still had not the slightest idea what the Latin inscription might refer to.

"We're really not getting anywhere with this," Angela said, closing one of the reference books with an irritated snap. "I'm going to start looking at the second inscription." She stood up and reached for her coat. "I'll be in the third café on our list, if you need me."

"Right," Bronson replied. "I'm going to keep flogging away at these for a while. Be careful out there."

"I will, but don't forget nobody's looking for me, at least as far as I know."

Angela had been working at the machine for only about twenty minutes when the door of the café opened. A police constable entered and walked across to the girl manning the counter.

"Good afternoon, miss," the officer said. "We're looking for a man who we believe was in this area earlier today using cybercafés, and we wonder if you remember seeing him in here."

He produced a photograph from a folder he was carrying and placed it on the counter. As he did so, Angela caught a glimpse of the face in the picture and realized in a single heart-stopping moment that it showed Chris.

"I'm sorry," the girl said, "I only started my shift

here a couple of hours ago, and I'm pretty sure he hasn't been in this afternoon. You could try asking the customers." She waved her hand to encompass the twenty or so computers in the café and the dozen people using them. "Some of them are regulars. What's he done, anyway?"

"I'm not at liberty to say, I'm afraid," the officer said. He walked across to the first occupied terminal and repeated his question. By the time he'd got to the third computer, all the people in the café were clustered around him, staring at the picture. Angela realized that if she *didn't* go and look, that would appear suspicious in itself. So, on legs that weren't quite steady, she walked across the room and peered at the photograph of the man she knew better than anyone else in the world.

"And you, miss?" the constable asked, looking directly at her.

Angela shook her head: "No, I've never seen him before. Quite good-looking, though, isn't he?"

A couple of girls in the group giggled, but the policeman seemed unamused. "I wouldn't know," he said, and turned to leave.

"This bloke," the girl behind the counter asked, "if he does come in, what should I do? Run away and hide in the loo, or make him a drink? I mean, is he dangerous, or what?"

The constable considered the question for a few moments. "We don't think he'd pose any risk to you personally, miss, but you should telephone the Parkside station as soon as possible. In case you need it, the number's 358966."

Angela returned to her computer and forced herself to remain at the machine for several more minutes, then stood up.

"Find what you were looking for, love?" the girl behind the till asked.

Angela shook her head. "I've *never* found exactly what I'm looking for," she replied, with a slight smile, thinking about her taste in men.

"The bloody police are looking for you, Chris," Angela announced, the moment she'd closed the hotel room door behind her. Quickly, she outlined what had happened in the café.

"So they knew I'd been using the Internet?" Bronson said.

"Yes, I told you. They even had your photograph, and they said you'd been in the area this morning."

"Jesus, these guys are good," Bronson muttered. "They even have the police doing their dirty work for them. They're a lot more dangerous than we thought."

"I can understand that the police are looking for you because of Mark's death, but how can they possibly know you've been using cybercafés?"

"I thought from the start that these Italians had an Internet-monitoring system running—that's why Jackie died. They must have a contact in the British police and be feeding him details of the searches we're running, which means we must be on the right track. We're going to have to get away from here, and quickly."

"Where to?" Angela asked.

"The answer must lie in Italy, where all this started."

"But don't you think that if the police are already looking for you in cybercafés, they'll be checking the ports and airports as well?"

"Yes, of course," Bronson said, "but I made sure I left my passport inside the house, and I've no doubt that by now they'll have got inside and seen it. They might have a token watch in place at the ports, but without a passport, they won't be expecting me to try to leave the country." He grinned suddenly. "Which is exactly what we're going to do. It'll be a lot harder for them to find us in Europe."

"I thought Interpol helped international cooperation between police forces."

"Dream on. Interpol is a wonderful concept, but it's also a huge system. To get anything useful out of it, you've got to fill in the right forms and talk to the right people, and even then it will take time to get the information disseminated. Anyway, it's not that difficult to get in or out of Britain without being detected, if you know how. You *have* got your driving license and passport with you?"

Angela nodded.

"Good. Now, what I need you to do is take this money"—he reached into his jacket pocket, pulled out a wad of notes and counted out a sum on the table—"that's just over fifteen hundred pounds. Use that as a deposit and go out and buy an old minivan. A Chrysler Voyager, Renault Espace, even a Transit van as a last resort, in your name, and get it insured for driving on the Continent."

"Then what?"

"And then," Bronson replied, grinning again, "we're going shopping for a new bathroom."

16

A little after six, Jeremy Goldman walked out of the museum gates and glanced in both directions before heading east along Great Russell Street. Angela's telephone call had bothered him more than he liked to admit and his feeling of unease had been increased by the incident with the Frenchman.

Earlier that afternoon, in response to a call from one of the reception staff, he'd gone down to meet a French archaeologist named Jean-Paul Pannetier who apparently knew him. The name hadn't been familiar to Goldman, but he'd worked all over the world with specialists from a number of disciplines, and such unannounced visits weren't that unusual.

But when he'd introduced himself to the visitor, the Frenchman had appeared confused and explained that he was looking for a *Roger* Goldman, not *Jeremy* Goldman, and then left the building. He'd been fiddling with a cell phone the whole time he'd been in the museum, and Goldman suspected that Pannetier had used it to photograph him.

That was peculiar enough, but what concerned him

more was that he'd checked his academic directories and been unable to find any reference to a Roger Goldman. Or, for that matter, to a Jean-Paul Pannetier. There was a Pallentier and a Pantonnier, but no Pannetier. Of course, he could have misheard—the museum had been quite noisy—but the incident, in conjunction with Angela's warning, did concern him.

So as he emerged into the evening bustle of Great Russell Street, Goldman was—for once—paying attention to his surroundings. But spotting anyone who might be lurking in wait for him was virtually impossible, simply because of the sheer number of people on the pavements.

At least he didn't have far to go—only to the tube station at Russell Square. He walked down Great Russell Street, casting occasional glances behind him, checking the traffic and the pedestrians, then turned up Montague Street.

Until that point, Goldman had seen nothing to concern him, but when he glanced back once more, he saw a dark-haired man starting to run directly toward him. More alarmingly, he locked eyes with a bulky man sitting in the driving seat of a slow-moving car, a man he instantly recognized as the "Jean-Paul Pannetier" who'd visited the museum that afternoon.

Goldman didn't hesitate. He stepped off the pavement and began running across the road, dodging through the traffic. A barrage of hoots followed him as he swerved around cars, taxis and vans, sprinting for the far side of the street and the safety—he hoped—of the tube station.

He almost made it.

Goldman glanced behind him as he ran around the back of a car, and simply didn't see the motorcyclist coming up fast on the vehicle's nearside. When he did see it, the bike was just feet away. The rider braked hard, the front suspension of his bike dipping, and Goldman instinctively leapt aside to try to avoid him.

The front wheel of the bike hit Goldman's left leg and knocked him sideways. Waving his arms to try to regain his balance, he stumbled and almost fell, then recovered himself. Again he risked a quick look behind him as he resumed his weaving run, still slightly unbalanced. The man he'd spotted was just a few feet away, and Goldman increased his pace.

But when he looked ahead again, all he saw was the front of a black cab. To Goldman, it was as if everything was happening in slow motion. The driver stamped on the brakes, locking the wheels, but the taxi just kept coming, straight toward him. Goldman experienced a moment of sheer terror, then the solid impact as the front of the skidding vehicle smashed into his chest. He felt a sudden searing pain as his ribs broke and organs ruptured, then only blackness.

II

Less than ninety minutes later, Angela stepped back into the hotel room.

"That was quick," Bronson said, looking up from the book he was studying.

"I found a garage on Newmarket Road selling secondhand cars," she said. "I got a Renault Espace, seven years old. It's a bit scruffy around the edges, but it's got a decent rating, good tires and most of its service history, all for two nine nine five. I haggled the salesman down to two and a half and told him to forget about the warranty, which was almost worthless anyway. Five hundred deposit and the rest on credit."

"Excellent," Bronson said, as he began packing away the reference books Angela had bought. "That's ideal. Right, let's get this show on the road."

While Bronson carried their few bags out to the car, Angela handed back the room key and paid the hotel bill in cash.

"So, now where are we going?" she asked a few minutes later, as Bronson swung the Espace off the A10 and onto the London-bound M11, just south of Trumpington. "I know you want to cross the Channel, but what was all that about a new bathroom?"

"The plods may be trying to find me, but they shouldn't be after you. And even if they are, hopefully they'll be looking for a Mrs. Angela Bronson, not a Miss Angela Lewis. We're going to fill the back of the car with flat-pack furniture and catch a ferry out of Dover. And I'll be under all the boxes."

Angela stared at him. "Are you serious?"

"Absolutely. The checks at Dover and Calais are rudimentary, to say the least. This is the simplest way I can think of to get across the Channel."

"And if they stop me?"

"You deny all knowledge of me. Tell them you haven't seen me for weeks. Act surprised that anyone's looking for me. You haven't heard about Mark's death, and you've recently bought a tumbledown ruin in the Dordogne—just outside Cahors, say—and you're taking a bunch of B&Q's finest flat-packs over to refit the bathroom."

"But what if they steer me into the inspection shed and start unloading the boxes?"

"In that case," Bronson said, "the moment they find me, you leap out and hide behind the biggest customs officer you can find. You're terrified, because I've forced you at gunpoint to help me escape from Britain. You're a victim, not a collaborator. I'll back you up."

"But you don't have a gun," Angela objected.

"As a matter of fact, I have." Bronson pulled the Browning from the pocket of his jacket.

"Where the hell did that come from?"

Bronson explained about the second, failed, burglary at the house in Italy.

"You do know that you could go to prison just for carrying a gun?"

"I do. I also know that the people we're up against have already killed at least once, so I'm hanging on to this and taking my chances with the plods."

"You *are* a plod, remember?" Angela pointed out. "Which makes carrying a weapon even worse."

Bronson shrugged. "I know, but that's my problem, not yours. I'll do my best to protect you."

Just more than an hour later, Bronson emerged from the B&Q warehouse in Thurrock with a laden cart. He loaded everything carefully into the back of the Renault, making sure that the upturned acrylic bath was in the center.

Then they were off again, crossing the Thames at Dartford and picking up the motorway for Dover. Bronson pulled off at the last service area before the port and parked the Espace in the most secluded section of the car park he could find.

"Time to pack me away," he said lightly, his tone not entirely concealing his concern. There was no certainty that the police would accept that he had forced Angela to drive him out of the country if his hiding place was discovered. He knew very well that they could both end up as unwilling guests of Her Majesty if it all went wrong.

He climbed into the back of the Espace and slid under the bath. It was cramped, but by pulling his knees up to his chest he was able to make himself fit. Angela stacked boxes over and around the bath until it was covered, then climbed into the driving seat and pulled out of the service area.

At the port, she bought a five-day return ticket at one of the discount booking offices and drove into the

Eastern Docks, following the "embarkation" signs. At the British Customs post she proffered her passport, which was swiped through the electronic reader with barely a grunt of acknowledgment. The French passport control officer glanced at the maroon cover and waved her through.

Just beyond the two booths was another "embarkation" sign, but as she accelerated toward it a bulky figure stepped in front of the car and pointed to his left, toward the inspection shed.

Angela cursed under her breath but smiled agreeably at him, and followed the road around into the shed. Inside, she dropped the driver's door window as one of the officers walked toward her and glanced into the back of the car.

"The French dream?" the officer asked. People who bought goods in Britain to try to renovate French ruins were not exactly a rare sight at Dover.

"Sorry?" Angela replied.

"A little stone house on the edge of a village in Brittany?" he asked with a grin. "In need of some light restoration?"

"Substitute the Dordogne for Brittany," Angela said, matching his smile, "and you've pretty much nailed it. And it's a town rather than a village. Cahors. Do you know it?"

The officer shook his head. "Heard of it, but I've never been there," he said. "So what's in the back?"

"Most of the master bathroom, or at least that's the plan, as long as I can persuade the builders to install it. Would you like to look at it?"

"No, thanks." He stepped back and waved her forward. "Off you go, then," he said.

Her heart thundering in her chest, Angela gave him a carefree wave, put the Renault into gear and drove toward the exit door, which opened automatically. They were through.

III

Angela milled about with the other passengers, wandered through the shop and finally sat down in one of the lounges to wait for the ferry to dock in Calais. But despite her appearance of absolute calm, inside she was almost frantic with worry.

What would she do if the French police were waiting for her on the other side of the Channel? Did Chris have enough air? Would she open up the back of the vehicle somewhere in France only to find she'd been accompanied by a corpse? What would she do then?

It was almost a relief when she heard the Tannoy announcement asking drivers to make their way to the car decks. At least the waiting was over.

Two hours after driving the Espace onto the ferry, Angela steered the car down the ramp onto French soil and joined the line of English cars heading toward the autoroute. She saw no police or customs officers, and nobody appeared in any way interested in her or anyone else disgorged by the ferry. Most of the drivers seemed to be taking the A26 Paris autoroute, but Bronson had told her to stay off the toll roads and head for Boulogne on the D940 instead. She was to look for a secluded parking place where he could escape from his pink—their choice of bath had been governed by size, shape and price, not color—acrylic prison.

As afternoon shaded toward evening, Angela drove along the coastal road past Sangatte and on to Escalles. Just beyond the village she found a deserted car park overlooking the sea and Cap Blanc-Nez. She parked the Espace in the corner farthest away from the entrance and checked that she hadn't been followed before opening the trunk and pulling away the boxes that covered the bath. Bronson gave a low moan as he crawled out.

"Are you OK?" Angela asked.

"I feel like I've gone over the Niagara Falls in a barrel," Bronson said, groaning and stretching. "Every joint and muscle in my body is aching, and I'm as stiff as a board. Have you got any aspirins or something?"

"Men!" Angela teased. "The slightest bit of discomfort and you turn into real moaners." She opened her handbag and pulled out a cardboard packet of tablets. "I'd take a couple if I were you. Do you want to drive?"

Bronson shook his head. "No way. I'm going to sit in the passenger seat and let you chauffeur me."

Twenty minutes later, they were heading south on the A16.

While she drove, Angela filled Bronson in on what she had found out before the police showed up at the Internet café.

"It looks to me as if the second inscription could be connected to the Cathars," she said.

"The Cathars? That's what Jeremy Goldman suggested, but I'm not sure that makes much sense. I don't know too much about them, but I'm certain they had nothing at all to do with first-century Rome. They came along about a thousand years later."

"I know," Angela said with a nod, "and their homeland was southern France, not Italy. But the verses do seem to have a strong and distinct Cathar flavor. Some of the expressions like 'the good,' 'pure spirits' and 'the word becomes the perfect' are almost pure Cathar. The perfects or *perfecti*—the priests—referred to themselves as 'good men,' and they believed their religion was pure.

"One of the problems about the Cathars is that virtually everything ever written about them was authored by their enemies, like the Catholic Church, so it's a bit like reading a history of the Second World War written entirely from the perspective of the Nazis. But what we do know is that the movement was linked to, or maybe even derived from, the Bogomil sect based in Eastern Europe. That was another dualist religion, one of several that flourished in the tenth and eleventh centuries."

"What did they believe? Why was the Catholic Church so opposed to them?"

"The Cathars thought that the God being worshipped by the Church was an impostor, a deity who had usurped the true God, and who was, in fact, the devil. By that definition the Catholic Church was an evil abomination, the priests and bishops in the service of Lucifer. And they pointed to the rampant corruption within the Church as a partial proof of this."

"I can see that must have pissed off Rome. But surely the Cathars weren't powerful enough to have any real influence?"

"That depends on what you mean by 'powerful.' Their power base, if you like, was in southern France, and there's a lot of evidence to suggest that the people of that region embraced Catharism as a very real alternative to the Catholic Church, which most people saw as wholly corrupt. The contrasts between the two religions were enormous. The high-ranking Catholic clergy lived in the kind of splendor you'd normally associate with royalty or nobility. But the Cathar priests had no worldly possessions at all, apart from a black robe and a length of cord to use as a belt, and existed solely on alms and charity. When they accepted the *consolamentum,* the vow they swore on becoming priests or *perfecti,* they surrendered all their worldly goods to the community. They were also strict vegetarians, not even eating animal products like eggs and milk, and were absolutely celibate."

"That doesn't sound like a lot of fun."

"It wasn't, but that regime was only practiced by the *perfecti*. Followers of the religion—they were known as *credentes*—were allowed a lot more latitude, and most only accepted the *consolamentum* when they were actually on their deathbeds when celibacy, for example, wouldn't have been much of a problem. I think the important point is that Catharism became popular in southern France precisely because the *perfecti* were so devout and humble. Significantly, the ranks of the Cathars were peopled by members of some of the wealthiest and most important local families. However you look at it, the mere existence of the religion *was* a real threat to the Catholic Church."

"So what happened?"

"At the end of the twelfth century, Pope Eugene III tried peaceful persuasion. He sent people like Bernard of Clairvaux, Cardinal Peter and Henry of Albano to France to try to reduce the influence of the Cathars, but none of them had any real success. Decisions by various religious councils had no effect either, and when Innocent III ascended the papal throne in 1198 he decided to suppress the Cathars by any means possible.

"In January 1208 he sent a man called Pierre de Castelnau, a papal legate, to Count Raymond of Toulouse, who was the then leader of the Cathars. Their meeting was very confrontational, and the next day de Castelnau was attacked by unidentified assailants and murdered. That gave Innocent the excuse he needed, and he called for a crusade against the religion. The Albigensian Crusade—the Cathars were also known as Albigensians—lasted forty years, and was one of the bloodiest episodes in the history of the Church."

"All very interesting," Bronson pointed out, "but I still don't see what any of that has to do with a couple of inscribed stones cemented into the wall of a house in Italy."

"Nor do I," Angela said. "That's the problem. But I've got a few more books to look at, so I might have some answers by tomorrow."

As the light began to fade, they started looking for somewhere to stay for the night.

"Our best bet is a small, family-run hotel somewhere. We don't want anywhere that we'd have to use a credit card."

"Don't they want to see your passport?"

"Those old French government regulations were abolished some time ago. These days the only thing that matters is whether or not you can pay the bill."

Twenty minutes later, they checked into a small hotel close to the center of a village not far from Evreux.

They had a late dinner, then walked around the village and found a small cybercafé with half a dozen computers.

"I'll just check my e-mail," Angela said, and bought an hour of time on one of the PCs.

Most of the stuff in her in-box was the usual dross that everyone with an e-mail account receives daily, and she swiftly ran down the list, deleting reams of spam. At the end of the list were a couple from the British Museum staff messaging system, and she opened those to read them. The first was just routine, reminding staff of a forthcoming event, but when she opened the second one, she sat back with a gasp of shock.

"What is it?" Bronson asked.

"It's Jeremy Goldman," she replied. "According to this, he was killed today in an accident, just down the road from the museum."

For a moment Bronson didn't say anything. "Does it explain what happened?" he asked.

"No, just that he was involved in a road accident in Montague Street and was pronounced dead on arrival at the hospital." She turned in her seat to stare at Bronson. "Do you think it was an accident?" Her face was white.

"No," he said. "And neither do you." He swore under his breath. "First Jackie, then Mark and now Jeremy. I'm going to hunt these bastards, and, by God, I'm going to bring them down."

17

I

It was going to be a long day: they both knew that. Bronson wanted to reach the Hamptons' house in Italy that evening, a journey of a thousand miles or so, which was just about possible if they stayed on the autoroutes. They got up at seven, eschewed the hotel breakfast, paid for the rooms and dinner in cash and then left.

When Bronson had gone to his room the previous evening, Angela sat up in hers, searching through the books she'd bought in Cambridge. She was tired, but the idea that had come to her while she'd been staring at the computer screen in the third cybercafé in Cambridge was now making more sense.

Now, while Bronson drove, she explained her theory, referring occasionally to a pocket book in which she'd recorded some notes in her small, neat handwriting.

"I think Jeremy was right," she began. "At least part of this puzzle *is* about the Cathars and the Albigensian Crusade, though perhaps not in the way he imagined. If we assume for the moment that the verses in the second inscription were written about, or perhaps even by, the Cathars, some of the references do begin to make sense. The most obvious example is the 'safe mountain.' That's an unusual expression, and there's no obvious reason why anyone should talk about any mountain as being 'safe,' unless you're a Cathar. If you are, the words are immediately recognizable as a direct reference to the citadel of Montségur: the name actually means 'safe mountain' in Occitan. It was the last major stronghold of the religion, and it fell to the crusaders in 1244.

"If you look at the first verse of the inscription, not only do the words 'safe mountain' make sense, but the first two lines probably describe the end of the siege itself: *From the safe mountain truth did descend, Abandoned by all save the good.*

"We talked a bit about this last night, remember? There were two general categories of Cathar. The priests were known as *parfaits* or *perfecti,* and the believers were called *credentes,* but what's interesting is that neither of them called themselves Cathars. In fact, there are some suggestions that the name—it's thought to derive from the Greek *'Katharoi,'* meaning 'the pure ones'—was only used by people outside the religion. The Cathars almost always referred to themselves as *'Bons Hommes'* or *'Bonnes Femmes'*—good men or good women—so when Montségur finally fell, you really could say that it had been 'abandoned by all save the good,' because the *parfaits* never left— they were executed on the spot."

"And the 'truth' that descended?" Bronson asked. "What the hell does that mean?"

Angela smiled at him. "I've got an idea about that, but there are a few other things you need to understand first."

"OK, Professor. Let's hear it."

"Right, so I assumed that these verses did have

something to do with the Cathars, and worked on that premise. I started at the beginning, with the title, the 'GB PS DDDBE.' You remember Jeremy thought these letters probably referred to an expression that would have been in common use in the fourteenth century or thereabouts, something as clear and obvious to people then as, say, 'RIP' is to us today?

"I wondered if the expression had been corrupted, its meaning altered or distorted, again like 'RIP.' Ask most people today what those letters stand for, and they'll say 'rest in peace,' but they don't. The initials refer to the Latin expression *'requiescat in pace.'* "

"But that means pretty much the same, doesn't it?" Bronson asked.

"Yes—'may he rest in peace'—but my point is that most people aren't even aware that when they say 'RIP' they're actually quoting a Latin expression, not an English one. So I wondered if this, too, was an old Latin expression that had been corrupted. But I was wrong. It wasn't. It was pure Occitan, and pure Cathar.

"I started with the 'GB,' but that didn't get me anywhere. Then I looked at the other initials, and particularly the last five, the 'DDDBE.' Once I made sense of those, the 'PS' was obvious, and then it was just a matter of finding out who 'GB' was, and that wasn't too difficult once I'd decoded the other letters."

"So those initials referred to a person?" Bronson asked.

Angela nodded. "I think 'GB' was Guillaume Bélibaste."

"Never heard of him."

"You wouldn't have, unless you've studied the history of medieval France. Guillaume Bélibaste was the last known Cathar *parfait,* and he was burned alive in 1321. That was the method of execution preferred by the Vatican for dangerous heretics, which, in the Middle Ages, simply meant anyone who disagreed with the Pope."

"So what does the title mean?"

"When any Cathar was about to die," Angela replied, looking down at her notebook, "prayers were said, prayers that started with a particular Occitan expression: *'Payre sant, Dieu dreiturier dels bons esperits.'* The initial letters of that expression spell 'PS DDDBE.' That roughly translates as 'Holy Father, true God of pure souls,' somewhat analogous to the beginning of the Lord's Prayer: 'Our Father, which art in heaven.'

"It was a common expression at the time, because you can still see it at several different locations in the Languedoc region of France. According to the books, there's a particularly clear example carved on a stone at Minerve in Herault, where a group of Cathars took refuge after the massacre at Béziers, where about twenty thousand people were slaughtered by the crusaders. But it was only a temporary reprieve. In 1210 some one hundred and eighty *parfaits* were burned alive there by the advancing crusaders."

"Is that what the Spanish called an auto-da-fé?"

"No. The execution of heretics never took place during the auto-da-fé. The expression simply meant an 'act of faith' and was conducted by the Inquisition. It was a very public spectacle that lasted for hours, sometimes days, and often involved thousands of spectators. It began with a mass, then prayers, followed by a procession of those found guilty of heresy and a reading of their sentences. Punishment would only be administered after the auto-da-fé had finished."

"Did people just come forward and confess, then?"

Angela laughed. "No, or not very often anyway. According to the records, most so-called heretics were snitched on by their neighbors, and it's reasonably certain the arrival of the Inquisition offered a wonderful opportunity to settle old scores. The problem the accused faced was that they were in a no-win position. If they admitted to whatever charges the Inquisitors leveled at them, they could face death at the stake. If they denied the accusations, they'd be tortured until they *did* confess.

"As far as the Inquisitors were concerned, there was no question of an accused person being innocent—the fact that an accusation had been made was sufficient proof of guilt, and all they had to do then was obtain a signed confession from the heretic. That almost always involved prolonged and inventive torture and took place in private, in specially equipped torture chambers. The Inquisitors were forbidden to spill blood, during either questioning or execution, so they made liberal use of the rack and the strappado to dislocate joints. They also roasted limbs over slow fires, usually the feet because the heretic had to be able to sign a confession once it was all over."

"Nice people," Bronson observed drily.

"Their aim was to cause the maximum possible pain for prolonged periods of time, and they specialized in methods that involved little effort on the part of the interrogators, so they had plenty of time to pray for guidance. Lighting a fire, for example, or hauling a victim up using the strappado took just a few minutes, but the heretic would be in agony for hours or days.

"One of their favorites was the iron boot. They'd put the victim's foot in an iron boot, then hammer wooden wedges all around the leg, crushing the shin and ankle. That was bad enough, but it was only the first stage. As a refinement, they'd pour water into the boot and leave the man overnight. The wooden wedges would absorb the water and expand, steadily increasing the pressure on the lower leg. After a few hours, while the interrogators were sleeping soundly or kneeling in prayer, the bones of the shin and ankle would be shattered, the muscles ripped to shreds, and for sure the man would never walk again.

"If execution was necessary, the only method approved by the Vatican was burning at the stake, again because that wouldn't spill the victim's blood, but even then there were refinements. Recanting at the last moment earned the condemned the mercy of being garrotted before the pyre was lit. Heretics who refused to do so would be made to suffer for even longer by the use of slow-burning wood. The executioners could also add fuel like wet or green wood that would generate choking fumes intended to kill the victims before the fire reached them—a small mercy. As a method of execution, burning offered considerable variety, and the Spanish and Portuguese were apparently very good at it. And they had plenty of victims to practice on."

"And the French?"

"My guess is they just chained their victims to wooden posts, lit the fire and waited for the screaming to stop."

Angela fell silent as the Renault Espace sped along the autoroute, heading southeast for the Italian border, with the back still full of the boxes they'd bought from B&Q.

"OK," Bronson conceded, "but I still don't see how any of that helps us. The Hamptons' house is in Italy, not France, and even if you're right and the second inscription *does* relate to the Cathars, the other one is written in Latin and is maybe fifteen hundred years older. So what possible connection could there be between them?"

"Well, I have a theory. It's a crazy idea, but it does answer at least one of our questions."

"Try me."

"First, we have to go back to 1244 and the end of the siege of Montségur, when the garrison of the fortress eventually surrendered. It had been a long, hard siege, but realistically there was only ever going to be one result, and everyone knew it. On the first of March that year, facing overwhelming odds and with food and drink reserves running low, the defenders finally capitulated.

"Now, this siege had occupied a significant number of men-at-arms for months, and had incurred huge costs for the crusaders. Plus, the Pope had initiated the Albigensian Crusade with the specific intention of completely destroying the Cathar heresy, and it was known that some two hundred *parfaits* had taken refuge in the fortress. In almost every other case, the defenders of towns and castles taken by the crusaders were slaughtered without mercy. So what terms do you think the crusaders offered?"

"Probably a choice between beheading, hanging or burning at the stake?"

"Exactly," Angela said. "That's more or less what any impartial observer would have guessed. Would you like to know what terms they actually offered?"

"Worse than that?"

Angela shook her head, and referred again to her small notebook. "Listen to this. First, the men-at-arms—that's the mercenary soldiers and others employed as the bulk of the garrison at Montségur—were to be allowed to walk away with all their goods and equipment, and would receive full pardons for their part in the defense of the fortress."

"Well," Bronson said slowly, "I suppose they weren't actually part of the heresy. I mean, they weren't Cathars, were they, just people employed by them?"

"I agree," Angela said. "Ever heard of a place called Bram?"

"No."

"It was another Cathar stronghold that fell in 1210

after a three-day siege, and there was nothing very significant in that. But shortly afterward, when the crusaders under Simon de Montfort tried to—"

"Simon who?" Bronson asked.

"Simon de Montfort. He was the commander of the crusaders at the time, and was trying to capture the four castles at Lastours, just north of Carcassonne, but he'd met furious resistance. To persuade the defenders to give up the fight, Simon's men took one hundred of the prisoners they'd captured at Bram and cut off their lips, noses and ears. Then they blinded them all apart from one man who only had one eye put out, so he could lead his companions in a bloody parade in front of the castles."

"Dear God," Bronson murmured. "Did the tactic work?"

"Of course not. It only made the defenders more determined to fight on, if only to avoid the same fate. The castles did fall, but not until a year later. That's just one example of 'God's mercy' as it was interpreted during the Albigensian Crusade.

"Or take the massacre at Béziers, where some twenty thousand men, women and children were slaughtered in the name of God and Christian charity. Before the attack, Bishop Arnaud Armaury, the Papal Legate and the Pope's personal representative, was asked by the crusaders how they could identify the heretics, because there were believed to be only about five hundred Cathars in the town. His reply in Latin was recorded as: *'Cædite eos. Novit enim Dominus qui sunt eius.'* That translates as, 'Kill them all. God will know his own.' And that's exactly what they did."

"I didn't know any of this," Bronson said. "It's just unbelievable. Anyway, back to Montségur. The crusaders were lenient with the soldiers, but I presume not with the Cathars themselves?"

"Wrong again," Angela said. "The *parfaits* were

told that if they renounced their beliefs and confessed their sins to the Inquisition they would be allowed to go free, but they would have to leave all their possessions behind."

"In other words," Bronson interjected, "both the Cathars and their soldiers were handed 'get out of jail free' cards. But why?"

"You haven't heard the best bit yet. The first anomaly was the leniency of the surrender terms. The defenders requested a two-week truce to consider the terms—terms that, if they'd been accepted, would have allowed the entire garrison to walk away from Montségur unharmed. That's the second anomaly: you wouldn't have thought they'd have needed more than two minutes to consider their options, not two weeks. Anyway, surprisingly, the crusaders agreed to this." She paused.

"And this is where it gets really peculiar. When the truce expired on the fifteenth of March, not only did all the *parfaits* reject the surrender terms unequivocally, but at least twenty of the non-Cathar defenders elected to receive the ultimate Cathar vow—the *consolamentum perfecti*—so condemning themselves to a certain and horrendously painful death."

"When they could have just walked away, they opted for death?"

"Right. At dawn on the sixteenth of March 1244, more than two hundred *parfaits* were taken out of the fortress and escorted down to the foot of the mountain. There, they were pushed into a hastily built wood-filled stockade and burned alive. None of them recanted their heresy, despite being offered every opportunity to do so."

For a few moments Bronson was silent. "That really doesn't make sense. Why would they reject the surrender terms after asking for two weeks to think about it? And, especially, why did the Cathars—and, from what you say, twenty-odd non-Cathars—decide their best option was to scream their way to death in the flames instead of simply walking away?"

"That's the interesting part. It's also worth pointing out that even when chained to the stake, the heretics were always given one last chance to recant."

"And then they could walk away?" Bronson asked.

"No, not at that stage. But as I said before, they would then be garrotted as an act of mercy rather than be burned alive. So what made the Cathars so sure of their faith that they were prepared to die in just about the most painful way imaginable rather than repudiate it?"

Bronson rubbed his chin. "They must have had one hell of a reason."

"There's a persistent story—I've found references to it both on the Internet and in the books I've studied—that suggests there *was* a definite reason for the delay in the Cathars' decision to accept or reject the surrender terms, and also for their willingness to perish in the flames. They were protecting their treasure."

Bronson glanced at Angela to see if she was joking, but her expression remained deadly serious.

"Treasure? But how could the deaths of two hundred Cathars by fire possibly help protect it?"

"I think—and this really is conjecture—that the Cathars were prepared to sacrifice themselves as a kind of diversion. They thought that once they'd died in the flames, the crusaders would be less inclined to mount a proper guard on Montségur and that would allow a few of their number to escape with their most precious possessions.

"And I don't believe we're talking about a typical treasure. No gold or jewels, nothing like that. I think their treasure was some kind of religious relic, an object of undeniable provenance that proved the veracity of the Cathar faith beyond any doubt. That might be enough, not only to persuade the committed members of the order to accept death at the hands of the crusaders, but also to convince the twenty non-Cathars to join them."

"So the treasure wasn't really a treasure at all, in the usual sense of the word?" Bronson interjected. "It was probably completely worthless in intrinsic terms—just an old bit of parchment or something—but priceless in what it proved?"

"Exactly."

"But what could it be?"

"Impossible to say for sure, but we can infer certain things about it from what we do know. If the sources I've looked at have got it right, sometime during that last night at Montségur, as the flames of the huge pyre at the foot of the mountain died away to a dull red glow, the last four *parfaits* escaped. They'd been hidden in the fortress by the garrison, and chose an extremely hazardous, but almost undetectable, route, using ropes to descend the sheer west face of the mountain.

"They took this risk because they were carrying the treasure of the Cathars. They reached the foot of the mountain and then vanished both into the night and from the pages of history. No one knows what they were carrying, where they went or what happened to them.

"If there's any truth in that story, then there are at least two points worth making. First, whatever the 'treasure' comprised, it had to be fairly small and not too heavy, because otherwise the four men couldn't have carried it during their perilous descent. Second, it had to be a physical object, not simply knowledge, or the four *parfaits* could have disguised themselves as soldiers or servants and left the fortress with the men-at-arms the following day.

"Now, this is all guesswork, unsupported by a single

shred of verifiable evidence, but it does provide a plausible explanation for what happened when the siege of Montségur ended. But what happened next on the mountain *is* in the historical record.

"Once the fortress was deserted, the crusaders, acting on the specific instructions of the Pope, tore it apart in a desperate search for some object, some 'treasure.' But whatever it was they were looking for, they clearly didn't find it, because they dismantled the castle, quite literally stone by stone. It's not generally known, but the citadel that now stands at Montségur was actually erected early in the seventeenth century, and no part of the original Cathar castle now remains at the site.

"For the next half-century, Rome ordered all traces of the Cathar heresy to be expunged from the landscape. As well as executing every *parfait* they could lay their hands on, the crusaders also continued their search for whatever had been secreted at Montségur, but without result. Eventually, memory of the 'treasure of the Cathars' passed into the mists of legend. And that's the story of Montségur as we know it today: a mix of historical fact, rumor and conjecture."

"But what the hell has that got to do with a six-hundred-year-old farmhouse on the side of a hill in Italy?" Bronson asked, waving his arm in frustration.

"It's all in the inscription," Angela explained. "The first verse of the Occitan poem can be interpreted as a specific reference to the end of the siege."

She read Goldman's translation of the verse from her notebook:

" *'From the safe mountain truth did descend*
Abandoned by all save the good
The cleansing flames quell only flesh
And pure spirits soar above the pyre
For truth like stone forever will endure.'

"The second line could describe the surrender of the garrison of Montségur, and the third and fourth the mass execution when the Cathars were burned alive. But I think the expressions 'truth did descend' and 'truth like stone forever will endure' refer to the escape of the four remaining *parfaits,* carrying with them some document or relic upon which the core of their faith—their unarguable 'truth'—relied. Whatever the object, it was so compelling in its implications that Cathars would rather die at the stake than renounce their beliefs."

"And the second verse?" Bronson asked.

"That's just as interesting, and again some lines seem to refer to the Cathars."

Again, she read the verse aloud:

> " *'Here oak and elm descry the mark*
> *As is above so is below*
> *The word becomes the perfect*
> *Within the chalice all is naught*
> *And terrible to behold.'*

"The expression in the second line was commonly used by the Cathars, and the 'word' referred to in the third line could be the 'truth' that guided the beliefs of the *parfaits*. The first line's nothing to do with the Cathars, but I think it's possible that the reference to the two species of tree indicates a hiding place."

"And the last couple of lines? About the chalice?"

"I'm guessing—I've been guessing all along, but now I'm *really* guessing—that they mean the object was secreted in some kind of a vessel—a chalice—and that it's dangerous."

Bronson began to reduce speed. He was approaching Vierzon, where the autoroute divided, and turned southeast for Clermont-Ferrand.

"So what you're suggesting," Bronson said, "is that

the Cathars had some kind of relic, something that confirmed their beliefs, and that quite probably would have been seen as dangerous by other religions? And the Pope started the crusade to recover or destroy it?"

"Exactly. The Albigensian Crusade was instigated by Pope Innocent III—and rarely was any pope so misnamed—in 1209."

"Right. So you think the Pope knew about this relic and believed it was secreted somewhere at Montségur? And that was why he ordered the different treatment of the Cathars and garrison there, and why, after the massacre, his crusaders demolished the fortress?"

"Yes. And if my reading of these verses is right, I think we may well find that the Cathar treasure was hidden somewhere in Mark's house in Italy!"

II

Back at their hotel near Gatwick, Mandino and Rogan had spent hours using their laptops to study the search strings the intercept system had recovered from the Cambridge cybercafés.

They seemed to have exhausted all their other options. They'd waited outside Angela Lewis's building, but her apartment lights had remained switched off, and neither her phone nor her doorbell was answered. Bronson's house was just as obviously deserted, and Mandino had now realized that both of them had disappeared. The intercept system was all they had left.

The biggest problem they'd faced was the sheer volume of information they had to work with. Carlotti, Mandino's deputy who'd remained in Italy, had sent them three Excel files. Two contained the searches input at the cybercafés he believed Bronson had visited, while the third and much larger file listed the search strings from the other half dozen Internet cafés

within the five-mile radius which Mandino had requested.

He and Rogan ran internal searches for words they
knew their quarry had been looking for, including
"LDA," "consul," "senator" and so on. Each time
either of them got a hit, they copied the following fifty
search strings and saved them in separate files.

Just doing that took a long time, and at the end of
it they were really no further forward.

"We're not getting anywhere with this," Mandino
said in irritation. "We already knew that Bronson had
probably worked out what the additional letters meant
on the Latin inscription. What I haven't found yet is
anything that looks like it might refer to the second
inscription."

Rogan leaned back from his laptop. "Same here,"
he said.

"I think what we need to do is try to second-guess
Bronson," Mandino mused. "I wonder . . ."

He did have one powerful weapon in his armory.
The book he held in his safe in Rome contained the
first few lines of the Latin text of the lost relic. More
important, it had a potentially useful couple of pages
that detailed the Vatican's attempts to trace the document's location through the ages.

"The house in Italy," he asked, turning to face
Rogan. "Did you find the exact date it was built?"

His companion shook his head. "No. I did a search
in the property register in Scandriglia, and turned up
several records of sales, but they were all quite recent.
The earliest reference I could find was a house shown
in that location on a map of the area dated 1396, so
we know it's been standing for at least six hundred
years. There was also an earlier map from the first
half of the fourteenth century that *doesn't* show any
building on the site. Why, *capo*?"

"Just an idea," Mandino said. "There's a section in

that book I was given by the Vatican that lists the groups
that might have possessed the relic through the ages. The
likely candidates include the Bogomils, the Cathars
and Mani, who founded Manichaeism.

"Now," Mandino went on, "I think that Mani and
the Bogomils were too early, but the Cathars are a
possibility because that house must have been constructed shortly after the end of the Albigensian Crusade in the fourteenth century.

"And there's something else. That crusade was one
of the bloodiest in history—thousands of people were
executed in the name of God. The Vatican's justifica-
tion for the massacres and wholesale looting was the
Pope's determination to rid the Christian world of the
Cathar heresy. But the book suggests that the *real*
reason was the growing suspicion by the Pope that the
Cathars had somehow managed to obtain the
Exomologesis."

"The what?"

"The lost relic. Pope Vitalian called it the *Exomologesis de assectator mendax,* which means 'The confession of sin by the false disciple,' but eventually it
became known inside the Vatican just as the
Exomologesis."

"So why did they think the Cathars had found it?"

"Because the Cathars were so implacably opposed
to Rome and the Catholic Church, and the Vatican
believed they had to have some unimpeachable document as the basis for their opposition. The *Exomologesis* would have fitted the bill very well. And the
Albigensian Crusade was only half successful. The
Church managed to eliminate the Cathars as a religious movement, but they never found the relic. From
what I've read, the crusaders probably came close to
recovering it at Montségur, but it somehow slipped
through their hands.

"Now," Mandino continued, "looking at the dates—

which seem to fit—I wonder if a Cathar placed the second inscription in the Italian house, or perhaps even built it. We know from what Hampton told us that the verses were written in Occitan. Why don't you try searching for words like 'Montségur,' 'Cathar' and 'Occitan,' and I'll check for Cathar expressions.''

Mandino logged onto the Internet and rapidly identified a dozen Occitan phrases, and their English translations, and then turned his attention to the search strings. Almost immediately he got two hits.

"Yes," he breathed. "Here we are. Bronson—or someone at that cybercafé—looked for 'perfect,' and then the expression 'as is above, so is below.' I'll just try 'Montségur.' ''

That didn't generate a hit, but "safe mountain" did, and when he checked, Mandino found that all three searches had originated from a single computer at the second cybercafé he believed Bronson had visited in Cambridge.

"This is the clincher," he said, and Rogan leaned over to look at the screen of his laptop. "The third expression he searched for was a complete sentence: *'From the safe mountain truth did descend.'* I'm certain that refers to the end of the siege of Montségur, and it also implies that the Cathars *had* possessed the *Exomologesis*—their 'truth'—and managed to smuggle it out of the fortress."

"And the searches are all in English," Rogan pointed out.

"I know," Mandino agreed, "which means that Bronson must have obtained a translation of the inscription from Goldman almost as soon as he got back to Britain. If he hadn't been hit by that taxi, we'd have had to kill him anyway."

They searched for another half hour, but found nothing further of interest.

"So what now, *capo*?"

"We've got two choices. Either we find Bronson as quickly as possible—and that doesn't look likely to happen—or we go back to Italy and wait for him to turn up and start digging in the garden, or wherever he thinks the *Exomologesis* is hidden."

"I'll book the tickets," Rogan said, turning back to his laptop.

III

"You're kidding," Bronson said.

"I'm not," Angela retorted. "Look at the dates. You told me that the Hamptons' house was built roughly in the middle of the fourteenth century. That was around a hundred years after the fall of Montségur, and about twenty-five years after the last known Cathar *parfait* was executed.

"And once in Italy, their first priority would have been to secrete their 'treasure'—the 'truth' they'd managed to smuggle out of Montségur at the end of the siege—somewhere safe. They needed a permanent hiding place, somewhere that would endure, not just a hole in the ground somewhere. I think they decided to hide the relic in something permanent, or as near as possible, and one obvious choice would be a substantial house, probably in the foundations, so that routine alterations to the property wouldn't uncover it.

"But they also wouldn't want to bury it beyond recovery, because it was the most important document they possessed, and they must have hoped that one day their religion would be revived. So whoever hid the relic would have needed to leave a marker, a clue of some kind, that would later enable someone, someone who understood the Cathar religion and who would be able to decipher the coded message, to retrieve it. If I'm right, then that was the entire purpose of the Occitan inscription."

Bronson shifted his attention from the unwinding autoroute in front of him and glanced across at his ex-wife. Her cheeks were flushed pink with the excitement of her discovery. Although he'd always had enormous respect for her analytical ability and professional expertise, the way she'd dissected the problem and arrived at an entirely logical—albeit almost unbelievable—solution, amazed him.

"OK, Angela," he said, "what you say does make sense. You always made sense. But what are the chances that the Hamptons' second home in Italy was the chosen location? It just seems so—I don't know—unlikely, somehow."

"But treasure—real treasure—turns up all the time, and often in the most unlikely places. Look at the Mildenhall Hoard. In 1942 a plowman turned up what is probably the greatest collection of Roman silver ever found, in the middle of a field in East Anglia. How unlikely is that?

"And what other explanation can you offer for the carved stone? The dates fit very well; the stone would seem to be Cathar in origin, and has been in the house since the place was built. The fact that the inscription's written in Occitan provides an obvious link to the Languedoc, and the contents of the verses themselves only make sense if you understand the Cathars. There's also the strong likelihood that a Cathar 'treasure' was smuggled out of Montségur. If it was, it had to be hidden somewhere. So why not in that house?"

18

"At last," Bronson muttered, as he steered the Renault Espace down the gravel drive of the Villa Rosa. It was well after midnight and they'd been on the road since about eight that morning.

He switched off the engine and for a few moments they just reveled in the silence and stillness.

"Are you going to leave it here?" Angela asked.

"I don't have any option. Mark locked the garage before we went to the funeral, so the keys are probably somewhere in his apartment in Ilford."

"House keys? You *do* have house keys, I hope?"

"I don't, but that shouldn't be a problem. Mark always used to keep a spare set outside the house. If that's missing, I'll have to do a bit of breaking and entering."

Bronson walked around the side of the house, using the tiny flashlight on his key ring to see his way. About halfway along the wall was a large light-brown stone, and immediately to the right of it what looked like a much smaller, oval, light-gray rock. Bronson picked up the fake stone and turned it over, slid back the cover and shook out the front-door key. He walked back to the front of the house and unlocked the door.

"Would you like a drink?" he asked, as he put their bags in the hall. "Scotch or brandy or something? It might help you sleep."

Angela shook her head. "Tonight, absolutely the only thing I need to get to sleep is a bed."

"Listen," Bronson said. "I'm worried about the people who are looking for us. I think we should sleep in the same room while we're here, for safety. There's a twin-bedded guest room at the top of the stairs, on the right. I think we should use that."

Angela looked at him for a few seconds. "We *are* keeping this professional, aren't we? You're not going to try to crawl into bed with me?"

"No," Bronson said, almost convincingly. "I just think we should be together, in case these people decide to come back here."

"Right, as long as that's clearly understood."

"I'll just check that all the windows and doors are closed, then I'll be up," Bronson said, bolting the front door.

With both Jackie and Mark gone, it seemed strange to be back here. He felt a surge of emotion, of loss and regret that he'd never see his friends again, but suppressed it firmly. There'd be time for grief when this was all over. For now, he had a job to do.

Bronson woke just after ten, glanced at Angela still sleeping soundly in the other single bed, pulled on a dressing gown he found in the en suite bathroom, and walked down to the kitchen to make breakfast. By the time he'd brewed a pot of coffee, found half a sliced loaf in the Hamptons' freezer and produced two only slightly burnt slices of toast, Angela had appeared in the doorway.

"Morning," she said, rubbing her eyes. "Still burning the toast, I see."

"In my defense," Bronson replied, "the loaf was frozen, and I'm not used to the toaster."

"Excuses, excuses." Angela walked over to the worktop where the toaster sat and peered at the two slices. "Actually, these aren't too bad," she said. "I'll have these, and you can burn another couple for yourself."

"Coffee?"

"You have to ask? Of course I want coffee."

Thirty minutes later they were dressed and back in the kitchen—apart from the bedrooms, it was the only place in the house where all the furniture wasn't covered in dust sheets. Bronson put the translation of the Occitan inscription on the table.

"Before we start looking at that, can I just see the two carved stones?" Angela asked.

"Of course," Bronson said, and led the way into the living room. He dragged a stepladder over to the fireplace and Angela climbed up to examine the Latin inscription. She ran her fingers over the incised letters with a kind of reverence.

"It always gives me a strange feeling when I touch something as old as this," she said. "I mean, when you realize that the man who carved this stone lived about one and a half millennia before Shakespeare was even born, it gives you a real sense of age."

She took a final look at the inscription, then stepped off the ladder. "And the second stone was directly behind this, but in the dining room?" she asked.

"It *was,* yes," Bronson replied, leading the way through the doorway, "but our uninvited guests removed it." He pointed at a more or less square hole in the wall of the room, debris from the extraction process littering the floor below.

"And they took it to try to recover the inscription you'd obliterated?"

"I think so. That's the only explanation that makes sense."

Angela nodded. "Right, so where do we start?"

"Well, the most obvious clue is the first line of the second verse of the inscription: *Here oak and elm descry the mark.* That could mean whatever's been hidden is in a wood or forest, its location indicated by the two different species of tree, but there's one obvious problem . . ."

"Exactly," Angela said. "This was probably written about six hundred and fifty years ago. The oak is a long-lived tree—I think they can survive for up to five hundred years or so—but the elm, even if it doesn't get hit by Dutch elm disease, only lives for about half that time. So even if this line refers to two saplings, they'd both be long dead by now."

"But suppose the author of this verse expected the object to be recovered fairly soon afterward, within just a few years, say?"

Angela shook her head decisively. "I don't think so. The Pope's opposition to the Cathars was so great that they must have known there was no chance of the religion surviving except as a covert, underground movement. Whoever wrote this line was anticipating a long wait before there would be any chance of a revival in their fortunes.

"And, in any case, it's far too vague. Suppose there *was* a stand of oaks next to a group of elm trees on the hillside behind the house. Where, exactly, would you start digging? And note that the line says 'oak and elm,' not 'oaks and elms.' Jeremy was quite specific about that. We can take a look outside if you want, but we'd just be wasting our time. That line refers to something made of wood. Some object fabricated from oak and elm that would already have been in existence when the verse was written."

Bronson waved his hand to encompass the entire house. "This place is built of wood and stone. It's full of wooden furniture, and I know that the Hamptons inherited a lot of it when they bought the property, partly because some of the pieces are far too big to be removed."

"So somewhere in the house there must be a chest or some other piece of furniture made of oak and elm, and there'll be a clue or something on it or inside it. Maybe another verse or a map, something like that."

The old house had an attic that ran the entire length of the building. Bronson found a large flashlight in the kitchen and they ascended the stairs. At first sight, the attic appeared almost empty but, once they started looking, it was clear that among the inevitable detritus that accumulates in old houses, like the empty cardboard boxes, broken suitcases, old and discarded clothing and shoes, and impressive collections of cobwebs, there were a number of wooden objects, all of which they needed to look at. There were boxes, large and small, some with lids, some without, bits and pieces of broken furniture, and even a number of lengths of timber, presumably from some construction project that had never come to fruition.

After almost two hours, they had checked everything. They were both covered in dust, cobwebs decorating their hair, their hands filthy, and they'd found exactly nothing.

"Enough?" Bronson asked.

Angela cast a final glance around the attic before nodding her agreement. "Enough. Let's get washed and have a drink. In fact, I know it's early, but let's have some lunch. At least that's the worst of the search over."

Bronson shook his head. "Don't forget this house has cellars too. And that means rats and mice, as well as spiders."

"You really know how to show a girl a good time, don't you? Think positive—maybe we'll find the clue before we have to go down there."

Searching the bedrooms didn't take as long as Bronson had expected, because there wasn't a huge amount to check. There were chests, wardrobes and beds which had been inherited with the property, many of them made of oak, but despite emptying every one there was no sign of anything that didn't belong to the Hamptons. There was also no indication that any of them were made from two types of wood, apart from three of the freestanding wardrobes that had an inlaid marquetry decoration, but the wood used on those pieces was certainly not elm: it looked to Bronson more like cherry.

"This isn't easy," he remarked, replacing a pile of bedding in a large chest at the foot of the bed in one of the guest bedrooms.

"I didn't expect it would be. This object was hidden more than six hundred years ago by people who'd been chased halfway across Europe by an army of crusaders who wanted nothing more than to burn them alive. When they hid the relic, they knew exactly what they were doing, and they would have made sure that no casual search was ever going to find it. Let's face it: we might not find it ourselves."

Bronson sighed, walked over to the corner of the room and pulled open the lid of another small chest made—like most of the others they'd looked at—of oak. As he bent forward to look inside it, a thought struck him.

"Just a minute," he said. "I think we're going about this the wrong way."

"What do you mean?"

"Think back to the Occitan inscription. What does the line actually say?"

"You know what it says: *Here oak and elm descry the mark.*"

"We've been assuming that the verse was telling us to find an object made of oak and elm, and that we'd find a chest or something with a lid made of the two woods, say, and when we opened it up there'd be a map or directions on the inside."

Angela sat down beside him on the floor.

"But if that was what the Cathars did, if the clue was as obvious as that, then by now surely somebody would have found it." Bronson continued. "This relic was of crucial importance to the Cathars, right? So if they just carved a map or something inside a chest or wardrobe, how could they guarantee that somebody wouldn't sell it or break it up for firewood a few years, or a few centuries, down the line? If that happened, the secret would be lost forever.

"And, just in case the property was ever raided by the crusaders, they wouldn't have wanted any visible or obvious clue. The inscribed stone was almost certainly covered with wood paneling, or maybe even plaster, and even if it was exposed, it could just be taken for a Cathar lament for the death of—oh— what's his name?"

"Guillaume Bélibaste," Angela supplied automatically. "So what're you suggesting?"

"It's possible that the clue, or whatever it is, isn't just on a comparatively fragile piece of furniture. I think we'll find it's built into the fabric of the house. We should be looking at the beams and the joists and the floorboards. We should be studying the actual materials—the wooden components—the Cathars used when they built this place."

Angela nodded hesitantly. "You know," she said slowly, "that just might be the most intelligent sugges-

tion you've made since we started this. OK, forget the
furniture. Let's start with the ceiling.''

The construction of the house was typical for buildings of its age. Thick wooden planks rested on huge
square-section beams, their ends inserted in sockets in
the solid stone outer walls, that formed each floor,
including that of the attic. The roof timbers were almost as massive as the beams, and covered with thick
terra-cotta tiles: the property had clearly been built to
last. The wood was blackened by age and smoke from
the two wide inglenook fireplaces, and the floorboards
had been polished by the passage of countless feet
over the centuries and were now covered with loose
rugs.

"Maybe the floorboards are made of both oak and
elm," Bronson suggested.

They worked through the house methodically, again
checking the attic first. All the floorboards appeared
to be made of the same dark-brown wood, painted
and varnished, which didn't look to Bronson as if it
was either oak or elm. And they couldn't see anything
on the floor that looked as if it might be a marker of
any kind.

They checked the first and then the second guest
bedroom: nothing. In the master suite, a good deal of
the floor was invisible because of the massive four-
poster bed that had come with the house and domi-
nated the room. They checked the floorboards that
were visible, without result. Then Bronson looked
thoughtfully at the bed.

It was a king-sized double with a carved wooden
base. At each corner a tapering and fluted dark-brown
wooden pillar terminated in a solid canopy close to
the ceiling, draped with a heavy dark-red material that
looked to him like a kind of brocade. The sheets had
been stripped off, and two three-foot mattresses rested

on the solid wooden base. It would take at least four or five strong men to move it.

"How the hell do we shift that?" Angela demanded.

"We don't. I'll wriggle under it and take a look. Pass me that flashlight, please."

"Find anything?" Angela asked, after he'd been under the bed for a few minutes.

"Quite a lot of dust, and that's all, so far. No, there's nothing here . . ." His voice died away.

"What? What is it?"

"There's what looks like a small circle on one of these floorboards. It could be a knot, but it's the first thing I've seen on the floor that looks out of place. I'll need to . . ."

"What? What do you want?" The excitement was rising in Angela's voice.

"A knife, I think, but not a kitchen knife. I need something with a strong blade. Have a look in Mark's toolbox—it's under the sink in the kitchen—and see if you can find a penknife or something like that. If I can scrape off the paint and varnish, I'll be able to tell if this is just a natural feature of the wood or something else."

"Hang on." Bronson heard her walk out of the room and down the stairs. A couple of minutes later she returned, carrying a heavy folding knife with a spike and a thick blade. She bent down and passed it under the bed to Bronson.

"Thanks, that's perfect. Here," he added, "could you hold the flashlight for me? Just aim it at my left hand."

He opened the knife blade, eased back slightly and began to scrape away at the paint. After a few minutes Bronson had managed to shift some of the multiple layers that covered the wood, but because of the oblique angle of the flashlight, he couldn't see clearly what he'd exposed.

"Let me have the flashlight, please," he said.

Angela handed it to him. "Well?" she demanded impatiently.

"It's not a knot in the wood," Bronson said, excitement coloring his voice.

"Not a knot?"

"No. It's some kind of an insert in the plank. It looks like two semicircles of different types of wood." There was a long pause. "And one of them looks like oak."

II

Bronson lay under the bed, looking at the small circle of wood he'd uncovered. The first thing he needed to do was pinpoint its location. He stuck the spike of the penknife into the center of the circle of wood and used it as a datum to measure its exact position with reference to the walls of the bedroom.

"I'm not sure how this helps," Angela said, as Bronson jotted down the measurements in a small notebook. "This floor is made of wooden boards laid on timber beams, so there can't possibly be anything concealed underneath them, simply because there is *no* underneath. If we go down to the dining room, we'll be able to see the beams themselves and the undersides of the floorboards."

"I know that," Bronson said. "But that circle of wood must have been placed there deliberately. It must mean *something,* otherwise why did they go to the trouble of doing it, and putting it in such an inaccessible position?"

"You're right . . . hang on a minute." Her voice rose in excitement. "Remember the second line of the Occitan verse: *'As is above so is below.'* Suppose the circle you found just acted as a marker, indicating something in the dining room? A mark on the ceiling that actually points you toward something hidden under the floor of that room?"

"God, Angela, I'm glad you're here. If I was by myself I'd still be drinking coffee and burning toast in the kitchen."

They walked quickly down the stairs and Bronson led the way through to the dining room. He took out the notebook and a steel tape measure, and began working out where the underside of the circle of wood had to be. When he'd more or less located its position, he and Angela stood side by side, carefully studying the timbers that formed the ceiling.

Bronson's measurements had indicated roughly where the bottom of the circle should be, but neither he nor Angela could see it in the ceiling beams. The undersides of the planks were uniform dark brown in color, the result of countless applications of paint and varnish through the ages.

"Are you sure you've got the right spot?" Angela asked. "I can't see anything."

"Neither can I," Bronson replied testily. "But this is where the measurements say it should be. And I've checked them twice."

They craned their necks, staring upward with total concentration.

"There," Bronson said at last, pointing. "I think I can see a circular mark on that plank. I'll need to get closer to be certain."

The blemish Bronson thought he'd seen was directly above the massive dining table. Using one of the chairs, he climbed up onto it. The wooden ceiling was still well above his head, but he could now see the mark much more clearly.

"Well, what do you think?" Angela asked. "Is that it?"

For a moment Bronson didn't reply. "I think so, yes. There's definitely a circular mark on the bottom of that plank, and it looks too regular to be a natural feature."

He climbed down from the table and both of them stared upward, then down at the table. It was a hulking structure, made of oak and easily able to seat a dozen people. Like the four-poster bed in the master suite, it was far too big to ever be removed from the house in one piece, and had obviously been assembled in situ when the property was built. Under the six column-like table legs was a large red carpet, worn and faded with age.

"We'll have to shift this to see what's underneath."

Bronson walked to one end of the table, grasped the top and strained to lift it, but the massive structure barely moved.

"Jesus, that's heavy," he muttered.

"Can I help?" Angela asked.

Bronson shook his head. "There's no way the two of us can lift it. The best we'll be able to do is slide it sideways on the carpet. We'll push it over here," he added, pointing toward one side of the room.

Angela helped him move the dining chairs away from that side of the table to clear a space.

"Lean your back against it," Bronson said, "and push with your legs. They're much stronger than your arms."

They stood at the side of the table, one at each end, and strained against it. For a few seconds, nothing happened, then they felt the first slight movement, and pushed even harder.

"It's moving! Keep going."

Once the table began to slide, it seemed to get easier, and within a few minutes they'd shifted it about ten feet to one side, well away from its original position.

"Well done," Bronson said, slightly out of breath. "Now, let's see what we've got."

They stepped directly under the circle on the ceiling

and looked down at the floor. Like most of the rest of the ground floor of the house, it was composed of parquet panels, each roughly half a meter square and containing about a dozen lengths of wood in a herring-bone pattern.

"This panel looks exactly the same as all the others," Angela said, disappointment clouding her voice.

Bronson took the knife from his pocket, bent down and began scraping away some of the accumulated paint and varnish. Immediately it was clear that the grains of the two central lengths of timber were different. He cleared sections on all the pieces of wood, and then did the same thing on the four adjacent panels.

"Look," he said. "The four surrounding panels are all made from exactly the same type of wood, but on this one the two central pieces—and *only* those two pieces—are different. It must be deliberate."

Bronson ran the knife around the edge of the panel, then slid the blade down into the gap and tried to lever it up, but it was far too heavy to move.

"Hang on a moment," he said. "I'll get something stronger from Mark's toolkit."

He went into the kitchen, rummaged around and picked out two large screwdrivers. Back in the dining room, he worked their tips into the gaps on opposite sides of the panel and pressed both of them down together, at first gently and then with increasing force. For a second or two nothing happened, then, with a sudden creak, the old wood began to lift. He readjusted the screwdrivers and pressed down again. The panel moved up a few more millimeters. On the third try, the screwdrivers slammed all the way down to the floor and the panel sprang free.

"Excellent," he breathed, reaching down to pick up the wooden panel and move it over to one side. They both peered down into the cavity that had now been revealed.

III

Outside the house, two men watched with interest as Bronson and Angela searched the dining room. When Bronson lifted the wooden panel, Mandino gestured to his companion. The endgame, he now knew, was near, and it looked as if the Englishman had found exactly what they were looking for. All they had to do was get inside the house and kill them both.

The two men ducked down below the level of the dining-room windows and headed for the rear door of the house. The bodyguard—Rogan was waiting in the car parked in the lane beside the property—pulled a collapsible jimmy from his pocket as they reached the door, but Mandino simply turned the handle—it wasn't even locked—and they stepped inside. Mandino led the way toward the dining room, the bodyguard—his pistol loaded and cocked in his right hand—just behind him.

The door to the room wasn't closed, and the gap between the door and the jamb was wide enough for both men to easily see and hear through. Mandino raised his hand, and they stopped there and just waited. Once they were sure the Englishman *had* found the *Exomologesis,* they would walk in and finish him off.

Bronson and Angela stared down into the square hole. It was stone-lined, about two feet across and eighteen inches deep. A musty odor—redolent of mushrooms, dust and damp—rose from it. Right in the center of it was a bulky object wrapped in some kind of fabric.

Bronson reached down into the cavity with both hands. "It's round, like a cylinder, or maybe a pot," he said.

The material that shrouded the relic crumbled away

even as he touched it, and he quickly brushed away the last remnants.

"It looks like a ceramic container of some kind," he said.

Angela breathed in sharply. Her excitement was tangible.

"Get it out so we can look at it. Take it to that end of the table, near the door," she suggested. "The light's better there."

Bronson lifted out the object, carried it carefully over to the end of the dining table and put it down gently. It appeared to be a green-glazed pottery jar, the outside decorated with a random pattern, and fitted with two ring handles. There wasn't a lid, but the opening was plugged with a flat wooden stopper, its circumference coated with what looked like wax to form an airtight seal.

"It looks like a Roman or Greek *skyphos,*" Angela said, examining the pot carefully. "That's a kind of two-handled drinking vessel. This is exactly what we should have expected, given the second verse of the Occitan inscription."

"Let's open it," Bronson said, picking up the penknife again.

"No, hang on a minute. Remember what else the verse said: *Within the chalice all is naught, And terrible to behold.* What if that refers to something physically dangerous inside the pot? Perhaps some kind of poison?"

Bronson shook his head. "Even if this was stuffed full of cyanide or something when it was hidden, the possibility of it still being viable after six hundred years is virtually nil. It would have decayed centuries ago. Anyway, I don't think the verse means the vessel contains something dangerous in that sense. It says whatever it contains is 'terrible to behold.' That suggests it's something dangerous to look at, and that probably means forbidden knowledge or a terrible secret."

"But the jar is clearly very old and it's possible that sudden exposure to the air might destroy the contents," Angela objected.

"I know," Bronson said. "But whatever's inside that pot was indirectly responsible for the deaths of both Jackie and Mark, and possibly Jeremy Goldman as well. I'm not prepared to wait around for weeks for some man in a museum to open it under controlled conditions. I'm going to take a look inside it right now."

"OK," Angela said, "but just wait a few seconds. We should photograph the stages in finding and opening this."

She pulled a compact digital camera out of her pocket and took several shots of the sealed pot, and a couple of the cavity in the floor.

"Go ahead," she said. "Unseal the lid."

Bronson took his pocketknife and carefully cut away the wax seal. He waited while Angela took another two pictures, then used the point of the knife blade to ease up the wooden stopper. It was stiff so he had to lift it by stages, but finally it came out of the neck of the vessel. Again Angela took pictures, before he removed the stopper completely, and then snapped a further image looking down directly into the pot.

"Before you reach inside it," Angela said, "wrap your fingers in a handkerchief or something. The moisture on your hands could damage whatever's in there."

"OK," Bronson replied, doing as she instructed. "Here we go." He reached inside the jar and pulled out a small cylindrical object.

Angela gasped.

"Be careful," she said urgently. "It looks like an

intact papyrus scroll. That's an incredibly rare find. Hold it for a second."

She trotted across the room, picked up a seat cushion from one of the dining chairs and put it on the table. "Rest it on that," she instructed.

"How rare, exactly?" Bronson asked, placing the relic where she indicated.

"Scrolls are fairly common, but it's the condition that matters. Over the centuries most scrolls, including those from sites like Qumran—you know, the Dead Sea Scrolls—have largely disintegrated. Papyrologists have had to study individual fragments and attempt to reconstruct entire scrolls piece by piece, trying to match up tiny slivers of papyrus."

"I didn't know papyrus could last that long—so how old do you think it could be?"

"Give me a minute, will you? It's not like looking inside a modern novel. Scrolls don't have publication dates." She drew a chair closer to the table and took a pair of latex gloves from her pocket.

"You've come prepared," Bronson observed.

"I'm always prepared," she said, "at least for some things."

For some time she didn't touch the relic, just looked at it, turning the cushion this way and that to reveal different areas of the scroll. Although her specialization was ceramics, it was obvious to Bronson that she knew quite a lot about early documents as well, and that it was a necessary part of her job. After a couple of minutes she leaned back in the chair.

"Right, from what I can tell it's early, precisely because it *is* a scroll. Scrolls normally had writing on only one side of the papyrus, though some later examples have been found with writing on both. This scroll looks as if it has text on one side only, so that's another indication that it's an early document.

"One of the obvious problems the ancients discovered," Angela went on, carefully checking the inside of the pottery vessel on the table, "was that the only way to find out what was written on a scroll was to open it and read the text, which is why someone invented the *sittybos*. That was a tag attached to the handle of the scroll to identify it to the reader or seller, and they used it the way we use the writing on the spine of a book these days. I've just checked the pot, and there's no sign of one in there, and there's nothing on the scroll itself."

"Which means what?" Bronson asked.

"Nothing very significant, just that there's probably not a lot written on the scroll. It suggests it's not what you might call a commercial document, that it's not a known text, which probably would have a *sittybos* attached. It's more likely to be a private text of some sort. I'm happy to take a quick look at it, but it's not my field and, no matter what you think, this should be examined by an expert."

Carefully, Angela opened the scroll, just far enough that she could see the first few lines of characters, then gently closed it again.

"It's written in Latin," she said, "and the letters are unusually large. I think the text is continuous, which also suggests it's early. Later writing would normally include both a *spatium*—that's a gap between the verses—and a *paragraphus,* a horizontal line under the beginning of each new sentence."

"So how old do you think it is?" Bronson asked, as they both bent forward over the dining table, their backs to the door, staring at the relic.

"If I had to guess I'd say second or third century A.D. It's got to—"

Angela screamed as someone grabbed her arm. She was pulled violently backward away from the table and slammed into the wall beside the door.

Bronson spun around. He'd heard no footsteps, no noise of any kind.

A heavily built man wearing a light gray suit had grabbed Angela and pinned her against the wall. But it was the other man who held Bronson's attention, or rather the semiautomatic pistol he was holding in his right hand. Because it looked to Bronson as if he knew exactly how to use it.

19

I

"You're wrong," the big man in the gray suit corrected Angela. His English was fluent and almost devoid of any accent. "It's first century."

"Who the hell are you?" Bronson demanded, silently berating himself for not checking that all the doors and windows had been locked.

Bizarrely, the man holding Angela could almost have been a banker or a businessman, judging by his appearance—immaculate suit, highly polished black loafers and neat, well-cut dark hair. Until, that is, Bronson looked into his eyes. They were black, and as cold and empty as an open grave.

In contrast to his companion, the man holding the gun was wearing jeans and a casual jacket. Bronson guessed these were probably the men who'd broken into the house. And killed Mark Hampton and Jackie and possibly Jeremy Goldman as well. Anger rose in him like a tide, but he knew he had to remain focused.

"Who we are isn't important," the bigger man said. "We've been looking for that"—he gestured toward the scroll on the table—"for a very long time."

Still holding Angela's arm, he strode across to the table and picked up the scroll while the second man kept his pistol trained on Bronson.

"What's so important about this scroll that both my friends had to die? You *did* kill them, I presume?" Bronson balled his fists, and forced himself to take deep, even breaths. He couldn't afford to get things wrong.

The man in the suit inclined his head in acknowledgment. "I wasn't personally responsible," he said, "but my orders were being followed, yes."

"But why is that old scroll so important?" Bronson asked again.

The man didn't respond immediately, but instead pulled a dining chair away from the table and pushed Angela toward it.

"Sit down," he snapped, and watched as she obeyed him.

He unrolled one end of the scroll, looked at the first few lines and nodded in satisfaction, then he slid it into the pocket of his jacket.

"I will answer your question, Bronson," he said. "You see, I already know who you are. I'll tell you exactly why this scroll is worth killing for. I think you know why I'm prepared to do that," he added. "You understand the situation."

Bronson nodded. He knew exactly why the Italian was happy to talk—the two intruders had no intention of leaving either him or Angela alive when they left the house.

"Who are these people, Chris?" Angela asked, and Bronson noted that her voice was steady but tinged with anger. She could have been inquiring about the identity of a couple of uninvited guests at a party. He felt a sudden rush of admiration for her.

Bronson focused on the big man. "Tell us," he said shortly.

The Italian smiled, but without any humor in his eyes. "This scroll was written in A.D. sixty-seven, on the specific orders of the Emperor Nero by a man who routinely signed himself 'SQVET.' The people who employ us have been looking for it for the last fifteen hundred years."

Bronson looked at Angela.

"What on earth do you mean?" she asked, looking shocked.

The Italian shook his head. "I've said enough. All I will tell you is that we believe the scroll holds a secret that the Church would far rather remain hidden. In fact, it suggests that the entire Christian religion was founded on a lie, so perhaps you can guess what's going to happen to it?"

"You—or your employer, which I presume is the Vatican—will destroy it as soon as possible?" Bronson suggested.

"That won't be my decision, obviously, but I imagine they'll either do that or lock it away in the Apostolic Penitentiary for all eternity."

Bronson had been watching the two Italians carefully. He'd tried to keep them talking, stalling for time while he figured out his next move.

The big Italian took a step back toward the door and glanced at his companion. "Kill them both," he hissed in Italian. "Shoot Bronson first."

And that was the moment Bronson had been waiting for. The second man half-turned his head toward the bigger man as he received his orders, nodded, and then began bringing his automatic up to aim at Bronson.

But Bronson was already moving. The Browning Hi-Power hadn't been out of his immediate possession since he'd left his house in England. He reached under his jacket, grabbed the pistol from his waistband, clicked off the safety catch and leveled the weapon at the Italian.

"Lower your weapon," he yelled, in fluent Italian. "If you move that pistol even one centimeter I'll shoot."

For several long seconds, nobody moved.

"Your choice," Bronson shouted, his eyes never leaving the man's weapon. "Take the damned scroll and get out of here, and nobody gets hurt. Try anything else, and at the very least one of you is going to die."

II

But even as Bronson aimed his pistol at the armed man about fifteen feet in front of him, the big man in the gray suit moved, as quick and lithe as a cat. He grabbed Angela by the hair, dragged her out of the dining chair and held her in front of him as a shield.

"Chris!" Angela yelled, but there wasn't a thing Bronson could do to stop him. If he'd fired, he'd probably have hit her.

In seconds, the big Italian had pulled Angela, struggling in his grasp, out through the door.

Bronson was left facing the second man. For a long couple of seconds they just stared at each other, then the Italian muttered something and moved his pistol. Bronson had absolutely no option. He adjusted his aim slightly and squeezed the trigger. The Browning kicked in his hand, the report of the shot shockingly loud in the confined space, the ejected cartridge case spinning away to his right in a blur of brass.

The Italian screamed and tumbled backward, his left shoulder suddenly blooming red. He clutched at the wound, his pistol falling to the floor.

Bronson ran forward and scooped up the weapon,

which he recognized immediately as a nine-millimeter Beretta. But he didn't even give the injured man a second glance. His whole attention was focused on Angela and whatever was happening behind the closed dining-room door.

His military training kicked in. Pulling open the door and stepping through it could be the last thing he ever did if the big man had a pistol, because he'd be a sitting duck, framed in the doorway. And that wouldn't help Angela.

So he stepped forward cautiously, flattened himself against the stone wall beside the door, and turned the handle. Then he peered through the gap into the living room. The big Italian wasn't waiting for him. He was almost at the far door, the one that led into the hall, one beefy arm around Angela's neck as he dragged her roughly across the floor.

Bronson wrenched open the door, stepped into the room, took rapid aim and fired a single shot into the stone wall beside the hall door. The Italian turned, his expression confused and almost frightened, and at that moment Angela acted.

As the big man paused, she lifted her right leg and scraped her shoe hard down the man's left shin and then drove her heel as hard as she could into the top of his foot.

The Italian grunted in pain and staggered backward, releasing his hold on Angela's neck as he did so. She dived to one side, getting out of Bronson's line of fire, as the big man hobbled toward the door.

Bronson aimed the Browning straight at the Italian, but he immediately vanished into the hall, and seconds later Bronson heard the front door slam shut. He ran across to the window and looked out to see the man jogging away from the house, his limp now markedly less pronounced.

Bronson turned back to Angela. "Are you OK?" he demanded.

Her hair tousled and her face flushed with exertion, Angela nodded. "Thank God for aerobics and Manolos," she said. "I always liked these shoes. What happened to the other one?"

"I winged him," Bronson said. "He's in the dining room, bleeding all over the floor."

"They were going to kill us, weren't they? That's why you drew the gun."

"Yes, and we're not safe yet. We need to get out of here as quickly as we can, in case that big bastard decides to come back with reinforcements."

"What about him?" Angela said, pointing toward the dining-room door, behind which moans and howls of pain could be heard. "We should take him to the hospital."

"He was going to kill us, Angela. I really don't care if he lives or dies."

"You can't just leave him. That's inhuman. We've got to do something."

Bronson looked again toward the dining room. "OK. Go upstairs and grab all your stuff. I'll see what I can do."

Angela stared at him. "Don't kill him," she instructed.

"I wasn't going to."

Bronson went into the downstairs lavatory, found a couple of towels and walked back into the dining room, the Browning Hi-Power held ready in front of him. But the pistol was unnecessary. The Italian was lying moaning in a pool of blood, his right hand trying to staunch the flow from the bullet wound in his shoulder.

Bronson placed the two pistols on the table, well out of reach, then bent down and eased the injured man into a sitting position. He pulled off his light-weight jacket and removed the shoulder holster he found underneath it. Then he folded one of the towels and placed it over the exit wound, laying the man down again so that the weight of his body would help reduce the blood loss.

"Hold this," Bronson said in Italian, pressing the man's bloody right hand onto the other towel, positioned over the entry wound.

"Thank you," the Italian said, his breath rasping painfully, "but I need a hospital."

"I know," Bronson replied. "I'll telephone in a minute. First, I need answers to a few questions, and the quicker you tell me, the sooner I'll make that call. Who are you? Who do you work for? And who's your fat friend?"

The ghost of a smile crossed the wounded man's face. "His name's Gregori Mandino, and he's the *capo-famiglia*—the head—of the Rome *Cosa Nostra.*"

"The Mafia?"

"Wrong name, right organization. I'm just one of the *picciotti,* a soldier," the man said, "one of the *capo*'s bodyguards. I do what I'm told, and go where I'm needed. I have no idea why we're here." He said it with such conviction that Bronson almost believed him. "But let me give you a piece of advice, Englishman. Mandino is ruthless, and his deputy is worse. If I were you, I'd get away from here as quickly as you can, and not come back to Italy. Ever. The *Cosa Nostra* has a very long memory."

"But why should someone like Mandino care about a two-thousand-year-old scroll?" Bronson asked.

"I told you, I've no idea."

The "need to know" concept was one Bronson was very familiar with from his time in the army, and he guessed that a criminal organization like the Mafia probably worked in a similar way. The wounded man very probably *didn't* know what was going on. Employed because of his skill with a gun—though he hadn't been quite good enough on this occasion—he would have been told only what he needed to know to complete whatever tasks he was set.

"OK," Bronson said. "I'll call now."

He quickly searched the man's jacket, found a handful of nine-millimeter shells and removed them. Then he scoured the floor, found the ejected cartridge case from the Browning and picked it up. The bullet that had hit the Italian had passed straight through his shoulder and buried itself in the edge of the doorframe, but he quickly removed it with one of the screwdrivers he'd used to lift the floor panel. That was all he could do to eliminate the forensic evidence.

Finally, he picked up the holster and the two pistols—and the *skyphos* as an afterthought—and left the room. Angela was waiting for him in the hall, both her bags at her feet.

"I've tried to stop the bleeding with a couple of towels," Bronson explained, "and I'll call the emergency services right now. You get in the car."

Fifteen minutes later they were in the Espace—the back of the car now empty as Bronson had unceremoniously dumped the bath and all the other boxes beside the Hamptons' garage—and heading west, away from the house.

III

Bronson steered the Renault down the road and glanced over at Angela. "Are you all right?" he asked.

"I'm furious," she snapped. Bronson realized that the shaking he had taken to be shock or fear was actually intense anger. Every sinew of Angela's body telegraphed her fury.

"I know," Bronson said, his voice deliberately calm

and measured, "it's a shame we didn't get the chance to examine the scroll, but we *are* alive. That's the most important thing."

"It's not just that," Angela retorted. "I was terrified in there, do you know that? I'd never even seen a real pistol until you waved that one at me back in England, and a few hours later I'm in the middle of a gun battle, and some fat Italian crook's dragging me around by my neck. That's bad enough. Then, just as we finally manage to decode the inscription and track down the relic, those two bastards come along and take it away from us. After all we've been through! I'm really pissed off."

Bronson smiled to himself. Good old Angela, he thought. Trust her to come back fighting.

"Look, Angela," he said, "I'm really sorry about what happened back there. It was my fault they got into the house. I should have double-checked that all the doors and windows were locked."

"If you *had* locked the doors, they'd probably still have got inside, and if we'd heard them coming we might have been involved in a shoot-out neither of us would have survived. As it is, thanks to you, we're both still very much alive. But it's a shame about the scroll."

"I brought the *skyphos* or whatever you call it. At least we've got that as a souvenir. It's obviously old— do you think it's valuable?"

Angela leaned over to the backseat and picked up the vessel to examine it properly—in the house she'd hardly had a chance.

"This is a fake," she said a few minutes later, "but a good one. At first sight it looks exactly like a genuine Roman *skyphos*. But the shape is slightly different: it's a bit too tall for its width. The glaze feels wrong, and I think the composition of the pottery itself isn't right for the first century. There are a lot of tests we could run, but it probably wouldn't be worth the effort."

"So we've been through all this for a fake?" Bronson asked. "And remind me. What, exactly, is a *skyphos*?"

"The name's Greek, not Roman. It's a type of vessel that originated in the eastern end of the Mediterranean, around about the first century A.D. A *skyphos* is a two-handled drinking cup. This one's in excellent condition, and if it had been the genuine article it would have been worth around four or five grand."

"So when was it made?"

Angela looked at the *skyphos* critically. "Definitely second millennium," she replied. "If I had to guess I'd say thirteenth or maybe fourteenth century. Probably made about the same time that the Hamptons' house was built."

Bronson glanced over at her. "That's interesting," he said.

"More coincidental than anything else, I'd have thought."

"Not necessarily, if you *are* right and they're more or less contemporary. I think it could be far more than simple coincidence that a fourteenth-century pot—and a fake at that—was deliberately hidden in a fourteenth-century house."

"Why?"

Bronson paused to order his thoughts. "The whole trail we've been following is obscure and complicated, and I'm wondering if that Occitan verse is even more complex than we thought, and that we're missing something."

"I don't follow you."

"Look at the verse," Bronson said. "It's written entirely in Occitan apart from one word—*calix*—and that's Latin for 'chalice.' When we follow the other clues in the riddle, we eventually find something that looks like a Roman drinking cup, but isn't. So the verse uses a Roman word for chalice, and we've recovered a copy of a Roman chalice. Doesn't that strike you as odd? Or at least convoluted?"

"Keep going," Angela said, encouragingly.

"Why did they go to all the trouble of manufacturing a fake *skyphos* when they could just as easily have buried the scroll in any old earthenware pot? It's as if they wanted to draw our attention to the Roman element in all this, back to the Latin inscription in the living room."

"But we've been over and over this. There aren't any other clues in those three Latin words. Or, if there are, they're bloody well hidden."

"Agreed. So maybe the Occitan verse is pointing us toward something else. Something more than just the location of the hidden scroll? Perhaps to the *skyphos* itself?"

"But there's nothing else inside it," Angela said, turning the vessel upside down. "I checked that when I was looking for a *sittybos*."

Bronson looked confused.

"Remember?" Angela said. "It's a kind of tag attached to a scroll that identifies its contents."

"Oh, right," Bronson said. "Well, maybe not anything inside it, but what about the *outside*? Is that just a random pattern on the side of the pot?"

Angela peered closely at the green-glazed pottery vessel and almost immediately she noticed something. Just below the rim on one side of the *skyphos* were three small letters separated by dots: "H•V•L."

"Now, that's odd," she murmured. "There are three letters inscribed here—'HVL'—and they obviously have to stand for *'Hic Vanidici Latitant.'*"

" 'Here lie the liars,' " Bronson breathed. "That's a definite link. So what's that pattern underneath the letters?"

Below the inscribed letters was what looked almost like a sine wave: a line that undulated in a regular pattern, up and down, and with short diagonal lines running below it, sloping from top right to bottom left. Below the wavy line was a geometric pattern, three straight lines crisscrossing in the center and with a dot at each end. Running along the lines were Latin numbers, followed by the letters "M•P," then more numbers and the letter "A." Beside each dot were other numbers, each followed by a "P." In the very center of the design were the letters "PO•LDA," and below that "M•A•M."

"It's not random," Angela said decisively. "Whatever these lines mean, they indicate something definite, almost like a map."

Bronson looked across at the *skyphos* Angela was holding. "But a map of what?"

20

Late that afternoon, the setting sun bathed the irregular rooftops and old walls of the ancient heart of the city of Rome with a golden glow. Pedestrians bustled to and fro along the wide pavements, and a constant stream of hooting and jostling vehicles fought its way around the Piazza di Santa Maria alle Fornaci. But Joseph Cardinal Vertutti saw none of it.

He sat down beside Mandino in the same café where the two men had first met. As the operation had been successfully concluded, he thought that it rounded things out nicely to hold their last meeting in the same place where they'd held their first. But this time Mandino had insisted that they meet in a small back room.

"You have it?" Vertutti asked, his voice high and excited. His hands were trembling slightly, Mandino noticed.

"All in good time, Cardinal, all in good time." A waiter knocked and entered with two cups of coffee. He placed them gently on the table and then withdrew, closing the door behind him. "Before I deliver anything, we have one small administrative detail to take care of. Have you transferred the money?"

"Yes," Vertutti snapped. "I sent one hundred thousand euros to the account you specified."

"*You* might think your word is sufficient proof, Eminence, but *I* know firsthand that the Vatican is just as capable of duplicity as the next person. Unless you have a transfer slip for me, this conversation will finish right here."

Vertutti pulled a wallet from his jacket pocket. He opened it and extracted a slip of paper, which he passed across the table.

Mandino looked at it, smiled, and then tucked it away in his own wallet. The amount was correct, and in the "reference" section Vertutti had inserted "Purchase of religious artifacts," which was a surprisingly accurate description of the transaction.

"Excellent," Mandino said. "Now, you'll be pleased to hear that we managed to retrieve the relic. I watched the man Bronson—Mark Hampton's friend—retrieve the scroll, and we interceded immediately. Neither Bronson nor his wife, who was also present at the house, have any significant knowledge of what the *Exomologesis* contains, and so they don't need to be eliminated."

Mandino said nothing to Vertutti about what he'd told them about the scroll, or the embarrassing fact that the Englishman had sent him running for his life and had actually shot one of his bodyguards.

"Very generous of you," Vertutti quipped sarcastically. "Where are they now?"

"They're probably heading back to Britain. Now that we've recovered the relic, there's nothing else for them here."

Mandino was again being slightly economical with the truth. He'd already instructed Antonio Carlotti to advise one of his contacts in the *Carabinieri* that

Bronson—a man wanted for questioning by the Metropolitan Police about a murder in Britain—was roaming at will around Italy. He'd even passed on details about the Renault Espace he'd seen parked outside the house. He was certain that the two of them would be picked up well before they reached the Italian border.

"So, where is the relic?" Vertutti asked impatiently.

Mandino opened his briefcase, removed a plastic container filled with a white, fluffy substance and passed it across the table.

Vertutti cautiously lifted out several layers of cotton wool to reveal the small scroll. With trembling fingers, he gingerly picked up the ancient papyrus. He held it up—the expression on his face reflecting his knowledge of both its age and its terrible destructive power—then carefully unrolled it on the table in front of him. He nodded gravely, almost reverently, as he read through the short text.

"Even if I wasn't sure about it," he said, "the way this is written is an indication of the author's identity."

"What do you mean?" Mandino asked.

"The writing is bold and the letters large," Vertutti said. "It's not generally known, but the man who wrote this suffered from a medical condition known as ophthalmia neonatorum, which was fairly common at the time. This disease caused a progressive loss of sight and a very painful weakness in his eyes, and in his case eventually left him nearly blind. Writing was always difficult for him, and he probably normally used an amanuensis, a professional scribe. That facility was obviously not available to him in Judea when he was forced to write this document."

Vertutti continued studying the relic for a few moments, then looked up. "I know we've had our differences of opinion, Mandino," he said, with a somewhat strained smile, "but despite your views of the Church and the Vatican, I would like to congratulate you for recovering this. The Holy Father will be particularly pleased that we've managed to do so."

Mandino inclined his head in acknowledgment. "What will you do with it now? Destroy it?"

Vertutti shook his head. "I hope not," he said. "I believe it should be secreted in the Apostolic Penitentiary along with the Vitalian Codex. Destroying an object of this age and importance is not something I believe the Vatican should contemplate doing, no matter what the context."

Vertutti unrolled the last few inches of the scroll. Then he leaned forward to examine something at the end of the document, below the mark "SQVET."

"Did you look at this?" he asked, an edge of tension in his voice.

"No," Mandino replied. "I only checked the beginning of it, purely to make sure it was the correct document."

"Oh, it's the correct document all right. But this— this changes everything," Vertutti said, pointing at the very end of the scroll.

Mandino squinted at the document. There were a few lines written in a different, smaller hand just above Nero's imperial seal.

Vertutti translated the Latin aloud, then looked at Mandino.

"You know what you have to do," he said.

II

Bronson and Angela found a small family-run hotel on the outskirts of Santa Marinella, on the Italian coast, northwest of Rome. It offered off-street parking in a courtyard at the rear of the building and seemed quietly anonymous. Bronson booked in, taking the last remaining twin room, and carried their bags upstairs.

The room was south-facing, light and airy, with a view over the courtyard. Angela opened her bag, lifted out a bulky bundle of clothes and laid it on the bed.

"We need decent light," Bronson said, moving one of the bedside tables over to stand it in front of the window.

Behind him, Angela carefully unwrapped the clothes, layer by layer, to reveal the *skyphos* nestling in the center of the bundle. She placed it gently on the table Bronson had moved.

Bronson removed the digital camera from his overnight bag. He crouched down between the table and the window so that the full light of the afternoon sun fell on the *skyphos,* making the old green glaze of the earthenware pot glow. He snapped a couple of dozen pictures of the vessel, from all sides and angles, then finally took a pencil and paper and made as accurate a drawing as he could of the inscribed lines and figures on its side.

"So all we have to do now," Angela said, as Bronson copied the photographs onto his laptop, "is work out what the hell that diagram—or whatever it is—means."

"Exactly."

They looked at the lines, letters and numbers.

"I still think it might be some kind of map," Angela suggested hesitantly.

"You may be right. But if it is, I've no idea how to decipher it. I mean, it's just three lines and a bunch of numbers. Maybe we should ignore it for the moment and look again at Marcus Asinius Marcellus and Nero. We guessed the literal meanings of 'MAM' and 'PO LDA,' but we never really deduced why they were inscribed on that slab. If we can do that, it might give us a steer."

"Back to the books?"

"You check the books. I'll use the Internet. Now

that those two Italians have taken the scroll, hopefully no one will be looking for us."

Bronson logged on to the hotel's wireless network on his laptop, while Angela leafed through the books that she had bought in Cambridge.

Bronson started by looking for references to Marcus Asinius Marcellus, because they surmised that he had probably been responsible for the Latin inscription on the stone in the Hamptons' house. They already knew Marcellus had been involved in a scandal over a forged will, and had only been spared execution by the personal intervention of Nero himself.

"That," Bronson said, "would have given Nero a lever he could use to pressure Marcellus into carrying out tasks for him. That would explain the 'PO LDA': *'Per ordo Lucius Domitius Ahenobarbus.'* What the letters on the stone meant was that the job—whatever it was—was done by Marcellus, but on Nero's orders."

"So perhaps we should look a bit more closely at the Emperor?" Angela said.

They transferred their attention to Nero himself and discovered, among other things, his implacable hatred of all aspects of Christianity.

"If that Italian henchman was telling the truth," Bronson said, "the scroll contained some secret that the Vatican definitely didn't want anyone to discover. Which would mean that whatever we're looking for is also connected with the Church."

"And if I'm right and those lines *are* a kind of map, that suggests Marcellus might have been burying or hiding something for Nero," Angela said. "It must have been something that the Emperor felt was so important that he had to entrust it, not to a squad of workmen or gang of slaves, but to a relative who owed him an enormous debt of gratitude."

"So what the hell did Marcellus bury?"

"I've no idea," Angela said, "but the more I look

at those lines, the more sure I am that *something* was buried, and this diagram must be trying to tell us where."

III

Mandino wasn't surprised to find the Villa Rosa appeared to be deserted. If he'd been in Bronson's place, he would have left the house as quickly as possible. He also knew that his wounded bodyguard was now in a Rome hospital, *Carabinieri* officers waiting to interview him about his gunshot wound, because the man had made a brief telephone call to Rogan.

The driver stopped the car in front of the house. Mandino ordered one of his men to check the garage, just in case the Renault Espace had been parked there. He wasn't about to make the same mistake twice. Moments later, the bodyguard ran back.

"The door's locked but I looked through the window. There's nothing in there," he said.

"Right," Mandino said. "Rogan—get us inside."

The rear door was jammed with a chair—Rogan could see that clearly enough through the glass panels in the door—so he walked farther on to the living room window where he and Alberti had broken the pane. The shutters were closed and locked, but they yielded easily to his crowbar. The glass hadn't been repaired yet, and in a few minutes Rogan was able to open the front door of the house for the others.

The two men walked straight through to the living room, and stopped in front of the fireplace.

"Are you sure it's there, *capo*?"

"It's the only place it can be. It's the only hiding place that makes sense. Get on with it."

Rogan dragged a stepladder over to the fireplace, then removed a hammer and chisel from the bag he was carrying. He climbed up until his shoulders were

level with the inscribed stone and started removing
the cement that held it in place. He drove the tip of
the chisel into the gap between the stone and the one
below it, and levered. The stone moved very slightly.

"This slab can only be a few centimeters thick,"
Rogan said, "but I'd like somebody else to help lift
it out."

"Wait there." Mandino gestured at one of the bodyguards who quickly removed his jacket and shoulder
holster, and grabbed a second stepladder.

Driving the tool into the space above the slab,
Rogan levered upward, and the top of the stone
moved forward. He shifted the position of the chisel
and pushed up again, then repeated the action on both
sides of the slab, until he was satisfied that the stone
had been freed off sufficiently to lift it out.

"Get ready to take the weight," he warned the
bodyguard.

Together the two men worked the slab back and
forth until it came free. Each held one side of the stone,
but Rogan immediately realized it wasn't that heavy.

"It's only about an inch thick," he said. He lifted it
himself and climbed down the ladder. He carried the
stone across to a small but sturdy table, where Mandino was waiting. Rogan held it up upright on its base
while Mandino eagerly brushed dust and mortar from
its back, searching for any letters or numbers.

"Nothing," Mandino muttered. The reverse of the
stone was unmarked apart from tiny cuts made when
it had been prepared. "Check the cavity."

Rogan climbed back up the ladder and peered inside the gaping hole above the fireplace.

"There's something in here," he said.

"What?"

"There's another stone lying in the cavity. It's not
been cemented in place. It's as if the first stone acted
as a door."

"Bring it down," Mandino instructed.

Rogan pulled the second stone out of the recess and placed it on the table beside the first one.

"No," Mandino said. "Not like that. Put it below the other stone. That's it," he added, as the two men maneuvered the slab into position. "Look, that's the lower section. That's the piece somebody must have cut off centuries ago."

The three men examined the markings on the stone.

"Is it a map?" Rogan asked, brushing the dust and dirt off the inscribed surface.

"It could be," Mandino said. "It'll take time to decipher, though. It's not like any map I've ever seen."

Religion held no sway over Mandino. He believed in the things he could see like money, and fear. But he was developing a grudging respect for the ingenuity of the Cathars. With their religion crumbling around them, they must have known that time was running out. But rather than risk either the stone or the *Exomologesis* falling into the hands of the crusaders, they decided to hide them both. They buried the scroll under the floor and split the stone in two, sealing the lower half inside the wall, where it would be safe from wear and tear. And then they left two markers visible. Two inscribed stones that showed where the two objects were hidden, but only if you knew exactly what you were looking for.

21

I

The Internet searches had helped, but not very much. Bronson and Angela now knew a lot more about the Romans in general, and Emperor Nero in particular, but still almost nothing about Marcus Asinius Marcellus, who remained a vague and insubstantial figure almost completely absent from the historical record. And they still had no idea what he had buried on Nero's orders.

In their room in Santa Marinella, Bronson examined the *skyphos* carefully while Angela studied one of their books about Nero.

"The one thing we haven't really looked at," Bronson said slowly, "is this drinking cup."

"We have," Angela objected. "It's empty now, because the scroll's gone, and we've copied that map thing off the outside. There's nothing else it can tell us."

"I didn't mean that, exactly. I've been trying to reconstruct the sequence of events. This pot is a fourteenth-century copy of a first-century Roman *skyphos*. But why didn't the Cathars use a contemporary vessel to hide the scroll? They could have made any old pot and inscribed that diagram on it. Why did they bother creating a replica of a Roman drinking cup? There had to be a good reason for doing that.

"The Occitan verse we found contained a single Latin word—*calix*—meaning 'chalice.' That was an obvious pointer to this vessel. But I think the fact that this appears to be a Roman pot points straight to the Latin inscription. Maybe this vessel and the two stones are all part of the same silent message left for somebody by the last of the Cathars."

"We've been over all this, Chris."

"I know, but there's one question we haven't asked." Bronson pointed at the side of the *skyphos*. "Where did that come from?" he said.

"The vessel?"

"No. The map or diagram or whatever the hell it is. Maybe we've got it wrong about the 'Cathar treasure,' or half wrong, anyway. They must have had the scroll—the clues we followed when we found it were too specific to be a coincidence—but just suppose the scroll was only part of their treasure."

"What else did they have?"

"I'm wondering if the Cathars found or inherited both the scroll *and* the stone with the Latin inscription on it."

Angela looked puzzled. "I don't see how that helps us. All that's on the stone are those three Latin words."

"No," Bronson said. "There is—or at least there was—more than that. Remember what Jeremy Goldman told me. He said that the stone had been cut, that the section cemented into the wall of the Hamptons' house was just the top half. In fact, that tip was the reason Mark and I started searching the rest of the house. We were looking for the missing lower section."

"But you never found it, so how does that help?"

"You're quite right. We didn't find it, but I wonder if we have now, or at least what was written on it. Think about it. How would you describe the carved letters on the Roman inscription?"

"All capitals, no frills. A typical first-century Latin inscription. There are hundreds of similar examples."

"And what about the Occitan verses?"

Angela thought for a moment. "Completely different. That was a cursive script. I suppose the modern equivalent would be a kind of italic."

"Exactly. Now your estimate was that the Occitan inscription was carved at about the same time as the *skyphos* was made, probably in the fourteenth century?"

"Probably, yes."

"Now look at the diagram on the side of the vessel, and the letters and numbers. The numbers are Latin—that's the first thing—and the letters are all capitals. In other words, although the *skyphos* and the Occitan inscription are probably contemporary, you'd never deduce that just by looking at the two texts. They appear completely different."

"So what you're saying is that if the *skyphos* was made by the Cathars, why is the decoration on the side so obviously Roman? Except that it's an obvious copy of a Roman drinking vessel, of course."

"Yes," Bronson said, "but I think that was quite deliberate. The Cathars made a copy of a Roman vessel to hold the scroll, and the decoration they chose for the *skyphos* is also Roman. More than that, the diagram is headed 'HVL'—*'Hic Vandici Latitant'*—just like the stone with the Latin inscription."

"Yes," Angela said, her voice suddenly excited. "You mean that what we're looking at here could be an exact copy of the map on the missing section of that stone?"

Bronson nodded. "Suppose the Cathars had possessed this stone for years, but they'd never managed to decipher what it meant. Perhaps the scroll itself refers to the stone, or to whatever was buried, and that convinced them that the map or diagram was *really* important. When the last of the Cathars fled from France and arrived in Italy, they knew their religion was doomed, but they still wanted to preserve the 'treasure' they'd managed to smuggle out of Montségur. So they split the stone in two, left one part—the top section—where it could be easily found, but hid the important bit, the diagram, somewhere else.

"To allow a fellow Cathar, or someone who knew enough about their religion, to decipher it, they prepared the Occitan inscription. The clues in that would lead to the scroll, safely hidden away in the *skyphos,* and on the vessel itself they left an exact copy of the diagram they'd never managed to understand. I think that map shows exactly where the 'liars' are hidden."

"But this isn't like any kind of map I've ever seen before. It's just lines, letters and numbers. They could mean anything."

Bronson nodded again. "If it was easy, the Cathars would have cracked it seven hundred years ago. I'm guessing here, but I think Nero must have insisted that the hiding place be located in an area that would never be found by accident, and that meant somewhere well outside Imperial Rome. Obviously the Emperor—or perhaps Marcellus—decided to make a map showing the location, so that the site could be found later if necessary. But to provide an extra layer of protection, they devised a type of map that would need to be deciphered."

"I see what you're driving at," Angela said. "But this jar is a lot smaller than the stone would have been. What about the scale?"

"I've been thinking about that, and I don't think it

matters. I know a bit about mapping and, as long as you know the scale, you can interpret a map of any physical size. That diagram"—he pointed at the *skyphos*—"isn't a conventional map because it hasn't got a scale, at least as far as I can see, and it doesn't show any features like a coast, rivers or towns. I've been trying to put myself in the position of the man who prepared it, trying to work out what he could have done to create a map that would endure, if necessary for centuries.

"If the burial place was outside Rome, he wouldn't have been able to use buildings as reference points, because the only structures he'd see out in the country wouldn't have been permanent. I mean, if he'd buried something in Rome itself, he might have guessed that places like the Circus Maximus would survive and used them to identify the location of the burial place. But in the country, even a large villa might be abandoned or destroyed within a generation or two. So the only realistic option he would have had would be to use very specific geographical features.

"I think Marcellus—or whoever made this—picked permanent objects, things that, no matter what happened in Italy, would always be visible and identifiable. I don't think this diagram needs a scale because it probably refers to a group of hills near Rome. I think the lines show the distances between them and their respective heights."

For a few seconds Angela looked at the diagram on the side of the *skyphos,* then down at the drawing Bronson had made, her fingers tracing the letters and numbers he'd copied from the vessel. Then she grabbed a book about the Roman Empire, flicked through it until she reached the index and turned to a specific page. It contained a table with letters and figures, but Bronson couldn't read it upside-down.

"That might make sense," she said, her eyes flicking

between Bronson's copy of the diagram and the table in the book. "If you're right and the lines represent distances, then 'P' would translate as *passus,* the pace step of a Roman legionary and equal to 1.62 yards. 'MP' would mean *mille passus,* one thousand *passus.* That's the Roman mile of 1,618 yards. The 'P' markings beside the dots would probably represent the heights of the hills, measured in *pes,* plural *pedes,* the Roman foot of 11.6 inches, and 'A' the *actus,* 120 *pedes* or about 116 feet."

"But would the Romans have been able to produce figures that accurate?" Bronson asked.

Angela nodded confidently. "Absolutely. The Romans had a number of surveying tools, including one called a *groma.* That had been in use for centuries before Nero's reign and would have allowed for quite sophisticated measuring. And you should also remember how many large Roman buildings are still standing today. They wouldn't have survived if their builders hadn't had quite advanced surveying ability."

Angela leaned over the keyboard of the laptop, typed the word "groma" into the search engine and pressed the "enter" key. When the results appeared, she picked one site and clicked on that.

"There you are," she said, pointing at the screen. "That's a *groma.*"

Bronson looked at the diagram of the instrument for a few moments. It comprised two horizontal arms crossed at right angles and resting on a bracket that was itself attached to a vertical staff. Each of the four arms had a cord at the end that formed a plumb bob.

"And they also used a thing called a *gnomon* to locate north—very roughly—and they could measure distance and height using a *diopter.*"

"So all we have to do now is work out which hills Marcellus used as his reference points."

"That sounds easy, but only if you say it quickly,"

Angela commented wryly. "How the hell are you going to manage that? There must be hundreds of hill formations outside Rome."

"I have a secret weapon," Bronson said, with a smile. "It's called Google Earth, and I can use it to check the elevation of any point on the surface of the planet. There are six reference points on that diagram, so all I have to do is convert the figures from it into modern units of measurement, and then find six hills that match those criteria.

"Then we find the liars."

II

On the way back from Ponticelli to Rome, Gregori Mandino telephoned Pierro and ordered him to wait at a restaurant on the Via delle Botteghe Oscure. By the very nature of the business he was in, Mandino had no office and tended to hold most of his meetings in cafés and restaurants. He also told Pierro to find detailed maps of the city and the surrounding area, and of the structures built in ancient Rome, and bring those with him, along with a laptop computer.

They met in a small private dining room at the back of the restaurant.

"So you found the *Exomologesis*?" Pierro asked, once Mandino and Rogan had sat down and ordered drinks.

"Yes," Mandino replied, "and I really thought that would be the end of the matter. But when Vertutti unrolled the scroll completely, there was a postscript to it that we hadn't expected."

"A postscript?"

"A short note in Latin accompanied by the imperial seal of Nero Claudius Caesar Drusus. It gave Vertutti quite a scare, because it implied that the scroll was only a part of what Marcellus had hidden on Nero's instructions, and wasn't even the most important part at that."

"So what else did he bury?"

Mandino told him what Vertutti had translated from the Latin.

"Are you serious?" Pierro asked, a slight but perceptible tremor in his voice. "I can't believe it. Both of them?"

"That's what the Latin text claimed."

The academic looked distinctly pale despite the warm lighting of the room. "But I don't—I mean—oh, God. You really believe that?"

Mandino shrugged. "My views are irrelevant. And I frankly don't care whether what's written on the scroll is true or not."

"Could those relics really have lasted two thousand years?"

"Vertutti isn't prepared to take the chance. The point, Pierro, is that we're still under contract to resolve this, so I'm expecting you to decipher what's on the stone."

"Where is it now?"

"We've left it in the car. Rogan has taken pictures of the inscription, and you can work from those."

Rogan handed over the data card from the digital camera.

Pierro slipped it into a document pocket on his computer bag. "I'd like to see the stone for myself."

Mandino nodded. "The car's just around the corner. We'll go and take a look at it in a few minutes."

"And what exactly is the inscription? A map? Directions?"

"We're not sure. It's definitely the lower section of the stone with the Latin inscription—we put the two pieces together and they match—but it seems to be just three straight lines, six dots and some letters and numbers. It's more like a diagram than a map, but it

must indicate where the relics are hidden, otherwise
there would have been no point in carving it in the
first place, and no reason for anyone to hide the
stone."

"Lines?" Pierro murmured. "You mentioned letters
and numbers. Can you remember what letters? Perhaps 'P' and 'MP'?"

"Yes, and I think 'A' as well. Why? Do you know
what they mean?"

"Well, perhaps. *Pedes* or *passus, mille passus* and
actus. They're Roman measurements of distance.
Whoever prepared the diagram might have picked
some prominent buildings or landmarks in Rome and
used those as reference points."

"I hope you're right," Mandino said. "We'll go and
look at the stone now, then you can get to work." He
got up and led the way out of the restaurant.

III

Bronson had been trying to find matches between the
heights shown on the diagram from the *skyphos* and
those on Google Earth for more than an hour.

"This could take forever," he muttered, leaning
back in his chair and stretching to ease his cramped
joints. "This bloody country is full of hills, and God
knows which ones Marcellus picked. And that's assuming he did use hills."

"No matches at all?" Angela asked.

"None. I've taken your conversions of the Roman
numbers and I've assumed a fudge factor of ten percent above and below, but even doing that I'm finding
hardly any hills on Google that even come close."

"How many?"

"Maybe eight or ten hills that fit the criteria, that's
all, and they're all down by the coast and quite a way
outside Rome."

For a few seconds Angela didn't respond, just stared at the laptop's screen, then she chuckled softly.

"Call yourself a detective?" she asked. "Do the initials 'AGL' and 'AMSL' mean anything to you?"

"Of course. 'Above Ground Level' and 'Above Mean Sea Level.' I—oh, hell, I see what you mean."

"Exactly. Google Earth measures the height of objects above sea level—it gives you their altitude—but Marcellus wouldn't have been able to work that out. He would have been standing on the ground close to the burial site. From there, the only thing he could measure with his *diopter* would be the heights of hills above his position, not their heights above sea level."

"You're right," Bronson said, despair in his voice, "and because we don't know what his elevation was, we're screwed."

"No, we're not. His elevation doesn't matter. Marcellus has given us height measurements for six hills, calculated from a single datum point. If the top of one hill was eight hundred feet above him and another was five hundred feet, there's a difference of three hundred feet. So what you should be looking at on Google Earth are the *differences* in height between any two hills."

"Yes, right, I see what you mean," Bronson said. "I've told you before, Angela, but I'm *really glad* you're here."

He took a sheet of paper and quickly chose two of the points on the diagram. He converted the Roman numerals into feet, using a table Angela had found in one of her books, and then worked out the difference between them.

"Now, let's see," he muttered, turning back to the laptop.

But he still couldn't find any two hills whose height difference fitted. After another hour, Angela took over for thirty minutes, but had no more luck than him.

"Frustrating, isn't it?" Bronson asked, as Angela pushed the chair back and stood up.

"I need a drink," she said. "Let's go down to the bar and drown our sorrows with copious amounts of alcohol."

"That's perhaps not the best idea you've ever had, but it's undeniably tempting," Bronson replied. "I'll just grab my wallet."

They found a vacant table in the corner of the bar. Bronson bought a bottle of decent red and poured two glasses.

"Do you want to eat in the hotel this evening?" he asked.

"Yes, why not?"

"OK. I'll just book a table."

When he returned to the bar, Angela was looking at the copy of the inscription Bronson had made. As he sat down she slid the paper across the table to him.

"There's another clue there," she said. "Something we haven't even looked at."

"What?" Bronson demanded.

Angela pointed at the wavy line that Bronson had thought looked something like a sine wave. "This is a purely functional inscription, right? No decoration of any sort. So what the hell's that supposed to be?"

"I don't know. Maybe the sea? Perhaps the northeast coast of Italy?"

Angela nodded. "You could be right, but whatever Marcellus buried had to be *really* important, otherwise why bother with the stone and all the rest? And if it *was* important, Nero wouldn't have wanted it to be stuck in a hole on the other side of the country. He'd have needed to keep it fairly close to Rome. I think that shape probably represents a line of hills, and Marcellus included it so that anyone looking for the site in the future would have something obvious that would help to identify the search area. I think that line's a deliberate marker."

"OK," Bronson said. "Finish that glass and let's get back upstairs."

Almost as soon as he sat down at the laptop he found something that might fit.

"Look at this," he said, pointing at the computer screen.

Just more than thirty miles east of Rome, between the communes of Roiate and Piglio, was a long ridge that peaked at about 1,370 meters, or 4,400 feet. The most distinctive feature of the ridge was its northeast slope, which was furrowed in a regular pattern.

"I see what you mean. It does look quite like the drawing on the side of the *skyphos*."

"That's the first thing," he said. "Now check this out." Bronson moved the cursor over the top of the ridge and noted down the elevation Google provided. Then he moved it to the end of another ridge lying almost due east, and jotted down that figure as well.

Angela picked up a pencil, quickly did the subtraction and then compared it to those they'd derived from the diagram on the *skyphos*.

"Well," she said, "it's not exact, but it's bloody close. There's an error of maybe eight percent over the Latin numbers, that's all."

"Yes, but we're using satellite photography and GPS technology, while Marcellus only had a *diopter* and whatever other surveying tools were available two thousand years ago. In the circumstances, I reckon that's definitely close enough."

"What about the other four locations?"

"Yes, I think I've found them as well. Watch."

Swiftly Bronson moved the cursor over four additional locations on Google Earth and noted down their heights, and again passed the paper to Angela to do the calculations.

When she'd finished, she looked up with a smile. "Not exact, again, but certainly within the limits you'd expect from someone using first-century surveying tools. I think you might have found it, Chris."

But Bronson shook his head. "I agree we've probably found the right area, but we still haven't pinpointed the physical location of the hiding place. I mean, the lines on the diagram cross, but not in a single point, which would have been the obvious way to locate the site. Instead they form a wide triangle."

"No," Angela agreed, "they don't intersect at a single point, but right here, in the middle of the diagram, are the letters 'PO LDA.' And between the 'PO' and the 'LDA' is a dot. That was a common device in Latin to separate words in a piece of text. Now, why put those letters again in the diagram itself? They were already carved into the top section of the stone, directly below the *'Hic Vanidici Latitant.'* If they were going to be repeated, surely they would have been placed at the bottom of the diagram, near the 'MAM'?

"But if this diagram shows the burial place of whatever Nero wanted hidden away, having *'Per ordo Lucius Domitius Ahenobarbus'* in the center of the map does make sense. In fact, it's a kind of double meaning. I think it means 'This was done on the orders of Nero' as well as 'This is the location of the burial place.' I believe those letters were placed in the middle of the diagram because the dot between the 'O' and the 'L' marks the site."

"Yes, that's as good a suggestion as any," Bronson said. "And tomorrow morning we'll drive over there and try to dig up whatever Nero ordered to be buried almost two thousand years ago."

22

Bronson had worked out that the straight-line distance between Santa Marinella and their destination was only about seventy miles, but he knew it would be more like double that by road.

"Seventy miles isn't that far," Angela said, finishing her second cup of coffee. They'd walked into the dining room at seven, the earliest time that breakfast was available.

"Agreed. On a motorway it would be an hour, but on the sort of roads we're likely to find, I reckon it's at least two hours' driving. But we've got a bunch of things to do before we get there, so it's going to take three or four hours altogether."

Bronson paid the bill and carried their bags down to the Renault Espace. His first stop was a newsagent's on the outskirts of the town, where he bought a couple of large-scale maps of the area northeast of Rome.

Five miles down the road, they found a large out-of-town commercial center and, just as Bronson had hoped, a hardware supermarket.

"Stay here," he said, "and lock the doors, just in

case. I won't be long. What size feet do you take? The continental size, I mean?"

"Forty or forty-one," she replied, "if you mean shoes."

"Shoes, feet, they're all the same."

Twenty-five minutes later he reappeared, pushing a laden cart. Angela hopped out as he approached and opened the trunk for him.

"Good lord," she said, eyeing the contents of the shopping cart. "It looks as if you've got enough there for a week-long expedition."

"Not quite," Bronson replied, "but I do believe in being prepared."

Together they transferred the equipment into the back of the Espace. Bronson had bought gloves, shovels, picks, axes, crowbars, a general toolkit, haversacks, climbing boots, flashlights and spare batteries, a compass, a handheld GPS unit and even a long towrope.

"A towrope?" Angela asked. "What do you need that for?"

"You can use it for dragging rocks or tree trunks out of the way, things like that."

"I don't like to mention it," Angela said, "but this Renault's definitely not the car I'd pick for an excursion up into the hills."

"I know. It's completely the wrong vehicle for where we're going, and that's why we're not taking it off the road. I have a plan," he said. "We're just going to use the Renault to get over to San Cesareo, on the southeast outskirts of Rome. I checked on the Internet last night, and there's a four-by-four hire center there. We'll leave the Renault somewhere in the town, and I've pre-booked a short-wheelbase Toyota Land Cruiser in your name. If we can't get up to the site in that, the only other thing we could use would be a helicopter."

*   *   *

It was approaching noon when Bronson parked the Renault Espace in a multistory parking garage in San Cesareo. Together they walked the few hundred yards back to the off-road vehicle hire center, and twenty minutes later they drove out in a one-year-old Toyota Land Cruiser which Angela had hired for two days, using her credit card.

"Was it safe, using my Visa?" she asked as Bronson pulled the Toyota to a halt in the parking bay next to the Renault.

"Probably not. The trouble is you can't hire a car *without* using a credit card. But I'm hoping we'll be long gone from here before anyone notices."

They transferred all their gear, including their overnight bags, into the Toyota, then locked the Renault, and drove away.

"That'll do nicely," Bronson muttered, spotting a couple of used-car lots on the outskirts of San Cesareo. Both looked fairly downmarket, the lots scruffy and the cars old and somewhat battered. They looked like the kind of places where cash transactions weren't simply welcomed, but insisted upon. And that suited Bronson very well.

He walked into the first one and haggled with the salesman for about twenty minutes, then drove out in a ten-year-old Nissan sedan. The paintwork had faded, and there were dents in most of the panels, but the engine and transmission seemed fine, and the tires were good.

"Is that it?" Angela asked, stepping out of the Toyota.

"Yes. I'll drive this. Just follow me and we'll sort everything else out when we get to Piglio."

The town wasn't far, and the roads were fairly clear, so they made good time. Bronson parked the Nissan in a supermarket parking lot which was well more than half full, and a few minutes later they drove away together in the Toyota.

On the way out of Piglio, Bronson pulled into a garage, went inside and emerged shortly afterward with a couple of carrier bags filled with sandwiches and bottles of water.

"Can you map-read, please?" Bronson asked. "We need a track or minor road that will take us as close as possible to the site, so we won't have to walk for miles."

The location suggested by the inscription on the *skyphos* was well off the main road, and thirty minutes later, after driving down increasingly narrow and bumpy roads, Angela asked him to stop the jeep so she could explain where they were.

"This is where we are now," she said, indicating an unnumbered white road on the map, "and this dotted line here seems to be about the only route up there."

"OK, the entrance to the track should be just around the corner."

Bronson pulled the Toyota back onto the tarmac, drove another hundred yards until he saw a break in the bushes that lined the road. He turned in through the gap and immediately engaged four-wheel drive.

In front of him, a rough but well-used track snaked up the slope.

"Looks like other jeeps have been up here," he said, "and perhaps a tractor or two as well. Hang on. This is going to be fairly uncomfortable."

The main track seemed to peter out after a couple of hundred yards, but tire tracks ran in several directions, and he picked the route that seemed to head for the high ground in front of them. He urged the Toyota up the slope and over the rutted and uneven ground for nearly another mile, until they reached a small plateau studded with rocks.

Bronson angled the jeep across toward the far side, where a low cliff rose up, and then stopped the vehicle.

"That's it," he said. "This is the end of the road. From here we walk."

They climbed out of the vehicle and looked around. Shrubs and trees grew in clumps all around them, and there was absolutely no sign of any human presence. No litter, no fences, no nothing. The wind blew gently in their faces, but carried no sound. It was one of the most peaceful places Bronson had ever visited.

"Quiet, isn't it?" Angela asked.

"Probably the only people who ever venture up here are shepherds and the occasional hunter."

Bronson turned on the GPS and marked the geographical coordinates it displayed onto the map. Then he cross-referred it to his interpretation of the diagram on the side of the *skyphos*.

"This is all a bit bloody vague," he muttered, "but I *think* we're in the right place."

Angela shivered slightly. "It's spooky. We're standing in about the same place that Marcus Asinius Marcellus did two thousand years ago," she said, gesturing toward the horizon. "The landscape we're looking at is pretty much identical to what he would have seen. You can even understand why he picked those six hills. From this spot they're the most prominent landmarks by far."

"Our problem is that we don't have any kind of detailed directions," Bronson said, "so we're going to have to check anywhere that looks a likely location. Neither these maps nor the diagram from the *skyphos* is going to be of much help to us now."

"And what do you suggest *would* be a likely location? If Marcellus buried something in the ground, there are definitely going to be no visible signs of that now, not after all this time."

"I don't think we're looking for an earth burial.

Whatever was hidden was too important for that, so I think the hiding place will be in a cave or man-made stone chamber. And the entrance would nave been covered, probably by rocks or hefty slabs of stone, so that's what we need to look out for."

II

Gregori Mandino picked up the phone on the third ring. He was expecting—and hoping—it was Pierro with the news that he'd cracked the diagram on the stone, but the caller was Antonio Carlotti, his deputy.

"Some unusual news, *capo*," Carlotti began. "You told me the Englishman and his ex-wife had probably left Italy by now to return to Britain?"

"Yes. Why?"

"We still have the Internet monitoring software running, and some relevant searches have just been reported from Santa Marinella."

"Where?"

"Santa Marinella. It's a small coastal town northwest of Rome."

"What searches?" Mandino demanded.

"More or less the same as those we detected from Cambridge. These came from a wireless network connection in a small hotel in the town. They were detailed searches for anything to do with Nero and Marcus Asinius Marcellus."

"That must be Bronson. What the hell is he *still* doing in Italy? And why is he *still* following this trail? When were these searches recorded? Today?"

"No—yesterday evening. And there are a couple of other oddities. Those searches were followed by one for a *groma*. It's an ancient surveying tool used by the Romans. And we traced other activity on the same network. Someone downloaded the Google Earth program. That's the—"

"I know what it is, Carlotti. Which areas did they look at?"

"We don't know, *capo*. Once the computer accessed the Google Earth server, we could no longer monitor its activities. The user was effectively working inside a closed system."

"I don't like the sound of this. Bronson's still in the area. He's finding out something about Roman surveying techniques, and the fact that he then went onto Google Earth might mean he's following some kind of trail. Anything else?"

"Yes. As soon as I heard about these searches I asked one of my contacts in the Santa Marinella area to find out who'd been staying in the hotel there. He called me back a few minutes ago. There were two English guests—a man and his wife—there last night, but the hotel staff didn't get their names because they paid the bill in cash. All the receptionist remembered was that they spent most of the evening in their room. And they know they used the Internet because they were charged for it. They were driving a British-registered Renault Espace and checked out early this morning."

"That confirms it, then. What did you do?"

"I tipped off one of my contacts in the *Carabinieri*. But it's the last piece of information that worries me most, in view of what happened with the scroll."

"Tell me."

"According to one of my other contacts in the *Carabinieri*, this morning a Toyota Land Cruiser was hired from a garage in San Cesareo, near Rome, by a woman named Angela Lewis, who paid for two days' hire by credit card."

"Damn," Mandino muttered.

"It looks like Bronson's following the same trail as us, though I don't understand how," Carlotti said.

"Are you sure that stone at the house hadn't been exposed before?"

"Definitely not, but somehow he must have got hold of another copy of the diagram showing the location of the burial. And if he's hired a jeep, he must have worked out where to start his search. Hang on a minute," Mandino said, as another thought struck him. "The Toyota was hired in San Cesareo this morning, you said?"

"Yes."

"Right, at least that gives us a starting point. Get the *Carabinieri* looking out for the Toyota."

"Already done, *capo*. Anything else?"

"No. Until we find out where he's heading, there's nothing more we can do."

Mandino ended the call, then dialed Rogan's number.

"Give the phone to Pierro," he instructed, as soon as Rogan answered.

"Pierro."

"Mandino. Any luck with matching the diagram?"

"Not yet, but I'm sure that with time we can—"

"We don't have time," Mandino snapped. "I've just heard that Bronson has hired a jeep from a garage over to the east of Rome, and that could mean that he's *already* deciphered the diagram. Where have you been looking?"

"Mainly to the north of the city, because I believe Marcellus owned estates in that area."

"It looks to me like Bronson's better at this than you are, Pierro, and you're supposed to be the expert. I suggest you start looking somewhere to the east of Rome, and quickly. If he finds the tomb before we do, I will be most displeased, and you *really* don't want that to happen. You know what's at stake."

23

I

"Anything?" Bronson asked, as Angela walked through the long grass toward him.

They'd been searching for about two hours and had found precisely nothing, apart from a handful of fired shotgun cartridges. At first they'd looked together, following a logical grid pattern, then split up in order to cover more ground.

"Sod all," Angela replied. "I'm fed up, hungry and thirsty. I'm taking a break."

The two of them walked back down the slope to the Toyota. Bronson opened the doors and turned on the engine, letting the welcome chill of the air-conditioning waft over them. Angela pulled out the packets of sandwiches and offered Bronson a choice.

"I'll have the chicken salad," he said, and ripped open the cellophane.

"Are you sure we're in the right place?" Angela asked, peeling apart a ham sandwich and looking with some uncertainty at the pinkish meat inside.

"Frankly, no. The dot on the diagram on the *skyphos* has to cover a fairly large area on the ground.

If someone had invented the compass and given one to Marcellus to provide accurate bearings, it would have been a hell of a lot easier. As it is, we're really stumbling around in the dark.''

"You'd really expect him to leave some sort of a marker so that he could find the exact location again if he needed to," Angela said. "All these cliffs and slopes look pretty damn similar to me."

"What kind of marker?"

"I don't know—an arrow carved on a rock, something like that."

"He might have done," Bronson pointed out, "but the mark might have weathered away to nothing over the centuries."

"That's very encouraging. Thanks."

"Let's have a drink," Bronson suggested, "and then we'll try again."

Three hours later they were still searching. They'd scoured the entire plateau from one side to the other. Bronson had climbed onto the upper slope of the feature and checked it out—but had found nothing—while Angela had clambered over the piles of irregular rocks that formed a kind of rough perimeter of the plateau itself.

Bronson was absolutely ready to call it a day and head back down the track when Angela suddenly called out to him.

"What's this?"

Bronson walked over to where she was standing, close to the low cliff that marked the upper edge of the plateau and a little way to the left of where they'd spent most of their time searching. About five feet above the ground, he could just see something that looked like a small letter "V" on a rock, maybe a couple of inches tall, but so faded and weathered that it was only when they traced the indentation with their fingers that they were sure it wasn't just their eyes deceiving them.

"Do you feel it?" Angela asked.

"I think so, yes," Bronson said, "but is it a 'V' or what's left of the letter 'M' or 'W,' or even a downward-pointing arrow? It's so weathered it could be almost anything."

Angela ran her fingertips over the rock on both sides of the indentation. "I can't feel any other letters," she said.

"There might not be any," Bronson suggested, "and I suppose a 'V' is more likely. Marcellus wouldn't have wanted anyone finding this by accident, so any marker he left would have been fairly discreet. He probably wouldn't have wanted his initials on the stone, either, but a simple 'V' for *Vanidici* makes sense to me."

"So what now?" Angela asked.

Bronson pointed down at the base of the rock face in front of them, where there was a jumble of boulders that had obviously remained untouched for years, possibly centuries. "We find out what's under that lot," he said. "Hang on here. I'll bring the jeep over."

He trotted back to the Toyota, started the engine and backed the vehicle up as close as he could to the rock face. He opened the tailgate and took out the crowbar, then inserted the tip behind one of the smaller boulders on top of the pile and levered it away from the rock. It tumbled away with a satisfying crash.

"Can I help?" Angela asked.

"No," Bronson grunted, "because these are sodding heavy rocks, and it's all I can do to shift them. But it might be an idea if you took pictures every time I moved a couple, just to document the scene."

Angela walked over to the Toyota to collect a bottle of water and the digital camera, and Bronson freed another boulder from the top of the pile. As it fell away he stared in disbelief at the rock behind it.

"Angela," he called, his voice slightly strained.

"What?"

"Forget the water," he said, "but bring the camera right away. We've found it."

Carved into the rock directly behind the boulder he'd just moved were three capital letters, protected from weathering by the stones that had covered them for centuries, and as clear and crisp as the day they were carved. "H•V•L."

" 'Hic Vanidici Latitant.' Here lie the liars," Bronson whispered softly.

In the ten minutes that followed he shifted all the boulders except for three large rocks at the base that were simply too big for him to move without using the Toyota to drag them, and he'd probably need a chain or steel cable to do so. Behind them, a flat and almost circular stone, clearly worked and with chisel marks still visible, rested against the rock face. Around its edge a kind of mortar had been used in an attempt to seal the gap.

"This is just amazing," Angela breathed. "It looks as if Jeremy got it wrong. Nobody would go to all this trouble just to hide a few books. This looks more like a tomb."

"They even tried to seal the entrance," Bronson said.

"That was probably as a precaution against scavengers, just in case Nero needed to retrieve the bodies he'd buried. He wouldn't have wanted to dig them up again only to find foxes or other animals had eaten the remains."

"And why the hell would he have needed to recover a corpse?"

"Oh, several reasons," Angela said. "The most obvious was a form of legalized robbery."

"You could rob a dead man?" Bronson asked, using a hammer and chisel to shift the sealing mortar from around the edge of the rock.

"It was rather more subtle than that. In the past, several crimes, notably treason and witchcraft, carried more severe penalties than just death. If an individual was found guilty, their entire assets could be seized by the king. There are quite a few recorded cases where corpses were dug up, dressed in fresh clothes and sat down in a courtroom to be tried for crimes like these, just because the reigning monarch wanted their lands. And, for obvious reasons, the accused couldn't speak in his own defense, so the verdict was usually a foregone conclusion."

"Bizarre."

"That's one word for it. How are you doing?"

"I've shifted the mortar," Bronson said, "so now I should be able to move it."

He slid the point of the crowbar behind the top of the stone and levered upward. There was a cracking sound and the top of the flattened rock moved an inch or two away from the face of the cliff.

"That's broken the seal," Bronson said, "but I'm going to have to use the Toyota to move it out of the way. It's too heavy for me to shift by myself."

He walked over to the Toyota and returned in a few moments with the heavy-duty towrope. He used the crowbar to lever the rock farther away from the cliff, so that he could drop the rope down behind it, secured the clip and then attached the other end to the towing hitch of the jeep.

"Keep well clear," he instructed Angela, "in case the rope snaps. In fact, you'd better get in the car with me."

He started the Toyota and moved it slowly forward until he'd taken up the slack in the rope, then began increasing the tension steadily. For a few seconds nothing happened, except that the noise of the Toyota's big diesel rose to a roar, and then the vehicle lurched forward.

"That should have done it," Bronson said. He turned off the engine and climbed out.

But when they looked behind the jeep, it was immediately obvious that it hadn't. The towrope had snapped cleanly in two just behind the tow hitch, and when they walked back to the rock face they saw that the round stone had barely moved.

"Shit. I should have brought a steel cable. I don't see how we're going to shift that."

"Maybe we should have rented a Toyota fitted with a winch," Angela said, staring at the stone. "Hang on a second, Marcellus wouldn't have had steel cables and turbo-charged diesels up here, would he? But he would still have had to be able to get back inside the tomb."

"Yes, presumably. So what?"

"So that's why the sealing stone is round. You've been trying to drag it away bodily. We should be able to roll it sideways."

"Genius," Bronson said. He crouched down at the side of the stone and began clearing away the earth and debris. Then he stood back.

"Bingo," he said. "There's a kind of channel cut in the rock here, like a track for the stone to roll along."

Bronson climbed over the rocks, to the other side of the stone, rammed the crowbar down at its base and levered. With surprising ease, the stone moved slightly, rolling an inch or two down the channel.

"Keep going," Angela urged.

Bronson heaved again and the stone rolled about a yard, so that they could both see exactly what lay behind it. Now visible was the entrance to a small cave, the opening too smooth and regular to be natural. Though they'd successfully removed the sealing stone, the three large rocks still partially obstructed the entrance.

"You can't move those big boulders," Angela stated.

"Not easily, and maybe not at all," Bronson agreed, "but I reckon I can crawl in through the gap."

"Suppose the roof caves in when you get inside?"

"Angela, that cave's stood here for the last two thousand years without collapsing, so as long as it can hold itself together for another ten minutes I should be fine."

"Well, just be careful."

"I'm always careful. Now pass me the flashlight and the camera, please."

Bronson slid the camera into his pocket and shone the flashlight inside the opening.

"Can you see anything?" Angela asked.

"Not much. I'll have to get right inside."

Bronson lay flat on his stomach, held the flashlight out in front of him, and crawled slowly inside the cave.

II

The small cavern was around ten feet long, seven feet wide with a curved roof about four feet in height at the center, tapering to a little more than half that at the sides. Bronson crouched down and looked around him, the beam of the flashlight dancing over the rough-hewn stone walls and the dusty floor.

It was immediately clear that Angela was right: the "liars" weren't books or documents. Lying along each side of the cave were two skeletons, both of them obviously very old and tremendously fragile. Tiny scraps of coarsely woven cloth still clung to some of the bones. The skull of one skeleton was lying about a foot from the neck vertebrae.

"What is it?" Angela called.

"Hang on," Bronson said, for a moment hardly trusting himself to speak. He was overwhelmed by an incredible sense of age, of time standing still. He reached out and touched the chisel marks on the stone walls. They were as sharp and clear as if they'd been made yesterday, though he knew the mason had died two thousand years earlier.

He sniffed the air. Faintly reminiscent of a church or cathedral, the cave had a dry, musty smell, overlaid with a faint hint of mushrooms. Really, really old mushrooms.

And then he looked down at the two pathetic piles of bones, feeling the hairs begin to rise on the back of his neck.

"There are two skeletons in here," he called, looking carefully at the detached skull. "Just dust and bones, and really old. But I don't think either of them died of old age."

"You mean they were murdered? How can you tell?"

"Hang on while I take some pictures. I daren't touch them—they'd probably crumble away to nothing if I did."

Bronson placed the flashlight on a rock so that its beam shone down the long axis of the cave and began to snap pictures of the interior of the chamber. He began with a panorama of the entire structure, photographing the floor, roof, walls and entrance, before moving on to the remains of the bodies. He took several of each one, first of the entire skeleton and then numerous close-up shots, concentrating on the skull and neck bones, especially a clearly severed vertebra on the first skeleton. On the second he took several pictures of the wrist and ankle bones, where the remains of rusted nails still protruded.

Bronson shivered, but not with cold. He looked around the tomb—a tomb as old as time itself—almost

fearfully, then stared down at the bones again, bones
that had been lying there undisturbed for two millennia. The bones of two men. One beheaded, the
other crucified.

III

The pilot swung the helicopter around so that its nose
pointed into the wind, then lowered the collective and
settled the aircraft on the ground. He turned slightly
in his seat and nodded to Mandino.

"Go," Mandino said, and gestured to his right,
where the four-by-four they'd spotted from the air was
parked about sixty yards away across the rough
ground.

One of the men slid open the side door and jumped
down to the ground. He reached back inside the helicopter, picked up a Kalashnikov assault rifle and released the safety catch. He waited for his companion
to appear, and then both men began running quickly
toward the target, their weapons at the ready.

Mandino and Rogan watched their approach from
the safety of the chopper. They hoped that Bronson
and the woman had led them directly to the tomb.
Mandino was impressed by their tenacity. In other circumstances, he might even have been prepared to let
them live.

The two men split up when they got to about thirty
yards from the vehicle, so as to approach it from different sides, and to offer two targets if it came to a
firefight. Mandino watched critically as they closed in,
but the result wasn't what he had expected. Both of
his men almost immediately slung their assault rifles
over their shoulders, peered inside the jeep, and then
jogged back to the helicopter.

The moment they were strapped in and wearing
headsets, Mandino fired questions at them.

"What happened?"

"It's the wrong jeep," one of them replied, panting slightly. "We were looking for a Toyota Land Cruiser, right?"

"Yes," Mandino replied.

"Well, that's a short-wheelbase Nissan Patrol. It looks similar, but it's a different vehicle. That one has a rifle rack in the back and the hood's cold. It probably belongs to a hunter or some local farmer who drove up here this morning and who's still out in the hills somewhere."

"Shit," Mandino muttered, and turned back to the pilot. "Get us airborne again. They must be up here somewhere."

With the scene recorded on the data card inside his camera, Bronson looked around the cave again. He couldn't understand why a couple of rotting corpses—even if one of them had been crucified and the other beheaded—could have been that important to the Roman Emperor. Dead bodies were not exactly a rare commodity in ancient Rome, so either there had to be something *really* special about these two victims, or there was something else hidden in the cave.

Bronson slipped the camera back into his pocket and shone the beam of the flashlight around the chamber, looking carefully at every inch of the rock. It wasn't until he surveyed the interior for a second time that he saw, at the far end of the cave, what looked like a worked rock, its sides and top squared off. Maybe that carried an inscription or something that would explain what he'd found.

He crawled across the floor, but when he reached it, he found that the stone was completely blank. It looked as if someone had flattened the top surface in preparation for an inscription, but had never finished the job.

It was only as he began backing away that he noticed a line of darker material running around the
lower part of the stone. He crawled back to study it
more carefully. He soon realized that what he'd assumed was a large worked rock was actually one flat
stone resting upon another, larger, stone like a lid.
The gap between the two had been sealed with what
looked to him like some kind of thick wax.

Bronson's pulse began to race. The two stones obviously formed a kind of safe, and whatever was hidden
inside the cavity had been secreted away from the
elements for two millennia. That made sense. It wasn't
just the bodies themselves that were important: it was
whatever had been buried with them.

He took a couple of pictures of the two stones, then
tried lifting off the upper slab. It was stuck fast. He'd
need to increase his leverage if he was going to be
able to move the stone lid.

Bronson crawled back to the mouth of the cave and
called out to Angela.

"I've found something else," he said, "but I need
the crowbar to get inside it."

"Hang on a minute."

For a few seconds there was silence, then Bronson
heard the clatter of steel on rock and the end of the
tool appeared in the narrow entrance to the chamber.

"Thanks." He crawled back to the far end of the
cave and slid the end of the crowbar into the sealing
wax. But the wax, or whatever it was, was a lot
tougher than it looked. He tried again, this time ram-
ming the tool firmly between the two slabs, then tried
to lever off the upper stone.

It remained obstinately in place. He was going to
have to break the wax seal around most of the edge
of the stone before he would be able to move it. He
guessed that the seal was airtight, which at least meant
that whatever was inside the stone "safe" would prob-

ably be in good condition. Bronson jammed the crowbar into the wax again, wrestled it sideways and then pulled it out.

There was a sudden rush of air from inside the object, almost like an exhaled breath, the sound of a faint sigh, and Bronson leaned back in alarm. Then he shook himself. It was just trapped air, obviously.

He began repeating the process all the way around the edge of the stone.

"There's another one," the pilot shouted, and again Mandino stared through the windshield in the direction the man was pointing.

Close to a rock face a couple of miles away was the unmistakable shape of an off-road vehicle. It was the third they'd seen, and Mandino was beginning to wonder if he'd overestimated Bronson. Maybe he'd hired the Toyota in preparation for the search, but hadn't yet identified the location where he was going to start.

"Check it out," Mandino ordered, and the pilot turned the helicopter toward the distant vehicle and began descending.

Bronson had cracked the seal around most of the stone, and again inserted the crowbar under the front edge of it and pressed down. This time the stone shifted very slightly. He increased the pressure on the crowbar gently. With a sudden crack, the wax seal finally surrendered its grip and the stone lid moved sideways and tumbled to the floor of the cave.

Bronson reached into the shallow recess. He pulled out two wooden tablets about the size and shape of modern paperback books, and a very small scroll. The latter was remarkably similar in appearance to the one they'd recovered from the *skyphos,* but he'd never seen anything like the tablets before. Each consisted of two flat pieces of wood, one of the long sides secured with a strip of what looked like a kind of wire as a rudimentary hinge. Small holes had been driven through the other three edges, and pieces of thread were looped through these, apparently as a means of preventing the object from being opened. All three relics appeared to be in excellent condition.

He took out his digital camera, checked that he still had plenty of space on the data card, and took several more pictures.

Outside the cave, Angela was leaning against a rock, her face upturned toward the sun.

She suddenly became aware of an unmistakable throbbing sound and peered around the rock. Still some distance away, but undoubtedly heading straight toward them, was a helicopter.

She scrambled down to the cave entrance and yelled inside.

"Chris! There's a chopper heading straight for us."

"There's someone moving down by those rocks," the pilot said, "next to the jeep. It looked like a woman."

"Excellent," Mandino muttered. "Now we've got them." He turned in his seat and nodded to Rogan. "Get ready," he ordered.

Bronson grabbed the two booklike objects and the scroll, and backed away hurriedly. At the entrance, he passed them to Angela, then wriggled out as quickly as he could. As he emerged into the daylight, he could see the helicopter flaring as it prepared to land about fifty yards away.

"Get in the car," he yelled.

They ran across to the Toyota and climbed inside. Angela reached over to the backseat, grabbed a towel she'd brought along and carefully wrapped the relics in it, then put the bundle in the glove box in front of her. Bronson started the engine, slammed the gear lever into first and powered the big vehicle across the plateau and away from the cave.

"For Christ's sake, land this thing," Mandino shouted, as he watched the Toyota roar away from the rock face.

He wasn't worried that Bronson had already driven off—he knew that the paved road was more than a mile away and that the chopper could easily catch up with the fleeing vehicle long before it got there. His first priority was to see what the Englishman had found.

"I can't," the pilot said. "The ground's so uneven I can't risk putting it down. There are rocks everywhere. The best I can do is bring it to a low hover so you and your men can jump out."

"Don't explain it to me, you idiot! Just do it."

The pilot lowered the collective lever until the right-hand skid touched the ground, then kept the aircraft level in a hover.

Mandino ripped off his headset and climbed out, followed by Rogan and the two *picciotti*. The four men ran across to the exposed cave entrance.

" *'Hic Vanidici Latitant,'* " Mandino said, staring at the three letters carved above the mouth of the chamber. If they'd frightened Bronson off before he'd managed to search the cave thoroughly, that would be the end of the matter. If the Englishman had taken anything away from the site, they'd have to stop him. And they'd have to do it before he got off the hillside. "You," he ordered, pointing at the smaller of his two men, "get inside and find out what's in there."

Obediently, the man stripped off his jacket and shoulder holster. Rogan handed him a flashlight, and he wriggled inside the cave.

Less than thirty seconds later, his head popped out again.

"There are only two skeletons in here," he called out. "Very old."

"Forget them," Mandino ordered. "I know all about them. What you're looking for are books or scrolls, anything like that."

The man vanished back inside the cave, but reappeared after a few minutes.

"There's nothing like that in there," he said, "but in the far corner there's a kind of stone box, just a hollowed-out rock with another flat stone used as a lid. It's empty, and there're some marks in the dust inside it. I think there was definitely *something* in it, but it's been taken out."

Mandino cursed. "Right, back to the chopper," he ordered. "We've got to stop Bronson, no matter what it takes."

24

Angela was strapped in tight, but had turned around in her seat to check behind them.

"Any sign of them?" Bronson yelled, over the roar of the engine and the crashing of the suspension as the Toyota bounced over the rutted and uneven ground.

"Nothing yet," she shouted back. "How far to the main road?"

"Too bloody far. That chopper'll overtake us any time now."

The helicopter lifted off the moment the four men belted themselves in, and turned immediately to the west, heading toward the edge of the plateau and the route Mandino knew Bronson must have taken to get back to the main road.

He turned around in his seat. "We *must* stop them before they reach the road," he said, and pointed to the man sitting beside Rogan. "You're the best shot. When we get in front of them, use your Kalashnikov, and try to disable the jeep. Aim for the tires and the engine if you can. If it won't stop, then hit the cab, but I'd prefer the two of them alive if possible."

The man took his AK-47 assault rifle, removed the

curved magazine and cleared the round from the breech. He checked that the cartridges were loaded properly, slammed the magazine back home and cocked the weapon.

"I'm ready," he said.

The other man reached over, slid the side door of the helicopter backward and locked it in the open position.

In the front seat, Mandino leaned forward, searching the terrain below the helicopter for the fleeing off-road vehicle. Then he pointed ahead, at a plume of dust rising from the rough and barely visible track that snaked down the side of the hill in front of them.

"There it is," he yelled.

The pilot nodded, pitched the nose of the helicopter farther down and accelerated, heading toward a point lower on the hillside.

Bronson was driving harder than he'd ever done in his life. He had no doubt who was in the helicopter. And he was equally certain exactly what would happen to them if they didn't get away.

Angela grabbed at Bronson's arm and pointed out to the left, where the helicopter was passing alongside, about fifty yards away at low level, effortlessly overtaking them.

"There it is," she shouted.

Bronson took his eyes off the road for a bare second. The chopper was close enough for him to see that one of the men was holding an assault rifle.

"Shit, they've got a Kalashnikov," he yelled. "Hold on tight."

The helicopter descended in front of them, dropping out of sight behind a clump of trees.

"Are they landing?" Angela asked, frantically.

"Probably not. The pilot will try to position the

chopper to block the track down to the road, so that the man with the Kalashnikov can shoot out our engine."

"So what can we do?"

Bronson slammed the brakes hard, then swung the wheel to the left. "We get off the track," he said.

He steered the vehicle well away from the rutted pathway, picking the best route he could between the trees and bushes, all the time keeping the jeep heading down the hill toward the road.

Bronson's guess had been right. The helicopter pilot had dropped the aircraft down almost to the ground, and it was straddling the track, its right side and the open door facing up the hill, the man with the Kalashnikov watching for his target.

But after a couple of minutes the Toyota still hadn't appeared.

"He must have turned off the track," Mandino said. "Lift off again and find him. This time don't lose sight of him when you descend."

In a few seconds the pilot spotted the jeep again. The Toyota was following an erratic and unpredictable course down the hill. The vehicle was swerving from side to side as Bronson drove around trees and other obstacles on the hillside.

"Drop down over there," Mandino ordered, pointing toward the base of the hill, where trees grew thickly and the track snaked through a gap between them. Bronson would have to drive through there if he was to get down to the road.

"Do you want me to land?" the pilot asked.

"No. Just get into a low hover and stabilize the aircraft. My man will need a steady platform to give him the best chance of hitting the target."

As the Toyota careered down the hill toward them, the helicopter swooped down. The Toyota was less

than a hundred yards away when the man with the
Kalashnikov began to fire single shots.

"Showtime," Bronson muttered as he saw the muzzle
flashes. He swerved the Toyota even more violently to
make it as difficult a target as possible. Then he took
his hand off the steering wheel just long enough to
pass Angela the Beretta pistol he'd taken from Mandino's bodyguard. It was smaller than the Browning
and he thought it would be easier for her to manage.

"Hold it in your right hand," he shouted over the
noise of the engine, "but keep your finger off the trigger." He glanced sideways quickly. "Now take hold
of the top of the pistol, that bit that's serrated, pull it
straight back and then let go."

There was a distinctive metallic clicking sound as
Angela pulled back the slide and released it, feeding
a cartridge into the chamber of the Beretta.

"Now look at the back of the pistol," Bronson continued, still weaving the Toyota unpredictably across
the rough ground. "Is the hammer cocked?"

"There's a little metal bit here pointing backward,"
she said, looking at the weapon.

"That's it. Now, holding it in your right hand, move
your thumb up until you find a lever on the side."

"Got it."

"That's the safety catch," Bronson said. "When you
want to fire the pistol, click that down. And keep it
pointing out of the window all the time, please," he
added, as Angela moved the weapon slightly in his
direction.

"God, I've never fired a gun before."

"It's easy. Just keep pulling the trigger until you've
emptied the magazine."

When they were about fifty yards from the helicopter, Bronson lowered the window on Angela's side of
the Toyota.

"Start shooting," he yelled.

Angela aimed the Beretta at the helicopter and flinched as she pulled the trigger.

Bronson knew it would be an absolute miracle if she hit the chopper. Firing a relatively inaccurate weapon from a vehicle traveling at speed over a plowed field was hardly conducive to accurate shooting. But helicopters are comparatively fragile, and if they could make the pilot think there was a possibility of a bullet damaging his craft, he might lift off and out of danger. In the circumstances, it was the best they could hope for.

As Angela fired her first shot, a bullet smashed through the windshield and passed directly between them and out through the Toyota's tailgate.

The shattering glass unnerved them both. Bronson swerved hard to the left, then right again, the Toyota barely staying upright.

Angela screamed and dropped the pistol. The weapon fell into the gap between her seat and the door. She scrambled to grab it, but couldn't reach.

"Christ, sorry," she shouted. "I'll have to open the door to get it."

"Don't. It's too late now. Brace yourself."

They had no options left. Bronson accelerated the Toyota directly toward the helicopter.

Mandino was shouting at the man with the Kalashnikov who, despite the closeness of his target, was still finding it difficult to hit it.

The gunman fired two more shots at the rapidly approaching vehicle, and then the action locked open on the AK-47 as he fired the last round. He pressed the release to disengage the empty magazine, grabbed another one and slammed it home, but in those few seconds the Toyota had covered another ten yards, and actually seemed to be accelerating. He cycled the action to chamber a round, selected full auto and brought the sights to bear again. At that range—now probably less than twenty yards—he simply couldn't miss.

The pilot watched the approaching jeep with increasing alarm. He lost his nerve when the Toyota got within about fifteen yards. He hauled back on the collective lever, gave the engines full power and the chopper leapt into the air.

At precisely the same moment, in the back of the aircraft, the gunman squeezed the trigger and sent a stream of 7.62-millimeter bullets screaming directly at the jeep. His aim was good, but the helicopter's lurch into the air took him by surprise and the shells plowed harmlessly into the ground.

"What the hell are you doing?" Mandino screamed at the pilot.

"Saving your life, that's what. If that jeep had hit us, we'd all be dead."

"He was playing chicken. He'd have swerved at the last moment."

"I wasn't going to take that chance. I've seen what's left after helicopter crashes," the pilot snapped, as he turned the chopper toward the main road, again following the plume of dust kicked up by the Toyota.

As the Toyota roared underneath the helicopter, Bronson accelerated even harder and turned back onto the rough track.

"Jesus Christ," Angela muttered. "I really thought you were going to hit it."

"It was close," Bronson conceded. "If he hadn't pulled up, I was going to try to swerve around the front of him."

"Why not the back?" Angela asked. "There was more room behind him."

"Not a good idea. There's a tail rotor there. If you

hit that, you end up looking like sliced salami. By the way," he added jokingly, "I hope you chose the fully comprehensive insurance option when you hired this. There seem to be a few holes in it now."

Angela smiled briefly at him, then peered behind them. "The helicopter's heading straight for us again."

"I see it," Bronson said, looking in the external rearview mirror. "But now we're only a couple of hundred yards from the road."

"And we'll be safe then?" Angela didn't sound convinced.

"I don't know, but I hope so. The last thing these guys need is publicity, and shooting up a car on a public road from a helicopter is a pretty good way of guaranteeing plenty of media interest. I'm hoping they'll just follow us and try to take us down when we finally stop. In any case, there's nowhere else we can go."

At the end of the track, Bronson glanced both ways, then swung the Toyota onto the road and floored the accelerator pedal. The diesel engine roared as the turbo kicked in and the big jeep hurtled down the road toward Piglio.

Mandino was hoarse from shouting instructions.

"Thanks to your total incompetence," he yelled at the pilot, "they've reached the road."

"I can take them there," the gunman said. "They'll have to drive in a straight line, and they'll be an easy target."

"This is supposed to be a covert operation," Mandino snapped. "We can't start blasting away with automatic weapons at a vehicle on the public roads." He tapped the pilot on the arm. "How much fuel have you got?"

The man checked his instruments. "Enough for about another ninety minutes in the air," he said.

"Good. We'll slow down and follow them. Sooner

or later they'll have to stop somewhere, and then we'll take them."

"I can't see the helicopter," Angela said, craning her neck at the window of the Toyota. "Perhaps they've given up."

Bronson shook his head. "Not a chance," he said. "It's somewhere behind us."

"Can we outrun it?"

"Not even in a Ferrari," he replied, "but I hope we won't have to. If we can just make it to Piglio, that should be enough."

Traffic was light on the country roads, but there were enough vehicles around, Bronson hoped, to deny their pursuers any opportunity to drop the helicopter down to the road to try to stop them. Then he looked ahead and pointed at a road sign.

"Piglio," he said. "We're here."

The helicopter was holding at five hundred feet. As the Toyota entered the town below them, Mandino instructed the pilot to descend farther.

"Where is this?" Mandino asked.

"A place called Piglio," Rogan said. He was tracking their location on the topographical chart, in case they needed to summon help from the ground.

It was a small town, but they couldn't risk losing their quarry in the side streets. The Toyota had been forced to slow down in the heavier local traffic, and the helicopter was almost in a hover as the men watched carefully.

"Keep your eyes on it," Mandino ordered.

"Nearly there," Bronson said, as he turned the Toyota down the side street, following the signs for the supermarket. Seconds later he swung the jeep into the parking lot, found a vacant parking bay, stopped the vehicle and climbed out.

"Don't forget the relics," he said, as Angela followed him.

She tucked the towel and its precious contents carefully into a carrier bag. "Got the camera?" she asked.

"Yes. Come on." Bronson led the way to the main entrance of the supermarket, where several shoppers were staring up at the helicopter, now in a hover about a hundred yards away.

"Land as close as you can," Mandino told the pilot.

"I can't put it down in the parking lot—there's not enough open space—but there's a patch of wasteland over there."

"Be as quick as you can. Once we're out, get back into the air. Rogan, stay in the aircraft and keep your mobile close."

The pilot swung the helicopter around to the right and descended toward the area of grass that adjoined the supermarket parking lot.

"The Nissan's right there, isn't it?" Angela said.

"Yes, but we can't just climb in it and drive away. That would be a dead giveaway. We'll wait here."

Bronson pulled Angela to the left-hand side of the entrance hall and carefully watched the helicopter.

"They'll have to land to let someone out to follow us on foot," he said, "and they can't put the chopper down out there in the parking lot—it's too crowded. Right, there he goes." He watched the helicopter move away and start to descend.

"We walk, not run," he said, squeezing Angela's hand. Without even a glance at the aircraft, they crossed to where Bronson had parked the Nissan. He unlocked it, climbed in and started the engine, then reversed out of the parking bay and drove the old sedan car unhurriedly away from the building.

Thirty seconds later Mandino and his two men ran

into the parking lot, heading toward the Toyota, the helicopter hovering above them.

But Bronson was already driving away, heading for Via Prenestina and Rome.

An hour later, after a careful search of the parking lot and the supermarket, Gregori Mandino was forced to face the unpalatable truth: Bronson and the Lewis woman had obviously escaped. The Toyota had been abandoned in the parking lot, and was already attracting attention because of the very obvious bullet holes in its windshield and bodywork. They'd peered in the back window and seen the tools and equipment that were still there. One of the men had stuck his knife blade into both front tires to ensure that their quarry definitely wouldn't be able to drive it away.

The three men had checked everywhere inside the supermarket, then extended their search to the surrounding streets and shops—and even the few cafés, restaurants and hotels—but without result.

"They could have had an accomplice waiting here for them," one of the men suggested. "So what do we do now?"

"It's not over yet," Mandino growled. "They're still somewhere here in Italy, in my territory. I'm going to find them and kill them both, if it's the last thing I do."

25

"We have to get an expert to look at these," Angela said.

They'd driven back to the Italian west coast and booked a twin room in a tiny hotel near Livorno. After a couple of drinks in the bar, and a very late dinner, they'd gone back up to their room. Bronson had plugged in his laptop and transferred the photographs to it from the data card in his camera.

He burned copies of the pictures he'd taken in the tomb onto four CDs. He gave one to Angela, put two of the others into envelopes to post back to his and Angela's addresses in Britain the next day, and kept one himself.

Only then did they unwrap the three relics Bronson had pulled out of the tomb. Angela spread towels on the small table in their bedroom, pulled on a pair of thin latex gloves and carefully transferred the three objects to the table.

"What are they, exactly?" Bronson asked.

"These two are diptychs. That's a kind of rudimentary notepad. Their inner surfaces are covered in wax, so somebody could jot down notes, and then simply erase what had been written by scraping something across the surface of the wax.

"But these are very special," she went on. "You see this?" she asked, pointing at a small lump of wax clinging to a thread looped through a series of holes pierced in the edges of the wooden tablets. The thread had broken in several places on both relics, but Angela hadn't attempted to remove it or open either of the diptychs.

Bronson nodded.

"The thread is called a *linum* and the holes are known as *foramina*. To prevent the tablets being opened, the thread would be secured with a seal, as this has been. That was usually done with legal documents as a precaution against forgers."

"So we've recovered a couple of first-century legal documents."

"Oh, these are more than that, much more. This seal is, I'm almost certain, the imperial crest of the Emperor Nero. Have you any idea how rare it is to find an unknown text from that period of history in this kind of condition? That wax seal around the stone in the cave seems to have preserved these almost perfectly. This is like the tomb of Tutankhamun—it's that unusual."

"Tutankhamun without the gold and jewels, though," Bronson said, looking more closely at the diptychs. "They both look a little tatty to me."

"That's just the paint or varnish on the outside. The wood itself seems to be in almost perfect condition. This is a *really* important find."

"Aren't you going to look inside them?" Bronson asked.

Angela shook her head. "I've told you before—this isn't my field. These should be handed to an expert, and every stage of the opening recorded."

"What about the scroll? You could have a look at that. You can read enough Latin to do that, can't you?"

"Yes," Angela said doubtfully. "I can try translating some of it, I suppose."

With hands that weren't quite steady, she took the scroll and slowly, with infinite care, unrolled the first three or four inches. She stared at the Latin text, the ink seemingly as black as the day it had been written, and read the words to herself, her lips moving silently as she did so.

"Well?" Bronson demanded.

Angela shook her head. "I can't be sure," she said, distractedly. "It can't be right—it just can't."

"What can't? What is it?"

"No. My translation must be wrong. Look, we have to find someone who can handle the relics profession- ally and translate them properly. And I know just the person."

II

"It's all been a bit of a shambles, Mandino, hasn't it?" Vertutti asked, his voice dripping scorn. The two men were meeting again—at the same café as previously— but this time the balance of power had changed.

"If I understand you correctly," Vertutti continued, "you actually had the relics within your grasp, and the Englishman at your mercy, but you somehow managed to let him escape with them. This debacle hardly in- spires much confidence in your ability to bring the matter to a satisfactory conclusion."

"You need not worry, Eminence," Mandino said, with a confidence that was only slightly forced. "We have several possible leads to follow, and you shouldn't underestimate the difficulties this man Bron- son faces. I know from my sources inside law enforcement that he has no valid passport, so he can't leave Italy by air or sea. Details of the vehicle he's driving have been circulated to all European police forces, and staff at the border crossing points told to look out for it. The net is closing in on him, and there's nothing he can do about it."

"Suppose he decides not to leave Italy?"

"Then tracing him will be even easier. We have eyes everywhere."

"I hope you're right," Vertutti said. "You must make sure he doesn't escape." He got up to leave, but Mandino motioned him back to his seat.

"There's still the matter of the bodies," he said. "You know their identities, obviously, so what do you want us to do about them?"

"The bodies, Mandino? What bodies? Ask any Catholic where those two men are buried and he'll tell you that the tomb of one man is right here in Rome and the bones of the other were sent to Britain in the seventh century."

"Sent by Pope Vitalian, Cardinal, the author of the Codex. He *knew* those bones weren't what he said they were. Vitalian would never have given away genuine relics."

"That's pure conjecture."

"Maybe, but we both know that the tomb in Rome doesn't hold the body the Vatican claims. What we've already found proves that, and now you *know* it's not true."

"It's true as far as the Vatican is concerned, and that's all that matters. Our position is that the bodies you found are exactly what the inscription above the tomb stated—they're the bones of liars—and of no interest to the Mother Church. And now the documents have been taken out of the cave, there's no proof whatsoever of what you're suggesting. Take some men up to the plateau and destroy the bones completely."

III

"So now we've got to drive all the way to Barcelona?" Bronson asked. "You can at least tell me why."

They were in the Nissan sedan, heading out of Livorno toward the French border. It was going to be a long drive, mostly because Bronson was determined to stick to the minor roads wherever he could, to avoid any possible roadblocks. There were more than twenty roads crossing the French–Italian border and Bronson knew the Italian police couldn't possibly mount a presence on every one, and would probably have to concentrate on the autostradas and main roads.

In truth, he wasn't too concerned about being stopped, because nobody knew that he was driving a Nissan. The police would be looking for him in a Renault Espace, and that car was tucked away in a corner of a parking lot in San Cesareo.

"About ten years ago," Angela replied, "just after I'd started work at the British Museum, I did a twelve-month stint in Barcelona at the Museu Egipti, working with a man named Josep Puente. He was the resident papyrologist."

"And what does that mean?"

"Papyrology is a generic term for the study of ancient texts written on a whole range of substances including parchment vellum—that's the skin of sheep and goats—leather, linen, slivers of wood, wax tablets and potsherds, known as *ostraca*. I suppose the discipline became known as papyrology simply because the most common writing material that's survived *is* papyrus. Josep Puente is a renowned expert on ancient texts."

"And I presume he can read Latin?"

Angela nodded. "Just like poor Jeremy Goldman, if you specialize in this field, you end up with a working knowledge of most of the ancient languages. Josep can read Latin, Greek, Aramaic and Hebrew."

Angela fell silent, and Bronson glanced across at her. "What is it?" he asked.

"There's another reason I want to go there," she said.

"Yes?"

"I didn't tell you what I read in the scroll, because I simply can't believe it. But if Josep Puente comes up with the same translation as I did, the museum would be the ideal place to announce the find to the world. He has the credibility and experience to be believed, and that's going to be important, because you have no idea what kind of opposition we'll face if we go public. Men with machine guns would be the least of our worries."

Bronson glanced at her again. "Tell me what you think you translated," he asked.

But Angela shook her head. "I can't. I might be wrong. In fact, I really hope I am. You'll have to wait until we get to Barcelona."

IV

Antonio Carlotti was not in the best of tempers. His boss, Gregori Mandino, was consumed by this ridiculous quest to track down the English couple and the relics they'd managed to find up in the hills near Piglio, but the bulk of the work involved seemed to have fallen on Carlotti's shoulders.

He was the man who'd had to supervise the Internet monitoring and related searches. He was the person whom Mandino had told to run down all the biographical details of Christopher Bronson and Angela Lewis, and who'd had to deduce where they were likely to go next. Mandino just demanded results and then made his own plans accordingly, usually with Rogan in tow.

To call Mandino's pursuit "single-minded" was to understate the case. He seemed to be letting all his other responsibilities slide and, as the Rome family *capo,* he had plenty of other things he should be doing. The quest appeared to be almost personal to him, and the one thing Carlotti had learned since he'd become a member of the *Cosa Nostra* was that you *never* let things get personal.

The bodyguard who'd been wounded at the property near Ponticelli was a good example. The Englishman, Bronson, had called an ambulance and then driven away from the house, and the man had been taken to a surgical hospital in Rome. But for Carlotti, a bodyguard who got himself shot was no use. He knew the man. He even liked him, but he'd failed in his duty, and that was enough. The two men Carlotti had sent to the hospital had distracted the police guard and then killed the wounded man, messily but quickly, before he could be properly interviewed by the *Carabinieri.* That was what Carlotti meant by not getting personal.

He was wondering what, if anything, he should say to Mandino next time they met when his cell phone rang.

"Carlotti."

"You don't know me," the voice said, "but we have a mutual acquaintance."

"Yes." The Italian was somewhat cautious.

"This concerns the Codex."

"Yes?" Carlotti said again, now on surer ground. "How can I help? My colleague has already left for Barcelona."

"I know. He gave me your number before he went. We need to meet. It's very important—for both of us."

"Very well. Where and when?"

"The café in the Piazza Cavour, in thirty minutes?"

"I'll be there," Carlotti said, and ended the call.

"So, how can I help you, Eminence?" Antonio Carlotti asked, as Vertutti sat down heavily in the seat opposite him.

"I think it's more how I can help you," Vertutti said. He leaned forward and clasped his hands under his chin. "Do you believe in God, Carlotti?"

Whatever Carlotti had expected, this wasn't it. "Of course. Why do you ask?"

Vertutti continued, ignoring the question. "And do you believe that the Holy Father is God's chosen representative on earth? And that Jesus Christ died for our sins?"

"Actually, that's three questions, Cardinal. But the answer's the same to all of them—yes, I do."

"Good," Vertutti said, "because that's the crux of the problem I face. Gregori Mandino would have answered 'no.' He's not simply godless: he's a committed atheist and a rabid opponent of the Vatican, the Catholic Church and everything they stand for."

Carlotti shook his head. "I've known Gregori for many years, Eminence. His personal beliefs will not prevent him from completing this task."

"I wish I shared your confidence. How much do you know about the quest he's undertaken?"

"In detail, very little," Carlotti replied, cautiously. "I've mainly been involved in providing technical support."

"But you *are* his second-in-command?"

"Yes. That's why you have my number."

Vertutti nodded. "Let me explain exactly what we have become involved in. This is a quest," he began, "that commenced in the seventh century under Pope

Vitalian. A quest that could affect the very future of the Mother Church herself.''

"And this *Exomologesis* is what, exactly?" Carlotti asked, having listened to Vertutti's explanation of the Vitalian Codex.

"It's a forgery," Vertutti explained, embarking on the wholly fictitious story he'd worked out the previous evening, "but a very convincing one. It's a document that purports to prove that Jesus Christ did not die on the Cross. Now," he added with a smile, "the faith of true Christians is strong enough to dismiss such a fabrication, and the Vatican can demonstrate the fallacy of the document itself, but the very existence of this scroll is enough to raise doubts about our religion. With people increasingly turning away from the Church, we simply cannot afford to have any such doubts expressed."

Carlotti looked puzzled. "But I thought Gregori had recovered the *Exomologesis.* I understood that was what had been concealed in the house outside Ponticelli."

"Mandino removed it from the property, but we found additional text at the foot of the scroll. It said a further copy of the document had been prepared, together with two diptychs which would provide proof of the validity of the scroll. Now, we know that these diptychs, like the scroll itself, must be forgeries, but we simply cannot afford for the contents of these documents to be made public. These three additional relics have been stolen by the Englishman Bronson and his ex-wife."

Carlotti still looked confused. "I know about Bronson, and I understand what you're saying, but Gregori will hopefully recover these objects when he reaches Barcelona."

Acting on Mandino's instructions, Carlotti had run exhaustive checks on the backgrounds of both Bronson and the Lewis woman. The only possible contact either of them had with academics based in Europe was Angela Lewis's previous work with Josep Puente, which was why Carlotti had ordered two of his men to watch the Museu Egipti in Barcelona, with detailed descriptions of what Bronson and Lewis looked like, and why Mandino was already on his way to Spain.

"That," Vertutti said, leaning forward earnestly to make his point, "is what worries me. Unfortunately, Mandino and I have never seen eye to eye over this matter, and he's told me that, once he's recovered these relics, he intends to make them public. With his religious—or rather anti-religious—views, that didn't surprise me, and he seems unconcerned that his action will do irreparable harm to the Church."

"So what can I do?" Carlotti asked.

Vertutti leaned even farther forward, lowered his voice and made the suggestion he'd been working on for the last three days.

Ten minutes later, Vertutti shook hands with Carlotti and headed back toward the Vatican. As he walked, he noticed he was sweating slightly, and it was not entirely due to the gentle heat of the Rome evening.

v

For a short while after Vertutti had left, Antonio Carlotti sat lost in thought. It had been, he reflected, a most unusual conversation. He'd noticed the slight traces of perspiration on Vertutti's forehead as the senior churchman worked his way through the lies he was telling. Carlotti's statement about only providing technical support was, of course, completely untrue: he knew just as much about the *Exomologesis* as Mandino did. But he'd guessed that he'd stand a much better chance of learning exactly what Vertutti was up to if he played dumb, and his decision had been amply vindicated.

Now all he had to do was decide whether to simply pass on what he'd learned to Mandino—which was the obvious and logical thing to do—and leave him to deal with Vertutti on his return to Rome, or do something else. Something that would, strangely enough, achieve exactly what Vertutti wanted, but at the same time benefit Carlotti himself. It was a big step to take, and before he acted he needed to be certain he could pull it off.

Finally, he pulled out his cell phone and made a long call to one of his most trusted men, a call that included the most specific—and highly unusual—instructions.

26

Two men walked out of Terminal B at Barcelona airport carrying only hand luggage and joined the queue for a taxi. The names in their Italian passports were Verrochio and Perini, and they were almost identical in appearance: tall and well-built, wearing dark suits, sunglasses with impenetrable black lenses shielding their eyes. When they reached the head of the line, they climbed into a black and yellow Mercedes cab and, as the driver pulled away from the rank, Perini gave him an address on the western edge of the city in heavily accented but fluent Spanish.

When they arrived at their destination, Perini leaned forward. "Wait here, please," he said. "I'll be about ten minutes, then we need to go into Barcelona itself."

Verrochio stayed in the car while Perini got out, walked a short distance down the street and entered the foyer of an apartment building. He checked a small piece of paper on which a few numbers were written, then pressed one of the buttons on the intercom. Lights flared on and he stared unblinking into the lens of a camera. A couple of seconds later the electric lock buzzed, and he pushed open the door and walked inside.

Perini took the elevator to the seventh floor, walked down a short corridor and knocked on a door. He heard the sound of movement inside and was aware of an unseen eye assessing him through the security peephole. The door opened and he found himself face-to-face with a swarthy, heavily built man wearing jeans and a T-shirt.

"Tony sent me," Perini said, in Italian, and the man beckoned him inside, locking the door behind him.

The man led the way into one of the bedrooms and opened a built-in wardrobe. He pulled out two black leather briefcases and placed them both on the bed.

"I can offer you Walthers or Glocks," he said, snapping open the locks on both cases.

Perini bent down to look at them. In one were two Walther PPK semiautomatic pistols in nine-millimeter, and in the other a pair of Glock 17s in the same caliber. Both cases also contained one spare magazine for each pistol, two boxes of fifty rounds of Parabellum ammunition and a couple of shoulder holsters.

Perini inspected the four pistols carefully, then replaced them in the briefcases.

"I'll take the Glocks," he said, finally.

"No problem. You'll need them for one day, I was told?"

"One day, perhaps two," Perini agreed.

"Is there sufficient ammunition?"

"More than enough."

"Good. Call me on this number when you want to return them." The man handed over a slip of paper.

Perini slipped it into his wallet. Then he snapped the locks shut on the briefcase containing the Glocks, shook the man's hand and left the apartment.

"Take us to the Plaça Mossèn Jacint Verdaguer,"

he instructed the taxi driver, as he leaned back in his seat.

The driver nodded. In a few minutes the vehicle was heading for the center of the city on the Avinguda Diagonal, the major road that divides Barcelona in two.

On arrival at the *plaça*, Perini paid the driver, including a modest tip, and the two men climbed out and stood waiting on the pavement until the taxi vanished into the stream of fast-moving traffic.

Verrochio pulled out a street map of Barcelona.

"We need to get over there," Verrochio said, pointing. They waited at the pedestrian crossing for the lights to change, then walked across the Diagonal and headed south down the Passeig de Sant Joan, before turning right onto the Carrer de Valencia.

"That'll do," Perini said, as they reached the junction with the Carrer de Pau Claris. Near the corner was a street café with chairs and tables outside. They stopped and took seats that offered them a clear view of the entrance of the Museu Egipti on the opposite side of the road.

When the waiter appeared, Verrochio practiced his Catalan by ordering two *cafés amb llet* and a selection of pastries, and settled down for what was probably going to be a long wait.

Once their coffees and food had been served, Perini nodded to his companion. "You go first."

Verrochio walked through the café to the toilet, carrying the briefcase, and returned in about five minutes. Ten minutes or so later, Perini did exactly the same thing. Anyone looking closely may have noticed that the briefcase appeared to be lighter once Perini sat down again at the table. This was because it was now almost empty, containing only forty-odd rounds of nine-millimeter ammunition. The two Glock pistols and loaded spare magazines were tucked in the shoulder holsters the two men were now wearing under their light jackets.

"This could be a complete waste of time, you know," Verrochio said, his eyes invisible behind his designer shades. "They might never turn up."

"On the other hand, they might arrive in the next ten minutes, so look sharp," Perini replied.

But after an hour, the strain of watching, with nothing to show for it, was beginning to tell on both of them.

"I'll read for an hour while you watch, then we'll change over, OK?" Perini said. "And let's grab another drink next time that waiter comes by."

"Sounds good to me," Verrochio replied, and shifted his chair slightly to ensure he had an unobstructed view of the museum entrance.

II

Getting to the museum wasn't easy. It was the first time Bronson had been to the city, and, once they'd left the main roads, they got lost in the maze of one-way streets.

"This is it," Angela said finally, looking up from her map to check the street signs as Bronson swung the Nissan around a corner. "This is the Carrer de Valencia."

"At last," Bronson muttered. "Now, if we can just find somewhere to park the bloody car . . ."

They found a space in one of the multistory parking garages near the museum and walked across the road toward the small gray-white building. It didn't look much like a museum to Bronson, who had a mental picture of stone steps and marble columns. Instead, the building was only about the width of a house, and

in fact didn't look unlike a large townhouse. Above
the central double doors were three floors of windows,
fronted by balconies with metal railings.

"Not very big, is it?" Bronson remarked.

"It's not meant to be. It's a small, specialist unit,
not a huge place like the Victoria and Albert, or the
Imperial War Museum."

Inside, they paid the six-euro admission charge. Angela walked over to the reception desk and smiled at
the middle-aged woman sitting behind it.

"Do you speak English?" she asked.

"Of course," the receptionist replied. "How can I
help you?"

"We'd like to see Professor Puente. My name is
Angela Lewis and I'm a former colleague of his. Is he
in the building?"

"I think so. Just a moment." She dialed a number
and held a short conversation in high-speed Spanish.
"He remembers you," she said with a smile, as she
replaced the receiver. "He's working upstairs in the
Dioses de Egipto room, on the first floor, if you'd like
to go straight up."

"Thanks," Angela said, and led the way toward
the staircase.

Almost as soon as they reached the first floor, a
short, dark-haired swarthy man trotted toward them,
his arms held wide in a gesture of welcome.

"Angela!" he called, and wrapped himself around
her. "You've come back to me, my little English
flower!"

"Hello, Josep," Angela said, smiling while disentan-
gling herself from his grasp.

Puente stepped back and held out a hand toward
Bronson, his movements quick and bird-like. "Forgive
me," he said, with a barely distinguishable accent,
"but I still miss Angela. I'm Josep Puente."

"Chris Bronson."

"Ah." Puente stepped back, his eyes flicking from one to the other. "But I understood that you two were . . ."

"You're right," Angela said, sighing and looking at Bronson. "We *were* married, then we got divorced and I've frankly no idea what we are now. But we need your help."

"And might that be because of what you're carrying in that black bag, Chris?" Puente asked.

"How do you know that?" Bronson demanded, astonishment in his face.

"It's not difficult to work out. Most people don't carry overnight bags when they tour a museum. I've noticed you've not let go of the bag, and you've been very careful not to knock it against anything. So, there's probably something inside that's fragile, and possibly valuable, that you need an opinion about. What have you brought for me to look at?"

Angela's face clouded briefly. "I'm not sure. We need to explain the sequence of events to you before we show you what's in the bag. Could we go to your office or somewhere private?"

"My office hasn't got any bigger since the last time you were here, my dear. I've a better idea. Come down to the basement. There's plenty of room in the library."

Angela remembered that the basement of the Museu Egipti housed a private library created by the museum's founder, Jordi Clos. She told Chris about it as they walked through the modern, open-plan public rooms where white, square-section pillars and stainless-steel handrails contrasted with the classic, timeless beauty of the three-thousand-year-old exhibits.

Puente led the way down the stairs, past the *"Privat"* signs and into the library.

"Now," he said, when they were seated, "tell me all about it."

"Chris has been involved in this from the start, so it's probably better if he explains what's happened."

Bronson nodded, and started at the beginning, telling the Spaniard how Jackie Hampton had died in mysterious circumstances at the house outside Ponticelli, his trip to Italy with Mark and what had happened while they were there, and subsequent events in Britain.

"The crux of this whole saga," he said, "appears to be the two inscribed stones. Until the Hamptons' builders uncovered the Latin inscription—"

" *'Hic Vanidici Latitant,'* " Angela interjected.

" 'Here lie the liars,' " Puente translated immediately.

"Exactly," Bronson continued. "Until the builders knocked the plaster off the wall above their fireplace, nobody was interested in the house or what it contained. But as soon as Jackie started searching the Internet for a translation of that phrase, well . . . you know the rest." He still didn't like to think about how she and Mark had died.

He explained how Angela had worked out the meaning of the second, Occitan, inscription, how they'd recovered the *skyphos* and the scroll from below the floorboards.

"And you've brought that for me to look at?" Puente asked eagerly.

Bronson shook his head and described how the scroll had been taken from them by the two Italians, and that the leader of the pair had claimed it dated from the first century A.D. and contained a secret that the Church wanted to keep hidden.

"So if you haven't got the scroll, what have you got?" Puente asked.

"We're not quite there yet," Bronson said. He told Puente how Angela had examined the *skyphos* and realized it was a reproduction, and guessed that the pattern on the side of the vessel was more than just an abstract decoration. Then he described their discovery of the ancient tomb up in the hills near Piglio, and what was inside it.

"Two bodies?" Puente interrupted.

"Yes," Bronson replied. "We have the photographs that I took inside the tomb, which I can show you. I believe that one of the bodies was beheaded and the other crucified. Above the entrance to the cave the letters 'HVL' had been carved, which we assume meant *'Hic Vanidici Latitant.'* "

Puente was lost in thought. "Why are you so sure that's how they died?" he asked, finally.

"On the larger of the two skeletons, one of the neck vertebrae was cut in half. As a police officer, I know that the vertebrae are very strong, and I can't think of any circumstances in which one of these bones could split like that after death. Beheading is the only scenario that makes sense."

"And the second body?"

"That was easy. The two heel bones were still pinned together by the remains of a thick nail, and there were traces of rusted metal in both wrists."

Puente looked shocked. "Are you sure?"

"I've got the pictures to prove it," Bronson reminded him, "and we could certainly find the tomb again—assuming that the Italians haven't blown it up."

"And you've still got the items that you retrieved from the cave?" Puente asked, a distinct tremor in his voice.

"There are two diptychs and a scroll," Angela said, as Bronson opened the leather case and began to unwrap the bundle that held the relics. "The diptychs are sealed, but I've looked at the scroll. That's the reason we brought them to you. I can't quite believe what I read."

Bronson placed the final part of the bundle on the desk and carefully unrolled it while Puente pulled on a pair of thin white cotton gloves. The moment the relics were revealed, he drew in his breath sharply.

"Dear God," he muttered, "these are in excellent condition, the best I've ever seen."

He placed a large sheet of cartridge paper on the table and arranged a couple of desk lights on either side of it. He picked up one of the diptychs and placed it reverently in the middle of the paper, then bent over it with an illuminated magnifier.

"I thought that might be Nero's imperial seal," Angela suggested, and Puente nodded.

"You're absolutely right," he said. "It is. And that makes this very rare and extremely valuable." He looked up at Angela. "You've no idea of the contents?"

"No. I only looked at the scroll."

"Very well. Some of the *linum* has disintegrated, so I can remove the sections of thread without damaging the seal."

"This *is* quite urgent, Professor," Bronson interjected.

"You must appreciate that proper examination of relics like these will take months or even years," Puente said, "but I can certainly run some very quick visual checks."

He unlocked a climate-controlled safe behind the table and took out three boxes containing scrolls and diptychs, and another two holding just fragments of papyrus. Then he placed the scroll and the second diptych on the cartridge paper, selected four diptychs and a couple of scrolls from the boxes and placed those on the paper as well.

"Comparative paleography is a very complex and meticulous science," he said, "but a quick comparison with these extant and dated relics might help indicate a likely period."

Five minutes later he looked up. "This scroll is very early, probably first century A.D., and the diptychs look as if they're from about the same period. I'll know better when I've opened them, and I'll also be able to tell you what the contents are."

He walked over to a cupboard and returned to the table carrying a camera. He took several photographs of the first diptych, then carefully removed the securing thread, placing the lengths beside the object. Then slowly, and with meticulous care, he opened the diptych. Before doing anything else, he photographed it.

Bronson leaned forward to stare at the relic but the result was disappointing. The two wax-covered surfaces looked like muddy-brown layers of paint, covered in faint scribbling.

But Puente's face lit up as he eagerly scanned the object.

"What is it?" Angela asked.

The Spaniard glanced up at her, then resumed his scrutiny of the diptych. "As I said, it may be years before we're certain of their age and authenticity, but to me this appears to be a genuine first-century relic. It looks like a *codex accepti et expensi.* That," he went on, glancing at Bronson, "was what the Romans called their records of payments and expenses. A kind of receipt book," he added.

"Is that all?" Bronson asked, feeling a stab of disappointment.

Puente shook his head, his eyes bright with excitement. "A receipt book makes for pretty dull reading, usually," he said, "but this one's rather different. It appears to be a list of payments—quite substantial payments, in fact—made by the Emperor Nero himself to two men over a period of several years. The recipients aren't named, but they have signed their initials against each amount. The initials they've used are 'SBJ' and 'SQVET.' Do they mean anything to you?"

Bronson shook his head, but Angela nodded, her face pale. "That's what I wanted to ask you about. I think 'SBJ' was 'Simon ben Jonah' and 'SQVET' was *'Saul quisnam venit ex Tarsus,'* or 'Saul who came from Tarsus.' "

"Who's rather better known to us today," Puente remarked, "as St. Paul."

"Hang on," Bronson interrupted. "That Italian told us the scroll we found in the *skyphos* was written by someone who signed himself 'SQVET.' Are you saying that was *St. Paul*?"

"I . . . I think so," Angela replied, her face pale.

"So who's 'Simon ben Jonah'?"

"Well," she said, almost reluctantly, "it could be St. Peter." She turned to Puente. "Is it genuine?"

"It's difficult to say for certain," Puente replied. Bronson noticed his hands were shaking. "All three of these relics could be fakes. Very early, and very good, first-century fakes, but fakes nevertheless. But if they *are* genuine, they could relate directly to the bodies in the tomb."

"How?" Bronson asked.

"You found two bodies," Puente stated, "one beheaded, and the other crucified. The very early history of Christianity is incomplete and often contradictory, and little is known about the fate of some of the early saints. However, St. Peter is believed to have been martyred in Rome by Nero in about A.D. sixty-three. The date's uncertain, but the manner of his death is believed to have been by crucifixion—upside-down, apparently—as he didn't feel worthy enough to occupy the same position on the cross as Jesus."

"But even I know that the bones of St. Peter have been found in Rome," Bronson interrupted.

Puente smiled briefly. "What people *know* is often very different from the truth. But you're quite right. The remains of St. Peter *have* been found in Rome— at least twice, in fact.

"In 1950 the Vatican announced that bones had been found in a crypt underneath the high altar of the Basilica of St. Peter, and conclusively identified them as those of the saint. But pathologists later identified the remains as parts of the skeletons of two different men, one much younger than the other, the bones of a woman plus bones belonging to a pig, a chicken and a horse.

"You might think, after such an embarrassing fiasco, that the Vatican would be more cautious about making such claims, but a few years later yet another group of bones was found in more or less the same area. These, too, were confidently proclaimed by the Vatican to be the mortal remains of this apostle. Another one of his tombs has been found in Jerusalem.

"The point is that *nobody* knows much about St. Peter, mainly because he only appears within the pages of the New Testament, and no contemporary writings mention him at all. Despite that, he's generally regarded by the Roman Catholic Church as the first pope. He was the son of a man named John or Jonah, hence his biblical name of Simon ben Jonah or Simon bar Jonah, but he was also known as Peter, Simon, Simon Peter, Simeon, Cephas, Kepha and, sometimes, as 'the fisherman' or the 'fisher of men.'"

Puente looked at Angela and Chris steadily. "No one actually knows if St. Peter ever lived. And if he did, nobody knows where his body was buried, or whether his remains have survived."

He spread his hands. "Until today, that is."

27

In the café down the street, Verrochio nudged his companion and pointed as Gregori Mandino and Rogan got out of a car on the north side of the Carrer de Valencia.

"And about time, too," Perini said. He stood up, tossed a ten-euro note onto the table to cover the cost of their last few drinks, and walked away from the café.

"Well?" Mandino demanded, as Perini stopped beside him.

"They're both inside the museum," Perini replied. "They arrived about three-quarters of an hour ago. Bronson was carrying a black leather case."

The four men crossed the road and entered the museum together.

"So what you and Angela are saying is that we found the last resting place of St. Peter, and that one of the skeletons—the one that had been crucified—was his. Is that correct?"

Puente shook his head helplessly at Bronson's question. "I'm a Catholic," he said, "and I've always accepted the teachings of the Church. I know there's been confusion about the bones they found in Rome, but I've always assumed that the apostle's remains—if they still exist—would be found *somewhere* in the city." He looked down at the diptych, then up again at Bronson. "Now, I'm not so sure."

"So is that the secret—the lie?" Bronson asked. "Is that what the Italian meant? That St. Peter's bones were *not* buried somewhere in Rome?"

"No," Puente said decisively. "Neither the existence nor the location of the bones would make any real difference to the Church. He must have been talking about something else."

"What about the second body?" Bronson demanded. "You're not going to tell me that was St. Paul?"

"It's at least possible. Again, it's not known exactly when he died, but it's almost certain he was executed on Nero's orders in A.D. sixty-four or sixty-seven."

"Paul was a Roman citizen," Angela added, "and so he couldn't have been crucified. Beheading would be the obvious method of choice, and that does seem to fit with the bodies we found."

"But why would Nero have been paying these two men money? And why would he then have had them both killed?"

"That," Puente said, "is the nub of the matter. Perhaps the second diptych or the scroll will provide some answers."

Tenderly, he closed the first diptych and placed it, together with the fragments of *linum,* in a cardboard box on the table. He reached for the second tablet and repeated the process of opening it, again taking photographs at every step.

"Now this," he said, when the relic was open on the table in front of him, "is different. This appears to be a confidential order, issued by Nero himself, giving specific instructions to Saul of Tarsus—he was also sometimes known as 'the Jew from Cilicia.' It's signed 'SQVET,' so presumably Paul accepted the assignment."

Puente sat back in his chair and rubbed his face with his hands. "This is unbelievable," he muttered.

"Take a look at the scroll, Josep," Angela suggested quietly. "That's what frightened me."

Puente moved the diptych to one side, picked up the small scroll and carefully unraveled it. He moved the magnifier over the text to begin translating the characters.

When he finished, he looked up at Angela, his face as pale as hers. "What do you think this means?" he asked.

"I only read the first few lines, but it referred to the 'Tomb of Christianity,' which held the bones of 'the convert' and 'the fisherman.' "

Puente nodded. "This scroll," he said, "was apparently written by a Roman named Marcus Asinius Marcellus."

"We worked out that he was acting as Nero's agent in some secret operation," Bronson said.

"Exactly," Puente replied. "From what I've read here, it looks to me as if he was pressured into acting by the Emperor—"

"That makes sense," Bronson interrupted. "We think Nero saved him from execution when he was involved in a plot to forge a will."

"Well, according to the scroll," Puente said, in a voice that was far from steady, "the author states explicitly that Christianity was a sham, nothing more than a cult started by Nero to serve his own purposes, and based on a handful of lies, and that these two men—the men we now know as St. Peter and St. Paul—were in the pay of the Romans."

II

"Check the whole building," Mandino instructed Rogan. "Start with the roof terrace and work your way down. I'll stay on the ground floor in case they're somewhere here. When you see Bronson and Lewis, leave Perini and Verrochio to cover them, and come and fetch me."

"Understood."

Rogan led the way up to the deserted roof terrace and worked his way back down, checking each level carefully.

"No sign of them, *capo*," he reported, when he returned to the ground floor. "Could they have slipped away somehow?"

"Not through the front entrance," Perini answered. "We were both watching it carefully. They definitely didn't come out again."

"There's a basement with a private library," Mandino told them, checking a museum information leaflet. "They must be down there. Let's go."

It was almost closing time as Mandino led the way toward the basement entrance. As they approached, a guard came over to them, raising his hand to stop them.

"Take him, Perini," Mandino murmured, as the man walked toward them, "but do it quietly, then lock the doors. We don't want any interruptions."

Perini drew his pistol and jammed it into the man's stomach.

"Verrochio," Mandino said, turning away, "take the receptionist. Rogan, secure the shop."

Under the silent pressure of Perini's Glock, the guard walked over to the main doors, which he closed and locked. Verrochio escorted the receptionist over to the museum shop, the sight of his pistol ensuring her silent cooperation. Two late visitors and the shop assistant stood quaking at the far end of the shop, their arms in the air, while Rogan covered the three of them. Perini produced a handful of plastic cable ties and handed them to Verrochio, who expertly tied up all five people, making them sit on the floor and lashing their hands behind their backs and tying their ankles together.

"There's hardly any money in the till," the assistant said, her voice quavering.

"We're not interested in the takings," Perini told her. "Keep quiet—that means no shouting for help—and you won't be harmed. If any of you yell out, I'll shoot. And I don't care who gets hurt. Do you understand?"

All five nodded vigorously.

Josep Puente had always taken pride in his faith. He was a Roman Catholic, born and raised. He attended mass every Sunday. But what he'd read that afternoon in the two diptychs and the scroll had turned his world upside down. And he really didn't know what he should do about it. He did know that the three objects—whether elaborate and convincing forgeries or genuine relics—were probably the most important ancient documents that he, or anyone else, would ever see.

When they heard the sound of approaching footsteps, none of them paid much attention. Then a man stepped through the doorway, flanked by three others, each holding a pistol.

"So, Lewis, we meet again," Mandino said, his voice cutting through the silence. "And where's Bronson?"

For several seconds nobody said a word. Angela and Puente were sitting on opposite sides of the library table, the scroll and the diptychs in front of them.

Bronson was out of sight, walking between the library shelves. The moment he heard Mandino speak, he drew the Browning pistol and crept back toward the center of the room.

He risked a quick glance around a freestanding bookcase to check exactly where the intruders were, then took four rapid strides across the room. Two of the gunmen saw him, but before they could react he'd cocked the Browning—the metallic sound unnaturally loud in the tomb-like silence—seized the back of Mandino's collar with his left hand and placed the barrel of the pistol firmly against his head. Bronson pulled the man backward, away from his armed companions, the pistol never wavering.

"It's time," Bronson said, "to find out what the hell's going on, starting with why you're here, Mandino."

He felt the man give a start of surprise.

"Yes, I know exactly who you are," Bronson said. "Tell your men to lower their weapons, otherwise the Rome family of the *Cosa Nostra* is going to be looking for a new *capofamiglia.*"

"The bodyguard, I suppose?" Mandino's voice was surprisingly calm. "Put your weapons away," he told his men, then turned his head slightly toward Bronson. "I'll tell you what I know, but it will take some time."

"I'm not in any particular hurry," Bronson said. "Angela, can you bring a couple of chairs over here? Put one behind the other, back to back."

Bronson pushed Mandino onto the front chair, and he sat down on the one behind, resting the muzzle of the Hi-Power on the chair back, so that it was just touching his captive's neck. Rogan and the other two men took seats between Mandino and the table where Angela and Puente were sitting.

"This story started," Mandino said, "in first-century Rome, but the Vatican's involvement only began in

the seventh century. I'm nothing to do with the
Church, but my organization—the *Cosa Nostra*—was
contracted to resolve this problem on its behalf. The
Mafia and the Vatican are two of the longest-lived
organizations in Italy, and we've had a mutually bene-
ficial relationship for years."

"Why don't I find that surprising?" Bronson murmured.

"In the first century A.D., the Romans had been
fighting the Jews for decades, and the constant military
campaigns were weakening the empire. Rather than
initiate a massive military response, Emperor Nero decided to create a new religion, based on one of the
dozens of messiahs who were then wandering about
the Middle East. He chose a Roman citizen called
Saul of Tarsus as his paid agent. Together they decided that a minor prophet and self-proclaimed messiah named Jesus, who had died in obscurity
somewhere in Europe a few years earlier after attracting a small following in Judea, was ideal. Nero
and Saul concocted a plan that would allow Saul to
hijack the fledgling religion for his own purposes.

"Saul would first achieve a reputation as a persecutor of Christians, as the followers of Jesus were becoming known, and then undergo a spiritual
'revelation' that would turn him from persecutor into
apostle. This would allow Saul to insinuate himself
into a position of power and leadership, and he would
then direct the followers—mainly Jews, of course—
into a path of peaceful cooperation with the Roman
occupying forces. He would tell them to 'turn the
other cheek,' 'render unto Caesar' and so on.

"In order to achieve this fairly quickly, Saul needed
to 'talk up' Jesus into far more than he ever was in
real life. He decided that the obvious option was to
portray him as the son of God. He concocted a variety
of stories about him, starting with the virgin birth and

finishing with him rising from the dead, and proclaimed these to be the absolute truth.

"To help him spread the word, he recruited a man named Simon ben Jonah—a weak and gullible man—who had known Jesus personally, but had regarded him as nothing more than just another prophet. Simon—who later became much better known as St. Peter—also entered Nero's employment, but toward the end of his life he began to believe his own stories. A third man—Joseph, son of Matthias, better known as Flavius Josephus—later joined them, but as far as we know he *was* a true believer. All three men preached Saul's version of events, attempting to recruit Jews who, because of their teachings as Jesus's 'disciples,' had become peace-loving people who no longer wished to fight the Romans."

"Are you seriously trying to tell us that Nero founded Christianity as nothing more than a device to keep the Jews quiet?" Angela whispered.

"That's precisely what I'm telling you. In the seventh century A.D., Pope Vitalian found a draft of a speech Nero never gave to the Roman Senate. It explained in detail exactly how Christianity began, and that it was an idea suggested by Nero himself. Pope Vitalian was appalled at what he read and began what would be a lifelong search for any other documents that might support or—hopefully—repudiate this horrific claim."

"And he found something," Bronson suggested.

"Exactly. In a bundle of uncataloged ancient texts he found a scroll that turned out to be a copy of what Vatican insiders began calling the *Exomologesis*. The name Vitalian gave to this document was the *Exomologesis de assectator mendax,* which translates as 'The confession of sin by the false disciple.' It was an admission that Nero's statements were true, and was handwritten by Saul."

"Dear God. So what did Vitalian do?" Angela asked.

"Precisely what the Church has been doing ever since: he hid the evidence. He prepared a document—now known as the Vitalian Codex—that explained what he'd discovered, and included the copy of the *Exomologesis*. The Codex also included one other piece of information derived from Nero's draft speech: it stated that the bodies of Saul and Simon ben Jonah had been buried in a secret location after their respective executions, a location that Vitalian referred to as the 'Tomb of Christianity.' He left instructions that each new pope, as well as a handful of carefully selected senior Vatican officials, was to be shown the Codex.

"But the *Exomologesis* that Vitalian had found was obviously a copy, specifically prepared for Nero, and there was a short note on it to that effect. The Pope ransacked the Vatican archives and every other document source that he had access to, but could find no trace whatsoever of the original scroll. A search was started for the relic, and the quest has been running ever since. Vitalian also instructed that the *Exomologesis* was to be destroyed as soon as it had been found, for the eternal good of the Church.

"Ever since the seventh century, each new pope has been initiated into the secret of the *Exomologesis* within the first four weeks of his papacy, but only once has any pope made a pronouncement about it, such was its power. In the early sixteenth century, Leo X, a Medici whose papacy ran from 1513 to 1521, made the somewhat enigmatic statement *'It has served us well, this myth of Christ.'* That one sentence has been the subject of speculation for the last five hundred years.

"The Vitalian Codex is held in the Apostolic Penitentiary—the most secure document repository in the whole of the Vatican—in a safe in a locked room inside another locked room. The official responsible for the document is the Prefect of the dicastery of the Congregation for the Doctrine of the Faith. He has custody of the relic, and normally only a handful of carefully selected senior cardinals from that Congregation are even aware of its existence."

"What did they think happened to the original scroll?" Bronson asked.

"Senior Vatican officials believe that the *Exomologesis,* and the stone that Marcellus had carved, disappeared during the chaos following Nero's expulsion from Rome, and passed through unknown hands before eventually being acquired by the Cathars. The scroll and the stone subsequently became the principal and most important items in the so-called Cathar 'treasure' spirited out of Montségur in 1244 during the Albigensian Crusade. And from that date until an English couple named Hampton began to restore a house they'd bought in Italy, both the scroll and the stone simply vanished."

Bronson took a deep breath. So this was why the woman he loved and his best friend had both died. The story had the unmistakable ring of truth, and provided cogent answers to almost all their questions. But there was one obvious matter that Mandino had glossed over.

"How did you know about the tomb up in the hills?"

"There was a postscript on the original *Exomologesis,* the scroll that had been hidden in the *skyphos.* It stated that two diptychs—relics that would prove what the *Exomologesis* stated—and another scroll had been buried with the two bodies. It also stated that the location of the tomb could be deduced from the 'stone Marcellus created.' That was why the Cathars guarded the stone so zealously, even though they had no idea how to decipher the diagram on it. All I had to do then was follow your trail, Bronson."

"But how do you know all this," Angela asked, "if you're not a member of the Vatican?"

"I was extensively briefed on the history of the quest by the last Prefect of the dicastery of the Congregation for the Doctrine of the Faith," Mandino replied.

"But why would a senior cardinal and member of the Roman Curia reveal all this information to someone outside the inner circle of the Vatican? And especially to a member of the Mafia?"

"Simply because they needed my help to find the *Exomologesis,* and I refused to give it until I knew exactly what the situation was."

Silence fell in the library for a minute or so as Angela, Bronson and Puente digested what they'd heard.

"Let's be clear about this," Bronson said at last. "What we're involved in here goes a long way beyond a mere matter of lost relics. Those three items on the table over there have the ability to topple the very foundations from under the Roman Catholic Church. If they're genuine, Christians all around the world could wake up one morning to find that their faith has been callously betrayed by the Vatican for nearly fifteen hundred years. Even if it could be proved that they're fakes, there would always be doubts and conspiracy theories about them, just like those surrounding the Turin Shroud. So the question is: what should we do with them?"

"*My* instructions are quite clear," Mandino replied. "I'm an atheist, but even I can see the incalculable damage that would be done to the Catholic Church and every other Christian religion if knowledge of their contents leaked out. For the sake of countless millions of believers around the world, these relics are simply too dangerous to be allowed to survive. They *must* be destroyed."

Bronson glanced around the room. Surprisingly, Puente nodded agreement, and even Angela looked undecided.

Suddenly Perini lunged across the room and grabbed Angela by the arm, spinning her around so that her body was between him and Bronson. In a fluid movement he drew his Glock and pressed it into the side of her neck, almost exactly mirroring Bronson's position behind Mandino.

Puente stepped forward and raised his arms in a calming gesture.

"Please, everyone, please," he said. "There's no need for bloodshed. No scroll or diptych, no matter how old or what text it contains, is worth a single human life." He stepped back to the table, picked up the scroll and the diptychs and held them above his head.

"We all now know exactly what these documents purport to be, and the destructive power of the information they contain," he continued. "I know the circumstances are far from normal, but can we please take a vote? What should we do with them? Angela?"

Perini jabbed her sharply with the pistol, and she answered hesitantly. "We should preserve them. Whether they're genuine documents or forgeries commissioned by Nero, they're relics of immense importance."

Puente nodded. "Chris?"

Bronson thought of Jackie, lying dead on the stone-flagged hall. Of Mark murdered in his apartment. And of Jeremy Goldman dying of terrible injuries in some London street. They had all died to preserve these relics. "We should keep them," he said, "obviously."

Puente looked down at Mandino. "We already

know your views," he said, and turned toward Rogan. "What do you think?"

"We destroy them," Rogan said. "Verrochio?"

The man standing beside him nodded. "Burn them."

"That's three to two who've voted to destroy them," Puente said. "You, sir." He turned to Perini, who was still using Angela as a human shield. "What's your decision?"

"Destroy them."

"I'm very much afraid," Puente said, "that I agree with the majority. We must think of the greatest good of the greatest number." He looked around the room. "It grieves me even to contemplate destroying objects so ancient, and so important, but in these unique circumstances I can genuinely see no other option. Mr. Mandino, if these three relics cease to exist, will that mark the end of your interest in this matter?"

"Yes. My instructions are to ensure they're destroyed."

"And if that is done, what will happen to those of us who've seen the relics, and who know what they contain?"

"Nothing, I give you my word. Without the objects, there's no proof of their contents," Mandino said.

Puente nodded. He seemed, Bronson noted, to have comprehensively taken control of the situation.

Puente stepped behind his desk and removed the data card from the camera he'd used. "All the pictures on this card are of these objects," he said. Taking a large pair of scissors, he cut it into four pieces. "Now I'll destroy the relics themselves. I'll do it right now, with all of you as witnesses, willing or not."

Puente pointed across the library at the side wall near the entrance door, and every eye followed his gesture. "That red box controls the smoke detectors and the fire alarm," he said. "Before I can burn these, somebody has to switch off the system, otherwise the sprinklers will cut in."

"I'll do it," Rogan said. He walked across to the box and flicked a couple of switches.

"Papyrus burns very well," Puente said, sorrow evident in his voice, "so this won't take long."

He placed a square steel plate on his desk, then picked up the scroll. He produced a cigarette lighter and held the flame to one end of it. Within a matter of seconds the tinder-dry papyrus was being consumed, and soon there was nothing left but a pile of ash. Puente opened the first of the diptychs and held the flame of the lighter against the inscribed wax until it dripped and melted onto the steel. The wood failed to catch, so he took a small hammer and with a few blows reduced it to dust and splinters. Then he repeated the process with the second diptych.

"That's it," he said, with a halfhearted attempt at a smile. "The world of organized religion is safe for all eternity."

For a moment or two nobody moved, as if the enormity of Puente's actions had turned them all to stone. Then suddenly Perini pushed Angela to one side, lifted his pistol and shot Rogan through the heart. Then he swung the weapon around and fired a second bullet straight into Mandino's chest.

28

I

"No!" Angela screamed, as Bronson instinctively dived to one side.

Mandino staggered backward and fell to the ground in a lifeless heap. When Bronson looked up, both Perini and Verrochio were aiming their pistols straight at him. He had no option but to drop the Browning.

Perini stepped forward and picked up the weapon, then he and Verrochio holstered their Glocks.

"What the hell's going on?" Bronson demanded.

"We were told to carry out a cleanup operation," Perini said. "Just in case you didn't know, Rogan"— he pointed at the body on the floor—"was responsible for killing your friends, and the *capo*"—he gestured at the other corpse—"gave the orders."

"But the scroll and the diptychs have been destroyed. Why did you have to kill them?" Angela asked.

"We had orders from Rome to tie up *all* the loose ends. Be grateful that you're still alive. Despite what he told you, Mandino intended to kill all three of you, and probably the handful of people in the shop as well."

"What are you going to do with us?" Angela asked. "We've read what was written on the scroll and in the diptychs."

"It doesn't matter what you read or what you know," Perini said dismissively. "Without the relics, nobody will believe you, and the only evidence left is that." He pointed at the desk and the sad pile of wood splinters and ash that was all that remained of the scroll and diptychs. "You won't see us again," he said, then he and Verrochio turned and walked away.

For several seconds nobody spoke, then Josep Puente stepped forward and put his arms around Angela.

"It's probably for the best," he said. "I'm so sorry, but if I hadn't destroyed the relics, we might all be dead by now. Come on, let's go upstairs so I can call the *Guardia Civil*."

While Puente used the telephone at the reception desk, Bronson went into the museum shop and released the staff and the two visitors, explaining that they'd have to wait in the building until the *Guardia Civil* had questioned them.

Four hours later, and well past midnight, Angela and Bronson were free to go. Puente's testimony and that of the other museum staff had cleared them of any involvement in the killings except as witnesses. Bronson would still have to satisfy the British police about the death of Mark Hampton, but the senior *Guardia Civil* officer had been able to confirm that he was now only wanted for questioning by the Metropolitan Police, and was no longer considered a suspect.

"Will they catch those two men, do you think?" Angela asked, as they headed toward the parking lot.

"Not a chance," Bronson said. "They would have

had an escape route planned in advance, because those two killings were obviously premeditated."

"Those men were all in the Mafia, so we're lucky to be alive. You heard what Mandino and that assassin said."

"Not necessarily. One of the few good things about the Mafia is that the organization has certain standards, and they don't normally kill innocent bystanders. If you're in their way, it's a different matter. I think those two men had very specific orders to ensure that the relics were found and destroyed, and that Mandino and, presumably, his number two were to die. In fact, I think what we witnessed tonight was a *coup d'état* in the Rome *Cosa Nostra*. If Mandino was the *capo*, there's been a power shift, and another *Mafioso* has now taken over as the head."

"Do you believe what that man said about Mark and Jackie? About who killed them?"

"I've no reason to doubt it," Bronson replied, "and I'd have been quite happy to pull the trigger on Rogan and Mandino myself. We've had a hell of a time these last few days," he added, his voice now low and bitter, "and all for nothing. Three people we knew are dead, and the relics we managed to recover have been destroyed, the secret they held now lost for all time. And the Catholic Church will just continue to preach its lies from pulpits around the world every Sunday as if they were literally the gospel truth."

"I wouldn't argue with any of that. But the important thing is that we're still alive. I don't see how we'd have got out of that basement if Josep hadn't done what he did."

"I know," Bronson said, "but it still rankles with me."

He fell silent, then somewhat hesitantly took her hand as they walked down the street. "I still can't quite believe Mark and Jackie have gone." His voice had softened as he thought again about his friends.

"Yes," Angela replied. "And Jeremy Goldman too—I really enjoyed working with him. Their lives are over, and I suppose you could say that a chapter of our lives has ended at the same time."

II

In the Museu Egipti, Puente was tidying the basement library. The bloodstains on the floor would need industrial cleaning equipment and, probably, special solvents, but they weren't his concern. He was only interested in the relics sitting on his desk.

One by one, he carefully replaced the scrolls he'd removed from the special safe. The last one wouldn't fit properly in the recess in the box, just as he had expected: it was a little too big. He would have to get a special container made for it as soon as possible. For the moment, he hunted around until he found a small cardboard box, filled it with cotton wool and carefully placed the scroll inside. Then he took a felt-tip pen and wrote "LEWIS" on the end of the box.

As he closed the safe he marveled again that none of the people in the room had thought to confirm that the scroll and diptychs he'd destroyed were the same ones that Angela had given him. Everyone had been focused on the guns, and on his deliberate piece of misdirection with the sprinkler system controls, and nobody had been really watching his hands.

It was a shame that he'd had to burn one of the museum's prized possessions, but the early-second-century text was utterly insignificant compared to what he was now thinking of as the Lewis Scroll. He was disappointed that he'd had to destroy two of the museum's few diptychs as well, but, in truth, they had been quite unremarkable, the writing on their wax surfaces almost completely illegible.

Not bad for an old man, Puente thought, chuckling to himself.

III

Bronson and Angela were heading out of Barcelona in the Nissan when Angela's cell phone emitted a faint double-beep, indicating that a text message had been received. She fished around in her handbag, pulled out the phone and looked at the screen.

"Who on earth's texting you at this time of night?" Bronson asked.

"I don't recognize the number—oh, it's Josep. He's probably just wishing us a safe journey." She opened the message and stared at the screen. The text was short, and initially meant nothing at all to her.

"What does it say?"

"There are just two words. In Latin. *'Rei habeo.'*"

"Which means?" Bronson prompted.

"The rough translation would be 'I have them,' I suppose. What can he mean by that?"

Then the penny dropped, and Angela smiled to herself. Then she laughed out loud. "I don't know how he did it," she said, "but Josep must have switched the relics we found for a scroll and a couple of diptychs from the museum's collection."

"You mean he destroyed three different relics?"

"Exactly."

"Brilliant," Bronson said. "Just sheer brilliance. I think that the pope and the Vatican—the whole of the Christian world, in fact—are going to go into massive shock when the professor publishes his research."

Angela laughed again. "So we did manage it after all. We decoded the clues and found the relics, and those bastards working for the Vatican didn't destroy them."

"Yes, that's a real result." Bronson glanced appraisingly at Angela's profile, shadowy in the darkness of the car. "Would you do it again?" he asked.

She turned and looked directly at him. "I don't see relic-hunting as a viable career, somehow. Was that what you meant?"

"Not exactly. I was thinking more about us spending a bit of time together. We didn't get on too badly, did we?"

Angela was silent for a few moments. "No promises, no commitment. Let's see how things work out."

They were both smiling as Bronson turned onto the *autovia* and headed north toward the snowcapped Pyrenees, the jagged peaks coldly illuminated by the full moon overhead.

AUTHOR'S NOTE

This book is, of course, a novel and to the best of my knowledge no documents resembling either the Vitalian Codex or the *Exomologesis* exist, or have ever existed, though without doubt there are numerous dark secrets lurking within the Vatican Library's 75,000 manuscripts and the estimated 150,000 items now held in the Secret Archives.

However, the central idea of this book is founded on fact because, despite my fiction, there is some historical evidence that St. Paul *was* an agent of Rome, employed by the Emperor Nero in precisely the manner I've suggested in this book. For more information about this, readers are directed to Joseph Atwill's book, *Caesar's Messiah.*

The hypothesis is that Paul and Titus Flavius Josephus—a first-century Jewish historian—were employed by Rome to foster a peaceful messianic religion in Judea in an attempt to reduce the rebelliousness of the Jews and their opposition to Roman rule. If true, this suggests an interesting piece of lateral thinking on the part of the Roman emperors.

St. Paul

Unlike St. Peter, we are at least certain that the man who became known as St. Paul actually existed. Quite a lot is known about him, and some of his writings survive to this day.

His birth name was Saul and he was born in about A.D. 9 to a wealthy Jewish merchant in Tarsus in Cilicia. He was a member of the tribe of Benjamin, and was an Aramaic- and Greek-speaking Pharisee, one of the most ancient of the Jewish sects. As a young man he was a violent opponent of Christ and was active in identifying those he saw as heretic Jews and delivering them for punishment.

Tradition holds that he was on his way to Damascus to continue his persecution of Jews when he was blinded by a light from heaven and underwent his celebrated conversion, after which he remained blind for some time. Once his sight was restored he became an ardent Christian. This apocryphal incident may have been inspired by ophthalmia neonatorum, a painful weakness of the eyes that left him almost blind in later life.

Whatever the reality of his "conversion" or motive in switching from persecutor of Christians to dedicated supporter of Jesus Christ, there are mixed views about his contribution to the Christian religion. One body of thought suggests that his views were so different from those of Jesus that his teachings are sometimes referred to as "Pauline Christianity."

The philosopher Friedrich Nietzsche viewed him as the anti-Christ, and the American Thomas Jefferson famously wrote that "Paul was the first corrupter of the teachings of Jesus" and actually tried to have his writings removed from the Bible.

St. Peter

As the Spanish scholar Josep Puente states in the book, St. Peter is found only within the pages of the New Testament, and there's no independent historical evidence to substantiate his existence. The two epistles ascribed to Peter were apparently written in sophisticated Greek and display such disparate characteristics that many commentators doubt they were written by the same person, and few serious researchers believe they could have been authored by a simple Aramaic-speaking fisherman. Despite all this, he's considered by the Roman Catholic Church to have been its first pope.

The Bones of the Apostles

Both men apparently died at the hands of the Romans, and in Rome, though neither death can be substantiated historically. Peter is believed to have died on either 29 June or 13 October A.D. 64, and he was apparently crucified upside down, while Paul was allegedly beheaded in A.D. 64 or A.D. 67—as a Roman citizen he could not be executed by crucifixion.

As for the final resting place of the bones of the two saints, the Vatican has shown a certain amount of confusion on the subject. Two entirely separate sets of bones, both found under St. Peter's Basilica in Rome, have been conclusively identified as those of St. Peter. The announcements were made in 1950 by Pope Pius XII and in 1968 by Paul VI.

The first set was inspected by an anthropologist in 1956 and found to contain five tibias—most human skeletons have a mere two, and at least one of those examined came from a woman—as well as pig, sheep, goat and chicken bones.

The 1968 bones, like the earlier set, included those

of various domesticated animals, plus those of a mouse, as well as fragments of St. Peter's skull. The skull fragments were something of an embarrassment, because what purported to be the apostle's skull had rested in the Basilica of St. John Lateran in Rome since about the ninth century.

Finally, to complicate the situation still further, in 1953 what appeared to be the skeleton of St. Peter was unearthed in Jerusalem on the site of a Franciscan monastery called "Dominus Flevit" on the Mount of Olives. The bones were in an ossuary inscribed, in Aramaic, "Simon Bar Jona" (Simon, son of Jona).

Bearing in mind that there's no evidence St. Peter ever lived, such confusion over his remains is perhaps not surprising, and such "duplication" of relics is not uncommon in the Catholic Church—although there were only twelve apostles, the remains of some twenty-six are buried in Germany alone.

According to the Venerable Bede in his *Ecclesiastical History,* St. Paul's bones were given by Pope Vitalian to Oswy, King of Britain, in A.D. 665. Given the Vatican's reluctance to surrender relics of any sort, this seems a somewhat unlikely fate for the skeleton. What happened to the bones after that isn't known.

The Cathars

Catharism was a dualist and Gnostic religion that possibly descended from the Byzantine Bogomils and, earlier, from Manichaeism. The Cathars believed that a benevolent god had created the human soul and the realm of spirit and light that lay beyond the earth. But an evil deity had then trapped the soul and forced it to suffer in the corrupt flesh of the human body: salvation lay only in death, when the soul could finally escape to the spiritual realm. Because they believed that the soul could also make this journey in the body of an animal, they were strict vegetarians.

They saw themselves as Christians, but rejected the Old Testament because they believed that the god who was described in it was the evil deity who had created the world to enslave the souls of mankind. They believed this god was actually the devil, and that the Catholic Church was therefore in the service of Satan.

Catharism was diametrically opposed to the medieval Catholic Church in almost every way, and the contrast between the two could hardly have been greater. Unlike the Catholic Church, the Cathars asked for nothing at all from their congregations except faith. In fact, they made material contributions to the society in which they lived. When a Cathar took the *consolamentum* vow and became one of the *perfecti,* he or she donated all their worldly goods to the community. They had no church buildings or property, and the movement rejected all the trappings of wealth and power. Unusually for the period, Cathars also treated women as equals, and ensured that the children in the community were properly educated. The obvious piety and essential goodness of the Cathar *perfecti* greatly appealed to the people of the Languedoc, and the heresy gained considerable power. That, predictably, was unacceptable to the Catholic Church, which could see its own power and influence in the area waning, and the inevitable result was the Albigensian Crusade.

The Albigensian Crusade and the Fall of Montségur

The events that I've described as taking place during the Albigensian Crusade, such as the massacre at Béziers, the mutilation of the prisoners from Bram and the ending of the siege of Montségur, are historically accurate.

The defenders of the citadel did request a two-week truce to consider the surrender terms offered by the crusaders, only to then reject them on 15 March 1244. One possible reason for this strange request was that the Cathar defenders wanted to celebrate an important ritual on the previous day, 14 March, possibly the so-called *manisola* festival.

The day before this, 13 March, was the spring equinox, another important date for the religion, and some records suggest that this was the date when at least twenty—perhaps as many as twenty-six—non-Cathars opted to receive the *consolamentum perfecti,* which would condemn them to certain death some forty-eight hours later.

For obvious reasons it hasn't been possible to establish as fact the story of the last four Cathars' escape from the doomed fortress carrying the "Cathar treasure," but there is considerable anecdotal evidence—some apparently deriving from records of later interrogations conducted by the Inquisition—that something like this event did actually occur.

The "Myth of Christ"

Finally, anyone who has ever properly researched the birth of Christianity must have wondered why no truly contemporary sources—apart from the books that now form the New Testament, which were anything but contemporary, being written between about A.D. 75 and A.D. 135—ever mention Jesus Christ.

In all, the Bible is a compilation of sixty-six books—thirty-nine in the Old Testament and twenty-seven in the New—that were written by some forty different individuals over a period of about 1,600 years.

It's generally acknowledged that the first list of the

present twenty-seven New Testament books appeared in a letter written in A.D. 367 by the Bishop of Alexandria, Athanasius. In Carthage in A.D. 397, a council decreed that only the canonical writings—the "agreed" twenty-seven books—were allowed to be read in church as divine scriptures: they were literally to be accepted as the "gospel truth." That decree essentially marked the creation of the New Testament.

All those other documents—and there were hundreds of them, including the Book of Jubilees, the Book of Enoch, the Gospel of Mary, the Protovangelion of Jesus, the Apocalypse of Peter and the Gospel of Nicodemus—that disagreed with this corpus of work were excluded and became known colloquially as "the banned books." And it's worth emphasizing that the selection was made on the basis of content, not authenticity or relevance, so the result was, by any standards, highly selective.

And even those books that *were* included are frequently at variance with each other, even the so-called "synoptic" gospels of Mark, Luke and Matthew, which appear to derive from an earlier common source, possibly the so-called "Q Document," now lost.

So, despite what is preached from pulpits in churches around the world every Sunday, the only evidence for the existence of the man upon whose shoulders rests the largest single religion in history lies within the pages of a single section of the Bible, a heavily edited, noncontemporary source. What this proves has been—and no doubt will remain—a source of worldwide debate by theologians and philosophers, believers and nonbelievers, for centuries to come.